TAKE YOUR LIFE

THE DCI PETER MOONE THRILLERS BOOK 2

MARK YARWOOD

EXCLUSIVE OFFER

Look out for the link at the end of this book or visit my website at www.markyarwood.co.uk to sign up to my no-spam Monthly Murder Club and receive two FREE and exclusive crime thrillers plus news and previews of forthcoming works.

Never miss out on a release.

No spam. You can unsubscribe at any time.

This novel is entirely a work of fiction. The names, characters and incidents portrayed in it are the work of the author's imagination. Any resemblance to actual persons, living or dead, events or localities is entirely coincidental.

BiscuitBooksPublishers © Mark Yarwood 2022

The author asserts the moral right to be identified as the author of this work Published by Amazon Kindle All rights reserved. No part of this publication may be reproduced, stored, or transmitted in any form or by means, electronic, mechanical, photocopying, recording or otherwise, without the prior permission of the publishers.

Once again, for Maggie,
who we miss very much

BOOK ONE

PROLOGUE

Her foot dug into the snow with a crunch, the icy burn of it biting into her bare skin, making her shiver even more than she already was. Her teeth chattered as her eyes filled with tears and she looked round at the white ground, the rocky hills surrounding her. She swept her head back, staring towards the car parked almost two hundred yards away.

Her car. She shook her head, pleading with the cold eyes that stared back at her, begging not to do what he wanted her to do.

The figure in the back seat sat up, and pointed his gloved hand at her, jabbing the air. She sobbed, her nose dripping, turning back round, searching for anyone who might help her. But she couldn't be helped, couldn't be saved, it was impossible. She looked down at the knife in her trembling hand that was turning blue. She looked up at the sky, saw a few flakes of snow falling, then lifted the blade to her throat. The knife was icy cold but she hardly felt it as she dug it against her flesh, then pulled it. It hurt and she stopped, more tears coming.

She bent her head, crying, the knife shaking in her hand.

Images flashed into her mind, things that might happen if she didn't do what he'd ordered her to do. She lifted the knife to her neck again, her legs giving way, landing on her knees in the snow.

She had no choice.

She dug the knife into her skin once more, then dragged it across. Blood dripped onto the snow, her hand shaking violently.

CHAPTER 1

The occasional wisp of snow blew across the windscreen of the car that DI Mandy Butler drove them in towards Dartmoor. They were on a narrow stretch of a never-ending road surrounded by rocky ground which was now mostly covered in a blanket of white. There was an incident response car far in front of them, the blue lights flashing.

Moone turned his eyes towards the mostly white ground to their left, spotting tiny ponies and the occasional muddy- looking sheep.

'You've got to be pretty sick to want to shag a sheep,' Moone said.

'What?' Butler stared at him.

'I mean, look at the state of their arses!'

Butler shook her head, huffed. 'So, your reason for not wanting to shag a sheep is their lack of cleanliness? Nice to know how your mind works, Moone.'

Moone shrugged, turning his mind to the job in hand. There had been nothing major to deal with over the last month or so, and Christmas had passed without much incident. Now this.

'They said it was a woman?' Moone asked.

'That's right. Possible suicide.' Butler put her foot down and roared the car round a dawdling pensioner a rusty vehicle. 'What's this meeting about?'

'Sorry?'

'The meeting with the Chief Super? What's it about?' She turned her eyes to him, burning them into his.

'I don't know. That's the third time you've asked me and I still don't know.'

'Fine. If it's bad news, like a demotion, I can take it.'

'It's not.'

'So, you do know?'

Moone let out a sigh. 'No, I don't.'

'Scout's honour?'

'Scout's honour.'

Butler made a sound in her throat that made Moone feel as if she still didn't believe him. He was as much in the dark as to why they were being summoned to Laptew's office in Crownhill, and he was just as perturbed as Butler, maybe more.

He didn't have time to think much more on it, as Butler took a lane off of Princetown, taking them past the prison, and allowing them a view down into it that made Moone shiver a little. Then they were back out into the white wilderness, stone walls surrounding a nearby massive field. The black silhouette of crows cut through the grey sky as they parked.

A couple of marked police cars were parked either end of the lane running alongside the field. Crime scene tape was twisting and flapping in the wind, tied to two telegraph poles. Uniforms were dotted around, while SOCOs were crossing the duckboards that lined the way to the only colour in their view.

Moone climbed out, looking around at the houses that were set far back, ramshackle cottages that looked ready to fall down. He stuffed his hands into his pockets and followed Butler as she headed towards a familiar face of one of the uniforms. He was a thickset, dark-skinned PC with a black goatee beard.

'OK, Dave?' Butler asked, wisps of her breath floating out of her mouth. 'What've we got?'

Dave turned towards the SOCOs. 'Dead woman. Charlene Bale. Thirty-two. Looks like suicide. Cut her own throat, they tell me. Lovely one for you, Mand.'

'Yep, lovely, just what we like. Have we got an ID, then?'

'Here.' Dave passed her a small evidence bag with the victim's driving licence inside. Butler walked on, heading for the duckboards, and hopping along them. Moone followed, taking time to look around and saw a couple more

SOCOs at work on the road. He turned back to see Butler approaching the SOCOs and caught up with her, suddenly desperate for a cigarette.

'You in charge, Nathan?' Butler said to a much older looking SOCO who had silver hair poking out of his white hood.

'Indeed, I am, DI Butler.' Nathan turned towards the body lying on the white ground. 'We're getting a tent set up. Looks like we're in for more snow.'

Moone stared towards the blood that flowed deep red against the white ground. 'What did she use?'

'We found a kitchen knife still in her hand. We'll check it for prints.'

Moone nodded. 'Quite a lot of blood.'

'Yes.' Nathan nodded. 'I don't think it killed her though. I think the pathologist will find that hypothermia got her first. Look at her feet.'

They were bare, discoloured, darkened where the cold had started to eat away at them. 'Why would you walk out here in bare feet?'

'What's it matter?' Butler asked. 'If you're going to do yourself in...'

Moone ignored her words and looked towards the road, then pointed his finger at the SOCOs at work along the lane and stared at Nathan.

'That?' Nathan said, looking where Moone was pointing. 'Tyre marks. Looks like a car was parked over there.'

'She was dropped off,' Moone said, his mind beginning to defrost a little. 'Someone dropped her off at the place she was going to kill herself? Who does that?'

Butler shrugged. 'Maybe her days were numbered. Maybe she was sick or something. Or maybe the Dartmoor hands got her! I don't know.'

'Dartmoor hands?' Moone looked between them.

'Ghostly legend,' Nathan said, rolling his eyes. 'Don't ask.'

'Perhaps one of her friends drove her here,' Butler said. 'Maybe she got a taxi.'

'Maybe.' Moone spoke the words, but something didn't sit right. It was the bare feet. 'If you were going to drop off someone and didn't want them to get very far...'

'You'd take their shoes,' Butler said and nodded. 'Shit. Are we looking at a murder?'

Moone turned towards the road, then started walking back along the duckboards a couple of steps. 'You said she definitely killed herself?'

Nathan took down his hood, his breath pluming from his lips. 'Looks that way. Lots of hesitation cuts. All fits so far. Who has the power to make someone off themselves like this? Cutting her own throat in the middle of nowhere?'

'He's right,' Butler said, looking round at the

scenery. 'Why not slit your wrists in a warm bath, or even take pills? This is something else...'

'Yep, it is.' Moone moved on, hopping along the duckboards, the wind biting at his cheeks as he reached the SOCOs taking photos of the tyre tracks. 'If someone drove her here, then maybe we'll catch the car on a camera.'

'Not much out here,' Butler said. 'But we might get lucky. What now?'

Moone looked at her. 'We know her name. Got her driving licence. Let's find where she lived.'

'Someone's about to have a bad day.'

The house Charlene Bale had lived in was in Salisbury Road, a lengthy road in an area called Lipson, a short walk from the city centre and Charles Cross police station. It was a tall-looking terraced house squeezed in with all the other grey looking homes. A lot of the houses were rented to students and some were a dumping ground for troubled families from other areas, Butler had informed him. Hence the rising burglary rate in the area, she said as they parked and got out.

They both climbed the three steps to the front door, but it was Moone who pressed the buzzer for the top floor flat. There were three in total, Moone noticed, including a basement flat.

Butler nudged him out of the way and pressed the buzzer a few times before the door was opened by a young blonde, frizzy-haired woman who looked as if she had just been rudely awoken. Moone took note of her checked pyjamas as he smiled awkwardly.

Moone showed his ID, 'DCI Peter Moone. DI Mandy Butler. Charlene Bale lives here? That right?'

The young woman blinked at them, frowning, and rubbing her eyes. 'Yeah, that's right. Has she done something?'

'Not exactly,' Butler said. 'What's your name?'

'Tess. Teresa Gregg.'

'Can we come in?' Moone asked, pointing into the hallway. 'Might be better.'

The woman hesitated, then opened the door, stepping back. 'Up the stairs. What's going on?'

Moone went into the kitchen, which was quite large, airy, modern and with a view of the roofs of the ramshackle houses that crowded the horizon. He turned and faced Butler and the worried and tired face of the young woman wiping hair from her cheek.

'I'm sorry, but it's bad news,' he said, the same old concrete lump sinking to the bottom of his gut. 'We've found a body just outside of Princetown. We're pretty sure it's Charlene.'

The woman stared at him, obviously trying to compute it all. Her head shook, she blinked for a few seconds. 'You sure? I mean... that can't be right... Charlene?'

Moone took out the evidence bag with Charlene's ID inside and passed it to Teresa. 'We found this on her. Is it hers?'

She took it, her hands trembling a little, then brought it close to her face. Her eyes widened. 'That's hers. But... what happened? I don't understand...'

Butler rested her back against the edge of the work surface. 'She was found in a field, in the snow. Looks like she took her own life...'

Teresa stared at her, then shook her head. 'No, not Charlene... she wouldn't... why would she?'

'Tess,' Moone said, making his voice gentler. 'This isn't ever easy, but can you think of any reason Charlene would want to harm herself?'

The young woman sniffed, stared down at the bag with the ID and shook her head. She looked at Moone almost apologetically. 'No, I can't. I really can't. I'm sorry.'

'No need to be sorry.' Moone looked at Butler as he drew a deep unhappy breath. Butler shrugged, reading his mind, so he said, 'Tess, can you think of anyone who might have wanted to harm her?'

Tess' eyes shot to him, stark confusion pouring over her pale skin. 'Hang on, you said...'

'I know. It's just we have to consider every angle.'

Butler straightened herself. 'Did she have

someone? A bloke or…'

Tess nodded. 'Yes, Darren. But he wouldn't do anything like this. I just don't get any of this…'

'Where was Charlene last night?' Moone asked.

'At Darren's.'

Moone took out his notebook. 'Can you give me the address and any family we need to contact?'

'And her job,' Butler added.

'What do you make of all this?' Moone asked as Butler drove them in the direction of Pennycomequick. Moone shook his head when he said the funny sounding name to himself, figuring that some ancient Plymothian had been having a joke when he came up with the name.

'Doesn't matter what we make of it, does it?'

Moone looked up at her. 'What do you mean? Of course it does.'

'It's a suicide… or at least it looks like it and we've only got flimsy material to say otherwise. Not even enough to make some granny pants.'

'But…'

'Moone, shut up and listen. When the Chief Super hears about this and the fact that it has most of the hallmarks of a suicide, then he'll want us to move on. It's a suicide, bang, job done.'

'You can't be serious?'

'Yes, McEnroe, I'm very serious. I've been here before. It's my second home. If it looks like a suicide, it is a suicide. Less paperwork that way and less cost.'

'Jesus.' Moone stared up at the roundabout and his old ridiculous looking friend, Isambard plonked right in the middle of it.

Butler parked along the road, outside a row of grimy new build houses that looked box-like and crammed in.

'This is where our boy lives,' Butler said and took them around to the side of the miniature estate and to a door at the centre of the row. Butler rang the bell, folded her arms and looked at Moone. 'You sulking now?'

'No, just annoyed.' He pressed the bell too.

'You haven't faced the Chief Super yet. Just you wait. You might want to get some blood pressure pills ready.'

The door opened and a tall, and quite broad young man with shaven strawberry-blond hair stared out at them. 'Yeah? What?'

Moone and Butler showed their IDs, but it was Moone who said, 'DCI Peter Moone and DI Mandy Butler. Are you Darren Taylor?'

Taylor ran a hand over his stubble, his eyes darting over the rest of the street. 'Yeah, what of it?'

'You went out with Charlene Bale?' Butler asked.

'Still do,' he said, folding his arms across his chest. 'What've I done?'

'Can we come in?' Moone asked.

'No.' Taylor puffed out his chest, set his dead eyes on Moone. 'What the fuck is this about?'

'I'm sorry,' Moone began. 'But Charlene has been found... she's dead.'

Taylor stared at him, taking it in. Then he smiled, gave a laugh. 'You're fucking having me on, aren't ya? Charlene? This a joke?'

'No joke,' Moone said. 'I'm very sorry. Can we come in?'

'Shit.' Taylor enclosed his face in his hands, let out a moan, then stepped aside for them.

Moone went into a small rectangular lounge where there was a beige sofa and a large TV with a game console attached. A cigarette smoked away in an ashtray on the coffee table next to a mug.

Taylor came in after Butler and collapsed onto the sofa, then hunched over, rubbing his face with his hands. 'Fucking hell. I can't believe this. Did someone... I mean, how did...'

'It looks like she took her own life,' Moone said, looking round the sparse room. 'Her flatmate said she was here last night.'

Taylor's head sprang up. 'That's a lie for starters. She didn't come here last night. She told me she was going out with Tess. What the fuck's going on?'

'That's what we're trying to find out.' Butler stepped closer to him. 'Did she have a car?'

'Yeah,' Taylor said and climbed to his feet. 'Little Ford Ka. Purple thing. She always parked it out...'

Moone looked towards the window, to try and see what Taylor was staring at. 'Mr Taylor, what is it?'

Taylor pointed to the window. 'It's out there. Parked along the street. I think that's hers.'

Then the boyfriend was down the hall, going out the front door with Butler going after him, calling him to stop. Moone hurried to keep up, jogging over the little strip of grass that sat opposite the grey box houses. Taylor reached the car, but Butler pulled him back, stopping him from touching the vehicle.

'Hang on,' she said, her hand gripping his elbow. 'Evidence.'

As Moone approached and took some latex gloves from his jacket and pulled them on, he saw Taylor nod, then search himself for a cigarette.

Being careful not to disturb anything, Moone used his index finger to try the passenger door. It clicked open, so he raised his eyebrows at Butler and said, 'We'd better get forensics over here.'

CHAPTER 2

'The car's been towed away?' Moone asked, leaning his head back against the wall as they both sat in the waiting area of the Chief Superintendent's office.

Mandy sighed, 'Yes, I said it had. I knew you weren't listening. Forensics will start giving it the once-over. But it's a waste of time.'

He looked at her. 'Why?'

'Because the Chief Super will want it filed away. Do you ever listen to me?'

Moone closed his eyes, then turned his head to face the office door. He was thinking it all over, wondering about the victim, trying to piece it all together. He almost shivered as he saw her being taken to the barren, snow covered field to take her last few steps in her short life. Alice, his daughter, barely sixteen, replaced Charlene and he felt immediately sick at the thought. A young woman, now dead, ready to be filed away as another suicide.

'We need to check her medical records,'

Butler said. 'See if she suffered from depression or anything.'

He opened his eyes, looked at her. 'So you're back on suicide too?'

'We've got to cover all the bases, haven't we? If we rule out depression or any mental illness...'

He nodded, then looked towards the office door as he heard it click open. The smart uniform of Chief Superintendent Laptew appeared in the doorway, his smiling, professional face sat above it.

'Moone,' he said, smiling a little more, opening the door wider. 'Butler. Come in. Come in. I've only got a little window left, so hurry on in.'

Moone dragged himself to his feet, and headed into the office, seeing the bright winter sun beaming into the room, casting the windows' shadows over the carpet. His eyes jumped to the plain clothed figure already sat by the Chief's desk, her legs crossed, her hay-coloured hair dragged back in a tight bob. Her red lips stretched into a smile that faded when Butler and the Chief joined them.

DC Carthew looked as if she'd lost weight, her face now tighter, her eyes sharper, her skin a little tanned.

'Of course you know Faith,' the Chief said and returned to his desk and sat back, smiling a little.

'Bloody hell,' Butler said, just loud enough

for Moone to hear. 'What a psycho bitch.'

Moone and Butler took the two seats in front of his desk. Moone smiled briefly at Faith, flashes of her sat astride their suspect, Colin Samson, ready to beat his skull in with a hammer.

There was silence for a moment, and Moone felt the awkward beat of it and caught the smile that passed between the Chief and Carthew. It was all there, in that one look and his mind repelled the images that came to him.

'I recently decided to promote Faith,' the Chief said, staring at Moone. 'After she acted so heroically during your last case together…'

There came a loud huff from Butler, that dragged all their eyes to her.

'I'm sorry, Mandy,' the Chief said. 'Did you want to say something?'

'Nope.' Mandy looked away.

The Chief sat back. 'Detective Sergeant Faith Carthew will be looking into a missing persons case. I thought that would be a good way to get her started. She can run it alongside any case you lot end up working on…'

'We're working on a case now,' Moone said, sitting up, his stomach tightening as he caught sight of Butler shaking her head.

'Really?' the Chief said. 'I didn't know that. I heard you were cleaning up a suicide…'

Moone shifted in his seat. 'Well, at first it looked like a suicide, but on closer examination…well, there's little things…'

'Little things?' The Chief Super raised his eyebrows.

'I heard she cut her own throat,' DS Carthew said, engaging Moone's eyes, a strange look in hers, perhaps a little anger.

'Is that right, Moone?' The Chief Super sat back. 'Does the physical evidence point to suicide? Did she cut her own throat?'

'Yes, it looks that way…'

The Chief stood up, nodding. 'Then sounds like suicide to me. Unfortunately, people find themselves in very dark places sometimes and it seems there's no way out.'

'That's true, sir, but I think this needs further investigation…'

'When there's a suicide, Moone, your job is to gather the evidence for the coroner, to help them come to a decision on the cause of death. You do understand that, yes?'

'Yes sir.'

'Good. I expect you to gather only the relevant details pertaining to the young woman's suicide. I don't want you digging around and making more of it than there is. We don't want to upset the families, or bring about any bad press. Do we?'

'No, I guess not.'

'Good. Anyway, I hope you three can lend each other a hand as you'll be working side by side…'

'Sir,' Moone said, standing up along with everyone else. 'It looks as if someone drove her to that spot… she had bare feet…'

The Chief stared at him blankly. 'So? So she had bare feet? She was there to kill herself, she was in a vulnerable and perhaps confused mindset… perhaps one of her friends drove her there. Either way, she took her own life. Just get it all neat and tidy and I'll sign off on it. Go on, Moone, Butler, go and get on with it.'

'Sir,' Moone said and followed Butler out of the office and into the waiting area. His PA was back, so they went on out into the corridor.

'I don't fucking believe that bitch!' Butler said, staring daggers at the Super's door. 'She's made DS! She's right behind me! Up the greasy pole? She's up *his* greasy pole!'

Moone played back the conversation, hearing his own boss tell him to tidy away the investigation and put it down as suicide. He shook his head, stared at Butler's red face, her angry words pouring out.

'And you!' Butler said, jabbing a finger at him.

'What have I done?'

'This is all your fault! You got her on your team in the first place, and we all know why! Why the bloody hell didn't you report her?! She was going to kill Samson! If you hadn't…'

'I wanted to help. I don't think she's crazy, just a bit…'

'A bit fucking what? Your kids haven't got any rabbits, have they, Moone?'

Moone smiled sarcastically. 'Very funny.'

They stopped talking when the office door opened.

'I'll meet you in the car,' Butler said and stormed off down the corridor, leaving Moone to face the smart suited, slimmer and deadlier looking DS Faith Carthew.

She sidled up to him, a subtle smile playing on her lips. She folded her arms, her eyebrows rising. 'So, Pete, looks like we'll be working together again.'

'In the same building.'

'In the same incident room. I'll have to watch myself round you. Don't want you getting any ideas.'

'You don't have to worry.'

'Promise?'

'Scout's honour.'

She smiled as her eyes changed, a glimmer of something passing through them, a hint of darkness clouding over her. 'We could've been so good together. We still could.'

'You were going to kill him.'

The friendliness sank away, the dark clouding in. 'I hope you haven't told anyone about that. I mean, it was only a momentary lack of judgement... I was all... het up.'

'Het up? That's what you call it?'

She smiled.

'I think we need to give each other a wide berth.' He went to walk round her, but her hand pressed against his chest.

'That's going to be impossible. You know it. I know it. I'm being fast tracked, Pete. Soon I'll be right behind you, so close you'll feel my breath on the back of your neck. One day, I'll even be your boss. Probably...'

'Good luck with that.' Moone walked on, his heart racing, his mind scrambling, a strange sort of panic travelling to every part of him.

By the time they arrived back at Charles Cross, Moone was ready to sell his own mother for a cigarette. But he'd promised Butler that he was going to try and give up again, so he knew he'd have to come up with an excuse.

'Right, home again,' Butler said as she parked and pulled on the handbrake.

'I need an espresso after that,' Moone said, shaking his head. 'I still can't believe that's it, he wants to tie it off. No investigation, nothing.'

Butler turned in her seat and gave him one of her stares.

'What?' he asked.

'You're not going to let that stop you, are you?'

'Well, I thought...'

'We've still got loose ends to tie up and family to talk to. It gives us some time to dig around.' She turned and climbed out. 'Stop faffing and go get us some coffees. And a bacon butty for me.'

'What's faffing?'

'It's what you do. You don't get anything done fast, you faff about.'

He rolled his eyes. 'Nice to know. See you in a minute.'

'And don't have a crafty fag!'

Moone ignored her clairvoyance and went back through the gigantic gates and back out into the road. He took out his pack of twenty cigarettes and the disposable lighter. He poked one in his mouth, lit it and stood there for a moment, enjoying the taste, the relaxation that massaged his mind. He backed himself against the gates, his eyes following the people coming up the street, sizing them up, trying to guess things about them. The third person he laid eyes on was a woman, probably in her late thirties. Average build, light brown hair that looked a little messy. He noticed her biting her nails as she reached a car. She struggled to find her car keys and when she did, she dropped them twice before she managed to open the car door. As she did, her eyes found Moone and stared at him.

He was frozen, mid drag, but managed a smile. Her eyes jumped from him to the police station, then back as she started crossing the road towards him. Moone straightened up, and dropped his cigarette.

'Excuse me,' she said, only a subtle West

Country accent in her voice that seemed to tremble a little. 'Do you work in there?'

'I'm a policeman, if that's what you mean.' He smiled again. 'Can I help?'

She looked worried, her eyes jumping round him as she seemed to weigh something up. 'What rank are you?'

'I'm a detective chief inspector. Is there a problem?'

Then she looked at him, her hazel eyes taking him in, seeming to burn deep into his, making him feel a little uncomfortable. 'I can't get anyone to listen to me. Least of all my family. No one in there wants to hear what I've got to say. I don't know what else I can do.'

Moone looked up the road, half remembering that he was supposed to be fetching Butler her coffee and bacon butty. 'Why don't we sit down in the cafe up the road and you can tell me about it.'

She looked up the street as she pulled at her hair, then nodded.

The woman, who said she was Mrs Ashley Whittle, bought them both a coffee and sat down at the table that Moone had settled at. Jake's wasn't particularly busy that morning, so they had most of the seating area to themselves.

Mrs Whittle put both her hands round her coffee in silence, her eyes darting round the room furtively.

Moone leaned forward. 'Why don't you tell me what's wrong, Mrs Whittle?'

'Ashley,' she said, and tried to smile.

'Ashley. Just talk to me.'

She nodded, sipped her coffee. 'Are you… are you married?'

'Was. Not any more. Are you?'

'I was. Happily, so I thought. Married to Simon Whittle for nearly ten years…' Ashley looked up at him with tears in her eyes. 'Then they, your lot, uniforms, are knocking on my door. My world fell apart. I was… happy, a strong person, confident. That all fell away that day…'

'Something happened to Simon?'

'They said he had killed himself. They said he'd gone to the roof of the civic centre…'

'I'm so sorry.' Moone put his hand across the table, but stopped himself, wondering what was coming from the woman, flashes of the young woman who had taken her life last night coming into his mind. His stomach turned over.

She looked up again, gave him the same sighing stare. 'I don't think… no, I know Simon would never kill himself… never. He had so much going for him… a new business… he was happy. Stressed sometimes, but not depressed. Never…'

Moone sat back. 'What about a note? Did he leave one?'

'No, nothing. But they told me that's not unusual…'

'It's not. Look, there's not much I can do…'

Her hand shot across the table and clasped his, her eyes full of tears again. 'Please. Look into it. I know there must be more to this. There must be. They never found his phone either. It wasn't at home. I mean, where is it? And I noticed money was missing from our bank account.'

'How much?'

'About two thousand pounds. The bank said it showed as been drawn out by Simon, but why would he if he planned... I don't understand any of it...'

'I appreciate your...' He stopped speaking, taking it all in, feeling the hairs stand up at the back of his neck and his gut started spinning. 'Ashley...'

She looked up, her teary eyes taking him in.

'I'm going to look into this. I'll do my best...'

He saw her eyes grow wider, then a smile come, and a light coming on inside her. 'Thank you. Whatever you can do or tell me. I just feel so lost.'

'Have you got a number I can reach you at?'

She took out her mobile in a hurry and brought up her number, which he entered into his phone. Then he thought some more. 'You said your family don't seem concerned?'

'Well, it's more his brother. Michael Whittle. I mean, he was shocked by it all, but he just seems happy with the verdict of suicide... not happy, but you know what I'm trying to say.'

'I do. Who looked into the case?'

'A police sergeant seemed to overlook it. But he just fobbed me off when I raised any issues. He's called Kevin Pinder.'

Moone made a note of it all, then smiled and stood up. 'Right, Ashley, leave it with me and I'll look into it. I'm not promising any miracles, but I'll do my best. OK?'

'OK,' she said, tears still in her eyes, a hopeful smile on her lips.

He smiled, then quickly left the cafe and headed back out into the street, his stride speeding up, his heart thumping a little more.

When he reached the incident room he found Butler at her desk, and DC Keith Harding working away in the corner. A few other detectives and civvies were at their desks, typing away or on the phones.

'Where's her phone?' Moone asked, heading to the whiteboard and writing Charlene's full name on the board.

Butler looked up. 'Where's the coffee? Where's my bacon bap? And why do you stink of fags?'

'Sorry, Mum. Did they find her mobile?'

Butler sighed and looked through some paperwork on her desk. 'No. No sign of it. Might be at her home or at the boyfriend's...'

'We need to check.'

Harding walked up to Moone. 'Is it true? Say it isn't true.'

'What?'

'Has Carthew made detective sergeant?'

Moone looked at him, saw the annoyance in his face. 'Sorry, Kevin. It's the whole fast tracked business...'

'For fuck's sake!' Harding turned towards Butler. Are you hearing this, Butler? She got DS over me! Bloody PC gone mad, it is.'

'It's worse than that, Kev,' Butler said, standing up. 'The next thing we'll know she'll be our bloody boss.'

'Right,' Moone said, trying to take his mind off the thought of Carthew and the fact that a psycho might be rising through the ranks at an alarming rate. 'Let's get on. Harding, I want you to check on Charlene Bale's phone, find out when it was last used and all that...'

Butler sidled up, squinting at him. 'You had a brainwave or something?'

'No. I just bumped into a woman who thinks her husband who supposedly killed himself, would never kill himself.'

Butler covered her face and let out a pained noise. 'That's most people who've been married to a person who's topped themselves!'

Moone nodded. 'I know, I know, it's probably nothing, but let's dig around. His phone was never found. Where was it last? Where's DC Chambers?'

'She's been assigned to Carthew,' Butler said and tutted. 'We're enough to deal with this.'

Moone nodded. 'OK. We need to check ANPR

for Charlene's car.'

'Already got on that,' Butler said. 'Nothing so far. I'll grab a team of uniforms and civvies to go through CCTV. We'll find it.'

'Good. I think we need to talk to the brother.'

'Whose brother? Charlene's?'

'No, the brother of Ashley Whittle's dead husband. Let's get his opinion on all this. I also want Sergeant Kevin Pinder brought in so we can talk to him. He handled Whittle's suicide.'

Butler made a disapproving noise in her throat.

'What does that noise mean?'

'It means you're about to get us in the shit again.'

'It's going to be fine. Trust me.' Moone gave her a reassuring smile as the incident room door opened and DSU Stack came in with DS Carthew at his side, both of them chatting.

'Let's get out of here,' Moone whispered to Butler, who nodded and grabbed her coat.

'Hang on, Moone,' Stack said, folding his arms over his broad chest. 'I just had a call from the Chief Super about you two. I'm to keep an eye on you both. Where you off to now?'

Moone adjusted his tie, avoiding eye contact. 'Off to talk to Charlene's family and clear all this up.'

Stack nodded, but his eyes dug into Moone, then Butler. 'Right. Don't fuck this up. Or you'll have me to deal with!'

CHAPTER 3

'We'll have to visit her parents after this,' Butler said, as she parked down Connaught Avenue off of Mutley Plain.

Moone nodded, his stomach filling with lead already at the mere thought of it. He climbed out, feeling the cold wind tug at him as he closed the door. 'Where do they live?'

'Out in Cornwall, in a little village.'

Moone headed back up the street and turned right towards a row of estate agents and solicitors, all glass fronted, people at desks working away inside. He spotted Wolfman House Solicitors which was a narrow office, wedged in between two of the letting agents. He went into the office, hearing a bell ting like an old style shop, and saw one of the young women office workers look up and smile. She had dark shoulder-length hair, an oval, quite pretty face, and was dressed in a light blue shirt.

'Be right with you,' she said, smiling at Moone then Butler who had just stepped in. 'Are you together?'

Moone showed his ID. 'You could say that.'

The young woman's face changed, the smile fading away for a moment until it was replaced by a more professional one. 'Who did you want to talk to?'

'Michael Whittle, if he's around.'

The young woman got up and headed to the back of the room and into another office. The door closed behind her, and no one came out for a while, so Moone signalled to Butler to follow him down.

He opened the office door, taking out his ID as he entered. The young woman turned round, revealing a man in his forties with greying light brown hair and a long, slender face.

'Michael Whittle?' Moone asked. 'DCI Peter Moone. We'd like a word with you.'

Whittle sat back, nodding a little. 'Thank you, Rachel. You can get back to work. How can I help?'

Moone watched Rachel turn and head out of the office, her blue eyes finding his, a smile appearing on her face. The look lasted a while longer than he expected and left him a little flustered for a moment.

'Your brother's suicide,' Butler said, huffing and staring at Moone.

Michael Whittle lost the half smile he was wearing, then pointed to the chairs opposite his desk. 'Why don't you take a seat?'

'Thanks,' Moone said, and pulled up a chair, while Butler remained standing, arms folded across her chest.

'I take it you've been talking to Ashley, my brother's widow?'

'Yes, we have.' Moone sat forward. 'She doesn't seem satisfied by the whole thing.'

'Is anyone satisfied by suicide?' Whittle raised his eyebrows. 'Look, I was as shocked as anyone. I still can't get my head round it, but Ashley... well, she was really hit hard by all this. For him to just go off and... it just messes with your head. And neither of us knew that he might... it's terrible.'

Moone nodded. 'I understand and appreciate you've been through a terrible time. Ashley said there was money missing from their bank account.'

'Yes, she told me the same thing. But I think I'm correct in thinking the bank said it must've been drawn out by him.'

'Yes, that's right. Any reason you can think of why he would draw out two thousand pounds before he killed himself?'

Whittle sat back, let out a sigh. 'I'm afraid not. I've been over all this with Ashley. There's no reason I can think of. I thought I knew my brother... we hadn't been that close lately, but I was confident that he would never surprise me... not like that, at least. What's this about? Are you investigating his death?'

'No,' Butler said, throwing daggers at Moone. 'We're not.'

'Why the interest?' Whittle asked.

'Just a similar case. Just going over old ground. No need to be concerned.' Moone stood up, taking his cue from Butler's fiery eyes. Then he stopped when he remembered the mysterious mobile phone. 'Your brother's mobile phone was never found. You don't know anything about that?'

Whittle stood up, showed his empty palms. 'Not a thing, I'm afraid. It's a mystery.'

'It certainly is.' Moone looked into the solicitor's eyes, trying to read them, noticing that Ashley had been right, and that he did seem pretty cool when it came to discussing his brother's death. 'Well, thanks for your time. We appreciate you must be busy.'

'No, it's fine.' Whittle smiled.

Moone turned to see Rachel was in the doorway, ready to come in or perhaps to usher them out. He let Butler go ahead and watched her storm out of the office, while he slowed down, took his time.

'It was an awful time for him,' Rachel said, so Moone turned and faced her.

'Must've been,' he said. 'I can't imagine.'

'Are you married or...'

'Was. Not any more.' He looked down at her left hand and saw no ring or even a mark where one might have been.

'Me neither. Never been close.'

'Did you know his brother?'

'A little. Only met him a couple of times. I could tell you a little about the family and Ashley. Maybe we could have a coffee or a drink?'

Moone's heart rippled to life, realising suddenly that a young attractive woman had asked him out. 'Well, I don't know. We're not supposed to…'

'Oh right. Yes.' She smiled awkwardly, nodding.

'But I suppose it's not really an official investigation… so there's no real harm.'

She smiled, raising one of her perfectly shaped eyebrows. 'That's more like it. Pick me up here tonight. About eight?'

'OK. Will do.' He smiled, feeling suddenly incredibly self-aware, then turned and walked out to find Butler waiting on the pavement. Her arms were folded, her eyebrows raised.

'What was that about?' she asked.

'Nothing. Just being nosey.'

'I hope you didn't tell her anything.' Butler turned and headed back to the car.

'Course not.' Moone turned his head towards the solicitors and saw Rachel had gone back to work, talking to someone on the phone. But her eyes found him, and she smiled.

Detective Constable Molly Chambers drove out towards Mannamead, finding the traffic growing heavier as they got past Mutley. She looked in the rear-view mirror and saw DS Carthew sat on the back seat, going through some statements. She had been a little annoyed to see her climb in the back, and had started to feel more like a chauffeur than a police officer. She shrugged it off like she did most things, storing it up to tell Tyler about it later over a large glass of wine.

She flinched a little when Carthew's eyes met hers.

'I suppose you think I'm being rude,' Carthew said, smiling only a little. 'But there's more room in the back. I don't expect you to chauffeur me about.'

Molly smiled, returning her eyes to the road where the traffic had started moving again.

'What's it been like,' Carthew said, sitting forward, 'working with Butler and Moone?'

'It's fine.'

'Just fine?'

'It's good. I mostly man the phones, while they get all the legwork and action.'

'I see. You'll get there. Look at me. You've just got to be a bit proactive.'

Molly smiled and nodded, burying the things she'd heard about Carthew, the rumours about the men she might have slept with...

'You've probably heard rumours about me.'

Molly looked up at the rear view mirror, saw Carthew's eyes were staring at her. 'Er... no, not really.'

'They only spread those rumours because they're jealous. I'm being fast tracked and they're not. I made myself known, pushed myself forward. Us women should stick together.'

'Definitely.' Molly spotted the road they wanted on their left, thanked heaven for it, and signalled to turn into it. 'Here we are.'

She managed to find a parking space a hundred yards away and on the opposite side of the road to the large, three-storey house they were headed for. Molly was glad to find that DS Carthew climbed out of her own volition and didn't wait for her to open the door for her.

They headed up the grey stone steps and Molly rang the bell beside the double wood doors.

'Let me do all the talking,' Carthew said as Molly heard the door being unlocked.

A slender woman with long, shiny dark hair and pale skin, wearing an elegant red dress was standing in the doorway. 'Can I help you?' the woman asked in a well-spoken voice.

Carthew took out her ID. 'DS Faith Carthew. This is DC Molly Chambers. We've come about your husband.'

The woman's large oval eyes took in their IDs, then their faces. 'More of you? I see. Have you found him?'

'I'm sorry, no,' Carthew said. 'Can we come in?'

The woman let out a subtle tired sounding breath, then opened the door wider, allowing them to enter a wide black and white tiled entrance hall.

Molly followed Carthew inside, her eyes jumping to a few modern art style canvases on the walls. The woman went around them, then directed them all into a high-ceilinged, minimalist lounge. A black grand piano sat in one corner, a leather sofa in the other. Molly could see no TV. How could anyone survive without a TV, she thought and suspected it must be hidden.

Mrs Audrey Beckett sat down on the sofa, and crossed her long, slender and pale legs. 'What news have you brought?'

'I'm afraid we haven't got much to report,' Carthew said, standing by the sofa, looking down at the lady of the house. 'This is more of a check-in. The case has been passed on to me. We're taking your husband's disappearance very seriously...'

'I should hope so. My husband has been missing for nearly two weeks. He hasn't run off with another woman, in case that's what you're thinking.'

'No, no one's thinking that, Mrs Beckett. For one thing there's been no activity on his bank account since he went missing.'

'Apart from the five thousand pounds that was withdrawn.'

'Five thousand pounds?' Carthew said, sharing her surprise with Molly. 'That's a lot of money. You didn't report this before, I didn't read…'

'I've only just become aware of it,' Mrs Beckett said, uncrossing her legs. 'Edward dealt with all the finances. It's only when I went to the bank that I realised the money had been withdrawn.'

'Did the bank say who withdrew the money?' Molly asked, noticing that Carthew flashed her a lot of anger that quickly subsided.

Mrs Beckett turned to Molly. 'It seems that my husband withdrew the money. It was an unusual thing for him to do… but if he had decided to start a new life, five thousand pounds wouldn't get him very far. Would it?'

'No, it wouldn't,' Carthew said. 'And you can't think of any other reason that your husband would want to hide away?'

'None at all.' Audrey Beckett got to her feet and carefully picked a piece of fluff from her dress. 'I'm not an emotional person. Inside I'm incredibly worried. Please find out what has happened to my husband. I need him home as soon as possible.'

'We'll do our best.' Carthew smiled, then signalled for Molly that it was time they were leaving.

Mrs Beckett showed them to the door, her dark eyes watching them as they walked down to the car and got in, still with very little emotion breaking her skin.

This time DS Carthew climbed in beside Molly as she started the engine.

'Turn it off,' Carthew said, turning to Molly.

Molly turned off the engine and stared at her boss, waiting.

'Five grand. That's a lot of money.'

'It is. But like she said, not enough to vanish on and start a new life.'

Carthew shook her head. 'No, it's not. So what was it for? I think we need to take a closer look at his life, his finances. Maybe he had debts that she didn't know about. Husbands hide lots of stuff from their wives, and sometimes they even have second families.'

'So do wives.'

Carthew stared at her, a hint of malice in her eyes. 'Yes, but men are the worst offenders. Take Moone for instance. He did the dirty on his wife. Typical man. Bastard. Come on, let's get back to the station. I think we're going to make a good team, you and me.'

Molly smiled, but quickly lost it as she started the engine, reversed, then took them out of the road. Her last words on Moone stayed with her, echoing in her mind. There was definitely something about DS Carthew that she didn't like or couldn't quite understand.

The house in St Ann's Chapel was set back quite far from the road, up a sloping gravel path. It was adjoined to another identical house, but separate from the few others along the road. Fields surrounded the houses, and a disused petrol garage sat opposite.

Butler parked up, then turned to stare at the whitewashed house. Moone noticed a Land Rover parked on the drive.

'Maybe they're home,' Moone said, climbed out and crossed the quiet road, spots of icy rain starting to tap at his head.

'I hate this bit,' Butler said as they crunched up the drive, then went up the stone steps to the front door. A dog barked loudly inside as footsteps came towards the front door.

A short woman, with curly blonde hair and a ruddy face looked out at them, her hand gripped to a large golden retriever's collar. 'Hello. Excuse Flossy. What do you want?'

Moone showed his ID. 'DCI Peter Moone. This is DI Mandy Butler. Are you Charlene Bale's mother?'

The woman's expression changed, her head turning to the side as she shouted, 'Tony! Get down here!'

Then she straightened herself, her skin looking more ruddy, as her eyes searched them both. 'What's happened?'

Moone's gut was tied in knots as he said, 'Can we come inside?'

Heavy steps came down the stairs and a thick set, grey bearded middle-aged man appeared behind her. 'What's going on?'

'We're from the police,' Butler said. 'We've got some bad news.'

It was Tony, the husband who managed to grab his wife as she started to fall, and Moone who rushed past the stairs and into the large farmhouse style kitchen he spotted. He brought back a glass of water and found them all in a large room that was filled with sunlight from the winter sun. The husband and wife were seated on a bulky brown leather sofa, her resting her head on his chest. He half stroked her hair, while also fighting off the dog that tried to get in on the action.

Butler stood by watching, her arms at her sides, a hint of sadness in her eyes.

'Here you go,' Moone said and handed the husband the water.

'What's happened?' Tony asked.

Moone stood back, choosing his words. 'Your daughter, Charlene...'

The woman buried her face in Tony's arms and began to sob. The man looked up, staring at Moone, his eyes a little wet too. 'Go on.'

'We're still investigating,' Moone said. 'But it looks at the moment as if she took her own life.'

The crying grew in intensity, Tony holding his wife tighter as she shuddered and sobbed, his face stolid. 'That's not right. Charlene would never... she would never do anything like that! You're wrong.'

'I'm very sorry,' Moone said. 'I'm just telling

you what we've found so far. Like I said, we're still investigating... there's questions we need to ask, but they can wait until a later date.'

'Ask them,' Tony said, his eyes filling up.

Moone nodded. 'Did Charlene suffer with depression... or...'

'Nothing like that. She was a happy young woman.'

'Can you think of anyone who might want to harm her?'

'No, I can't...'

The mother came out of her husband's grip, sniffing, and wiping her swollen and red eyes. 'Everyone... everyone... they all... they loved her... didn't they, Tony?'

'Everyone. But someone must have wanted to hurt her. Someone took away our girl. You find them! You find the person, this bastard who took her life.'

Moone looked at Butler, and she raised her eyebrows, then nodded towards the door.

'We'll leave you alone,' Moone said. 'We'll send a family liaison officer, and keep in touch.'

The husband nodded as his wife began to cry again, so Moone backed away, watching them, aching all over for them. He made a mental note to get in contact with his kids and make sure they were all safe and happy.

'Come on,' Butler said, pulling him by his arm. He turned and followed her along the hall, the dog behind him, sniffing him. He forced the dog back and shut the front door, then breathed the cold, but bright winter air.

'I hate all that,' Butler said, then turned and went down the steps to the driveway.

He followed, but stopped at the bottom of the steps as he heard his phone ringing. Harding was calling.

'Moone,' he said. 'What is it?'

'Thought you'd better know that the tyre tracks in the snow you found matched Charlene Bale's car.'

'So she or someone drove her there, then left her with no shoes?'

'Looks like it. We also took a look at her mobile phone records. The phone went off just by Princetown. Not been on since.'

'Thanks. We're coming back.'

CHAPTER 4

DC Molly Chambers was back at her desk, typing something up when Moone entered the incident room. Harding was on the phone, while Butler was elsewhere, perhaps getting them a coffee, he hoped. He went over to Chambers and smiled when she looked up.

'Boss,' she said. 'All OK?'

'Fine.' He looked round the room. 'Where's your new partner in crime?'

'DS Carthew? Not sure. Must be something important. Left me with the paper trail.'

'Missing persons case, yeah?'

'Yes. Two weeks. No trace.'

He nodded. 'We've got two suicides, supposedly, but I'm not convinced.' Moone turned to Harding. 'Have you got any more for me, Harding?'

Harding had just put down the phone and looked over. 'Not much, boss. Just the tyre tracks and the knife. Her tyre tracks. The knife only had her prints on it. Still no idea where her mobile phone is. Why wouldn't it be on her?'

'Not at her place?' Moone asked.

'Search team hasn't found it.'

Moone went over to the whiteboard, picked up a marker and made some notes. 'So where would it be? And where is Simon Whittle's mobile? What about Charlene's finances? Any money missing?'

'Not sure. I'll have to get in touch with her bank.'

'Do it, please,' Moone said.

'Excuse me, DCI Moone,' Molly said, raising her hand.

Moone gave a laugh. 'Moone will do, and you don't have to raise your hand. What is it?'

'You mentioned missing money. When we went to see Audrey Beckett today, the wife of the missing man, she mentioned money going missing. Well, she said it looked like the husband had taken out five thousand from their account, something he normally wouldn't do.'

Moone's neck hair rose and prickled once again. 'Five grand? Right, we definitely need to know if Charlene took any money out before she allegedly killed herself.'

'Could be a coincidence,' Harding said. 'Your missing guy's probably done a bunk.'

'On five grand?' Moone said, then his eyes jumped to Butler as she came through the door, followed by a stocky, dark-haired uniform.

'DS Pinder's here,' Butler said. 'Thought

you'd want a word.'

'Yep,' Moone said. 'Let's find an interview room.'

Sergeant Kevin Pinder was already sat at the desk in the interview room, his arms folded, only turning his head to watch Moone and Butler enter and sit down.

'Thanks for coming in,' Moone said, smiling slightly.

'It's not a problem,' Pinder said, leaning forward. 'I was in the station anyway. What's all this about?'

'Simon Whittle?' Moone said. 'Is that name familiar to you?'

Pinder seemed to think for a moment, then nodded. 'Yes, the guy who jumped from the civic centre. A bad day for all involved.'

'You oversaw the whole thing?' Butler said.

Pinder stared at her. 'Yes. That's right. It was decided it was a straightforward suicide and so I was given the job of gathering all the relevant information and statements for the coroner. You know how it works.'

'Yes, we do.' Moone looked down at his notes. 'Who decided it was a suicide and there shouldn't be any further investigation?'

Pinder sat up, seemed to tense. 'It came from above. I reported the circumstances, and I was told to treat it like it seemed to be, just a suicide.'

'How long have you been on the force?' Moone asked.

'Nearly ten years.'

'You get a feeling for things, don't you? What's right, what's not?'

Pinder shrugged. 'I suppose.'

'What was your feeling about Simon Whittle's suicide?' Moone looked up at him, engaged his dark green eyes.

'Didn't matter what my...'

'But we want to know,' Butler said, sounding pissed off.

Pinder nodded. 'OK. Yeah, if you must know, I wasn't happy with it. At least I wasn't after I talked to his wife and found out there didn't seem to be any real history of depression or anything. Then there was the missing money and the missing mobile...'

'Did you raise these concerns?' Moone asked.

'Of course.'

'With who?'

'My inspector. He passed it on, but in the end I was told to write it up as suicide and pass it on to the coroner. What else could I do?'

Butler sighed and sat back. 'If they'd passed it on to us lot, that would mean an investigation, more money spent, more of the budget gone...'

'Exactly,' Pinder said, nodding. 'It's the way it always is. You looking into it, then? Reopening the case?'

Moone looked down at his notes, let out a breath. 'I don't think they'll let us. They won't want all this coming out. We're looking into a similar case. Young woman, cut her own throat.'

'I heard about that,' Pinder said, shaking his head. 'I hate stuff like that. You don't reckon she did it to herself?'

'Looks like she did,' Moone said. 'But I'm not convinced she wanted to...'

'Then why would she?' Pinder asked.

Moone shrugged. 'I don't know. I really don't. Thanks for talking to us, Sergeant. You can go now.'

Pinder nodded, then got to his feet, seeming to hesitate as he went for the door.

'You all right, Pinder?' Butler asked.

'Not really,' he said. 'The whole business never sat right with me. I feel like I should've done more. If I can help out, be of any use...'

Moone looked up at him, saw for the first time that he seemed to be genuinely upset by it all. He was quite aware of how it ached and burned to live with regret and pain. 'I'll see what I can do about having you seconded to our investigation, if it ever takes off. Don't hold your breath.'

'I'd appreciate that if you can.'

'I'll try. Scout's honour.'

Pinder nodded, then left the room.

'Poor bastard,' Butler said, sitting back, then tutting.

'Bet it was the Chief Super pushing for a clear-cut suicide verdict.' Moone put away his notes.

'Course it was. Less paperwork and the murder rate stays reasonably low.'

'What're we saying then? Why did these people kill themselves? A seemingly happy young woman, and an also seemingly happily married businessman?'

Butler sighed. 'I don't know. Why don't you tell me, Sherlock?'

'I don't bloody know. But somebody drove Charlene to her death, then parked her car outside her boyfriend's place… '

'Then maybe it's him. Maybe he drove her there…'

'Why? Are you saying he somehow got in her head, somehow mentally tortured her until she agreed to take a knife to herself?'

'Wouldn't be the first time a boyfriend or husband mentally abused their other half, would it?'

Moone blew out his cheeks as he opened the door. 'No, but it doesn't feel right. Let's get him in, find out if he knows anything else and see if he's got an alibi. But I'm not convinced. I mean, why would he park the car outside his place? Why not hers? And if you want it to read as a suicide, then why not leave the car where it was, out there in Dartmoor?'

'I don't know, Pete. I don't know. But I do

know we're going to get bloody moaned at when the Chief Super finds out what we're up to.'

'That might happen sooner than you think.' Moone walked on ahead, then heard the quick tap of Butler's heels as she came after him.

'What does that bloody well mean?'

'It means... well, the missing persons case that DS Carthew is working on, I think might be connected to our suicides. Come on, I'll go over it in the incident room.'

When Moone got inside the incident room, he stopped dead, nearly causing Butler to bump into his back. DS Carthew was back, going over her missing persons case with Molly Chambers in the corner opposite his team. His stomach took a swan dive as his eyes met Chambers' and they exchanged awkward glances. He carried on, clapping his hands together and suddenly feeling like his old boss. Now he was the senior officer that everyone was supposed to look up to and it scared the shit out of him. Harding, the other members of the team and the civvies came towards the whiteboard and sat down, while Butler rested her backside on her desk, arms folded.

'Right,' Moone started. 'As you know, we're dealing with an apparent suicide. Charlene Bale drove or was driven to a field near Princetown last night and then she cut her own throat. She was barefoot, which has raised some concerns.'

'Excuse me, DCI Moone.'

Moone turned to see Carthew approaching as she said, 'Aren't you supposed to be collecting all the evidence together for the coroner?'

He stared at her, feeling the eyes of the room on him. 'Yep. I'm investigating, clearing up some issues. That's what we do.'

'But you're treating this like it's a murder investigation.'

'Thank you, DS Carthew, but I believe you're working on a missing persons investigation.'

Her smirk faded as the anger took hold of her face, a dark cloud arriving over her head. 'Quite right. Something I will do efficiently, by the book, unlike some round here.'

Moone watched her return to her desk, where she started talking to Molly quietly about their case. He watched for a moment, gathering his thoughts, hoping to hell that her case and his was not connected at all. He was never that lucky.

'Boss?'

Moone broke out of his nightmare when he heard Harding's voice. 'Sorry. Yes, so there are questions arising, like who drove her car out of Princetown and back to her boyfriend's place.'

'Could be the boyfriend,' Butler said.

'We need to talk to him again,' Moone said. 'What if they weren't the loving couple he makes out?'

'I checked up on her finances,' Harding said.

'And?'

'Eight hundred pounds was withdrawn from her account a couple of days before we found her. Bank says she took it out.'

Moone rubbed his eyes. 'So, what do we think is happening here? That's both Whittle and Bale who've taken large amounts of money from their accounts before they, well, whatever happened to them.'

'Only two of them did this,' Butler said. 'Could be a coincidence. Maybe they both just wanted to give someone some money before they ended it all.'

Moone nodded, then looked over at DS Carthew and saw she had stopped her little chat to focus her attention on them. She was staring, but when Moone looked at her, she turned away and began talking to Molly again. He walked over, his stomach churning, trying to find the right words.

'So,' he said, looking between Carthew and Molly. 'How's your investigation going?'

Carthew stared at him, emotionless. 'Fine. Nothing to see here.'

'I see. Missing husband? What's he called?'

'Edward Beckett,' Molly said, then fell silent when Carthew glared at her.

Moone nodded. 'No sign of him? Any activity on his bank account?'

'None,' Carthew said. 'But it's none of your business, is it?'

'Any large withdrawals before he went

missing?'

Carthew stood up, her eyes jumping to Molly, the burn of anger in them. 'Whoever's been talking to you, they've got it wrong. Beckett's alive somewhere. He's done a bunk, started a new life. So don't start getting any funny ideas. This is my case, a missing person case and I'll find him. Right, Chambers let's get a coffee then find an office somewhere, and get some peace and quiet.'

Molly turned to Moone and gave him an apologetic shrug as she grabbed all their files and rushed out to follow Carthew.

'That went well,' Butler said, and sighed. 'Anyway, she's probably right. He's probably done a bunk. Just a coincidence.'

'There's no such thing,' Moone said, turning to the whiteboard and staring at the photograph of Charlene Bale. 'Someone once told me that. I believe them. Let's look up any similar cases over the last few years...'

'What?!' Butler stormed over. 'You're joking? You are joking, aren't you? You heard the Chief Super. We're supposed to be gathering all the data for the coroner! This is not a murder investigation, Moone!'

'What if it is? What if someone was blackmailing them, hence the withdrawals, then they force them to take their own lives...'

'How, exactly? How does someone force you to kill yourself?'

He shrugged. 'I don't know. But I know if someone was pointing a gun at my kids' heads and telling me to cut my own throat, I'd do it. I'd have to.'

Butler pinched her nose. 'All we've got is two suicides. That's it. Don't go jumping to conclusions.'

'Let's get the boyfriend in.'

'Excuse me, DCI Moone?'

Moone swung round to see one of the civvies, a full-bodied woman with tied back greying blonde hair, putting her hand in the air.

'Yes,' he said, going over. 'Sorry, I don't know your name.'

'Anita,' the civvy said as she sat at her desk, staring at her monitor. 'I've been going through the CCTV footage. I think I've picked up Charlene Bale's car heading past Derriford.'

Moone went round her desk, followed by Butler and Harding. On Anita's monitor was a grainy image of the car heading towards a junction. Charlene was driving, her face perhaps drawn, her eyes wide. It was hard to tell from the image, but Moone thought she could have been scared.

'So, she drove herself?' Butler shrugged. 'See.'

'Run the footage, Anita,' Moone said, and leant in close when the footage started to play. Then he saw it, just as the car was moving past the junction, the camera capturing the back seat.

'Stop!'

Anita paused it, so Moone pointed to the back seat, where a leg and hand could just be made out. 'Look, someone's on the back seat.'

'Where?' Butler leaned in. 'Shit!'

'Who sits on the back seat as you drive yourself to your suicide?' Moone asked, looking them over, feeling the prickling up his spine.

'The boyfriend?' Butler asked, then went back to her desk and slumped into her seat.

'Maybe. Like I said, let's get him in and see what he has to say.'

About an hour and a half later, Moone and Butler stepped into an interview room to find Darren Taylor sat there, a cup of water by his hand. Moone realised how tall he really was, now sat uncomfortably under the desk, his legs out at awkward angles. Moone took a seat, noting his light blue polo shirt and matching trousers, some kind of emblem on his chest.

As Butler sat down, Moone said, 'Thanks for coming in, Darren.'

He nodded, looking glum. 'You found anything out?'

'Not a great deal,' Moone said, looking down at the file he'd brought with him. 'But we will. What's the uniform for?'

Darren looked down. 'My work. A cleaning company. I'm supposed to be there by now.'

'We'll try and get you on your way as soon

as.'

'I keep thinking 'bout it,' Darren said, shaking his head. 'Char wouldn't do that. No way. I mean, if she was, like, upset or...'

'You would've known?' Butler said, leaning forward.

Darren nodded. 'I'm dying for a ciggy.'

Moone felt his pain. 'After this. So, Charlene never came over last night?'

'No, I told you. She told me she was staying at hers.'

'But her car was parked outside your place,' Butler added.

Darren looked at her. 'Yeah, but I don't know why. Why would she leave it there?'

'We don't think she did, Darren,' Moone said and opened the file. He took out a photo, a still from the CCTV and pushed it across the desk. 'Look at the back seat. That was taken as Charlene drove towards Dartmoor last night.'

Darren looked down, staring at the image. He looked up. 'Who's that?'

'We don't know.' Moone sat back. 'We were hoping you could enlighten us.'

Darren looked between them. 'It's not me. Have you seen her car? It's one of those little, shitty things. If that was me, I'd have my knees round me fucking ears.'

Moone moved the photo back towards himself, looking at it again, realising that Darren was right. But he nodded, then dragged out another image, caught on the way through town. He showed Darren as he said, 'You shouldn't have driven that way.'

Darren stared down at it, becoming paler, fidgeting. His head came up, a little pleading in his eyes. 'Yeah, that's me. I know it looks bad, but I can explain.'

'Go on.' Butler folded her arms. 'I can't wait.'

'Me and Char had a row a couple of nights ago,' Darren said, hanging his head. 'I was driving home the other day, and I went past her place. I sees her up the road, talking to some fucking bloke. Snarky looking bastard. I said to her about it, but she said it was someone from work, nothing to it. But you should've seen the way she was smiling and...'

'What about her car?' Moone asked, watching him carefully.

'I took it. I had a spare key for it. Walked up there and took it.'

'Why?' Butler asked. 'To piss her off?'

Darren shook his head. 'No. She'd have to come and get it, wouldn't she? Then we could talk and, you know...'

Moone sat back. 'So, you had a row, and you're admitting to stealing her car?'

Darren stared at him, his eyes widening. 'It wasn't stealing, I just...'

'You took it without her permission.'

'I know, but it's not like...'

Butler huffed. 'You're just giving us a reason

your prints will be all over her car...'

'No! I've driven her car before, taken it to get fixed... I didn't do this... please, I'm telling you. That's not me in that photo, I'm not the bloke in the back...'

Moone looked down at the photographs, thinking, realising they hadn't got very far. 'Who was this bloke you saw her with?'

Darren raised his broad shoulders. 'Don't know. He was suited, slick hair and all that. Up his own arse, probably. Looked the sort.'

'She didn't say his name?' Moone asked.

'No.'

'But he worked with her? At the library?'

'So she said. Look, I don't know what's going on. Things between us had been up and down, had been since she went and saw this bloody psychic woman. Load of old bollocks, if you ask me.'

'Psychic woman?' Moone asked.

'Yeah, she went there a few weeks back. Then she started acting all weird, trying to work out all the stuff she'd told her. She was really taken in by it all.'

'What's her name, this psychic?' Moone asked, taking out his notebook.

'I can't really remember,' Darren said. 'Think her last name began with an "r". Foreign sounding.'

'Revello?' Butler asked.

'That's it, I think.' Darren nodded. 'Anyway,

she must've fucked with her head, cause she wasn't herself after that.'

Moone stood up. 'Right, thanks for coming, Mr Taylor.'

'That all?' Darren stood up.

'Yep. We'll let you know if we need anything more. The uniform outside will show you out.'

Darren looked between them, then headed to the door, almost sheepishly, then went out.

'What do you reckon?' Butler asked, following Moone on their way out.

'I don't think he's anything to do with it.'

'To do with what though?' Butler asked. 'You still think someone forced her to do it?'

Moone stopped in the corridor, rubbed his face, thinking it all over. 'I don't know. But who was in the back of the car? It's not Darren, that's for sure. Someone was with her, sat on the back seat as she headed to her death. Why in the back, unless they had a knife or gun pointed at her. Why was she barefoot? So she couldn't run very far?'

Butler blew the air from her cheeks. 'Jesus. Anyway, why did you want the name of this psychic?'

'Revello? You seem to have heard of her.'

'Everyone in Plymouth has.'

Moone smiled. 'I bet. Have you been to see her?'

'I'm not answering that.' Butler turned and started walking back to the incident room.

'You have, haven't you?'

She stopped, folded her arms. 'Why did you want her name?'

'Because if Charlene Bale did go and see her, then she's bound to have told her something about her life, her worries. People only go to see psychics when they're at a crossroads or in trouble. I think Charlene Bale was in some kind of trouble. That's why she died. I'm starting to believe someone killed her.'

CHAPTER 5

Sarah MacPherson looked at the text message again. There was no name with the number, only the short message. She looked round the cafe again as she sat at the back, hearing the kids crying, the chatter of the customers echoing round the cave-like interior. She put down her phone, her heart beating faster, her stomach full of black moths. She sipped her milky coffee, watching people enter, suspecting that each person who came inside was the person who had sent the message.

She read it again:

'I know all about you,' it said. 'Gorge Cafe, 1pm.'

She'd replied to the message to ask what they meant, but nothing came back. She was trembling as she sat there, feeling everyone was staring at her, as if they knew what she had done. It was such a long time ago, but it always came back to her, usually on bright days, the good days when everything seemed better. The darkness would creep in, the flashes of that day. The sickness rose up, her heart now filled with the black moths. She always saw her sadness as moths, evil looking things, but she didn't understand why.

The door to the cafe kept opening, the cold wind coming in with it, making her shiver even more than she already was. The meeting time came and went, and her coffee grew colder. Eventually she got up, looking round to see if anyone was staring at her, watching. It had been someone's idea of a sick joke; but why would they say what they said in the message? Her mind tried to make sense of it, tried desperately to come up with an explanation that didn't result in her secret being exposed. She wanted to cry, but she held it all in as she headed through the customers just arriving, fighting to get out of the cafe and onto the cold street.

As she headed for the bus stop, tears forming in her eyes, she heard her phone beep. She took it out as she got under the bus shelter, spits of rain hitting her face.

The same phone number.

Her heart beat faster as she opened the message.

'I see you,' it said. 'You will pay for what you did.'

'Who are you?' she typed.

Pause.

'I want money. Do not go to the police. Go to

them and the world will know what you did.'

'Why are you doing this?'

Nothing. No more messages, and she stood there in the crowded bus stop, the bus having arrived, her eyes filling up with tears. She sniffed, her mind spinning, the adrenaline pumping through her veins. Who knew? Who would do this? She had left it all behind, started a new life, so who could possibly know?

'You all right, my luvver?'

Sarah looked up with blurry eyes and saw the elderly woman looking at her with sympathy. She smiled, nodded, and thanked her. She managed to get on the bus and sat at the back, staring at her phone, wondering how much money they would want. Where the hell would she get the money from?

Butler drove them up towards Mutley Plain, then along Mannamead Road and into Eggbuckland Road. Agatha Revello lived in a pleasant looking white painted house with a red roof in Higher Compton. A large brick porch jutted out the front of the house, and a flight of white steps led down to a long driveway. Moone noticed the battered mobile home that sat on the drive as they parked up and got out.

'You've been here before, then?' Moone said, trying not to smirk, but failing miserably.

Butler turned her annoyed eyes on him. 'Not a word, you. I was going through a difficult time.'

'I'm sure you were.' Moone started up the flight of steps, aching for a cigarette with each one.

'You never read your horoscopes in the paper?' Butler joined him at the top step.

'Only for a laugh.' He rang the bell and waited, taking out his ID.

The front door opened a moment later, revealing a skinny man, easily in his mid-forties, dressed in a grey shirt, with thick glasses on, and greasy brown hair thinly covering his scalp.

'Have you got an appointment?' the man asked.

Moone showed his ID. 'Will this do? DCI Peter Moone, DI Mandy Butler. Is Agatha Revello home?'

The man, looking a little perturbed, turned and stared into the darkness of the house. '*Mum! Police are here!*'

Then he looked back at them, blank faced, staring at them through his thick glasses that made his eyes seem gigantic. 'Come in. I suppose. Mum will come and...'

He let them in and stood awkwardly in the doorway as they walked across a thick red carpet down a hall lined with photographs of an elderly woman with various people, some of which Moone thought he recognised.

'Keep going,' the man said, waving them into the dark hallway. 'Conservatory.'

Moone saw the glass door at the end of the hallway and knocked. Seconds later, a young woman with curly blonde hair came out clutching a CD, tears in her eyes. The woman glanced at Moone, then Butler, then hurried towards the front door.

It was dark in the conservatory, but a couple of red bulbs glowed in the corners, allowing him to see the shape of a small elderly woman sat at a round, wooden table. Moone flinched when he made out her sharp little eyes staring deeply into his.

'Agatha Revello?' Moone asked.

'Madam Revello,' she said, trying to sound posh, he thought, although her Plymouth accent wasn't very well hidden. 'Have you an appointment?'

'Like I said to your son,' Moone said, showing his ID. 'We're the police.'

'I knew you were coming,' she said, taking a pack of tarot cards from the table. 'I saw it in my cards this morning.'

Moone turned and saw Butler was staring at the woman, a look of astonishment on her face. 'I'm sure you did.'

'You don't believe?'

'Can't say that I do. Anyway, we'd like to ask you a few questions…'

The woman signalled to the seat opposite her. 'Then sit down and I'll tell you what I can.'

Moone sat down, letting out a sigh. The

woman suddenly pushed the deck of tarot cards towards him, touching his hand with them. Then she dragged them back, started shuffling them a little, her small dark eyes staring into Moone.

She put down a few cards, smiling to herself, then looked up at him. 'You've had a lot of tragedy in your life, Peter.'

Moone gave a laugh. 'Who hasn't?'

'I see a woman, blonde, beautiful...'

'Jesus, just listen...'

'She died. You blame yourself...'

Moone's head shot up, staring at her, his stomach turning over. 'I just want to ask you about...'

'You worry a lot about... a young girl. Your daughter?'

'Good guess.'

'Begins with the letter A. Anna? No, it's... yes, it's Alice?'

Moone tried to keep his face deadpan, not to give away anything. She was reading him. Cold reading, they called it, a con person's game. 'We want to talk to you about *this* young woman.'

Moone took out his phone and showed Agatha the photo of Charlene Bale. 'You recognise her?'

The woman picked up a pair of spectacles and put them on. She nodded. 'I remember her. She was lost. Poor child. I tried to help her. I tried to warn her, too...'

'About what?' Butler asked, stepping close to Moone.

'There was darkness in her life,' Agatha said. 'Great darkness. She was troubled about the past.'

'Did she say exactly what was troubling her?' Moone asked, getting tired of all the dramatics.

'No, but it was there. All around her, like a dark cloud hanging over her. Even her aura was shrouded in darkness.'

'I didn't think you told people the bad things,' Moone said, smiling. 'Isn't that one of the psychic's rules?'

The old lady looked into him, staring, those dark eyes picking around in his mind, or trying to. Reading him. Definitely trying to read his face. 'I have a duty to say something… If I see something bad, like with you, Peter.'

'Me?' Moone laughed.

'What do you see?' Butler asked.

Agatha looked at the cards. 'Darkness. It's coming for you, Peter. It has a shape. A pleasant shape. You have to be careful when it comes to love.'

Moone didn't bother holding in his sigh, then thought about Simon Whittle, and wondered if he had been a believer. He brought out the photograph he'd managed to find from the Evening Herald and showed it to Agatha. 'You ever read for this man?'

The psychic looked down at the

photograph. 'I read for a lot of people. It's possible.'

'Do you have an appointment book, some kind of record?'

'People like to keep their secrets.'

'We're dealing with a death here.' Moone got to his feet. 'That young woman, she's dead...'

'I tried to warn her...'

Moone let out an empty laugh, let her see his utter disrespect for her profession. 'Did you, really? I'm going to need you to come up with some kind of appointment book...'

'I don't keep one. I'm very sorry she died.'

'I bet you are. Another punter, a lost soul looking for someone to tell her it'll be all right. What a laugh. Come on, Butler.'

Moone turned and headed to the door but stopped when he heard the woman say his name.

'Peter,' she said. 'Be careful when it comes to love. It can bring as much darkness as it does light.'

'Good one.'

'It might even take your life if you let it.'

Moone looked into the woman's dark eyes that burned into him. He felt the hairs stand up on the back of his neck again, but he shrugged it off, and headed back out into the darkness of the hall and then out the front door where the low winter sun burned into his eyes.

'You all right?' Butler asked, following him down the steps.

'Yep, fine.' Moone searched his jacket and found the last of his cigarettes and shakily lit one, then took a deep puff.

'That shook you up, didn't it?'

Moone looked up at her as he blew out some smoke. 'What shook me up was all her bollocks. Charlatan.'

'She knew quite a bit about you. That thing about love and darkness, you know who that's about, don't you?'

'Why don't you enlighten me?'

'Faith Carthew. If you don't steer clear of her, she'll be the end of you.' Butler climbed in the car and started the engine, and he could see her watching him, her eyebrows raised. He got in eventually and stared straight ahead.

'Where now, then?' she asked.

'Let's find out if Simon Whittle ever visited Madam Revello.'

'Really? What, now you think that old dear's forcing people to commit suicide? Look, I bought into your forced suicide theory, but now I'm not so sure...'

'Somehow, someone knew something about Charlene Bale. Psychics know stuff about people, and they can even get you spilling your guts without you even knowing it...'

'If there is some mastermind behind all this. Probably just plain old suicide.' She pulled the car away from the kerb. 'Come on, then, let's go and talk to his widow.'

The wind seemed to be beating at her outer door, rattling the letterbox, the eerie whistling travelling through the entire building. Sarah was still trembling a little, a cup of tea in her hand, staring at her phone as if it might suddenly give her some answers.

She could call the police, report whoever was sending her the messages; but she knew that the messages said little, definitely nothing threatening. No, she couldn't call them anyway, just in case they did know all about her, did know the truth of what she had...

The buzzer of her flat screamed out. Her hand jumped, knocking over her cup of tea, the milky liquid pouring along her kitchen work surface and onto the floor. She grabbed handfuls of kitchen towels and started to mop up the mess.

Buzzzzz. Buzzzzz.

She jumped up, angry, tears in her eyes. Nothing went right.

She ran up to the intercom and pressed the door release. She heard the wind and rain come in with whoever was at the door.

'Hello?' a man's voice said.

She opened her door and looked down the stairwell, into the threadbare carpeted hallway. There was a man in a hooded winter coat, a package in his hands.

'Hi,' she said. 'Who do you want?'

The man looked down at the package. 'Sarah MacPherson?'

'That's me.'

'Needs to be signed for,' he said and started walking up the stairs.

When he got to the landing, he held out a small tablet device and said, 'Got a pen or pencil?'

'Can I use my finger?'

'No, don't work, I'm sorry.'

'OK, hang on,' she said, then went back inside and towards the kitchen to find her pot of pens and paper clips, and all the other stuff she kept inside in case of some kind of stationery emergency. She grabbed a biro, half laughing at her pathetic life, then swung her head round towards the door.

She thought she heard the front door close. She listened out, then heard the creak of someone walking, sounding like it was coming from the living room.

She headed towards the landing, expecting to see him standing there, the package in his hand still.

The door was shut. The man wasn't there, but she could smell something, a scent, something familiar. Out of the corner of her eye, she saw movement and swept round to see someone sitting in her front room, on the sofa. Their hooded head was turned away

'What're you doing?' She stepped in, her heart racing, her hands trembling with a mix of fear and anger.

Then her breath was sucked out of her. He turned to look at her, his face covered by a black stocking, his skin distorted beneath it. He lowered the hood, sitting up a little.

'Sarah,' he said, almost quietly. 'Sarah. I've always liked that name.'

'What do you want?' She thought about running as she half turned her head towards the door.

Then he put a hand in his coat, took out a large kitchen knife and laid it next to him on the sofa. 'You did receive my messages?'

Her heart thumped uncontrollably, the realisation flooding her mind, her body, every inch of her alive, trembling. 'Why did you send them? I don't understand...'

'You know. *I know.* You asked what I wanted before.' He stood up, making her back away. 'I want money.'

'Money?'

'Thing is, I haven't got time for all that other business. The bank, you drawing cash out... so, I ask, how much do you have on you?'

'Money? I don't know. I've got some...' Money. All he wanted was money, and he wore a mask, like a burglar or bank robber. *He was mugging her*. Her mind clicked in, telling her to remember every detail she could.

'How much?' He picked up the knife from the sofa and she realised for the first time he was wearing flesh-coloured latex gloves.

'I, I, think about, two hundred.'

'That'll have to do. Fetch it.'

She backed away, watching the knife as he toyed with it, swapping hands, then up at his eyes that she could hardly see through the stocking mask. She couldn't make out eye colour or hair colour. Perhaps it was light brown, maybe darker, it was so hard to tell.

She hurried to her bedroom, where she had the money stashed in a locked metal box under her bed. She grabbed all the money and walked back into the lounge. He was sitting again, waiting, the knife resting on his lap.

She held out the money. He held out his gloved hand, so she carefully stepped closer, stretching her arm until the money touched his hand. He snatched it away but didn't bother counting it, just stuffed it in his coat.

'Good, Sarah,' he said, softly. 'That was very good.' He stood up, holding the knife at his side. 'Now I need you to do something else for me...'

'What?'

'I need you to take off all your clothes.'

Moone could feel the car being pushed around by the wind. Butler gripped the wheel as she took them over Tamar Bridge, heading into Cornwall. He looked up at the grey-painted bridge, the suspension chains, the towers that creaked in the wind. Beneath them, water was dark, uninviting, and he imagined the iciness of it, and felt his stomach break out into a horde of ants, running manically away from the imagined horror of falling, falling into the dark waters…

They drove on, into wide open fields, then turned off into the country lanes until they were running alongside a village that sat far too close to the road for Moone's liking. Butler parked along from an old post office and pub.

'Here we are,' she said and climbed out.

Rain had started and the usually picturesque village was shrouded in a grey cloud that seemed to hang low in the air and wrap itself around the world.

Moone knocked at a corner house, a cottage with black-painted timber on the outside.

After a little while the black door was unlocked and Ashley Whittle looked out at them, the recognition slowly coming to her eyes. 'Sorry,' she said, opening the door properly. 'I couldn't place you for a minute. Come in.'

Moone stepped into the low-ceilinged cottage that had been decked out with real wood floors, generally modernised inside, including a large chrome and white kitchen. That's where she led them, and they all stood looking out the French windows and onto a long garden and the woodland beyond.

Ashley Whittle picked up the kettle. 'I take it you've got news. I feel a bit nervous now.'

'No need to be,' Moone said, noticing Butler

was standing by the door, arms folded, looking around the place.

'Did you find out anything?' Ashley put the kettle on.

'Not a great deal, I'm afraid. But I wanted to ask you something.'

She stood back, her face reddening even more than it already had, and folded her arms. 'OK. Ask away.'

Moone smiled a little. 'This may sound strange, but did Simon believe in mysticism, psychics and all that sort of thing?'

She let out a breath of relief, then a short laugh. 'OK, sorry, I didn't know what you were going to ask then. Well, he was pretty open-minded...'

'It's just that we wondered if he might have visited a psychic recently.'

'Madam Revello,' Butler said, in almost a huff.

Ashley looked at her. 'I don't think I've heard of her. If he had gone to see her, he hadn't told me, and that's something he would've told me, I'm sure.'

Moone nodded, a little disheartened that his theory had taken a nosedive. He turned to look at Butler and saw already that she had her usual look of derision on her face. 'Thanks, Ashley. We just thought we better ask.'

She nodded. 'It's fine. What bearing does it have?'

'I'm not sure at this point.' Moone thought of something else, his stomach tightening. 'There's something else. Bit more delicate.'

'OK.'

'Was there anything in Simon's past, anything he wouldn't want anyone knowing about?'

Ashley Whittle's surprise filled her eyes, then she shook her head. 'No, there's nothing he ever talked about to me. I'm sure I would know if there was. Is this to do with the money? You thought maybe blackmail?'

'It is a possibility.'

'I thought the same, but I can't think of anything.'

'He never had an affair?' Butler asked, her voice cold, hard.

Ashley's face grew scarlet again, her eyes widening for a moment. 'No! He'd never. I know he wouldn't have…'

'It's OK, we're sorry,' Moone said, flashing a pissed-off look at Butler. But she shrugged and turned away.

'I know you have to ask these questions,' Ashley said, tears coming to her eyes. 'But the answer is no, definitely not.'

'Thanks.' Moone smiled again. 'We'll leave you in peace now.'

She was shivering, standing on the landing, a towel wrapped around her. He was sat on the edge of the bath, the water running into it, roaring, echoing in the small bathroom. He stared at her, the knife by his hand, his eyes burning to her through the stocking mask.

'Drop the towel,' he said, his voice barely a whisper.

'Please, please, don't…' Tears filled her eyes, her head shaking.

He picked up the knife. 'The towel. Drop it.'

With trembling hands, her eyes filled with tears, she undid the towel and dropped it. Then she wrapped her arms around herself, trying to keep at least her breasts covered.

'I'm not interested in your body,' he said. 'I'm excited, but not by the sight of you. I want you to get into the bath.'

She stepped into the room, hearing the tap dripping, the sound of it filling her ears.

'Just get in,' he said, standing up, and gesturing to the water.

'*Why?*'

'Just get in and I'll tell you. Come on, the water's nice and warm.'

Half covering herself, she edged around him, still staring at the water, seeing the steam rising. Awkwardly, she lifted her leg and dipped it in. It was hot, but not scalding. She trembled and stared at him, the knife in his gloved hand.

'Go on,' he said, so she stood in the water, then lowered herself down until she was up to her shoulders in the water, still shivering, her teeth chattering as if the water was filled with ice.

He sat down again, staring at her before he reached into his pocket and brought out something in his gloved hand. He put it on the soap dish, then sat back.

The object glinted in the light from the bathroom spotlight. Her eyes widened, the horror filling her as she stared at the double-edged razor blade.

She looked up at him, unable to speak, shaking her head.

'I want you to take that,' he said softly. 'I want you to take it and cut your wrists.'

CHAPTER 6

As the cold winter evening drew in, Moone and Butler had decided to talk to Charlene Bale's flatmate the next day. So Moone returned to the caravan park and entered his mobile home, the end of a much-needed cigarette between his lips. He stubbed it out, then opened his fridge to find a cold beer and sat on the corner sofa and turned on the TV. He turned and watched the grey sea raging in the distance, the grim clouds crowding in, his mind travelling to the moors, Charlene Bale's frozen body lying on the snow-covered ground. He saw her frost-bitten feet, the blood against the snow. He shook his head, imagining her car where it had been parked that morning, someone sat at the steering wheel. *Who were they? A man? A woman? A man. A man had been photographed in the back of her car. Average build, white. Not a lot to go on.*

His mind wandered, going back through the day.

Rachel.

He sat up, his heart beating, wondering what the time was. He breathed out. He had time for a quick shower before he headed out to Mutley to meet her, but as soon as he started getting ready, he started imagining Butler's response if she'd known he was going on a date with a much younger woman. No, not a date, just a drink. *With a possible witness*. He was kidding himself.

He parked back at Connaught Avenue, then took a slow walk towards the high street, hands in pockets. He suddenly found himself half expecting to be stood up, almost hoping he would be. She would expect him to be entertaining, but the way his mind was set, filled with images of the dead, he felt a little empty. Then he looked up, his heart flickering into life as he saw a slender female shape held in the soft glow of the street light.

He smiled as he reached Rachel, adorned in a mid-length black dress, a dark red warm-looking overcoat on top.

'Hi,' she said, smiling too.

He looked round at the street, feeling his nerves race up his chest, rushing to his face and making it glow. 'Where did you want to go?'

She turned and looked towards the glow of the Hyde Park pub. 'I quite like it in there, plenty of corners to hide out in. Fancy it?'

'Sure.'

They sat in a dark corner, away from the crowded bar, and the television screens that played the latest music videos. Moone bought Rachel a glass of wine and a pint of beer for himself, then sat down. Music played in the distance, some pop tune that Moone didn't recognise, and he was suddenly aware of the difference in age between them.

'Thanks,' she said, taking her wine and sipping it.

'I've never been in here before,' Moone said, looking around.

'How long have you lived down here? You're from London, right?'

'That obvious? About five months, give or take. You? You don't sound like you're from down here.'

'Don't I?' She laughed. 'Born and bred. I guess I just never picked up an accent. How old are you?'

Moone laughed, nodding. 'Very, very old. Forty-seven.'

She smiled. 'That's not old.'

'Old enough.'

She leaned forward, half closing her eyes. 'Well, I like an older man. Always have.'

He felt his face burn along with his desire unfolding and rising with a creak of old bones.

'That's good, then,' he managed to say before his phone started to ring in his jacket pocket. 'Sorry, got to get this.'

'It's OK,' she said, lifting her wine to her lips.

He got up and stepped away, praying it wasn't work.

'DCI Peter Moone,' he said, turning to watch Rachel, who seemed to be looking round the pub.

'Evening,' a man said. 'It's Sergeant Kevin Pinder. Hope I'm not disturbing you.'

'No, not at all,' he said, watching the evening ride off into the sunset. 'What can I do you for?'

'I'm on duty tonight. First response team. I'm at another suicide…'

Moone pressed his phone to his ear as he hurried outside into the light rain and wind. His heart began to lurch into action as he said, 'What is it this time?'

'Got a young woman in a bathtub. Cut her wrists. Thought you might want to take a look as there are a couple of things bothering me. I'll text the address.'

'I'll be there as soon as I can.'

Moone sighed and looked up at the pub, his stomach somersaulting as he knew only too well what he had to do now. He trudged back inside the pub and stood with a sad look on his face.

'Work?' she asked, tilting her head to one side.

'Sorry.'

'It's OK. Walk me out before you race off to the scene of the crime.'

She got up and slipped her coat on before

they headed through the crowd of customers and out onto the street.

'I feel bad,' he said, as they stood on the corner of Connaught Avenue.

'Don't,' she said and stepped towards him, raising a hand that lightly brushed his shirt front. Then the same hand touched his face, as her mouth moved towards his. He kissed her back, feeling himself put his arms round her. The kiss lasted a few seconds but remained with him long after she smiled and said, 'Until next time,' then turned and walked away.

The blue lights were flashing. Moone blinked and covered his eyes as he headed down the tree-lined lane, rainwater dripping from their bare branches. The action seemed to be centred around an old Victorian semi-detached house. An ambulance was parked close by, the paramedics were standing chatting to one of the uniforms.

Moone spotted Sergeant Pinder talking into his radio, and went over, waiting for him to finish.

'You got here bloody quick,' Pinder said, his radio still squawking, joining in with the other uniforms' radio noise. 'I take it you were in town? Out were you?'

'Sort of.' Moone smiled, then looked up at the building, wondering what he would find inside.

'Don't tell me it was a date?'

Moone laughed and shrugged.

Pinder shook his head. 'If I'm good for one thing, I'm good for ruining someone's night.'

'Don't worry about it. So, suicide?'

Pinder shrugged. 'That's for the coroner to decide.'

Moone nodded. 'Let's take a look.'

Pinder took him into the house, opening the front door and avoiding a white-suited forensic officer coming out with a large metal case. Then they went up the narrow threadbare stairs and up to another open door. Moone went ahead, walking across the landing, his eyes jumping to where all the action was. There was a figure in the bathroom, a slender hooded shape in a light blue forensic outfit. Moone went in, his eyes immediately jumping to the blood-red water in the bathtub, the young woman lying sunk in the water, her head and her shoulders barely above the water. Her eyes were closed, her skin milky white.

The hooded figure turned to Moone, revealing that it was, in fact, none other than Dr Lee Parry, the Home Office pathologist.

'Evening, DCI Moone,' he said. 'I can't say it's a good one.'

'No, it doesn't seem to be. Slit wrists?' Moone's eyes jumped to the bloody razor blade sitting on the soap dish, a puddle of pink water around it.

'Looks that way.' The pathologist leaned over the bath, then dipped his gloved hand into the red water, and brought out the woman's arm. Moone saw the multitude of cut marks along her left wrist. The doctor let the arm rest back in the water, then straightened up.

'Did she do it herself?' Moone asked and saw the doctor's dark eyes stare at him questioningly.

'You don't think she did?'

Moone shrugged. 'I'm just asking. All above board?'

Parry gave a strange sort of empty laugh. 'As above board as it could be. There are a couple of troubling matters.'

'Like what?'

The doctor raised her arm again. 'Several cuts, some deep, some shallow. Hesitation marks. I wouldn't usually expect to see so many in this situation, but this isn't an exact science. The human mind is so complex.'

'I see. Anything else?'

'Well, most of the cuts are horizontal. The last couple are vertical. The correct way, if you want to really finish yourself off.'

'That's strange, isn't it?' Pinder asked, from behind Moone.

Parry looked over Moone's shoulder. 'I'd say so.'

'Time of death?' Moone asked.

'Judging by lividity, and temperature of the water, I'd hazard a guess at about four hours ago.'

'So, about three-ish this afternoon.' Moone nodded. 'Who found her?'

'Her best friend,' Pinder said.

Moone turned and faced him. 'She just happened to turn up?'

'It's a guy. She sent him a text. Must've been just before she went.' Pinder pointed towards the damp lino floor next to the bath. 'Found the phone there. Bagged up now. No blood on it, pretty clean...'

'What did she say to him?' Moone asked.

'Goodbye. I'm sorry.'

'That's enough to bring your friends running.'

'A cry for help?' Pinder asked.

'Not the way the last cuts were administered,' Parry said. 'This is all a bit...'

'What?' Moone asked.

'Did you show him the package?' Parry said, looking questioningly at Pinder.

'What package?' Moone asked as Pinder pointed a thumb behind him, then took him through to the lounge.

Pinder stopped at the sofa, where there was a small open cardboard box, the kind that Amazon or similar online shops send their products in.

'So, she got a delivery before she died?' Moone asked, looking into the empty box.

'Looks like it but so far I can't see anything new in the flat,' Pinder said. 'Thing is, look at the address label and stamp. They're not real. Someone copied it all and stuck it down on the front of the package.'

'To look like a real package? That's interesting. Maybe if someone else staged all this, this is how they got in.'

'Is that what you think? Someone killed her and made it look like suicide?'

'Something like that. We need the forensic people to examine this scene, and the box.'

'Your boss won't like it,' Parry said from the landing.

Moone shook his head, then went over to Parry. 'Very true. Did you carry out the post-mortem on Charlene Bale?'

'I did.'

'What did you find?'

Parry pulled off his latex gloves. 'I found a young woman who had sliced her own throat. Lots of hesitation marks, as I'd expect to see. But why were her feet bare? She had the beginnings of frostbite on her feet and fingers. I think she was digging her fingers into the snow, trying to drag herself. Some of her nails were broken.'

Moone rubbed his face, then looked at Parry. 'I'm going to need your help.'

'My help?' Parry looked confused. 'I thought that's what I've been doing?'

'The Chief Super wants to write the first one off as suicide. Chances are he'll feel the same about this one.'

'You want me to argue the case for murder?' Parry picked up his medical case.

'At least that these last two cases don't seem quite, well, straightforward.'

Parry sighed. 'He's not going to like it, but my testimony is supposed to go towards influencing the coroner's decision...'

'Exactly. We can't let the coroner just rule this as suicide. We can't.'

'There's not that much to go on,' Pinder said, having sealed the package in an evidence bag.

Moone pointed to the package. 'He or she left that behind for us to find. We've also got the footage of a man in the back of Charlene's car as she drove to her death.'

'Where did the razorblade come from?' Pinder asked. 'Why would she have one of those? Did she go out and buy it for this? If we can't find any receipts...'

Moone pointed a finger at Pinder. 'Good. Let's have a look around. Let's take all this to the Chief Super tomorrow.'

Parry let out an unhappy sigh. 'OK. I'll make myself available. Not got too much on tomorrow, apart from this poor young woman. Give me a ring tomorrow. I'm going to go and try and get some sleep.'

Moone nodded as he watched the doctor head off down the stairs.

'I'm behind you,' Pinder said, then laughed. 'Not just right now. Tomorrow, I mean, if you need me. I don't like the smell of this. Something funny's going on, and I want to put things right, especially when it comes to Mrs Whittle. I didn't do all I could...'

'I think you did your best. Thanks though. I'll let you know tomorrow.'

'You going to talk to her friend?'

Moone started heading down the stairs. 'Let's leave it until the morning. Get his details and we'll go and see him.'

'Will do.'

When Moone got outside, he smelt it on him, as well as felt it all inside, all crammed in. Another life gone, another young person extinguished. As he shakily took out a cigarette and lit it, he made a mental note to check her financial records. If there was missing money...

Then he pictured himself sitting in front of the Chief Super, ready to lay it on the line. All of a sudden, his cigarette didn't taste so good and he stubbed it out and started heading for his car.

Sleep hadn't come easy like he'd known it wouldn't, his mind trampling all over the case again and again. In the morning, he fetched a cappuccino for Butler and an Americano for himself, then headed into the incident room where he found the usual crowd gathered.

Butler, Harding and Chambers were hunched round a desk, chatting, then stopped when Moone came in. He noticed they all had coffees already, so put Butler's on her desk.

Butler swung round on her chair, then looked him over before she said, 'You look rough. Late one?'

'Yep.' Moone sipped his coffee, staring at the whiteboard. 'Another suicide last night.'

'So I heard. Terrible.'

He looked at her. 'It wasn't suicide…'

'Oh shit, here we go.' Butler went over and slumped at her desk, starting to log into her computer.

'Several cuts to her wrists…'

'People do that…'

'Then a couple the vertical way, *the way you do cut yourself if you want to do it properly*.'

Butler faced him and folded her arms. 'So, she Googled it? She learnt what to do…'

'From what I heard the phone didn't have any blood on it, if she decided in the middle…'

'Not necessarily…'

'There was a package…'

'What package?'

'It was open, on the sofa, but the label was fake, printed off. I think someone came to her door, pretending to deliver a package and then they got inside…'

Butler sighed, then picked up the coffee he had brought with him. 'This mine?'

'Yes. Parry's on my side. So is Pinder.'

'Pinder? You've got him on this?'

'He was with the responding team. They

both agree, last night and Charlene Bale's suicide, well, there's something not right with it all.'

Butler sipped her coffee, shaking her head slightly. 'Pinder just wants a leg up.'

'I'm going to the Chief Super with all this.'

She stopped drinking and put the coffee down. 'You're going to put all this to the Chief Super? You're fucked in the head, Pete. You know what he's going to say…'

'He can't. Not with the figure in Bale's car, the package, any of it. He's got to give us more time before a coroner gets to rule on this.'

Butler stared at him, then put her face in her hands, and took deep breaths. 'When are you thinking of speaking to him?'

'Today. I'll call and make an appointment.'

'All right. Let me know when…'

'You don't have to come.'

She gave an empty laugh. 'Course I do. You can't be trusted on your own, London boy. Right then, where do we go from here with this thing?'

'We talk to the best friend of the young woman who died last night. I've got his work address. He's a nurse.'

Butler stood up. 'Then I'll get my coat.'

DC Chambers headed into the conference room that had now been taken over by DS Carthew and used as her own personal incident room. Carthew was at the front of the room, standing in front of a small whiteboard she had nicked from somewhere. There was a thick-set, red-headed WPC sitting at one of the desks, using a laptop.

Carthew turned round and faced Chambers, hands on hips. 'Are you done gossiping with your old colleagues, Chambers?'

'I just needed stuff from my desk.' Chambers took a seat and waited, still thinking about the possibility that their missing persons case was linked to Moone's investigation. But she knew that bringing it all up to Carthew was a sure way to get herself in the shit.

Carthew folded her arms. 'Well, since you've been gallivanting about, me and PC Robins have been looking at the CCTV footage from the bank and from the place he was seen, which was the shopping mall a couple of hours later. It looks like he had a cup of coffee on his own in Costa, then left. That's the last anyone saw of him.'

'How much did he withdraw?' PC Robins asked.

'Five thousand,' Chambers said. 'Not enough to start a new life somewhere. They had plenty of money in the bank, so if he wanted to...'

'What's your theory, then?' Carthew asked, her eyebrows raised.

Molly shrugged. 'He had debts the wife didn't know about? Or... I don't know really.'

'Go on, what were you going to say?'

'Maybe he was being blackmailed.'

'By who?' Carthew came closer, hands

behind her back.

Molly shrugged. 'I don't know...'

'Is this your theory or DCI Moone's?'

She was frozen for a moment, her mouth moving a little, but nothing coming out. She was also very aware that the PC had turned to look at her. 'It's just that, well, I know DCI Moone...'

Carthew held up a hand. 'DCI Moone is clearing up a suicide, just a suicide. But just like him, he's got to make something out of it. We're looking for a missing man, who's probably done a bunk...'

Carthew stopped speaking when she heard her phone ringing, which was lying on the corner of the desk, vibrating along it. She stared daggers that were coated in excrement at Molly, then answered the call.

'Sorry, yes,' Carthew said. 'I was looking into...' DS Carthew started nodding, her face losing colour. 'OK, yes, we're on our way.'

Carthew put the phone down, then stared down for a moment, before taking a few controlled breaths and looking up at Molly. 'Well, seems our missing man has been found...'

'That's good news,' Molly said.

'No, it really isn't. He's been found hanged.'

CHAPTER 7

Moone was standing on the edge of the accident and emergency department of Derriford Hospital, watching the doctors and nurses running back and forth, while gurneys and beds crowded the waiting rooms and the corridors. Moone had been faced with the absolute chaos of many a London hospital, but he hadn't expected to see Derriford in a similar state.

'He's over there,' Butler said, nudging him back into reality. 'That's Daniel Acton.'

She seemed to be pointing towards a curtained-off bay, where a quite young, mixed-race man in scrubs was looking after a frail elderly woman.

Moone headed over, taking his ID out as the young male nurse started to take the woman's blood pressure. 'I'm DCI Moone, this is DI Butler.'

The young man flashed a look at them while fixing the cuff around the woman's arm. 'I'm a little busy right now.'

'It's about Sarah MacPherson,' Moone said

and watched as Daniel Acton nodded, frowned and then finished what he was doing.

'I'll be with you in a sec,' he said, then took the woman's temperature, wrote something down, then took them down the corridor, where things were a little less noisy.

Acton folded his arms, leaning against the wall, staring at them as they got closer.

'I can't believe it,' he said, looking down towards his feet. When he looked up, his eyes were a little wet.

'I'm sorry for your loss,' Moone said. 'You got the text from her in the afternoon, is that right?'

'Yes, that's right. I knew something was up straight away. It just didn't sound like her. I just can't get my head round it. Why would she suddenly do this? It doesn't make sense...'

'You don't know of any reason why she would?' Butler asked.

'No,' Acton slightly shook his head, letting out a harsh breath. 'Far as I knew she was happy. OK, we didn't see each other as much as we'd like, but, well, that's life. Now I feel guilty that I didn't...'

'Don't start blaming yourself,' Butler said. 'You'll go crazy that way.'

Moone stepped closer, lowering his voice. 'Can you think of anything in her life that troubled Sarah?'

Acton's brow creased up. 'What do you

mean?'

'Well, did she ever tell you about anything that happened in her life that someone might use against her?'

'Could someone blackmail her?' Butler asked, with a heavy breath.

'Blackmail? Sarah?' Acton shook his head. 'No, I don't think so...'

'There's nothing she talked about, nothing that...' Moone began, but saw the nurse's face change. 'What is it?'

'Well, there was this night out,' Acton said, folding his arms. 'She didn't often drink a lot, but it was her birthday and we had some Prosecco. Anyway, she started crying. She'd been talking about when she was up at Marjon...'

'Marjon?' Moone asked.

'Marjon University,' Butler said, waving away his question. 'Go on.'

Acton nodded. 'She was talking about this terrible thing she'd done. She'd hurt someone or done something. I couldn't get a straight answer out of her, then I got her back to her place and she passed out on her sofa. I didn't like to press her on it, so I just left it. Maybe I should've got her to talk about it. Do you think it's what made her, I mean, do what she did?'

Moone shrugged. 'We're still looking into it. When was she at Marjon?'

'Finished about five years ago, I think.' Acton kicked himself away from the wall. 'My matron's giving me the evil eye, so I'd better get back to work.'

'OK,' Moone said. 'Thanks. Here's my card. Give me a call if you think of anything more.'

Acton took it, nodded, and then tried to smile at them. 'She didn't have any real family. She was adopted, but they died a few years back. I don't know who to call.'

'Wish we could help,' Moone said.

The nurse smiled, then hurried off into the madness, the noise. Moone watched him, then sighed, glad he wasn't working for the NHS. No, he just had the dead to deal with, to try and find some kind of footnote for them, especially for the murdered. He wouldn't be able to live with himself if the accountants, the budget keepers like the Chief Super got their way and filed it all away as just suicide.

'Come on, stop faffing,' Butler said and started walking towards the exit. 'We need to go and talk to Charlene Bale's flatmate.'

Moone caught up with her. 'We also need to go and talk to the Chief Super about all this.'

'Don't remind me.'

The allotments near the top of Peverell Park Road were sealed off by police tape, with uniforms standing guard at either end. Anyone wanting to get to the doctors surgery or the child's playground behind it, would have to go along the high street and around. Molly Chambers followed DS Carthew as she slipped under the cordon, the rain starting, being thrown at them diagonally by the wild wind. They both signed the crime scene log and were let into the allotment. Chickens were clucking and pecking the ground in a small hen house to the left as they headed past a few fenced-off plots. A uniform pointed the way to DS Carthew, directing her over to a large battered old shed a couple of hundred yards away.

A couple of times, Carthew looked round as if to see if Molly was still following, but only shot her a look of annoyance before she hurried on.

Paramedics and more uniforms were standing by the shed, the wind and rain pushing them about, tugging at their waterproof jackets. The shed door was open. Carthew showed her ID, as did Chambers, and then went inside. Molly tried to keep it all in when she saw the figure hanging from a wooden beam that ran the length of the shed. It moved slightly, side to side, but then she realised the whole structure seemed to be moving, the wind shoving it now and again. The body had its hands out in front, tied together.

'Found about an hour ago,' a gravelly West Country voice said behind them.

They both turned to see a tall, slender uniform wrapped up in a waterproof. He had short, greying spiky hair, and deep-set eyes.

'Inspector Tremain,' he said. 'First response.

One of the other growers kept some equipment in here. That's when he found this.'

'Awful,' Molly said and watched the deep-set eyes take her in for a moment.

'Not the worst I've seen,' Tremain said. 'Who's in charge here?'

'DS Carthew,' Molly said, pointing to her boss.

'DS Carthew,' Tremain said, stepping closer. 'Don't be fooled by the hands tied in front of the body...'

'No, I'm not.' Carthew turned round. 'I've seen this before. Stops them changing their minds. If the hands were behind the body, then I'd be worried.'

'I didn't recognise you for a minute,' Tremain said. 'Not out of your uniform. Good to see you.'

Carthew nodded. 'Have photos been taken?'

'Yes, everything has been taken care of apart from informing the family.'

Molly watched Carthew as she stepped over to a workman's desk in the corner, where an evidence bag was filled with the suicide victim's personal effects.

'Definitely Edward Beckett?' Carthew picked up the bag, seeming to weigh it.

'That's what the ID says.' Tremain gripped his radio as it started squawking. 'But someone'll need to take a look at him, someone in his family. Are you going to notify the family, or do you want us to do it?'

'We'll take care of that. Don't suppose you found five thousand pounds on him?'

Tremain huffed out a laugh. 'About twenty pounds in his wallet. Anyway, they'll be coming to take down the body soon. I'll be outside if you need me.'

Carthew sighed heavily, then turned to face Chambers, her arms folded. 'Don't say a word.'

'I wasn't going to, boss,' she said.

'Moone's not going to be put in charge of this. This is a suicide, nothing more.'

'What happened to the money?'

'Maybe he's got a secret love child, I don't know. Either way, we have to go and inform his wife.'

As Carthew stormed towards the open doorway, Molly stepped aside, her stomach sinking, a hollow kind of sorrow filling her as she looked up at the hanging figure.

Carthew stopped at her side, leaning in towards her. 'Not a word to Moone about this, or I'll rip your hair out, got it? Let me deal with him. Understand?'

'OK.' Molly watched her leave the shed, then saw the figures in white outfits entering the small space, and quickly squeezed her way out. All the time she argued to herself about whether she should talk to Moone about it or not.

They managed to track Teresa Gregg down to

one of the make-up counters in Dingles, a large department store situated at the top of Plymouth's City Centre. As they went through the glass door of the entrance, Moone was clouded by a whole smorgasbord of scents, both male and female, all mixing together to make a kind of flowery tear gas. Then he noticed the smartly dressed women at the counters, all in the same sort of uniform, their faces plastered in seemingly every bit of foundation and lipstick the shop sold. He stopped dead, pulling Butler back to him as he pointed towards a horde of women that had an orange-hued appearance.

'Which one's Teresa Gregg?' he asked. 'They all look identical. Why do girls do that these days, plaster themselves in so much make-up that they are unrecognisable?'

'Contouring, they call it,' Butler said and sighed. 'My other half's daughter does it.'

'You have a stepdaughter?'

'Yes, but she doesn't have much to do with me.'

'I see. You're a dark horse.'

Butler made a strange noise, then hurried to the counter and leaned over it. 'Teresa Gregg?'

One of the orange-faced women turned round, her face full of surprise until she recognised them both.

'Hi,' she said, looking a little sheepish. 'Is everything OK?'

'Hello again,' Moone said, 'We'd just like to

ask you a couple more questions.'

'Hang on,' she said, then went over to an older lady, who started shooting them looks before Teresa came back over.

'There's a cafe upstairs,' Gregg said.

'Then let's go get you a cuppa,' Moone said.

They sat round a table near the back of the large restaurant, overlooking the grimy roofs of the rest of the shops. Teresa Gregg stirred her tea, staring down into it, shaking her head occasionally. Then she looked up, her eyes filled with tears.

'I still, I just can't believe it,' she said. 'Not Charlene.'

'That's why we needed to talk to you,' Moone said and sipped his coffee. 'Can you think of anything that might have been troubling her? Anything in her past that she might have mentioned?'

Teresa stared off towards the other customers and the tills. 'I'm not sure really. I don't remember her mentioning anything. Nothing that would make her, well, do that.'

Moone sat back, nodding.

'No one might've tried to blackmail her?' Butler asked, leaning forward. 'That's what my colleague's trying to get at.'

'Blackmail her?' The young woman stared back at Moone. 'No. I don't even think she had that much money. I don't know why anyone would try and blackmail her.'

'OK,' Moone said, shooting a look at Butler. 'Then is it possible for us to take a look at her room?'

'I guess so,' Teresa said, then she looked uncomfortable, running her hand over the table. 'Her parents have been in touch. It was her dad who, well, got in touch. He was so, so, upset. I could hear it in his...'

'We'll just take a quick look around,' Moone said. 'We'll be very careful, we promise.'

She looked up. 'What are you looking for?'

'Honestly, I'm not sure. We just think there might be other factors at play and we're trying to get a clear picture of what happened.'

Teresa nodded, reached for her coat and bag, and then took out a set of keys. 'You'll need my keys.'

Butler reached across the table and snatched them up, then got up. 'Thanks, we'll get back as soon as we're done. Come on, Moone.'

Moone was smiling kindly at the young woman and standing as he heard his phone start to ring. He said goodbye to Teresa Gregg, then took out his phone as he followed Butler towards the tills, avoiding the queues of mostly elderly people lining up to get served.

'DCI Moone,' he said.

'This is Chief Superintendent Laptew,' the voice said, making Moone stand still, his stomach lurching.

'Yes sir, what can I do for you?'

'I need you and DI Butler to come back to Crownhill and see me as soon as you can.'

'Anything wrong?'

'You could say that. But we'll discuss the issues when you get here.'

'Right, we'll be right over.'

The call was ended, leaving Moone standing at the centre of the restaurant, looking up to see Butler with a frown on her face and coming back towards him.

'All OK?' she asked.

'Not really. That was the Chief Super asking us to go and see him.'

Butler's face sank and she turned away, then spun round again, pointing a finger at him. 'You know what this bleeding well is, don't you?'

'The suicides?'

'Yeah, the bloody suicides. He's got wind of all this. Now we're in the shit! Well done.'

Moone followed her as she headed out of the restaurant and stepped onto the down escalator. 'How is this my fault? We're supposed to be making sure they did commit suicide...'

'Which they did...'

'Maybe. But I think someone forced their hand in this. The money, the man in the back seat, the bare feet...'

Butler turned round, getting shorter as they went down. 'It's not me you've got to convince, it's Laptew! Laptew and all the bloody accountants. Come on, let's just go and get told off.'

'Stop fidgeting,' Butler snapped as Moone was adjusting his trousers as they waited outside the Chief Super's office.

'OK, Mum.' He sat back and folded his arms as the office door opened and Laptew came out.

'Come on in,' he said, opening the door and standing back.

Butler went in first and Moone heard her sharp intake of breath as she muttered, 'Don't fucking believe it.'

When Butler carried on in and sat down opposite Laptew's desk, Moone got a clear view of what had annoyed her. DS Faith Carthew was sat next to the Chief Super's desk, legs crossed, a mug of coffee in her hand, looking rather smug. Moone sat down, starting to question whose office they were sitting in exactly.

The Chief Super took his seat and sat back in it, swinging it slightly. 'So, what's been happening with these suicides? I hear you've been involved in two now, is that right?'

Moone sat forward. 'I attended the scene of a second suicide last night...'

'Why?' Laptew asked, leaning forward, staring at him.

'I got wind of it and I was, well, I was curious.'

'I hear you have a theory.' The Chief Super

raised his eyebrows. 'Let's hear it.'

Moone shrugged. 'Well, it's not so much a theory…'

Butler huffed. 'We feel that there's something off about both the suicides.'

'Off?' Laptew looked towards Butler. 'What constitutes off?'

Moone cleared his throat. 'In the first suicide, Charlene Bale's suicide, there's the bare feet, and the fact someone dropped her off. Not forgetting we have CCTV footage of someone in the back of her vehicle as she was heading towards her final destination…'

'Someone was sitting in the back of her car?' Laptew leaned forward, seemingly interested, nodding. 'What about this other suicide?'

'Sarah MacPherson. As far as we can ascertain, she had no history of mental illness, depression or anything. Supposedly in the middle of it all, she texted her best friend. She had sliced her wrists, but there was no blood on the phone… Then there's the open package…'

'Package?' the Chief Super asked.

'Yes, but it was fake, printed to look like a real package.' Moone heard how it all sounded, then took a deep breath. 'Look, sir, I know what we're supposed to do, but all this, these little, odd, things, they just don't sit right with me. If you can give us a little more…'

The Chief Super held up a hand, flashing his eyes over to Carthew. 'You can stop there, Moone.

Very well, I get that there are things in these suicides that warrant further investigation. In fact, Carthew's missing person, Edward Beckett has turned up. He was found hanged.'

'Jesus,' Moone said. 'Where was he?'

'An allotment they used to use,' Carthew said. 'Think they had one of those back-to-nature fads at one time...'

'Let's not get off course,' Laptew said, clearing his throat. 'Now, I don't know if these suicides are related, but I'm not stupid, I know there's something amiss here. But it all needs a thorough looking into. So, that's why I've decided DS Carthew and you DCI Moone should work together on this...'

'Excuse me?' Butler asked, sitting forward.

'Yes, DI Butler?' Laptew said. 'Well, I see. As you're an acting DI now, you can work alongside DC Harding and DC Chambers. I've been told there's a few other cases that need clearing up.'

Moone looked at Butler's profile, and noted the way her cheeks prickled with spots of red, her neck too. Then he noticed DS Carthew, the way she was subtly smiling as if she'd just won a long game of chess.

Shit.

'Sir,' Moone said, but the Chief Super was already up and saying something to Carthew in her ear.

'You two can wait outside,' Laptew said, waving them out.

'That conniving bitch!' Butler said, half in a growl as they both stood in the corridor.

'We can sort this out,' Moone said, his mind racing to find how they could exactly sort it out.

She stared at him. 'Can we? Yeah, right, now you've abandoned me for the psycho woman!'

'I haven't abandoned you! Listen, she's using this to get a leg up...'

'Leg over more like.'

'She's not interested in me. I'm old news. She thinks that if she can help me solve this, then she'll be on her way.'

'Yes, but...'

They both stopped talking as his phone started ringing out in his pocket.

'You'd better take that. Might be important.' Butler huffed, then turned away.

Moone answered the unrecognised call, and said, 'DCI Peter Moone.'

'Hi, it's me, Rachel,' the voice said.

Moone straightened up, turning sharply away from Butler. 'Hi. You OK?'

'Yes, I'm fine.'

'Sorry about the other night.'

'It's all OK. You're forgiven.'

He smiled. 'How did you get my number?'

'You left a card with Mike, my boss.'

'Oh, yes...'

'I was wondering what you were doing for lunch today.'

'Lunch? I don't know. Probably still

working...'

'I'll be at the Early Bird cafe on Mutley Plain at one, if you want to join me. Up to you.'

'OK. I'll try my best to be there.'

'You'd better. See you then.'

She hung up, so Moone put his phone away and found Butler standing close by, staring at him, eyebrows raised.

'What?' he asked.

'Who was that?'

'No one.'

'Your new bit of stuff? Thought as much. Who is she?'

'Remember we went to see Michael Whittle?'

Butler closed her eyes and let out a heavy huff. 'Please, tell me it's not the young, short-skirted, eye-battering PA thing?'

'All right, I won't tell you.'

'Her? She's young enough...'

'I know, I know. I think I'm going to meet her for lunch and tell her, you know, that it's a bit...'

'Weird?' Butler nodded. 'Yep, I think you'd better. Anyway, listen, before the psycho bitch comes out, remember you need to go over to Bale's place and have a look round. We never asked MacPherson's BFF about the psychic thing either.'

Moone nodded. 'I know. I'll get on it. Can you and Harding check MacPherson's finances?'

'Yeah, OK, I suppose so. But watch your back with...'

Butler stopped talking when the outer door opened and DS Carthew came out, her eyes jumping to them both.

'I'll be seeing you back at Charles Cross,' Butler said, throwing daggers at Carthew.

When Butler had stormed off, Carthew came over, arms folded across her chest. 'She doesn't like me.'

'No, she doesn't.' Moone nodded, then smiled. 'Probably because of the whole, you know. In the house and all that.'

'Because I saved your lives?'

'I appreciate that you saved my life.'

Carthew stepped closer, staring into his eyes. 'I'm glad to hear it. Because I was starting to feel you had it in for me.'

'No, I don't.'

'Good. Because if I start to feel like you're not on my side, then, well, I don't know what I might do. Right, let's get to work, shall we?'

Moone watched her head off down the corridor, realising that he was up to his neck in it, the dark waters rising, and his limbs were starting to ache.

Shit.

CHAPTER 8

Acton was at home, having finished his shift and was probably sleeping. But that didn't deter Faith Carthew, who was set on going around to his place and waking him up. Moone found himself driving them, heading towards the flat, which was situated just off Beaumont Road, in a low-rise block. Moone kept looking at Carthew, trying to recognise her as the same PC he'd taken under his wing a few months back. Her hair was different, more blonde than red, and she had obviously been going to the gym a lot. She had metamorphosed and appeared from her cocoon, but not as a creature more beautiful. Yes, she was still attractive, but now there seemed to be a hardness to her, a sharp cunning that he had not noticed before.

'What are you staring at?' Carthew asked, flipping through her notebook.

'I wasn't,' he said and turned off Beaumont Road and slowed, heading towards the park just up a little way.

'Yes, you were. I could feel your eyes on me. It's fine. I'm used to it these days. You lose a few pounds, dress smarter and the eyes of men seem to follow you. You're all very shallow.'

'You don't have to lecture me. I know, I'm a man.' He parked up outside the building, then turned to her. 'But we're not all like that.'

She gave a humourless laugh. 'No, I suppose not. You're not, are you, Moone? You're a really moral guy, aren't you?'

He opened the door. 'I've had my failings. I know I'm not perfect, not by a long shot.'

'No, not by a long shot.' She climbed out and headed to the door, taking her time.

'Maybe we shouldn't go banging on this guy's door yet.'

'We've got questions for him, haven't we? What was it again?'

Moone sighed. 'I want to know if he's visited Madam Revello...'

'A psychic? Why, exactly?'

Moone stared at the intercom next to the door, reading the names listed beside them, trying to fend off her question, knowing she thought he was crazy like everyone else.

'Go on,' she said, nudging him.

'Because psychics don't read minds, they read you, get you to volunteer information and you don't even realise. I know, it's a bit crazy...'

'No, I like it. If there is someone out there trying to blackmail these people, then someone like a psychic might've wormed their way into their heads.'

'Thanks.' He stared at the buzzer again. 'Guess we better wake him up.'

Carthew nodded and pressed his buzzer a couple of times. Then Moone looked up when he saw movement inside and the muffled sound of a door opening. A head popped over the bannister at the top, and then a figure came down the stairs and opened the door.

Acton looked out at them, not looking like he had been asleep at all.

'Sorry if we woke you,' Carthew said, showing her ID. 'DS Carthew, you remember DCI Moone?'

'Yes, yes, I do,' he said, pulling a robe around his partly naked body. 'Has something happened?'

'We just need to ask you some more questions,' Moone said. 'Can we come in?'

'Yeah, sure, come up.' The male nurse turned and trudged back up the stairs to his flat with Moone following close behind.

Moone found himself in a small, tidy flat with magnolia walls. DS Carthew shut the door behind her, so Moone followed Acton into a small living area with a kitchen to his left, separated by a small island.

Acton sat down on a beige sofa and looked up expectantly at Moone. 'What did you want to ask?' he said.

'This might sound like a weird question,' Moone said. 'But do you know if Sarah ever visited a psychic?'

Acton gave a sad little smile. 'Yes, she did. We both did. Was my idea. I was going through a strange time in my life, I didn't know which way to turn...'

Moone looked up and saw a rainbow flag over a large, framed collage of photos. 'I'm sorry, but was the psychic called Madam Revello?'

There was a flash of shock across the nurse's face. 'That's right. I don't get it though, what's that got to do with Sarah doing... Do you think that she said something to her? Something that messed with her head?'

'We're not sure at the moment,' DS Carthew said. 'We're following a line of enquiry.'

Acton hunched over, nodding, but Moone caught sight of the sadness that washed over his face as he said, 'It was my idea. I thought it would be a laugh, that we might, you know, sort of...'

Moone heard a sob come from the nurse, then sniffing, but he remained frozen to the spot, feeling awkward, useless. There was movement out of the corner of his eye. Faith was moving past him, then she was sitting beside him. Her hand touched Acton's back, rubbing it as she said, 'It's OK. Let it out. This is not your fault. Don't ever think that...'

Moone stood and watched, observing DS Carthew being so empathetic, but his mind found it almost impossible to reconcile to the woman he'd seen almost beat to death another human being. People were complex, he knew that, and even killers had moments of regret, of emotion.

Moone pulled himself back out of his confusion. 'Did she tape it for you, the reading, I mean?' Moone asked.

Acton looked up, nodding, sniffing. 'Yeah, she did. She put it on a CD.'

'Have you got a copy we could listen to?'

'Sorry, we only paid for one CD. They seemed a bit pricey. I suppose Sarah would have it somewhere. She was amazed at how much she knew about her. I think she was a bit freaked out by it really. She listened to it a lot.'

Moone stepped forward, his mind buzzing. 'So she must still have it somewhere?'

'I'd think so.'

Carthew looked up at Moone but didn't say anything.

'Come on, DS Carthew,' Moone said. 'Let's get on. Are you going to be OK?'

Acton nodded, and wiped his nose. 'Yeah, I'll be OK. Thanks.'

When they got outside, Carthew asked, 'What was that about?'

Moone reached the car and turned to her. 'We need to find that CD. If Sarah MacPherson did spill her guts to Madam Revello, giving her blackmail material, then we'll have the evidence.'

'OK, let's go.'

Butler was at her desk, going through some of her and Moone's paperwork, filling in reports, still seething a little to be replaced by DS *fucking* Faith, *bleeding* Carthew. She wasn't convinced that Moone had even tried to put up a fight and had pretty much rolled over to have his balls tickled. Men, she huffed and looked up when the door to the incident room opened.

DSU Stack came in, talking to someone on the phone, then put the phone away and stood before her desk, his arms folded across his bulky chest. 'So, he's given you the boot, then?'

She gave a humourless laugh. 'Wasn't his choice, was it, boss?'

Stack looked round the room. 'No, don't suppose it was. Better this way, though, isn't it? You don't want to be running around with that cockney... wanker.'

She stood up and stared into Stack's eyes. 'No, not when we've got our own born and bred wankers right here!' She smiled, then went over to Harding, not even turning when she heard Stack call her a 'bitch' under his breath before leaving.

'Nice one,' Harding said.

Butler rolled her eyes. 'I'll pay for that. What've you found?'

Harding sat back in his seat. 'Plenty of suicides over the last couple of years. Tamar

Bridge, train tracks, hangings. Are we going to look into every suicide that's ever happened?'

'No, just the ones that raise questions. What about money being withdrawn or any financial irregularities?'

Harding half closed his eyes and looked at her.

'What?' she said.

'Nothing. But aren't we supposed to be leaving this to Dempsey and Makepeace?'

Butler laughed. 'Yeah right. She might be close to Makepeace, but he's no Dempsey. Hasn't even got a big gun!'

Harding raised his eyebrows. 'You seen it, have you?'

'Don't start rumours. I'm practically a married woman...'

'But you're not though, are you? He's never popped the question.'

Butler stared at him for a moment. 'Right, so have we got any suicides where money has gone missing?'

'Well, there's one that jumped out at me. Martin Jessop jumped off a bridge in Cornwall in the early hours about three years ago.'

'Martin Jessop? I know that name...'

'Yeah, because he was on our books. Jessop was just about to be arrested for a series of sexual assaults around Plymouth.'

'Right. That's why he killed himself, wasn't it?'

Harding shrugged. 'Theory was he couldn't live with what he'd done. But I noticed that his poor widow told us about eight thousand pounds had disappeared from their account.'

'So, like our suicides?'

'Well, not quite.' Harding started tapping at his computer.

'Not quite? Hurry up. Are you men all faffers?'

Harding brought up a news article, which Butler leaned in to read, seeing that it was about an elderly solicitor who had been arrested for stealing money from clients and then had absconded to the Caribbean somewhere. She sat back and looked at Harding. 'So?'

Harding shrugged. 'Well, it's similar, isn't it?'

'Not really. The guy commits suicide, probably because he's going to be exposed as a pervert. He just so happens to have had money stolen from him by this Philip Stannard. I don't really see the connection.'

'OK, fine. I thought it was worth bringing up.'

Butler huffed and stood up. 'Well, it wasn't really.'

'He did do work for Edward Beckett.'

Butler stopped as she was heading for her desk. 'Beckett? Who's just been found hanged? What work?'

'He helped when he sold his house.'

Butler hurried back to his desk. 'How do you know that?'

'Beckett's mentioned in the article. He's one of the people Stannard ripped off.'

'Really?' Butler scanned through the article, then huffed a little, thinking it all through. 'Come on then, let's go and look into it.'

Harding did a double take. 'Me and you?'

'Yes, why not?' Butler grabbed her coat. 'Harding and Butler for a change.'

Harding stood up, adjusting his shirt and tie. 'All right. But you realise you've made us sound like a packet of cigarettes, don't you?'

'Just get your coat and stop faffing.'

Moone snapped on his gloves as he went up the narrow staircase to Sarah MacPherson's flat, following DS Carthew. That's what she was now, he reminded himself, plain old DS Carthew, a rank and a surname. Not Faith any more.

An image flashed into his mind. *Her,* lying on his bed, smiling, looking up at him.

He shook it away as he stepped into the living room, looking round at her neat and ordered possessions.

Another image. Carthew, sitting astride their suspect, raising a hammer.

He looked round at her, watched her coming in, her eyes scanning everything, his mind rewinding to Acton's place.

'What was that all about back there?'

he asked as he started looking through the bookshelves.

She looked at him, her gloved fingers on a CD. 'Sorry?'

'With Acton. The whole back rubbing...'

She shook her head, returning to the job in hand. 'You mean the being kind? Having sympathy?'

'Yes, I know, but it's just...'

She faced him, arms folded across her chest. 'I know. I know what I did, I was there. I lost it. I'm trying to sort it...'

'Are you?'

'I'm seeing someone.' She started on the CDs again.

'Who?'

'Anger management. A private practice thing. I'm trying to get it under control.' Then she stopped, looked at him, stared into his eyes then came over. 'I'd really it if you'd give me a chance. Please don't say anything to anyone about it, not until I've had a chance to try and, well, deal with it all.'

He looked into her eyes but didn't see anything that led him to believe that she was lying. 'OK. I'll give you the benefit of the doubt.'

She smiled a little, touched his arm, then went back to her searching. He looked down at his arm, still feeling her touch, telling himself he shouldn't be feeling anything for her. But he did.

Rachel. That's who he should be thinking

about. He checked the time and started to wonder how exactly he was going to navigate his way to lunch with her after excusing himself from being partnered with Carthew.

'Where would you keep a CD like that?' Carthew said.

Moone shrugged.

Carthew pointed behind him, in the direction of the bedroom. 'Maybe by your bed?'

Moone followed her into a small bedroom. The bed took up most of the space, along with a dresser and a bedside table. Pictures of sunsets and photos of friends lined the walls. Moone felt sadness wash over him as he was standing there, imagining the young woman asleep in the bed, happy, dreaming, and not in the morgue, cold.

Carthew was already crouched at the bedside table, going through the drawers.

'Bingo!' Carthew stood up, holding a CD in a black case. "Madam Revello reading" was written in gold ink across the front.

Moone smiled. 'We need to go over to Charlene's place, see if we can find her CD and then give the keys back to her flatmate.'

'OK, let's go, then. We can listen to this on the way.'

Butler stepped up to the grand house, imagining that there was probably a piano inside somewhere. She looked round to see Harding trailing behind, his hands in his pockets.

'Come on,' Butler said. 'Hurry up.'

Harding joined her on the top step, facing the large double doors. 'Are you sure about this?'

She stared at him, frowning. 'Yes, I'm sure. We have to look into these things and ask questions. It's our job.'

Harding shrugged, so Butler pressed the ornate doorbell and waited, puffing out the air from her mouth.

The door opened after a short while, revealing a young woman with long, silky black hair, pale skin, dressed in a dark blue dress.

'Mrs Beckett?' Butler asked, showing her ID. 'DI Mandy Butler.'

'Sophie,' the young woman said. 'I think you want my sister. She's not in a good way, I'm afraid.'

'We appreciate that,' Butler said. 'It's not a good time. But we need to ask some questions...'

Sophie looked round, back into the house then at Butler again. 'Perhaps I might be able to answer them.'

'Maybe. Why don't we come inside?'

Sophie opened the door wider, letting them in, then took them into a large, wood-floored kitchen, filled with white and chrome units. The sister rested her back on a huge Aga-style oven and folded her thin pale arms across her chest. 'What did you want to ask?'

Butler looked round at Harding and saw he was looking down, avoiding eye contact. 'Your sister, she and her husband had money stolen from them by Philip Stannard? Is that right?'

Sophie nodded. 'That's correct. What has that got to do with Edward's death?'

'We're not sure. We're trying to look into something...'

'But you think somehow having this money stolen... what? You think that caused him to do what he did?'

'Again, we're not sure. Do you know if he knew a man called Martin Jessop?'

The door of the kitchen creaked open, and they all looked round to the tall frame of Audrey Beckett coming in, her dark eyes burning out.

'We knew Martin Jessop,' Audrey said, folding her arms. 'He and my husband were friends. And no, we didn't know anything about any of that...'

Butler waved away her words. 'We're not suggesting you did, Mrs Beckett...'

'Then what is this?' Audrey raised her eyebrows. 'You don't have other cases to work on? No other crimes to solve? I find that hard to believe. So, you thought why not sink yourselves into some ineffectual activities, like coming around here and asking ridiculous questions? My husband is dead. He took his own life, rather than to talk to me, to give me the chance to help him...'

Butler watched as the distraught woman prodded her thumb hard into her own chest, her eyes wide, her lips trembling. Butler approached her, putting on her kindest look, which she had been told before always fell short of kind.

'I'm sorry,' Butler said. 'So very sorry for what you're going through. We're just trying to get an idea of what's going on here...'

Audrey Beckett straightened herself, a stern look in her eye. 'I'll tell you what is going on here. Two police officers are in my home, harassing me because they cannot be bothered to busy themselves with finding murderers or rapists...'

Butler sighed. 'We'll show ourselves out.'

Butler walked on, heading through the house, hearing Harding's footsteps coming quickly behind her. They went out the front door and shut it behind them. Butler turned to Harding, then pointed a finger at his face.

'Not a word, you!' she said.

'I wasn't going to say anything,' he said. 'Except that didn't go very well.'

Then the front door opened and the sister was coming out. Butler smiled at her, then said, 'Sorry for upsetting your sister...'

'It's OK,' Sophie said. 'I just wanted to add to what my sister said. They did know Martin Jessop. After it came out about him, well, Edward was beside himself. He felt tainted by it all.'

'Do you think that might be the reason why...' Harding asked.

Sophie shook her head. 'No, not at all. Edward was happy. My sister can be, well, a bit of a bitch, to be honest, but he was happy. Yes, Stannard stole money from them, but he stole from a lot of people and it was only a few thousand, nothing to them.'

Butler nodded. 'OK, thanks for letting us know.'

'It's OK.' Sophie smiled. 'There is someone else who had money stolen from him by Stannard, and he was friends with Edward.'

'Who?' Butler asked.

'Colin Darwin.'

Butler let out a laugh. 'Darwin? As in The Realm stores?'

'Yes. He had a few thousand conned out of him by Stannard. He's kept it quiet because of his reputation, but I know because Edward told me.'

'Thank you,' Butler said. 'You've been very helpful.'

CHAPTER 9

'Have you got somewhere to be?' Carthew said as she drove them towards Charlene Bale's flat. They had just left the build-up of traffic along Mutley Plain. Moone looked up from his phone, having just noted that his lunch date was about twenty minutes away.

'It's OK,' he said, put his phone away and stared up at the houses racing past.

'No, go on,' she said. 'Where do you need to be?'

'Just supposed to be having lunch with someone.'

'Lunch? With a witness or...'

'It doesn't matter.' He smiled.

'I see. I get it. You've got a lunch date, but you didn't want to hurt my feelings.' Carthew signalled, checked her mirrors, then pulled over and parked. 'Go on then, Moone, run along to your date.'

'But we've got...'

'I'll sort it out. Believe it or not, Pete, but I'm

not holding a candle for you. Not even an ember.'

He laughed. 'Thanks -I think! Anyway, I'll meet you back at the nick?'

'Yep. Go on.'

He climbed out and turned to face the car, but Carthew had already revved it and headed back into the road and off.

The Early Bird Cafe was sat in the middle of Mutley Plain, just on the corner of a street, next to a shop that seemed to have closed down. He stepped in to find the place quite busy, with the kitchen staff hurrying around and preparing the food at the back of the place in a corner kitchen. He spotted Rachel by the window, a coffee already in front of her. She smiled up at him, the glow of the winter sun behind her, making her outline shine hazily. She had her hair up, and she was dressed in a cream shirt and dark blue pencil skirt.

'Hi,' he said, 'Do you want another coffee?'

'I'm fine. You have to order at the counter.'

He fetched an Americano from the counter and then sat down, scrambling around inside his head for something charming and witty to say, but only a tumbleweed passed in front of him.

'How's the case going?' she asked.

'Oh, it's going,' he said, sipping his coffee. 'I just don't know where.'

'When you ran off the other night. Was it a murder?'

'I really don't know. Sorry, I can't really talk about it.'

She nodded. 'Did you want to eat something?'

'Did you?'

'I'm not very hungry.' She smiled. 'But I don't live far from here. Just round the corner really.'

'OK...'

'Thought you could come back to mine...' She leaned towards him, a smile on her lips as she raised her eyebrows.

'Come back to yours?'

'Or aren't you allowed to do that sort of thing while you're on duty?'

'I think it's frowned upon, but I've never been one for playing by the rules.'

'Good.' She stood up and put on her jacket. 'Come on, then.'

Moone found himself being let into a nice, first-floor flat, well decorated, just a few minutes walk from Mutley. As Rachel shut the door behind him, he turned, remembering why he had decided to meet her for lunch; which was to break her heart, to seal off a relationship that could go nowhere.

But she put her arms around his neck, lifting her mouth to his, kissing him and driving him back towards the sofa. He fell onto it, her on top of him, her hands pulling at his tie.

'You sure about this?' he managed to ask as

she pulled his tie over his head, jerking his collar up to his chin uncomfortably.

'Definitely,' she said, getting off of him while she unbuttoned her shirt, then revealed her pink bra that cupped her lightly tanned breasts.

Whatever Moone was thinking, whatever doubts he was having, disintegrated as she pulled up her skirt and sat astride him, half unbuttoning his shirt, half kissing his mouth, his neck. He ran his hands over her legs, feeling the black nylon that covered them, and then his eyes fell on the stocking tops. He pulled her face to his, telling himself to enjoy it while it lasted, because things like this, this good, never really lasted. Life was short, he said in his head and kissed her.

Butler sat staring at the massive store in front of her, situated along Billacombe Road, on the way to Plymstock. She stared at the gigantic "The Realm" sign that was spread over the front of the place.

Harding lowered his window, letting in the stink from the Tamar, the deep belch of what lay beneath the tide, mixing with the local fish factory.

'Shut that bloody window!' she snapped.

Harding huffed and shut it again, then folded his arms. 'You're not seriously considering going in there, are you?'

'I'm thinking about it. Why, you scared?'

'He's pretty much a billionaire, he raises money for local charities, and he's got a photo in there of him with the Prime Minister!'

'I've seen that photo. Probably bloody photoshopped. What's your point anyway?'

Harding let out a harsh breath. 'My point is, that chances are he's got a lot of clout down the local lodge. You know, funny handshake, all that business. He probably belongs to the same lodge as the Chief Super.'

Butler rubbed her face, her heart sinking as she realised Harding was probably right for once in his life. 'Shit.'

'Come on though, you haven't really got anything to go on, have you? So Darwin gets ripped off just like this other fella, Beckett...'

'And Jessop. Don't forget Jessop.'

'Yeah, and Jessop. Yeah, they both top themselves, but where's the real link? What's that got to do with these other girls killing themselves?'

'I don't know. But I'm starting to get this feeling in the pit of my stomach that something's going on here...'

'You're spending too much time with Moone. He sees conspiracy everywhere.'

'He was right last time, wasn't he?'

'Yeah, but close your eyes and throw a dart and you're bound to hit the bullseye eventually. How many poor bastards did he get in the eye with a dart during his time in the smoke?'

Butler turned and stared at the store. 'All right, you win. Start the engine. Let's get out of here.'

'Good.' Harding started the car, put it in reverse and started to head out towards Billacombe Road.

'What the fuck was with the darts thing though?'

Harding shrugged and signalled. 'I don't know. I like darts.'

'Jesus. Go on, get us back to the station.'

Moone looked at his phone, saw that his lunch was almost over, and then put it down on the bedside table. Rachel turned over and faced him, her chest a little red, a smile on her face.

'Not bad for an older guy,' she said, then caressed his bare chest.

'I'm glad you appreciate the talents of a more mature man.'

'Yes, I do occasionally pick up an old age pensioner, but I tend to find they run out of puff.' She laughed, then kissed him.

'Nice. This doesn't usually happen to me...'

'What? Sex for lunch?'

'Yep. That sort of thing. There's a chance if this continues, I might starve to death.'

'But you'll have a smile on your face when they find you.'

Moone laughed. 'True.'

'Want to do it again?'

'Give me a chance to get my breath back!'

Rachel sat up. 'No, I meant in general. Maybe we could do something at the weekend, like a proper date. Go to the cinema or something.'

He nodded, then sat up. 'Yes, I'd like that.'

'Plus, you'll probably get in free with your pensioner card or whatever you lot have.'

'You cheeky sod!' He pushed her back on the bed, then kissed her. 'I've got to go back to work.'

'So have I. Mike likes his staff to be punctual.'

Moone found his shirt and slipped it on. 'He a good boss is he, this Michael Whittle?'

'As good as any.' Rachel found her underwear and put it on. 'Better than your boss, I bet.'

'You're not wrong. My boss wants everything tidied away, even if it stinks.'

Rachel found his tie and helped put it around Moone's neck and started doing it up. 'But you're not going to listen to him, are you?'

'No, not if I can help it.'

'For what it's worth, I don't think Simon killed himself.'

'You don't? Why's that?'

She finished knotting his tie, then stood back. 'He just wasn't the type. He used to look forward to each day. You know the type, the sort of person who jumps out of bed in the morning...'

'Yep. I hate them. So you knew him pretty

well?'

'Not really, just listened to Mick when he talked about him. He loved his brother. He didn't let on, but he really did.' Rachel pulled on her skirt and zipped it up.

Moone was about to talk some more but his phone beeped at him. He picked it up, then saw Butler had sent a message: 'U still on lunch?'

'No, just about done. Why?'

'I need a word with u. See u at the station.'

Moone put away his phone and looked up to see Rachel was fully dressed and touching up her make-up and half looking at him.

'Work?' she asked.

'Yep. The call to action.' He walked over to her, searching for what to say, still not convinced that a relationship with her was the right way to go. Then he found himself wondering what Alice would think if she ever found out. What the hell would Angela say?

Rachel smiled at him. 'I like you. You've got a nice smile and trustworthy eyes.'

He laughed. 'Trustworthy eyes? Never heard that one before. People usually compare me to a dog.'

'A dog? Really? Interesting. Right, I think it's time we both got back to work.'

Moone could feel his cheeks burning as he headed up the stairs to the major incident room. He stopped as he saw Butler coming towards him, arms folded across her chest. She looked at him like a snake about to devour a mouse.

'Why're you smiling like the cat who fell in a bucket of cream?' she asked, pulling a face.

'No reason.'

'Stop it. You look like a sex pervert.' Her face changed, her eyes widening. 'Did you have sex?'

'No!' He tried to walk past her, but she caught his elbow.

'You did! You were supposed to call it off, not bang her brains out.'

'I know, I know.'

Then Butler's face softened a little. 'Could be worse I suppose. Could've been DS Carthew you were banging.'

'Anyway, what's going on?'

'Well, I went to see Mrs Beckett today. Turns out she and her husband had money stolen from them by Philip Stannard...'

'Who's that?'

'Who's Stannard?' She let out a huff and nodded. 'No, of course you don't know, London boy. Philip Stannard was a solicitor, an elderly chap who everybody liked and respected. Turned out though that he was skimming money off people, little by little. Apparently, he'd been doing it for years. They reckon he got away with a couple hundred thousand.'

'He got away?'

'Oh, yeah, they reckon he had some fake passports made and did a bunk to South America or somewhere. They were just about to nab him when he ran off.'

Moone whistled. 'OK, so what's this got to do with our suicides?'

'Beckett was ripped off by him, so was another man called Martin Jessop, who went on to kill himself by jumping off a very high bridge in Cornwall.'

Moone rubbed his face, trying to make the connection. 'I still don't get it. We've got two dead young women and possibly Simon Whittle on our books. We've got reason to believe that their deaths were suspicious, but this...'

Butler sighed. 'You too? Come on, don't you think it's all a bit odd?'

'It's definitely all a bit odd, but we've got nothing tying your Beckett and the guy who jumped off the bridge...'

'They knew each other. Beckett, Jessop and Whittle. I've just checked with Ashley Whittle and yes, they all knew each other. It's got to be more than a coincidence.'

Moone stood back, thinking. 'Three of them dead?'

'That's right.'

Moone pushed through the doors and into the incident room where he saw Harding, Chambers and Carthew working away at separate desks. They all looked up, watching him, then Butler as they stepped up to the whiteboard.

'Right then,' he said loudly, so everyone could hear him. 'Gather round.'

Harding, Chambers and Carthew came over and rested themselves against the desks at the centre of the room.

Moone looked them all over, avoiding the curious gaze of Carthew as he said, 'Our recent suicides may have a link to some other suicides. Martin Jessop, Simon Whittle, and Edward Beckett all crossed swords at some point. Two of them were victims of Philip Stannard...'

Harding raised a hand. 'Sir...' He seemed to look sheepishly towards Butler before he said, 'It's just that Jessop took his own life before it all came out...'

'What came out?' Moone asked.

Butler huffed. 'He's referring to the fact that Jessop had been committing assaults in Central Park. The inquest said that it was likely that he couldn't live with what he'd done. Likely. Not proven one hundred per cent.'

Moone pinched his nose, nodding. 'OK, well, let's dig a little deeper, find out exactly how these men knew each other and anything else that might've pushed them to take their lives. We need to see if there's a link to Charlene Bale or Sarah MacPherson...'

'There isn't going to be one,' Carthew said, her voice full of disbelief. 'These men have nothing to do with these women killing themselves. There's nothing linking them...'

'You don't know that!' Butler snapped. 'Or do you know everything about them?'

Carthew squared up to her, her cheeks growing even more scarlet. 'No, I don't. But I'm not so blinded that I can't see this is just a wild goose chase. Remember those kids in that small Welsh town a few years back? Loads of the kids killed themselves. But there was no link, they found no reason but boredom, despair or depression...'

'She's got a point,' Harding said, then shrunk back when Butler glared at him.

Moone stepped in, feeling the tension practically living and breathing between them. 'OK, maybe we were getting ahead of ourselves. Let's concentrate on what we do know.'

'What's that?' Butler said, still sending eye daggers at Carthew.

Moone picked up a marker and tapped the whiteboard. 'We know someone was in Charlene's car when she went to kill herself. And I'm pretty sure that someone gained access to Sarah MacPherson's flat by pretending to deliver a package to her.'

Moone looked over at the door as he heard a knock. Sergeant Kevin Pinder was standing there, an evidence bag at his side that seemed to contain a metal box.

'Come in, Sergeant,' Moone said. 'We were just having a briefing.'

Pinder came in, looking a little unsure, and

nodding to the team. 'Sorry to interrupt, but I thought I'd better come and tell you what I've found.'

'Go on,' Moone said, watching Pinder putting the metal box on the desk.

'Found this hidden under Sarah MacPherson's bed,' Pinder said. 'Talked to her friend and he told me she'd been saving up some money in this. Saving for a holiday. It's empty now.'

Harding stepped forward, looking down at it. 'I didn't find any large amounts of money missing from her account.'

Moone nodded. 'So, whoever entered her home might have emptied this.'

'Why?' Butler asked. 'So he's a thief?'

Moone shrugged. 'I don't know. But what if it's not about the money? What if that's a kind of trophy, taking something from them?'

'I listened to the CD,' Carthew said, making everyone turn to her. 'There was plenty both of them told the psychic woman, but nothing there that anyone could blackmail them with…'

Moone sighed. 'I still think Madam Revello has had a hand in this somehow.'

Butler huffed. 'Only because you hate psychics.'

Harding sat at his desk and started typing as he said, 'She's got her own website. Not many Plymouth psychics bother with that.'

'Really?' Moone went over and looked

over Harding's shoulder and took a look at Revello's website. 'Then she's moving up in the world.'

'There's a few local celebs left testimonials,' Harding said. 'Local newsreader, that young swimmer fella. All sorts on here.'

'Bring up the rest of the testimonials.'

Harding clicked on the page Moone wanted. There were quite a few comments, most of them by local everyday people thanking Madam Revello for turning their lives around. Then Moone's eyes sprang to one of the names.

'Look, here, right near the bottom,' he said, tapping the screen.

'Who is it?' Butler joined him. 'What? M. Jessop? It can't be the same one, surely?'

'Only one way to find out.'

Butler stared at him, shaking her head. 'You're thinking of going to talk to his widow?'

'I'm thinking about it.'

'All right, but why don't we go and see Madam Revello again and see if Jessop did use her services, how about that?'

'OK. Let's go and talk to her.'

Harding laughed. 'She probably already knows you're coming.'

CHAPTER 10

'You realise she's probably very pissed off,' Butler said as she drove them to Madam Revello's house in Higher Compton.

'Who?' Moone looked at her, his mind wrenched away from the case and his wonderings about how everything possibly fitted together. Part of him had raised doubts, wondering if he might have it wrong and Carthew was right. But what did come up from deep in his thoughts, stank as bad as if it had been pulled from the deepest part of the River Tamar.

'DS Carthew,' she said, swinging the car into Efford Road.

'Oh shit!' Moone sat up. 'I didn't even think...'

'Not to worry, I'm sure she'll get over it.' Butler let out a short-lived laugh as she parked up outside Madam Revello's house. 'What do you think her part is in all this?'

Moone climbed out, the wind pushing at

him, while the rain started to tap at his head and face. He looked up and saw the bleak greyness of the afternoon sky. 'I don't know. What if she was giving extra private readings, ones not recorded, where Bale or MacPherson spilt more of their life story?'

'I don't buy it.' Butler walked up the steps and rang the doorbell. 'This woman has been charging twenty quid for a reading since I was a nipper. She could be charging a lot more. She's just not the type to be ripping people off or blackmailing people.'

'I'll take your word for it.'

The door opened, and the son looked out at them through his thick glasses.

'Remember us?' Moone asked, showing his ID.

'Mother's with someone,' he said, stepping back into the darkened house and allowing them to step inside.

Moone followed the middle-aged son, watching his slow, laborious movements as they reached the conservatory that was curtained off like before.

'Nasty weather,' the son said.

'Yep,' Moone said. 'There's a storm coming.'

'Mother doesn't like storms. They scare her.'

'Surely she can see them coming.' Moone stifled his smile.

'She's not a weather presenter,' the son said.

Nothing more was said, but Moone turned

to see Butler telling him off with her eyes, her head shaking. Then the door of the conservatory opened and a young man appeared. He took one look at them, then walked on, followed by Madam Revello's son. Moone and Butler were left to enter the darkened room and found the elderly woman sitting at a small table.

'Have you come for your fortune told this time?' Revello said, a slight smile on her thin lips.

'No, not this time.' He sat down in the chair reserved for customers while Butler stood, arms folded, behind him. 'We've come to see if you know this man.'

Moone took out his phone and brought up a photo of Martin Jessop that he showed to Madam Revello. 'Ever read for this guy?'

She peered at the photograph, then shook her head. 'I don't know I'm afraid. There's been so many customers over the years.'

'He left a comment on your website, a testimonial.'

Revello sat back, staring at him. 'Then I must have read for him. As I said, there have been so many clients over the years.'

'You don't have some kind of record?' Butler asked, her voice sounding kinder to Moone than he had ever witnessed before. 'It's just that we need to find out if you did read for him or not.'

The elderly woman smiled up at Butler. 'I read for you once. How's life with your other half now? Are things better?'

'You remember me?' Butler said.

'Of course.'

Moone let out an exhausted breath. 'Then why can't you help us?'

The woman turned her eyes to Moone, a little annoyance in them. 'Very well. My son has a photo album with lots of our customers in it. Have a look through, maybe this man will be in there.'

Moone nodded and sat back a little, staring into her dark eyes. 'That's more like it.'

'Do you want me to finish your reading?' she asked, picking up her deck of tarot cards.

He went to stand up. 'No, thanks.'

Then her hand was on his, grasping it tightly, forcing him to sit back down. 'What're you doing?'

'I see darkness,' she said, refusing to let go, even though he tried to pull his hand away. 'I see a woman. A woman shrouded in darkness. She doesn't know which way to turn. She needs help.'

'What does she look like?' Butler asked, her voice full of enthusiasm.

Revello let go of Moone's hand and shook her head. 'I never see that clearly. But there's danger surrounding her. I'm not sure if it's for herself...' She stared at Moone. 'Or for you.'

Moone stood up, a bubble of annoyance rising in him. 'Believe what you want... In the real world, we've got a possible killer to find.'

'They don't want to die,' Revello said.

'They've got no choice in the end.'

'What do you know about it?' Moone said, anger soaking his words. 'What do you feed their minds with? Death? Misery? What do you tell them when the tape's not running?'

Revello sat back, closed her eyes and shook her head. 'I don't expect you to understand, but I help them. If I see darkness, then I try and reroute them.'

'Did you see danger in their futures?' Butler asked. 'In Charlene Bale's or Sarah MacPherson's future?'

'I see so many clients. You'd have to listen to their CDs.'

'We did,' Moone said. 'There was nothing on there like that.'

The woman raised her shoulders. 'Then I didn't see any darkness for them.'

Moone huffed. 'Let's go, Butler.'

'Don't go there this evening,' the old lady called out to Moone as he was about to step out of the conservatory. 'Or it will surely take your life.'

Moone gave her a look of pity, then headed through the house until he found the son in the lounge, sitting at a desk with a large PC and monitor in front of him.

'I hear you have a photo album of the people your mum reads for,' Moone said.

The son's thick glasses turned on him, but he remained silent. Then he got up, went to a shelf thick with books about the occult, and removed a large photo album and handed it to Moone.

'Can I?' Moone asked, pointing to a worn black leather armchair.

The son shrugged as Moone realised he didn't know the man's name. 'I'm sorry, Mr Revello, I don't know your name.'

'Ian,' he said. 'Ian Speare.'

'Not Revello?' Butler asked, leaning over Moone's shoulder as he opened the book.

'That's just a stage name,' Ian said, then pointed to the door. 'I'd better make Mother a cup of tea.'

'Revello.' Moone huffed. 'I knew it.'

'Just keep turning the pages.'

Moone took out his phone to find the photo of Martin Jessop, only half concentrating on the photos in the album.

'Hang on!' Butler said. 'Turn back the page.'

Moone turned back the page and watched as Butler's finger tapped at one of the photographs.

'Who's that?' he asked. 'That's not Jessop.'

'No, but it is Colin Darwin.' Butler pulled the book away from him, laughing to herself. 'Fancy a big shot like Darwin coming here. It's hilarious.'

Moone followed her round the room. 'Who's Colin Darwin?'

Butler shot him a look as if he had stripped down to his pants. 'Darwin? You must've heard of him. He's a local billionaire. Runs a small chain of shops called The Realm.'

'Oh, I think I bought my kettle and toaster there.'

'More than likely you did. Now we've got a connection.'

'Have we?'

'Yes. Jessop and Beckett and Whittle moved in the same circles. Jessop came here. Darwin also rubbed shoulders with them, and he's in here too.'

Moone rubbed his chin, feeling the stubble burn his palm. 'It's thin. We don't even know what the connection is to the girls.'

'This place. That's the common denominator here. I don't think Madam Revello's the culprit, but something's going on.'

'What now, then?'

'Let's go and see Colin Darwin and hear what he has to say.' Butler raised her eyebrows and Moone thought he detected a look of almost glee in her eyes.

They sat outside the huge store, in the packed car park, staring at the building, the engine quietening. The rain and wind were battering the car, pushing at it, sweeping across the tarmac. Customers were coming out, running to their cars.

'What's the story with this guy?' Moone asked, looking at Butler.

'A self-made billionaire,' she said. 'And an arsehole.'

'I think the two go hand in hand, don't they?'

'They certainly do with him. Thinks of himself as a bit of a Del Boy. Started out working in Panier Market, down the bottom of town.'

'Now look at him.'

'Still an arsehole,' Butler said and pushed open her door, then hurried through the wind and rain towards the store entrance.

Moone followed, pulling up his coat's collars and jogging to the automatic doors. He found Butler standing just inside, near the long row of tills. The place was packed out with customers filling the aisles.

'Where do we find him?' Moone asked, but Butler had already moved off, taking out her ID as she approached a middle-aged woman in a grey suit.

'Excuse me,' Butler said to the woman, showing her ID. 'Police. We need a word with your boss, Colin Darwin.'

'I'm afraid he'll be busy,' the woman said, a little bewildered.

'Where's his office?'

The woman's eyes jumped towards the back of the store, where there was a second level. 'Well, up there, but, you'll need...'

But Butler was striding on, her ID still in her hand, heading for the escalators. Moone caught up, joining her as she waited behind a long line of trolley-pushing customers.

'I'm sensing you resent him,' Moone said.

Butler turned on him, an eyebrow raised. 'Oh, do you? Why would I resent him?'

'I don't know. Because he's a local, a Plymouth boy who's done well for himself...'

'So? Good for him.'

'Does he do a lot for local charities?'

'So I've heard.' Butler stepped onto the escalator and Moone followed. 'Doesn't make him less of an arsehole.'

'Do you know him?'

Butler didn't say anything, just remained stiff, her arms folded until she stepped off the escalator and then started storming on again towards the back of the floor. Moone could see there were offices back there. Something was eating at Butler, he could feel it and it seemed like it had a lot to do with the man they were headed to see. He caught up, thinking some damage control or diplomacy might be needed.

There was a door marked "Colin Darwin", which Butler went through, with Moone following. They found themselves in a small office, an attractive young blonde woman sat at a desk, staring up as they came in.

'Darwin?' Butler asked, pointing to another door behind her.

The woman stood up. 'I'm afraid Mr Darwin is busy. You need to make an appointment...'

Butler showed her ID. 'No, we don't. We're the police.'

The young woman looked flummoxed for a moment, hovering by her desk and then she started backing up towards the door. 'OK, I'll go check with him.'

'Good, you do that,' Butler said, huffed and rested her backside on the PA's desk. 'You need an appointment… Jesus.'

'She was just doing her job.'

Before Butler could say anything, the young woman came out again with a smile, her cheeks a little flushed. 'Mr Darwin will see you now.'

'About time,' Butler said and pushed past her and into a large office. There was a podgy, suited man sitting behind a long desk, right behind a computer. Behind him was a wall of glass, but on each other wall there were photographs of him with various celebrities, including the Prime Minister.

The podgy man didn't get up, just sat back in his chair, running his hands through his thick greying hair.

'I've been told you're the police,' Darwin said, looking them up and down.

'That's right,' Butler showed her ID.

Darwin sat up, staring at it, nodding. 'I take it this isn't about a parking dispute or something?'

'No, it's not,' Moone said. 'It's about suicide.'

Darwin laughed. 'Suicide? Whose suicide? Look, I haven't got time to entertain you two all day. I've got people to see, deals to make. My shops don't run themselves...'

'You knew Martin Jessop,' Moone stated, making Darwin stare at him through half-closed eyes.

'I know lots of people.'

'What about Edward Beckett?' Moone asked.

Darwin held his poker face. 'I know Edward Beckett. He's just starting out...'

'He's dead,' Butler said. 'Hanged.'

The businessman stared at her for a moment, then stood up. 'Is that a sick joke?'

'We don't make jokes.' Butler folded her arms.

Darwin leaned on his desk, shaking his head. 'Edward? Eddie, dead? He killed himself?'

'That's what we're looking into,' Moone said. 'You did know Martin Jessop?'

'Yes, like I said, I knew him, knew lots of business people. Then all that business happened with him. I had to distance myself from all that, didn't I?'

'Did you?' Moone asked.

'Of course. I had a growing business. This is a family store. They all are. You bring your family here, to shop, and to eat in the restaurant. I couldn't be associated with all that.'

'It's not that we're interested in,' Butler said. 'We don't care how well you've done for yourself...'

'Don't I know you?' Darwin asked, pointing a chubby finger at her.

'No, you don't. Now, let's...'

'What's her name?' Darwin asked Moone. 'I mean, you have to identify yourselves...'

Moone sighed, avoiding Butler's glare. 'DI Butler. I'm DCI Moone.'

'Butler!' Darwin clicked his fingers. 'You were at school with me. Devonport Sec. That's it. Well, look at us now. You a copper, and me, well, I'm a billionaire. Got stores opening all over the country.'

'You were a cock then, still are a cock.' Butler stared at him, arms folded across her chest.

Darwin stared back, a little anger reaching his eyes before he let out a laugh. 'I know the Chief Superintendent. Play golf with him. How about that?'

Moone saw the light fade from Butler's eyes, so he said, 'Madam Revello.'

Darwin stared at him. 'Who?'

'Madam Revello.'

'A psychic,' Butler said, the light in her eyes coming back on. 'You went to see her a few years back. Maybe for business advice.'

Thunder travelled across the businessman's face. 'Never heard of her. Now, if you'd like to bugger off, I'd like to get some work done. Got money to make. I mean, how much do you lot make? Not that much I'm guessing for risking your necks. You coppers should get another job.'

Butler gave a sickened laugh. 'Did you hear that, Pete? Us coppers should find another job?

And what, the streets police themselves, do they? You arsehole.'

'You did go and see her,' Moone said, leaning on Darwin's desk. 'We've seen your photo, taken with her.'

The businessman, now red-faced with anger, his eyes burning out to Butler, growled, 'So what if I fucking did?'

'You had money stolen from you by Stannard, didn't you?' Moone asked.

Darwin faced him, his eyes full of suspicion. 'How do you know about that?'

'Can't tell you. But it wouldn't look good that getting out, would it? Did Jessop know? Beckett? What about Simon Whittle? I've heard you mixed in the same social circles.'

'So what if we did? What're you implying?'

Moone shrugged. 'Nothing. Just a bit of a coincidence that your business friends all knew you'd been fleeced by Stannard. You, a high-flying businessman. They all knew and now three of them are dead.'

Darwin didn't say anything for a moment, but his face reddened, his index finger rising, pointing at Moone. 'You're saying that you think...? *Get out! Get out of my office! Now!*'

'Come on,' Butler said. 'Let's leave this arsehole in peace.'

Moone followed her out, ignoring the cries of Darwin for them to go off and have sex with themselves.

When they were sat in the car, listening to the rain hitting the car, Butler said, 'I think we might've pissed him off.'

Moone nodded. 'Just a tad. Hit a sore point though, didn't I?'

'You really think he knocked them off?'

'No, he seemed genuinely shocked to hear about Beckett. But I think he knows more about all this.'

'He knows the fucking Chief Super. We're fucked.'

'So, you were at school together?'

'Drop it. Let's concentrate on how fucked we are.'

'We're not fucked yet.' Moone stopped talking when his phone started ringing. He took it out. 'Oh dear, here we go. DCI Peter Moone.'

'Hi, it's Doctor Parry.'

'Thank goodness,' Moone said, breathing out. 'What can I do for you, Doctor?'

'I've found something that I need to show you.'

'OK, we'll be right there.' Moone ended the call and then looked at Butler. 'The ace hasn't fallen yet. Let's go.'

They found Dr Parry dressed in his green scrubs, his skin looking so pale against his outfit and his dark stubble as he stood over the morgue table. He waved them in with his latex-gloved hand, then pulled back the sheet on the table, revealing the white body, with a slight grey tinge. It was Sarah MacPherson's body, Moone realised as he stepped closer. She looked so small and fragile on the large metal table. The wounds on her arms had been sewn up, as had the post mortem incision up her chest and sternum.

'What've you found?' Moone asked, looking over and seeing Butler standing, arms folded by his side, a look of unease on her usually stern face.

Parry lowered the sheet further, then lifted her left arm. 'Bruising. Ante-mortem bruising, I believe.'

'Really?' Moone looked closer.

'I believe so. Thing is, it is difficult to determine what is an ante or post-mortem bruise. But generally post mortem injuries need much more force than an ante-mortem injury. In this case, you can clearly see the shape of a hand on her left arm where he gripped her.'

'So he held her while she cut her wrists?' Butler asked, looking away.

'I think so.' Parry nodded. 'Sometimes these bruises take a day to show up. He must've gripped her arm quite tightly.'

'Couldn't it have been her own hand?' Moone asked.

'No.' Parry shook his head. 'No, it was his left hand, as he was stood by the bath. No mistaking it.'

'What're we saying then?' Moone asked,

feeling the hairs on the back of his neck prickling.

'It's what she's saying.' Parry covered her up. 'She's saying she was murdered.'

CHAPTER 11

Moone's feeling of elation, which seemed a little out of place seeing as he'd just visited the morgue, was quickly replaced by unease. He stepped out into the corridor to find DS Carthew waiting for him, leaning against the wall, arms folded.

'I'll meet you at the car,' Butler said, hurrying on, and flashing a sarcastic smile at Carthew.

'Parry reckons we're looking at a murder,' Moone said and pointed a thumb behind him.

'Chief Super wanted us working together on this,' Carthew said, straightening herself.

'I know, it's just that...'

'I think we make a good team.'

'We do, it's just that...'

'We've got history, I get it.'

Moone nodded, grasping any lifeline handed to him. 'Exactly. That's my fault.'

'True. But I've got a proposal...'

'Go on.'

Carthew looked round the corridor for a moment. 'Well, I think we need to clear the air. Talk things through...'

'Ok...'

'Tonight. I come to your... home, and we clear the air...'

Moone's stomach tightened. He saw and heard Madam Revello. He told himself off for even taking the old dear's ridiculous utterings seriously, but then he had a flash of Carthew with a hammer held high above her head. 'I'm not sure...'

'That's my one condition. We talk tonight, I leave, and you get to go back to working with your girlfriend again. I won't even tell the Chief Super. So, what do you say?'

'We talk, you go home. That's all?'

'Yes, so don't get any ideas.'

'I won't. OK. About eight, then?'

'I'll see you then.' Carthew smiled a little as she turned and walked away. It was a smile he had trouble reading, although he didn't have any trouble at all reading Butler's face as he reached her.

'What the bloody hell was that about?' she asked, her eyebrows almost jumping off her head.

'She wants to talk.' Moone kept walking, not really wanting to get into an argument.

'A talk? You know what that means, don't you?'

Moone faced her. 'No, it's not like that. She's going to come round tonight...'

Butler's face filled with horror. 'You're joking? Please tell me, you're joking. Tonight?'

'What's wrong with tonight? Oh, right, I get it, Madam Revello's mysterious prediction.'

'Don't go there tonight,' Butler repeated. 'It will surely take your life.'

'It. No mention of a woman. Anyway, she's coming to me. I'm not going anywhere. Let's just forget it.'

Butler stared at him, shaking her head. 'Your funeral. Anyway, where now?'

As if in answer to her question, Moone's phone started ringing again. He sighed, then took it out. 'DCI Peter Moone.'

'DCI Moone, you and DI Mandy Butler are wanted at Crownhill station,' the woman's voice said. 'The Chief Superintendent would like to talk to you immediately...'

Moone rubbed his temple as panic flapped its wings and took flight around his body. 'Right, OK, we'll be there as soon as we can.'

As Moone put his phone away, he looked up at Butler as she said, 'Please tell me that was a call out to a murder.'

'I wish. Chief Super wants us.'

'Shit!'

'That arsehole,' Butler said under her breath as they sat in the waiting area, looking towards the

Chief Super's PA as she typed something up.

'We don't know it's to do with Darwin,' Moone said, with no real conviction in his voice. His mind was racing, as it always seemed to be these days, trying to put all the pieces together while wondering what Carthew really wanted. First and foremost, she wanted to climb the ladder, but he didn't have the power to help her up. She already had the Chief Super in her pocket, so why was she bothering with him?

'Of course, it's to do with Darwin.'

Moone turned to her. 'What happened between you two at school? Were you two, you know...?'

Her eyes blazed. 'No! He wishes. Just leave it.'

The door of the Chief Super's office opened and he stood there in his uniform, minus the jacket, his fists at his side. Moone noticed that he didn't smile at all as he ordered them to come in. Butler exchanged a fearful look with him as they headed towards the gallows and sat down.

The Chief Super sat down and looked at them both. 'You can guess why I called you in.'

'Colin bleeding Darwin, by any chance?' Butler asked and huffed.

Laptew's eyes jumped to her, not a hint of humour in them. 'Colin Darwin is an influential member of our community. As a businessman, he brings many jobs to our city, and as a philanthropist...'

'We get it, sir,' Butler said. 'But he's also part of our investigation...'

'An investigation into a few suicides. I don't understand why you're interviewing Mr Darwin...'

'Not just suicides,' Moone said, gaining Laptew's attention.

'Go on, DCI Moone.'

Moone sat up. 'Well, I've talked to the Home Office Pathologist, and he's found several inconsistencies. He pointed out that someone, more than likely a man, gripped Sarah MacPherson's arm shortly before she died. I believe he did this as he administered the final cuts that ended her life.'

Laptew sat back, closing his eyes for a moment. 'OK. So, we know at least one victim, possibly two were aided in their suicides...'

'We have to treat them as suspicious,' Moone said.

'I understand that. But what has Colin Darwin got to do with these deaths? You don't believe he's involved, surely?'

Moone cleared his throat. 'We were following a line of enquiry. Darwin knew Jessop, and Beckett and Whittle. There's something tying them all together, we just don't know what it is yet, but we think it has something to do with Philip Stannard.'

The Chief Super let out a heavy breath. 'Him? Stannard? He's off sunning himself somewhere by all accounts.'

'I've been wondering about that,' Moone said. 'How do we know he did do a bunk?'

Laptew sat forward. 'We don't for sure. But they found out that he'd been skimming off his clients' accounts. Had nearly half a million hidden away. He'd also had a couple of fake passports made. They only found one of them. Chances are he skipped out on us.'

Moone nodded. 'Makes sense, I suppose.'

'You're not convinced?' The Chief Super sat back. 'Well, either way, I don't want you bothering Colin Darwin again. Got it? Is that understood? I promoted you two, but I can easily rescind that.'

Butler opened her mouth, so Moone quickly said, 'Understood, sir. We won't bother him again.'

The Chief Super seemed to look them both over for a moment before he opened a drawer and took out a small business card. 'I've always been one for keeping the press onside. They want to learn what they can from us, and sometimes we can learn from them. There's a local reporter, Carly Tamms. She's been doing pieces on suicide recently and seems she's got wind of our spate of suicides. Get in touch with her, would you, Moone? Keep a few things close to your chest. Don't let on that we're treating the deaths as suspicious, but see what she knows.'

Moone took the card that was being held out

to him and sat back reading it. 'Will do, sir.'

Laptew nodded. 'DS Carthew tells me you've all been working well as a team.'

'She did?' Butler asked, sounding shocked.

Laptew nodded. 'Yes. Keep it up. I have high hopes for you all, especially DS Carthew. She's going places that one.'

'Thanks, sir,' Moone said and signalled for Butler to follow him out of the office.

When they got down the corridor, Butler grabbed him by his arm and said, 'What was that? I have high hopes, especially for DS Carthew. Jesus. I hope she gets knee pads with her position.'

'Very funny.'

Butler looked away, shaking her head. 'I almost feel sorry for her. Having to…'

'We don't know anything's going on,' Moone said. 'But thing is, Carthew is an adult, and she obviously knows what she's doing, or thinks she does. I think she needs help. Maybe we can help her.'

Butler huffed. 'How exactly?'

'I don't know. Be kind. Show her kindness. Take her under our collective wings. Let's not be her and us. Like he said, we're a team.'

Butler breathed out. 'OK, right. Kindness. I'll suffocate her with it if I have to.'

Moone laughed. 'Come on. Let's get back to the station.'

Then Moone stopped and turned to her.

'Actually, I was thinking of visiting Michael Whittle's workplace again...'

'So you can see your girlfriend?'

Moone smiled sarcastically. 'No, I was thinking, seeing as his brother moved in the same social and business circles as Beckett and the others, then he might know something about Stannard.'

Butler shrugged. 'Sounds like you're clutching at straws to me. But seeing as they were both solicitors, him and Stannard, he might know something. I don't want to play gooseberry, so I'll let you find out. I'm going to start on our paperwork.'

Sergeant Pinder reached the top of Peverell Park Road and pulled up at the junction, about to turn left into Outland Road. He signalled, listening to the indicator clicking away, his eyes jumping to the rear-view mirror. Rain was starting to hit his back window, and beyond it, he could just make out the allotments where they had found Edward Beckett.

The lights changed, and he turned left but signalled again and pulled in and parked up near the children's playground. He climbed out, pulling up his hi-vis waterproof jacket and headed towards the allotments.

There was an elderly couple just inside the compound, so he asked them to let him in. He walked on, feeling the wind pushing him sideways, starting to lash his body with rain. The shed was a hazy triangular outline at the end of the section, police tape sealing it off. He took out his penknife and cut the tape, then let himself in.

He looked up, listening to the rain battering at the outside, the building creaking like it was a boat at sea. He imagined Beckett still hanging there, swinging slightly.

He picked up the chair that lay on its side and climbed up, staring towards the beam where the noose would have been attached. He looked down at the room, at the shelves where the dusty tools were hung. There were books too, all gathering dust. Then his eyes jumped to one of the shelves where there was a gap. He got down off the chair and went over, noticing that the dust had been recently disturbed. When he looked round, he saw a book lying on the nearby work-bench in the far corner.

He went back to his car, battered by the rain and wind again, and fetched some latex gloves, then went back into the dusty shelter of the shed. He put his fingertips on either side of the book and lifted it. He bent his head and saw the message that had been scratched into the wood beneath it.

'I don't want to die,' it said.

Moone pushed open the door of the solicitors, Wolfman House, and was greeted by chatter. All the staff seemed to be either talking to each other or clients. Moone made eye contact with Rachel, nodded and sat on the hard-looking leather chair by the window. Rain started hammering at it, echoing inside the place. Rachel kept looking over at him, while she talked to a young couple. When she was done, she came over and stood by him, smiling. An ache started within him, flashes of the afternoon rippling into his mind.

'Back already?' she asked, raising one eyebrow. 'Couldn't stay away from me?'

He smiled. 'Well, something like that.'

'Business, is it?'

'I'd like to talk to your boss again.'

'He's with a couple at the moment, but should be free soon.'

'Good. I'll wait.'

She smiled, then sat next to him. 'I was wondering, what are you doing tonight?'

Moone's stomach tightened, an image of Carthew coming to mind, the awkward conversation he was going to have with her. What exactly did she want to talk about, anyway? 'I'm a bit busy tonight.'

'Oh, right I see.' She nodded and looked a little annoyed or at least red around the cheeks as she stood up.

'It's not like that.' Moone got up. 'Believe me, I'd love to do something with you...'

She turned, her face brightening again. 'Then do it.'

'I've got a meeting. But I'll see what time it finishes…'

She moved closer, putting her hand round his, making an excited thrill rush up his arm and right around his body. It was stupid, he told himself, but he felt like a passenger on a runaway train with no way to pull on the brakes.

'Doesn't matter what time,' she said, her voice a whisper. 'Just come round.'

Her head turned then towards the back of the shop, where a couple were saying goodbye to Michael Whittle. The solicitor's eyes jumped to Moone as the couple left, and a polite smile formed as he greeted him halfway. Whittle put out his hand and shook Moone's.

'Back again so soon?' Whittle said, directing Moone towards his office.

'Just had a couple more questions for you.' Moone took a seat opposite Whittle's desk as the solicitor retook his seat.

'Well, if I can be of any help,' Whittle said, sitting back and smiling. 'What did you want to know?'

'Well, it's just that I recently learned that your brother, Simon, socialised with some other businessmen who happened to have all committed suicide…'

Whittle let out a heavy sigh. 'I'm afraid the business world can be a harsh one. I warned Simon about going it alone, the risks, but unfortunately he didn't listen to me.'

'Well, I just find it a bit strange that three businessmen who knew each other all committed suicide. Not only that, they all had dealings with a man called Philip Stannard.'

Whittle looked up at him, a look of curiosity filling his eyes. 'Really? In what way? I know Simon had a little money stolen by Stannard...'

'So did Edward Beckett and Martin Jessop.'

Whittle sat up. 'OK. But I'm having trouble following this. I mean, Jessop killed himself because of, well, what he'd done... to those young women...'

'That's what we've presumed. We still don't know why your brother committed suicide. His widow certainly doesn't.'

'Ashley, I think, doesn't like to think that Simon was suffering in silence like so many young men do these days. Depression is getting to be a pandemic.'

'That's what you think? That he was depressed?'

Whittle leaned forward. 'I know he was. He told me. Ashley and my brother found out a few years ago that they couldn't have children. It hit him hard. He didn't let on, didn't want to upset Ashley, but the old dark cloud of depression slowly arrived.'

'I see. What about Stannard? Did you know him?'

'Only a little. Like everyone thought, he seemed to be a mild-mannered, forgetful old solicitor. We were all shocked to find out that he'd been stealing all that money from his clients. We're not the best loved of professions, but he brought a new shame to us all.'

Moone nodded, trying to look earnest while thinking the same, that his experience of solicitors was only bad. 'Do you think he did a bunk to South America?'

Whittle sat up, looking a little surprised. 'I thought that was the police's theory on it. I did actually hear from someone that he had two fake passports made...'

'Yes, but only one was recovered. One of his colleagues helped him have the passports made. But there's little evidence that he ever left the country.'

'But surely if he was still here...'

Moone stood up, noting that time was getting on, and he only had a couple of hours before his awkward meeting with Carthew. It was getting dark out and didn't want to travel back through the country lanes in pitch darkness.

'It's just a theory,' Moone said. 'Right, I'd better go. I'll be in touch if I need anything else.'

Whittle held out his hand and Moone shook it. 'Believe me, Detective. I don't like the thought that my brother took his own life, but I know how troubled he was inside.'

Moone smiled, nodded, but couldn't think of any more to say. He turned and headed out, half noticing Rachel was absent from her desk. Just as well, he thought, feeling his longing growing. Then he found his mind travelling to Mrs Whittle, who didn't know why her husband had left her. She needed to know if he had indeed taken his own life, but Moone still wasn't completely convinced.

There was a figure on the street when Moone pushed through the glass door, and he found Sergeant Pinder waiting for him as a lighter rain fell on the pavement.

'There's something you need to see,' Pinder said, pointing a thumb behind him.

The wind and rain had started again, coating Moone's face as he followed Sergeant Pinder towards Pounds Park at the top of Peverell Park Road, where the allotments were. The wind pushed him sideways and made the trees creak high above him. The fences rattled too, making an eerie sound as Pinder let them both into the compound.

'It's at the far end,' Pinder said, raising his voice over the wind and rain.

Moone nodded, pulling his jacket collar round his neck, and looking towards the outline of the large shed at the far end. 'That's where they found Beckett?'

'That's right.'

There was a light glowing from inside the shed, and when Moone stepped inside, sheltered from the wind and rain, he found a SOCO in a white hooded suit, taking photos of something on a workbench in a far corner.

'They found him hanging there,' Pinder said, pointing to the beam above their heads.

Moone nodded, trying and failing to stop the imagined image of a man hanging from a homemade noose. Moone pointed to the corner. 'That it?'

'Yeah.' Pinder directed him over to the workbench and let him see where the book had been removed. Moone moved closer, bending over the bench, reading the words that had been scratched into the wood.

'When did he have time to do this?' Moone asked.

'Maybe he left him in here, locked him in. You can bolt it from the outside.'

Moone nodded, looking round the shed, hearing the wind and rain attacking it. He shivered a little at the thought of being left in there, told to kill yourself or... Or what? 'I think you might be right about that.'

Moone checked his phone, saw that time was getting on, and it wasn't that long until he'd have to meet with Faith Carthew. 'Right, I have somewhere to be. Thanks for this. Come to the incident room tomorrow and you can brief the team.'

Pinder smiled a little, then Moone turned and headed for the door, the wind and rain still blasting outside.

'DCI Moone,' Pinder called out and caught up with him. 'Sir...'

'Yes?'

'Forget it...'

'No, go on.'

'It's just that, I see you've got Faith Carthew working with you...'

'That's right. DS Carthew now. What about her?'

'It's just that. Well, it's just...'

'You can talk to me. It's fine.'

Pinder nodded. 'I've heard stories about her. Not very pleasant ones. She's, well, she's trouble from what I've heard. She seems to be getting fast-tracked, but, well, I've heard she's dangerous.'

'Dangerous?' Moone saw her with a hammer in her hand, held over Samson's head.

'That's what I've heard. From other uniforms she's dated...'

'Let's talk about this tomorrow. I've got to go.'

Moone turned, his stomach digging a trench for itself as the wind tugged and pushed him about. In about half an hour he'd be meeting with her. What the hell did she want?

Moone's headlights glowed along the road, lighting up the corners of the country lane that were thick with darkness. His mind raced on, an uneasy feeling having long since overtaken his gut. He entered the caravan park without even being aware of it and took the long road that ran the whole way up to the back of the campsite. He turned left, heading towards the plot where his mobile home was situated. He was tired and wanted to go to bed, not have a long-winded, pointless chat.

Then he saw something through the darkness of the trees, a light flickering as he turned the bend and passed the rows of mobile homes. He stared as he slowed down, watching the red and orange light dancing about, a slow, terrible realisation growing inside him as he stared towards his own home.

He pushed open the door and ran towards his caravan, watching the flames eating away inside the window.

A massive blast knocked out the window and the roar of the flames filled the air. Moone stepped back, feeling the warmth, the burn of the fire that was devouring his home. He hardly noticed his neighbours who had come out, all panicked and loud.

'Is that your place?' someone asked him, but he could only stare, watching the blaze of flames blackening his home, turning it into a rectangular-shaped skeleton.

He was watching the flames dance, sending black smoke into the night air, when he saw a figure move round the caravan and then come towards him. The light of the fire caught them, allowing Moone to see DS Carthew walking towards him, her eyes taking in what was happening to his home.

She reached him and stood shoulder to shoulder with him. He turned and looked at her, staring at her profile.

'That's a terrible thing to happen to your home,' she said, then looked him in the eye. 'Isn't it?'

He said nothing, so she smiled, then said, 'Lucky you weren't home.'

Moone stared back at her as she smiled, then turned and walked away, sinking back into the darkness.

CHAPTER 12

There was very little street lighting along the road in Devonport where PC Karen West has been posted after the incident. She stood up straight, watching the dark corners of the street, her hands resting on her stab vest. Her feathers were still a little ruffled from being posted to guard the house alone in such a rough neighbourhood. At least the rain had let off a little and reduced to a few spits instead of a downpour. Still, it was cold. But she would be relieved in half an hour, she'd been told. But that had been two hours ago, and so far no one had even come to give her support. 'Cuts,' she grumbled under her breath.

Her attention turned to the house for the moment, at the crime scene tape across the front door, which looked like it had been given a few kickings in its time. About four hours ago, a woman, more a skeleton than an actual living human, was taken from the building. The paramedics had tried to save her, but it was too late. A needle had been found sticking out of her foot, between the toes. An overdose of heroin had been suspected, but a post-mortem would need to be carried out before it was labelled death by misadventure. There had been two other occupants found in the house; one was a long-haired, greasy, skeletal young man who had been found passed out on the floor. The other was a much older, hood-wearing man who had a dog with him, something like a Staffy. Both of them had sloped off into the night, after having had their details taken.

PC West turned round when she heard squawking and spotted the seagulls coming down to attack a bin bag left out at the end of one of the gardens. She could hardly make out what they were up to, just their wings flapping as they danced and pecked angrily at each other.

Her eyes rose, focusing towards the end of the street where she thought she saw a change in the dim light. She stared, then stepped closer, recognising a human shape coming in her direction. Then slow footsteps, getting louder, disturbing the seagulls and causing them to fly off up to one of the roofs.

The figure kept coming, hitting the occasional puddle, and as the little light available lit up the figure, she saw that the person was carrying something in his arms. The man wore a hood, much like the hooded man who had sloped off with his dog hours earlier.

'I need to get inside,' the man said, his voice

barely a whisper. She could barely see his face, just his mouth, which was much less obscured by the hood and the shadows.

'It's a crime scene,' she said. 'You need to find somewhere else to go.'

'I need to get inside to get something to dig with.'

'What?' She looked down at the creature in his hands, wondering why it had hardly moved. 'Is that dog OK?'

The hood lowered. 'No. It's dead.'

'Dead? What the bloody hell happened?'

'He jumped off the roof.'

'What? What do you mean?'

The man looked up again. 'I was on the roof of the car park in town. He suddenly made a run for it and dived off the roof. Killed himself. Couldn't live without her, I guess.'

'Dogs don't kill themselves!' A wave of anger flooded West, and she found herself wanting to grasp the druggy by the neck. She calmed herself and brought back her professional expression. 'Why did you do it?'

'Do what?'

'Kill the dog?'

'I didn't.'

'Dogs don't kill themselves.'

'He did. I need to go inside...'

West rubbed her face, the anger rising again. 'You can't. I've told you, it's a potential crime scene. Your friend's dead. Doesn't that mean anything to you?'

'She wasn't my friend.'

West jumped back as the man suddenly released the body of the dog, letting it thud against the pavement. Then he swept round and started walking off.

'Where do you think you're going?' she called out.

'You bury him.'

The shape of the man sunk into the darkness of the street and West was left with the carcass of the dog. She knelt, put a hand on his flank, feeling his fur. His body was still quite warm. She looked up, trying to see where the junkie had gone to, annoyance and tiredness swelling inside her, mixing together. She should have been relieved from her duty two hours ago. She stood up, confused, unsure of what to do.

She called it in and was put on to the on-duty inspector. Tony Harris.

'Say it again,' Inspector Harris said.

'He just dumped the dog right in front of me, sir,' she said. 'Any chance of getting relieved?'

Harris sighed. 'I'll get someone there as soon as I can. You say he wanted to get into the house?'

'Yes. I reckon he must have some drugs hidden in there.'

'OK. I'll send someone to relieve you. Do us a favour, West, have a look around inside.'

'Go in there?'

'Yes, are you OK to do that? Try and see what he was after. Better wear some gloves.'

She held back her sigh, not wanting to sound too pissed off or scared. But she was, very scared and just as pissed off.

'No problem.'

'That's my... well, you're doing a great job. I'll send someone now to relieve you.'

PC West put away her phone, then turned and faced the building. She pulled on a pair of latex gloves then took out the keys to the temporary lock and bolt that had been put on the front door, then took out her torch and Casco baton. She had her pepper spray too, just in case. She undid the lock and went in, staring into the darkness. She found a light switch along the long hallway, but as she expected, nothing happened when she flicked it. It was almost pitch black inside the building and all she could smell was the odour of smoked cannabis, heated heroin and human sweat. There was damp too and general squalor. How can anyone live like this, or choose to? But they didn't choose to, the addiction did, and once it had eaten everything, all the money, the family ties, then this was where they found themselves.

She ran her hand over the wall, feeling the coolness of it, trying to find her way. She shone her light ahead, watching the golden ball of light climbing the stained walls as she crept along. She stopped dead as she heard a noise like a door being shut.

'Hello?' she shouted, her heart thumping in her chest. 'Anyone there? This is the police! You shouldn't be in here. This is a crime scene.'

She looked up. There was a creak of a floorboard, then footsteps somewhere above. She swung the light, trying to find the staircase and turned the way she had come. Then she froze, feeling something had reached out and brushed her hair.

'Who's there? Don't do that again!'

She lifted the light, shining it around. Then she breathed out, half laughing as she saw a fake severed arm hanging from the bare light fitting above her. Maybe left over from Halloween, she thought and went on, heading for the stairs. There was hardly any carpet, and each step creaked as she went up, shining her torch as she climbed.

'I'm warning you,' she said. 'This is the police. You're trespassing on a crime scene!'

She shone her torch into the first room. It was bare, with old flowery wallpaper peeling from the walls. Half the carpet was missing and grey mattresses and sleeping bags were shoved in the corners. She swept her torchlight over the room, into each corner, her heart rate rising again, but saw nothing out of place.

Her head spun round towards the wall, the sound of movement coming from the next room. Now her blood was up, pumping round her heart at full speed as she hurried out of the room and onto the dark landing. Her eyes had adjusted a little and she could see the dark grey shapes of the walls and the broken banisters. She found the door to the next room and stopped, her heart beating madly, instinct telling her to go back downstairs and call for reinforcements. She shook her head, took out her Casco baton and flicked it out to full length.

'*Right, if anyone's in there*!' she shouted. '*You're going to be in trouble! Come out now!*'

The door was ajar, just a little, enough for her to slip through. But the windows had been covered, and so the room was inky black. She shone the torch around, picking out the corners, the thud of her heart in her ears as she slowly moved the light around. She stopped the torchlight, having caught something. She moved it back slowly to whatever it was.

A shape. A man crouched down by a mattress, wearing a hooded top like the man who had dumped the dog at her feet.

'You!' she said, trying to sound commanding. 'What do you think you're doing?'

The man slowly, inch by inch, stood up. He remained facing the wall.

'Turn around,' she said. 'Let's get a look at you.'

But he didn't move.

'Hey! You heard what I said!'

Then he lurched sideways, vanishing from

her torchlight, the sound of his shoes hitting the floorboards. She swung the light in panic, her heart thumping again. Nothing. She swung the light around, her eyes jumping round the room, fearful of the dark corners. Footsteps, moving, fast.

She swung round and saw him move, dodging the light.

Then nothing, no movement, and hardly any sound but her heavy breaths, her heart thumping in her ears.

Where was he?

'I'm the police,' she said, her voice shaky.

Then she heard something, swung the light, and saw him, racing at her, holding something high in his hand. She swung the baton, but the object hit her on the head. A fist hit her stomach, blasting the air from her lungs, knocking her to her knees. The torchlight rolled across the floor, lighting up the doorway as the hooded man ran out, his shadow cast upwards and across the ceiling.

She pulled herself up and followed, hurrying, her Casco still gripped in her hand, listening to his racing footsteps fading away.

When she reached the front door, it was swinging open, so she ran out to the front of the house. There was no one, not even the sound of someone running away, just the noise of angry, complaining seagulls attacking and ripping apart another bin bag of rubbish.

An incident response car turned into the road, then pulled up in front of the house.

Inspector Harris got out, followed by another PC she recognised from Crownhill.

'What's happened?' the Inspector asked, staring above her eyes.

'Someone broke in,' she said, her heart still racing, slowing bit by bit. 'Did you see anyone running off?'

'No one. You'd better get that looked at.' The Inspector pointed to her left eye.

She touched it, winced and looked at her gloved fingers that were now coated with blood.

'By rights, I should be tucked up under my duvet by now,' Sergeant Pinder said, as he climbed out of the incident response car and headed across the road towards the Bank pub, near the Theatre Royal. PC Ray Thomas was with him as they headed round the back of the theatre. Between the theatre and the pub, there was a group of large bins. Seagulls flew off as they approached. There was a couple nearby, quite young, sitting on a wall.

Thomas pointed to the couple, so Pinder nodded and went over towards the pile of bin bags. The sun was coming up, the black sky now turned a dark mauve colour. The wind was sharp, chilled, and bringing spots of rain.

The first thing he noticed was the shoe, an old battered brown brogue, lying close to the bin bags. Then there was the sock-covered foot, one of the white toes poking out of a hole in it. Pinder moved some of the bin bags after putting on a pair of blue surgical gloves. He looked over the body, then into the hard, pale face of the dead man. He was sure by this point that he wasn't just sleeping things off. His skin was milk white, his veins deeply blue under his flesh. He was cold to the touch, cold as metal left to freeze. No pulse in his neck. He only wore what was once a yellow T-shirt that was now covered in unidentifiable stains. Pinder caught sight of his arms, both covered with needle scars. Intravenous drug user, he said to himself and stood up. He noticed something poking out of the man's jeans pocket and carefully removed it, and realised it was a dog leash. No dog.

Where was the dog?

'They found him here about half an hour ago,' PC Thomas said, pointing a thumb to the young couple.

'Drug user,' Pinder said. 'Probably an overdose. Getting more and more frequent, this. Better call it in.'

'I heard West ended up in ER this morning.'

Pinder turned to face him. 'Karen West?'

'Yeah. Didn't you two...?'

'What happened to her?'

'Some druggy assaulted her then did a runner...'

'Is she OK?'

'Cut to her head, but all right, I think. Getting fucking dangerous, this job. Far too bleeding dangerous if you ask me! When you get called out, you never know what you're going to face.'

Pinder sighed. 'You can say that again. Well, better call this in.'

Thomas nodded, looking grimly at the body, then grabbed his radio and started talking into it. Pinder carefully looked for any other signs of foul play, then for ID, but didn't find anything apart from some coins in the man's pocket that didn't add up to much. As he moved him, he spotted a used syringe on the ground, a little blood swimming about inside.

'They're on their way.' Thomas came over, saw the needle and let out a breath. 'Why do they fill themselves full of that shit?'

Pinder stood up. 'Beats me. Where's West now?'

'Gone home. Why?'

'Thought I might pop round and see her.'

'I'm sure she'll appreciate that.'

Pinder waited for the whole circus to arrive before he left the scene and drove over to Plympton where he knew PC West shared a house with another couple of uniforms. She lived in one of those strange houses, built on a hill, where the stairs go down to the living area and kitchen. He parked, then walked up the drive to the house that was painted mostly white with a little bright red thrown in around the edges. He knocked, guessing that West would not be asleep, not after the night she'd had.

She answered the door dressed in grey jogging bottoms, a white vest top, and wrapped up in a red dressing gown. Her hair was tied up and he grimaced when he saw the large plaster over her left eye.

'That looks rough,' he said as she opened the door to let him in.

'My eye or my face?' she said, sounding tired, and a bit grisly.

He went down the stairs that started halfway down the hallway and went down to a large kitchen. 'Your face's still gorgeous.'

'Don't let your missus hear you say that.' Karen overtook him and sat at the kitchen table opposite a mug of coffee. 'Want one?'

He shook his head and sat down. 'So some junkie did that to you?'

'Yeah, I was guarding a house in Devonport. Young woman died inside. Looks like an overdose. Her two friends were let go. Well, a few hours later one of them turns up carrying his dead dog in his arms. Wants to get inside the house...'

'What?'

'Exactly. Wants something to bury the dog with. Told me it jumped off the roof of the car park...'

'The dog killed itself?' Pinder said, half laughing, hardly believing what he was hearing.

'I know. I tell him to get lost and he dumps the dead dog right in front of me and leaves. Then I have to go in the house and make sure it's secure, the Inspector's orders. I should've been relieved two hours before!'

'Bloody cuts.'

'Tell me about it. Anyway, I hear a noise upstairs. I investigate and he attacks me with a club or something. Then he disappears.'

Pinder made a noise in his throat, thinking as he sat back.

'What?' West picked up her coffee and took a sip.

'It's just that we found a dead drug addict in town. Looks like an overdose. Found a dog lead in his pocket.'

West sat up. 'Shit, I bet that's him.'

'Maybe. What time did this all happen?'

'About one, two in the morning.'

Pinder let out a laugh. 'Couldn't have been him, then. Doctor reckons he'd been dead for over nine hours. That doesn't add up.'

'Was he wearing a hoodie?'

'No, just a yellow, stained T-shirt.'

West frowned. 'The junkie with the dog was wearing a yellow, stained T-shirt when we talked to him after we found his friend.'

'Stained jeans? Brown shoes?'

'Yeah. Come to think of it though, the guy

this morning didn't have a stained, yellow T-shirt on. I don't think. It was a dark Jumper or shirt. Yeah, think it had collars. But he was wearing the same stinking hoodie. What the bloody hell's going on?'

'I don't know. What was he after?'

'Don't know. But I found him looking at one of the sleeping bags. Drugs maybe?'

Pinder got up. 'Maybe. I think I should take a look. Because what if this person that thumped you, killed the junkie and his dog, took his hoodie, and then turned up at the house?'

CHAPTER 13

Moone was hardly aware of Butler getting out of her car across the police station car park as he slammed his car door and stormed towards the building. He was doubly pissed off for not having a chance to grab his usual Americano and for having spent a sleepless night in a hotel.

'What's going on?' Butler called out. 'I've never seen you move so fast.'

He carried on, heading into the building, his fists clenched at his sides, not knowing what he would say, what he would do.

'Oi!' Butler grabbed hold of his arm, then swung him round. 'What's happened?'

'What's happened?! My bleeding caravan, my home, was burnt down last night! I came home to find it burning away!'

'Jesus. Do they know what happened?'

'No, but I know! Just as I was standing there, out of nowhere, fucking Faith bleeding Carthew turns up, walks right up to me and tells me it was lucky I wasn't in there! You should've seen the look in her eyes.'

He shook his head, then turned round, ready to storm in and give Carthew what for.

Then his arm was up, twisted the wrong way, and he was turned round, being marched into a nearby room.

'Ow!' he shouted and spun round to see Butler shutting the door behind her. She straightened up and folded her arms across her chest as she said, 'Where's your proof?'

'I know she...'

'You might know she did it, but you need proof. Remember evidence?'

Moone shook his head, the raw anger subsiding, knowing she was right. 'The evidence went up in smoke last night, along with my clothes and everything else.'

'What did the fire crew say?'

'Nothing much yet. Their chief said he'd come by today to tell me what they find.'

Butler nodded, then stepped up to him. 'You can't say anything to her.'

'What?'

'If she did this, if that was some kind of warning or something, then you can't let her see you're freaked out.'

'How the bloody hell am I meant...'

Butler grabbed his shoulders. 'Put on an Oscar-winning performance. As far as you know it was an accident, you left the stove on or something...'

'She's a psycho. We're working with a nut job.'

'I know. But as far as we know she's not killed anyone...'

'She nearly killed Samson!'

'Yeah, nearly. We can't show our hand. We've got to bluff this out.'

'Do you play poker?'

She laughed and let go of him. 'No. But I know this is what she wants. We're at war, Pete. She's declared war. But you can't have a war if one side refuses to fight. The real art of war, is confusing your enemy. This way, we'll wind her up. You with me?'

Moone rubbed his tired eyes, then looked up at her, realising that she was right. 'All right. But I need a bloody coffee.'

'And a change of clothes by the look. I'll send out a uniform to get you a suit and shirt and an Americano. What hotel you staying at?'

'Duke of Cornwall.'

'That's a lovely hotel. What're you complaining about?'

Moone puffed out the air from his cheeks, then stared towards the incident room, imagining Carthew already there, working away, not a care in the world, waiting for him to come in all flustered. He smiled a little.

'Good idea, Mandy. Send out for that suit, and a tie and shirt. Coffee too. I want to go in there all fresh and smelling of roses.'

'Not smelling of smoke and sweat would be a good start.'

He smirked at her, stuck up two fingers then headed to the toilets to freshen up.

An hour later, Moone strolled into the incident room smiling, decked out in his new apparel, sipping his takeaway Americano. Out of the corner of his eye, he could make out DS Carthew at a desk working away.

'Right, team,' he said, rubbing his hands together. 'Gather round. Got some new stuff to go over.'

Everyone assigned to his team started to wheel their chairs over to the whiteboard, gathering around as Moone took out a few more photographs he'd collected from the crime scene manager.

He looked over at DS Carthew, putting a smile on his face, an action that almost burned his jaw off. 'DS Carthew, you going to join us?'

She looked up at him, staring into his eyes for a moment before putting down her pen and getting up. Her expression was blank for a moment before she put on a smile.

'Certainly, sir,' she said and stood facing the whiteboard.

Moone looked over his team, made up of the usual suspects and a few civvies. The door of the incident room squeaked open and Moone turned to see Sergeant Kevin Pinder enter with a female uniform behind him.

'Right, everyone,' Moone said. 'I was about to send you to sleep with my boring cockney accent, but now Sergeant Pinder's here.'

'Sir,' Pinder began, looking round at the faces of the team. 'Can I have a word?'

'Sure.' Moone headed towards the door. 'Butler, brief them on what's on the board, please.'

In the corridor, Moone faced the two uniforms, with Pinder standing slightly in front of the female uniform. 'What is it?'

'This is PC Karen West,' Pinder said, turning to gesture to his colleague.

'Nice to meet you, West,' Moone said. 'I take it you've got something for me?'

West nodded. 'Well, I was standing guard outside a house last night. Place is a doss house for drug addicts in Devonport. We got a call out because a girl had overdosed. The paramedics did their best but it was no good. Anyway, there was a couple of other junkies with her. They took their details and let them go. No signs of foul play, so no cause to arrest them or anything. One of them was this junkie, wearing a hoodie. Had a dog with him. A staffy. Anyway, while I'm guarding the house later on, he comes back, or at least I thought it was him...'

'But it wasn't?' Moone asked.

She shook her head. 'Can't have been. The junkie with the dog was found dead this morning in town, near some bins round the back of the theatre. Been dead for nine hours. The guy who came back couldn't have been the junkie we let go, but he was wearing his hoody, and he was carrying the dog.'

'Carrying the dog?'

'The dog was dead,' Pinder said. 'He said it committed suicide.'

'Dogs don't commit suicide,' West said. 'He dumps the dead dog at my feet and goes off. But when I'm searching the house, someone breaks in. It's him again, but he hits me with something and makes his escape. I'm sure he was after something in that house.'

Moone nodded. 'So what you thinking? He murdered the real junkie with the dog, and pretended to be him to get into the house?'

Pinder shrugged. 'At the moment, looks like he died of an overdose, same as the woman in the house.'

Moone leaned against the wall, staring at them, wondering. 'So, what's this got to do with my case? You think there's a connection?'

Pinder stepped closer. 'Well, I wouldn't, but we managed to ID the young woman as Lily Carver.'

'Who's she?' Moone asked.

'Daughter of a local millionaire businessman. Used to own a chain of pubs and a couple of clubs back in the day, along with some flats he rents out. She went missing a year or so ago. History of drugs, petty theft.'

'OK, this is starting to fit in,' Moone said. 'Good. I mean, not good. We need to find this other junkie who was in the house...'

'We've got people looking for him,' Pinder said. 'We were about to break the news to Lily Carver's parents...'

'OK, I think me and Butler better tag along. Give us a couple of minutes. Go and have a coffee or something.'

Pinder nodded and they turned and walked off in the direction of the canteen.

Moone watched them, thinking, then turned back towards the incident room to find Butler finishing telling the team about the message scratched inside the shed where Edward Beckett hanged himself.

'So,' she said, folding her arms across her chest. 'You know your duties, so get on with them. We'll meet again this afternoon.'

Moone saw DS Carthew still resting against a desk, arms folded, so he went over. 'Carthew. I want you and Harding to go over to Marjons. Acton, Sarah MacPherson's best friend, mentioned some incident at Marjons that seemed to bother her. Dig around and find out if there's anything to it.'

Harding nodded, then took a regretful look at Carthew. But Carthew stepped towards Moone as she said, 'Nice suit, boss. Suits you, pardon the pun. Hope you've got somewhere to stay. I've got a spare room.'

'Thanks, but I'm in a hotel. Right, come on, Butler, let's get going.'

'...the Chinese authorities have now cut off the city of Wuhan, which has a population of eleven million people,' the reporter said on BBC Radio Devon. 'They hope to stop the spread of Coronavirus to other parts of the country...'

Butler turned off the radio as Moone parked up, the windscreen wipers squeaking as they tried to clear the torrent of rain hitting the glass. 'Jesus. Sounds bad over there.'

'They always panic like that over new versions of the flu,' Moone said. 'Probably won't get over here.'

'Famous last words.'

Moone huffed, watching the incident response car that was parked in front of them. Satnav had directed them to Plymbridge Road, Glenholt, where there was a stretch of land surrounded by greenery and woodland. They were parked outside a house that looked like something from the Grand Design show. It was mainly glass and steel, lying like a string of metal boxes over the hillside, part of it held up by struts.

'Sold for just over one million,' Butler said, looking down at her smartphone. 'Some people have got more money than sense.'

The two uniforms made a run for the door,

and got under the thick stone awning that jutted out of the wall of glass that made up the entrance. The door was opened, but Moone could hardly make out who opened the door and then let them in.

'How long do we give it?' Butler asked.

'Ten minutes?' Moone turned to her. 'What're we going to do about her?'

'Carthew?'

'Who else? Give it a year or so and she could be our boss!'

'Not on my watch.' Butler huffed and shook her head.

'Then what do we do?'

'We wait for the right moment.'

Moone gave a humourless laugh. 'And when the fuck Is that?'

'We can't rush this. She thinks she's got the upper hand...'

'She has!'

'No, we have. She's not going to fuck with us. We let her think we're beaten, let her relax and that's when we strike...'

'How?'

'I'll think of something, don't you worry.'

'You keep thinking, Butler. That's what you're good at.'

'Is that a film quote or something?' She stared at him.

'Butch Cassidy and the Sundance Kid. Best film ever.'

'You're sad, Moone. Let's go and talk to these poor people.'

Butler got out, pulling up the hood on the raincoat she was wearing as she braved the downpour, leaving Moone to follow. He caught up with her as she reached the frosted glass double doors, sheltered under the giant awning. Butler pressed the buzzer, and the door was opened by PC West who let them into a wide open, wood and glass foyer. Moone looked up at the glass ceiling, where the rain hammered down. There was a steel staircase to their right, leading up into the rest of the house, but West took them down to the left, where another set of steps led them to a large living area, also surrounded by glass. A large man, with thinning grey hair and a hard-looking face was sitting on the brown leather sofa, staring into space. Sergeant Pinder was standing near him, talking, answering the man's questions.

'They're the detectives I mentioned,' Pinder said, gesturing towards them as they entered the room.

The man, Mr Carver, turned to take them in, but didn't seem to take much notice as he said, 'I knew it was bleeding coming.'

Moone heard his London accent and stepped closer. 'I'm sorry for your loss. Is there a Mrs Carver?'

The man pulled himself up with a groan. 'Lynda died a year ago, give or take,' he said, then looked at Moone and pointed a finger at him. 'You from London? Whereabouts?'

'Enfield. Born and bred.'

'Bethnal Green. We had sod all when we were kids. Shared a bed. One of you pissed in it you all had to sleep in it.'

Moone smiled. 'I'm DCI Peter Moone. This is DI Mandy Butler...'

'Overdose?' Carver asked.

'That's what it looks like.'

The man walked over to the wall of windows that were covered in streaks of rainwater and stood there, staring out. 'Got about three million quid under my belt and no one to leave it to.' Carver turned to look at Moone. 'She has an older brother. Nathan. She was already a wild child, out all night, taking God knows what. So she thought she would get Nathan in on the act. Thing is, Nate wasn't like her, his mind wasn't like hers. He couldn't take it. You know what he did?'

Moone shook his head.

Carver stared at him, a little wetness filling his eyes. 'He found a bridge, no, that's wrong. It's a viaduct in Cornwall. Takes himself up there. All on his own...'

Carver looked away, staring out into the rain again. Moone waited, feeling more was coming, his mind curious about the suicide of his son.

'Breast cancer,' Carver said. 'Spread quickly.

Nothing they could do.'

'I'm sorry.'

'I suppose, maybe she did it to even the score. Do you think?'

Moone saw Carver looking at him, his eyes digging into him for answers. 'I couldn't say. But we have to ask certain questions...'

'What?' Carver came over. 'Get on with it.'

'Can you think of anyone who would want to harm your daughter?'

'Ruling out foul play? No, I can't. Not unless you mean me? I suppose I had reason, but how could I do something like that to my own flesh and blood?'

'Happens all the time, I'm afraid,' Butler said.

Carver turned to her. 'I would never. But I know how you lot think. I've known a lot of villains and a lot of coppers. You got any evidence it wasn't an accident?'

'No,' Moone said. 'We've just got to make sure, dot all the I's. We'll be in touch if we need any more information. Again, I'm sorry for your loss.'

Carver nodded, so Moone turned and headed out, allowing Butler to go before him. As he reached the centre of the wide foyer area, Pinder caught up with him.

'What did you make of that?' Pinder asked. 'About the son's suicide?'

Moone stopped. 'I wonder if it's the same

viaduct. Because if it is the same viaduct...'

'Could be a coincidence,' Butler said. 'Tall building to jump off. Everyone that jumps off the Tamar Bridge, are they all connected? No. Come on, let's leave him in peace.'

Pinder nodded to them both as his radio started to beep and then squawk at him. Moone followed Butler out into the wild wind and rain where they made a mad dash for the car. They slammed the doors as they got in, huffing, wiping the raindrops off their coats.

'You think it's all linked, don't you?' Butler said. 'Doesn't matter what I say, does it?'

'Just a bit funny, isn't it? Daughter of yet another businessman dies mysteriously? There's something fishy going on here. Can't you feel it?'

'All I can feel is the water in my shoes and my damp coat clinging to me. I need a bloody coffee.'

'Hang on,' Moone said, taking his hand off the key.

Sergeant Pinder was rushing towards them through the rain, so Moone lowered his window. 'What is it?'

'They've located Henry Crown, the other junkie staying in a house in North Prospect.'

Moone started the engine. 'Good. Get him to Charles Cross.'

CHAPTER 14

DC Harding followed DS Carthew into the wide open space of what used to be the Porters Lodge of Marjons, the College of St Marks and St Johns. Now it was all high ceilings and glass patched onto the old brick buildings of the old college. A lot of money had been poured into the place over the last few years, but the skeleton of the educational creature was much the same, Harding decided.

There were a couple of receptionists at a large crescent desk, both young women.

Carthew showed her ID, 'We need to talk to someone about a student who used to study here about five years ago.'

One of the receptionists, who had long dark hair, stared towards the other, lighter-haired young woman. 'Tish, who should they talk to?'

'Five years ago?' the blonde one asked, frowning. 'Depends on what you need to know.'

'There was some kind of incident,' Carthew said. 'Possibly involved a young woman called

Sarah MacPherson.'

'You know who you should talk to,' the darker-haired one said. 'Paul Banner. He was the student union president about then. He knows everything about everyone. If there was an incident, he'd know all about it.'

'Where is he?' Carthew asked.

'He'll be in his office or around campus somewhere.' The blonde took out a smartphone and waved it, smiling. 'I'll text him.'

'I didn't know you had his number,' the dark-haired one said.

The blonde shrugged and carried on texting him.

As they waited in the main corridor that cut through most of the main buildings of the university, Harding scrambled around for something to say, watching Carthew typing something on her phone, a deep look of concentration on her face.

'You've come far,' he said, putting on a friendly smile.

She looked up, staring at him as if he'd passed wind. 'What's that supposed to mean? I've come far? Quickly, you mean? As if I haven't earned it?'

'I didn't say that...'

She put away her phone and moved closer to him. 'I suppose you're one of Peter Moone's little fan club...'

'No...'

'He rides up from London and you all can't wait to kiss his arse.'

'Not at all.'

'Well, let me tell you, his days will be short-lived. They need new blood. I've been told so. He's had his day in the sun.'

Harding was about to ask her what she was getting at, but then a man in about his late twenties, dressed in light blue shorts and a student union T-shirt came jogging up to them. His tanned, chiselled face was stretched into a smile filled with too many white teeth. He brushed shoulder-length blond wavy hair from his face as he said, 'Paul Banner, student union president.'

Carthew showed her ID. 'DS Carthew. This is my colleague. We need to ask you a few questions.'

Banner held up his hands, his smile still shining. 'Not in trouble, am I? Don't take me away, officers!'

Harding almost gave a polite laugh, but saw the way Carthew's face was set in official police business mode and refrained. 'We just need to ask you a few questions.'

Banner nodded, losing his smile a little. 'I've got to get back to my office for a meeting in a little while. Walk with me?'

Carthew gestured for him to start moving, so he did, turning on the spot but keeping his eyes on them as they caught up.

'Where're you from?' Harding asked him.

'Worcester,' Banner said. 'For my sins. Decided to come down here though. More of a social life, I'd heard.'

'What halls were you in?' Carthew asked.

'Halls?' Banner asked, turning down another corridor that took them out into the centre of the university and the cold day. 'Dix Hall. It was party central. All organised by myself, thank you very much.'

'Did you know Sarah MacPherson?'

Banner took them back into the building, then up a short flight of steps. He stopped and faced them, his hands in his pockets. 'Sarah MacPherson. That name's familiar. Have you got a photo? Better with faces than names.'

Harding took out his phone and showed him MacPherson's photo.

Banner studied it, smiling a little. 'Yes, I knew her. She was in Dix, too. Not one of the wild child girls, but I remember her. Something happen?'

'She's dead.' Carthew stepped up to him, quite close, making Banner look strangely at her, a little uncomfortable. 'Do you remember an incident involving her?'

'An incident? What sort of incident?'

'We don't know. Something that might have affected her.'

Banner stepped back a little, raising his shoulders. 'Nothing untoward happened, if that's what you mean. I made sure nothing like that happened in my halls.'

'You can't think of anything at all?' Harding asked.

'The only thing I can think of,' Banner said, looking upwards. 'There was this film that somebody took...'

'What film?' Carthew stepped closer again.

'There's this guy, Dan, he had this girl in his room. He's a bit of a player, and that's putting it mildly. Anyway, he's got this girl in his room and some cruel bastard takes some footage through his window. It ends up online. I mean, the poor girl. You can see, well, everything, including her face...'

'Sarah MacPherson?' Harding asked.

'No. I think her name was Cassie something. Like I said, I'm bad with names.'

'What happened to her?' Carthew asked.

Banner shrugged. 'Don't know. I know she left uni. Couldn't face the limelight, and I can't say I blame her. Whoever put that online, well...'

'Did Sarah MacPherson have anything to do with this Dan person?' Carthew asked.

'Don't know. You can ask him though.'

'Can we?' Carthew asked.

'Yes, he works at a little hotel I bought cheap a couple of years ago. The Sussex Hotel. He basically runs it for me.'

'OK. Thanks we'll talk to him.'

'Prepare yourself,' Butler said as she had one hand on the door to the interview room.

Moone was confused for a second as she went in, then realised what she had been getting at the moment the scent of the tall, bony man reached out and grasped his nostrils. That was one of the joys of dealing with smackheads, he recalled, the lack of personal hygiene. The man had shoulder-length scraggly greasy hair and a wispy red beard that barely covered his white, taut face. There was not an ounce of fat on him, Moone noted as he sat down, looking over his unwashed jeans and jumper.

'Henry,' Moone said, trying to rise above the stench. 'I'm DCI Peter Moone.'

'What do I get for this, bey?' Henry said, chewing his bottom lip.

'I'm sorry?' Moone said, noticing Henry had a distinct lack of teeth, and the few he did have were a strange dark colour.

'You might get something if you're lucky,' Butler said, sitting forward. 'If you tell us the truth, Henry.'

'Don't no one call me Henry.'

'No?' Moone asked. 'What do they call you?'

'No one don't call me nothing.' He sniffed, grinding his few teeth. 'Just you, scumbag fucka. All that shit.'

Moone sat back, folded his arms. 'You were removed from a house in Devonport last night...'

'Was I, mate?' Henry scratched at his wiry beard, then his hair. 'News to me.'

'A young woman died. Lily Carver. That name mean anything to you?'

'Lily? No, don't know nobody by that name. How she die?'

'Overdose.'

Henry rolled his eyes up to the ceiling. 'No drug user dies of that if they know what they's doing. Infection, that sepsis thing or something, maybe. Not overdosing.'

'It happens,' Butler said.

Henry nodded. 'Not saying it don't. Unlikely though, ain't it, luv? Na, she weren't no professional. Just on vacation maybe?'

'How many of you were in the house that night?' Moone asked.

The junkie raised his eyebrows, gave a gravelly laugh. 'You says I was in some house, I got to take your word for it. Where was this house?'

'Devonport.'

'Fuck me. Ain't they all? Sorry, can't help ya, mate.'

Moone leaned forward. 'You must remember being there. It was you, the woman, and a guy with a dog...'

There was a flicker of something across the druggy's face. 'A dog. A staffy. Lovely thing. Loved me, it did. Dogs always love me. Couldn't give a shit about people, but dogs, fucking lovely things...'

'The dog's dead,' Butler said, blank, expressionless. 'Sorry.'

The junkie shook his head, looking genuinely upset as he spat out his words. 'Dead? Fuck! That's fucking awful. Did someone do something to it? Fucking scumbags...'

'Someone chucked it off a roof,' Moone said. 'So, you do remember that night?'

Henry shrugged. 'Sort of. I remember the filth all over the place, pulling and pushing me round. Remember the dog, poor fucking thing. Who did for the dog?'

'We don't know. But we're trying to track them down. There was three of you there...'

'Four.' Henry scratched his head.

'Four. Including the dog...'

'No, five if you include the dog...'

'Five? Who was the other person?'

The junkie shrugged. 'Don't know. I didn't know who I was either right about then.'

'What did they look like?' Butler asked.

'I don't fucking know. All I knows is there was four people in that house. He wasn't partaking though...'

'He?' Moone leaned in again, flinching at the stench, the waft of bad breath. 'It was a man? You're sure?'

'Yeah, I'm sure. Sort of.'

'But you can't describe him?'

Henry sat back. 'I could, but you gots to

remember that my mind ain't running at full speed when I'm on that stuff.'

Moone nodded, then exchanged disappointed looks with Butler as he sat back.

'That it?' Henry asked, looking between them. 'You ain't gonna ask me what he sounded like?'

'What did he sound like?' Moone asked.

'Tried to sound like a local, but the accent wasn't right. He was putting it on, and I think I told him. He didn't say nothing, well not much after that.'

'You didn't catch a name?' Butler asked, standing up with a huff.

'Na, no name. But like I said, he weren't no local bey.'

'Bey?' Moone repeated.

'Boy,' Butler said. 'Come on, Moone. We're not going to get anything more from this one.'

Moone followed her out, then shut the door after them, thinking all the time, imagining a fourth person in the house.

'You don't give any credence to what he just said, do you?' Butler was staring at him.

He shrugged. 'I don't know. I really don't know what to believe at the moment.'

'He's a heroin addict. Anyway, the uniforms found a dead woman and two men in that house. Not three…'

'He could've helped her with the overdose then slipped out.'

Butler huffed. 'The accent thing? Not a local. What a load of crap.'

Moone sighed, having to admit to himself that the word of a drug addict didn't count for much, even though he had his suspicions that maybe there was some truth in his account. Then his mind rewound to the other dead drug addict found behind the Theatre Royal. The autopsy would have been carried out by now or would be close to it. He looked at Butler. 'Let's go and talk to Dr Parry. He might be able to tell us something about the dead drug addict and maybe something about Carver's dead son.'

'Good idea, let's go,' Butler said.

As they climbed out of their car, the clouds parted a little, allowing the sun to shine on the Hoe and the few people walking along it, most walking dogs or with kids. Harding saw the lighthouse and glow of sunlight that it was bathed in, then followed Carthew down the narrow street that was lined with hotels and bed and breakfast places. The Sussex hotel was the penultimate building, a slender place, with a red and white awning, the name of the hotel printed in large gold letters.

The sound of vacuuming came from inside and as they stepped into the hallway, they could see an archway to their right that led into a dining area. A middle-aged, quite large woman was vacuuming and singing to herself.

Carthew walked up to her, showing her ID, causing the woman to start, then turn off the vacuum.

'Oh, dear,' the woman said. 'You gave me a fright, my luvver.'

'Sorry, I'm sure. Is there a Daniel Pritchard round here?'

The woman groaned as she stretched. 'That's the manager. General dogsbody, if you ask me, poor luv. Hang on.'

The woman scurried off deeper into the hotel, calling out to Pritchard. Eventually a young man appeared dressed in a grey, expensive looking shirt, and dark trousers. He had short dark hair, tanned skin. He had his hands in his pockets as he had whispered words with the cleaner, his eyes jumping suspiciously towards Carthew and Harding. Soon he came over, hands still in his pockets, a look of boredom on his face.

'I hear you're the police,' he said, looking them over casually.

Carthew showed her ID. 'That's right. DS Faith Carthew. We need to ask you some questions. Why don't we sit in the dining area?'

Pritchard nodded, then gestured back towards the dining room. 'What's this about?'

Carthew sat down at a table, while Harding decided to remain standing, watching the young man as he sat down, leaning back in his chair.

'Sarah MacPherson,' Carthew said.

'Who?' Pritchard asked.

'She was at uni with you. Marjons.'

His brow crumpled as he sat up. 'Right. Has she said something? I mean, I don't remember...'

'She's dead.'

'Dead? But what's that, I mean, that's awful, but I don't know...'

'There was a video of you going round the internet for a while.'

Pritchard folded his arms. 'Yeah, but it was taken down. I don't get what this...'

'Did you have a relationship with Sarah MacPherson?'

'At uni? I didn't really have any relationships at uni, if you know what I mean? I met a lot of girls...'

'I see. I'm wondering if it's possible that Sarah MacPherson took the video of you as a kind of revenge porn thing...'

He shrugged. 'I don't know. It's possible. Like I said, I don't remember her...'

Carthew took out her phone and brought up the photo of Sarah MacPherson. Pritchard leaned in, staring at the photo before he started nodding his head. 'Yeah, I remember her. She got all serious with me, went a bit off the rails when I said I wasn't interested in anything serious. Jesus. She's dead? You don't think...'

Carthew huffed out a laugh. 'No, this hasn't anything to do with that. But she was upset about an incident at uni. We're wondering if this was it. Can you think of anything else?'

He shook his head. 'No, like I said, it's all in the distant past. Water off a duck's back. Maybe she did take the video, I don't know. Anyway, I should get back to work...'

'This what you studied for at uni?' Carthew asked, looking round the place.

Pritchard stood up. 'No. Not at all. I was going to set up my own gym, had plans to buy a leisure centre. But it all fell through. Me and my missus invested some money with a local businessman, but he ran off with most of the money...'

'Stannard?' Harding asked, flickering out of his dream.

'Yeah, that bastard. Still haven't got the money back, and probably won't. Here I am, stuck managing this... shit hole.'

'What's the deal you had with him?' Harding asked.

Pritchard looked up at him as he said, 'Have you seen how they've been redeveloping North Prospect Road?'

'Yeah.'

'Well, he said he was looking for investors to buy up some of the property with him. His plan was to build some kind of health centre and gym for the locals. Course, I saw it as the perfect opportunity, but then he goes and runs off with the cash.'

Harding turned to Carthew and saw her raise her eyebrows at him as she said, 'Where exactly were the houses he wanted to buy up?'

Dr Lee Parry took them into the autopsy room and started washing his hands, his gaunt, stubble-covered face turned towards Moone and Butler.

'You have to know how to wash your hands properly,' he said, soaping his hands and massaging his fingers and palms under the water.

'I think I do,' Butler said. 'Been doing it for most of my life.'

Parry gave a laugh. 'There's a virus in China and it'll be here eventually. Got a friend who's been looking into it, specialist in infectious diseases. It looks bad.'

'I'll take my chances,' Butler said. 'We're here about Lily Carver and the unidentified drug addict found behind the Theatre Royal.'

'Don Layton,' Parry said, nodding. 'They identified him. It's quite unusual to have a drug addict, especially a heroin addict die of an overdose. Of course, it happens, but they usually know what they're doing...'

'Do you think someone could've doctored what they were given?' Moone asked.

'I'm waiting for lab results. But my experience is, we will find too much heroin in their system. It can make the user pass out, and even stop breathing. If they don't die, then brain damage can be the result.'

Moone ran his hand over his beard. 'So someone could've said, "here, have all this heroin", and next thing…'

'If he was out of it enough or didn't really care.'

Moone nodded, let out the air from his lungs.

Butler stepped closer to Parry as she asked, 'Heard of Nathan Carver?'

Parry frowned. 'Might have. You'll have to be more specific.'

'Committed suicide by jumping off Bickleigh viaduct nearly three years ago,' Butler said.

Parry nodded. 'Yes, that's right. It was a couple of days before he was found. Drugs in his system. Put down as suicide.'

'What did you think?' Moone asked, staring at him.

'I know that look,' Parry said and smiled. 'You want me to say I thought it was suspicious. But I couldn't say either way. No signs of a struggle or ligatures. Yes, drugs in his system, but he was a drug user, if I remember correctly. The coroner ruled suicide, using his past mental health issues as a factor.'

'Jessop leapt from there,' Moone said.

Parry looked up, his smile gone. 'Yes, that's true. That's the only connection, isn't it?'

Moone shrugged. 'I don't know. We've got nothing concrete, but there's something there, I can feel it.'

Parry smiled sympathetically. 'I think you might be clutching at straws. Sorry.'

'Don't be sorry. It's just me making a mountain out of a mole hill.'

Butler shook her head and huffed. 'Right, when you two have stopped coming out with every hackneyed phrase in the book, can we get on?'

Moone laughed. 'OK, let's go.'

He was about to say goodbye to Dr Parry, but his phone started ringing. It was an unrecognised number. He mouthed an apology, then slipped out into the corridor to answer the call.

'DCI Peter Moone,' he said, leaning against the wall.

'Hi, this is Carly Tamms,' a young sounding woman said. 'The journalist?'

'Oh, right. Sorry, I'm a bit busy at the moment...'

'You've been looking into some recent suicides, that's right, isn't it?'

'Listen, I can't really discuss an ongoing...'

'Your boss, Chief Superintendent Laptew, said you should talk to me, didn't he?'

'Yes, that's true.'

'How about we meet for a coffee in a little while.'

Like I said, I'm busy...'

'I have information for you.'

Moone straightened up. 'What information?'

'Meet with me later and I'll tell you. It's about suicide and the cases you've been looking into. Believe me, you'll want to hear this.'

CHAPTER 15

Carthew decided to drive and took them towards the Britannia Pub, then up to the roundabout where Tesco's sat, still closed after a fire, and around to North Prospect Road. They passed the new build developments that had replaced the old houses that had been torn down a few years before.

Carthew parked at the end of a row of older houses now boarded up, ready to be redeveloped. Harding leaned towards her, looking up at the old houses, the shabby, small front gardens, and the rails put alongside the steps to help the elderly occupants.

'Do you mind?' Carthew said, looking at him as if he'd licked her cheek.

'What?'

'You're invading my personal space.' She pushed open the door, then climbed out, and walked towards the houses.

Harding followed with a grumble of annoyance sitting heavy in his stomach. He shrugged it off and stood by Carthew as she took out her notebook.

'Those three,' she said, waving her finger over three particularly decrepit-looking houses. 'Apparently, Stannard put in plans to have them torn down and turned into a leisure centre.'

'Puts in plans, so it looks official. Probably even had drawings.'

'More than likely.' Carthew turned round, staring across the street, looking both ways. 'Where's this guy from Plymouth Homes?'

Harding turned around to face the complex of shops and the library that had been slotted in between the development of new build houses across the road. He saw a young man wearing square glasses, dressed in a grey suit, coming their way, a courier bag over his shoulder.

'Hi,' he said, as he quickly crossed the road, putting his hand out to Harding. 'Tim Morrell. Which one of you...'

Carthew flashed her warrant card. 'DS Carthew, I'm in charge. We need to get into these houses. Have you got the keys?'

Morrell nodded, then opened his bag and took out a bunch of keys. 'Got them here. My boss asked me to ask you what this is about.'

'I'm sure he did,' Carthew said. 'Let's open up this first house.'

'It's a woman,' Morrell said, flipping through the keys. 'My boss, I mean. Sandra King.'

'That's wonderful. Open up, if you'd be so

kind.'

Morrell's face flushed as he pushed his glasses tighter to his face, then hurried up the stone steps to the battered, light-blue front door. 'Don't you need, you know, a warrant or something?'

'No,' Harding said, standing on the other side of Morrell as he searched the keys again. 'It's an unoccupied property. We can do whatever we like.'

'Oh right,' Morrell said, then unlocked the door. 'Here we go.'

Harding went in behind Carthew as the door creaked open and the daylight let them see the shadows and shapes on the walls. The carpets were dusty, as were the walls and the bannisters of the stairs. A pile of junk mail was sitting on the welcome mat. A musty smell greeted them as they walked into the dark grey of the hall.

Harding took out his phone and turned on the torch app, then shone it into the small front room. There was an old flowery armchair in the corner and a seventies-style coffee table, but nothing else. Dust was thick across the carpet and there were faded rectangles on the wall where photos used to hang.

'I'll wait here,' Morrell said from outside the door.

Carthew headed up the stairs, ignoring him, then came down again a couple of minutes later.

'There's nothing here,' Carthew said. 'Let's check the next house.'

The light was slowly fading, the winter sun dipping below the horizon bit by bit as Moone walked from his car and up across wild and muddy land. He could see outcrops of rock formations in the distance where clusters of whiteness still hung about. There would be more snow, the weather was saying. It hardly ever snowed in Plymouth for some reason, but the moors were always covered in the stuff about this time of year. There was no one around for miles, and he soaked it up for a moment, enjoying the isolation, imagining for a moment that he was the only person left on the planet. It soon became an unsettling thought.

Then he saw a shadow move, stretching out towards him as the sun glowed over Bickleigh Viaduct. He reached the bridge, then stepped towards the edge, looking down at the grass and mud below, his stomach flipping a little. He'd never been that great with heights and his brain rebelled against him by sending images of him hanging over the edge, gripping on for dear life.

He walked away and headed towards the silhouetted female figure at the other end, their shadow stretching out towards him.

Carly Tamms seemed to be in her mid-twenties, pretty, with shoulder-length wavy, light brown hair and quite tall. She smiled as she held out a takeaway coffee.

'Americano?' she asked, raising her perfectly shaped dark eyebrows.

He nodded, looking round at the darkening view. 'Thanks. So, you're Carly Tamms?'

'In the flesh,' she said, resting her back against the wall, the wind bustling her hair. 'And you're DCI Peter Moone. Up from London.'

'I live here now.'

'Welcome to Plymouth.'

'Thanks.' He smiled.

'Why here?' she asked, raising one eyebrow and sipping her coffee.

'Haven't you worked it out?' He took the lid off his coffee.

'Well, there has been a scattering of suicides here. Not many. Two over the last three years…'

'Bingo.'

Carly looked round at the view, shielding her eyes from the lowering winter sun. 'Nathan Carver and Martin Jessop. One had issues with drugs, and the other had other issues. What's the link, apart from this place?'

'I'm not saying there is a link. Maybe I'm just a policeman who's worried about an epidemic of suicides involving young members of our city.'

Carly half closed her eyes, staring at him for a moment, before pointing a finger at him. 'No, I've looked you up, DCI Moone and you've worked some pretty high-profile cases in your career in the Met. You even received a medal for bravery, and by the way, I'd love to talk to you...'

He held up a hand. 'I really don't want to talk about that. How about you talking to me about what you've learned?'

She gave him another suspicious smile, then took out her notebook. 'OK. I don't suppose you've had a chance to take a look at suicides overall?'

'No. Is this where you tell me that there's nothing out of the ordinary about any of this...'

'Oh no. Definitely not. I've been looking at the stats. In 2017 there were 17 suicides registered in Plymouth. In 2018, there were 26. In 2019 there were 45! That's nearly doubled in one year!'

Moone walked to her side, looking down at her notes, mulling it all over, thinking that he needed not to give too much away. 'That's certainly a steep curve.'

'Steep? I know things are tough these days, but that many in Plymouth in one year?'

He stepped away, thinking. 'What do you know about Philip Stannard?'

Her face was swamped with curiosity as she said, 'As in the solicitor who ripped everyone off? Only what I've read, and the fact that he was supposed to have legged it to South America or the Caribbean. Why? Do you think these suicides have something to do with what he did? Were a lot of the suicides you've looked into connected with Stannard? Did he rip them off?'

'You ask a lot of questions.'

'I'm a journalist, remember? I've spent the last couple of years looking into suicide, trying to find out why so many people decide to take their own lives. I started looking into social media, and trolls. My thinking was that our society was...'

Moone raised his eyebrows when she suddenly stopped talking. 'What?'

'It's none of those things. I mean, yes, they contribute, but there's something else going on here. Now you're looking into it. What do you think's going on here?'

'Honestly, I can't really talk about it...'

Tamms made an unhappy face, putting her coffee down on the wall. 'Jessop killed himself here. People think it was the charges being brought against him, but what if it was something else? You mentioned Stannard. Everybody seems to think he ran off to the ends of the earth after he ripped all those people off.'

'What do you think?' Moone sipped his coffee.

'Maybe he killed himself, you just haven't found his body yet.'

'Nice idea. But we would've found his body by now.'

'OK, then someone murdered him for whatever reason...'

'Who?'

'I don't know.' Carly sat down, letting out a

harsh breath full of disappointment.

Moone laughed. 'You sound like me. Grasping at straws. Right, listen.'

Carly sat up, staring at him, her eyes ignited.

'I'm trusting you to not go off and print what I say.'

'I won't. I promise.'

'Scout's honour?'

She smiled. 'I wasn't in the scouts.'

'Never mind. I'm wondering if someone forced these people to kill themselves...'

'How?'

'I don't know. They must have something on them. They've learned their dirtiest secrets...'

'But who would want to do that?'

'Someone incredibly sick. They'll look just like you or me, but they're hiding in plain sight. This might've even started as a way to blackmail people, to get money, but I think they realised they liked the power...'

'You sound like you know them.'

Moone let out a tired laugh. 'Yep. That's because I've met a fair few in my time.'

'In the Met? You must have some interesting stories.'

'A few. I'll tell them to you sometime. None of that gets in print. I'll give you an exclusive story when the time is right. Not before. Got it?'

'Of course.'

Moone's phone started ringing in his

pocket, so he took it out and saw that Harding was calling him.

'Moone,' he said. 'What's happening?'

'We're in North Prospect Road,' Harding whispered. 'We're outside some houses that Stannard was going to buy...'

'Why're you there?' Moone asked.

Harding lowered his voice. 'It was DC Carthew's idea.'

Moone sighed. 'Go on.'

'We went into the second house. There's a bad smell... I think you should be here.'

'Right. I'll be there as soon as I can.'

Moone text Butler on his way, telling her to meet him in North Prospect Road. It didn't take him long to find the right houses, as three incident response cars were parked at the end of the road, next to the turning into Ham Drive. Then he spotted the white suits of the forensic team entering the penultimate house.

Carthew came out, dressed in a white forensic outfit as he approached, removing her hood. Her eyes jumped to him and filled with thunder as Moone reached her.

'What the fuck are you doing here?' she asked.

'A little bird told me that you'd found something.'

She looked round and spotted Harding, who quickly looked away, pretending to look at his phone. 'I can guess which little bird. How's life in a hotel?'

He stared into her eyes, noticing the smile on her lips. He smiled back, nodding as he said, 'Not too bad actually. What the hell was I doing in a bloody caravan? No room service in a caravan.'

'Someone did you a favour, then.'

'Someone? Probably an accident. The fire investigator's going to pay me a visit later. So, what have we got?' Moone pointed to the house.

Carthew turned and faced the old building. 'Deceased male, badly decomposed. Shoved under floorboards.'

He stepped towards the house. 'Jesus. Stannard?'

'Hard to tell, but I'm thinking it probably is him. I talked to a guy who runs a hotel down on the Hoe. Said Stannard ripped him off. Was meant to meet him here.'

Moone looked at her. 'You think he killed Stannard? Revenge?'

'He had the motive.'

Moone nodded, 'I suppose he did. Better get him in. Right, I'd better take a look.'

'Knock yourself out.'

Moone headed over to the SOCO van and suited up in one of their forensic outfits, then stepped into the house that was now brightly lit by the spotlights set up in every corner. It only took him a couple of steps before the aroma greeted his nostrils, then travelled to his gut, churning it over and over. The white bodies of the SOCOs came and went, their shoes scraping the dusty carpet. He stepped into the front room, where the carpet had been torn back. The floorboards had been taken up. He covered his mouth, his eyes on the SOCO photographer who was taking snaps of the remains. He held his breath and moved round, trying to get a good view of the decomposed body, half noticing that Dr Parry was kneeling close by the gap in the floorboards. Parry looked up, giving him a big smile that unnerved Moone as the terrible smell tried to invade his senses.

'Is it him?' Moone asked, concentrating on the shape of the man, still wearing a suit.

Parry stood up. 'If you mean Stannard, it's going to be hard to tell. He's badly decomposed. I'd say possibly the right age, but won't be able to tell you much until he's on the table. But I'm guessing it probably is.'

'Any chance you know the cause of death or can guess?'

Parry lost his smile and pointed his purple-gloved finger at the head. 'His skull looks as if it's suffered several blows. Blunt force trauma. I'd guess that was what killed him, but obviously that's just conjecture at this stage.'

Moone looked around at the SOCOs and noticed Butler entering the room, all decked out in a forensic outfit. 'Was there any ID on him?'

'Nothing,' one of the white suits said, but Moone found it hard to tell which one.

'Stannard?' Butler asked, her face poking out of her hood. 'You look like a wally, by the way.'

He stared at her. 'Oh, right, and I suppose you look like Kate Moss. Jesus. We don't know if it's him, but it's got to be, hasn't it?'

'That's marvellous. Now we've got to find his killer.'

'Let's talk outside. The smell's making me want to vomit.'

Butler followed him out into the grey day, the clouds having swooped in, the wind blowing, a light rain having started. They stripped off the forensic outfits and then Moone found himself hankering for a cigarette, anything to take away the smell that was clinging to his nostrils. He felt contaminated.

'If that's Stannard…' Butler said.

'It's got to be,' Moone stared at her and got a sarcastic grimace back.

'OK. So who killed him?'

Moone looked around the street, the rain dotting the grey pavements. 'I don't know. Maybe whoever's going round forcing people to kill themselves...'

'We still haven't proved that. We haven't got anything concrete...'

'No, we haven't. You're right. But now we've got a dead body with its head caved in.'

'What's the next step?'

'Interview Daniel Pritchard,' Carthew said behind them. They both turned to face her, but it was Moone who said, 'He's another of the people Stannard ripped off?'

'That's right,' Carthew said. 'He said he met Stannard here a couple of times. But there's another link to our suicides...'

'What's that?' Butler asked.

Carthew ignored her and kept her eyes on Moone as she said, 'Pritchard was the guy who was filmed in his room when he was in the middle of sex with some other student. He had a fling with Sarah MacPherson, then cast her aside. I think MacPherson was the person who filmed him, or the one who uploaded it. Either way, there's a link. I just don't know what it all means.'

Moone put his face in his hands, enclosing himself in the red darkness he found there, trying to think. He looked up as the rain grew stronger. 'Can't say I do either. Do you know that suicides in this city nearly doubled last year?'

'So?' Butler asked. 'People get depressed. They can't face living...'

'They doubled!'

'What're you thinking, then?' Butler asked, with a huff.

Moone shrugged. 'Maybe this bastard, whoever they are, has been doing this for a while. Maybe they were tied in with Stannard somehow. Probably got ripped off by him, or knew what he was up to. Knocked him off...'

'Then what?' Butler shook her head, an exhausted laugh falling from her lips. 'He starts going round sweet-talking people into killing themselves? It doesn't make sense.'

'None of this makes sense.' Moone turned away from her and saw Carthew was still there, watching him. 'What do you make of it?'

'I think you're onto something,' Carthew said.

'Oh, you would,' Butler groaned, then faced Moone. 'By the way, the forensics on Charlene Bale's car came back.'

'And?' Moone said.

'Clean. Someone had given it a very thorough valeting.'

Moone huffed out a laugh. 'Of course they have. They dropped her off, then removed all the evidence they were ever there.'

'Are we going to interview Daniel Pritchard?' Carthew asked, staring right at Moone.

'You and me?' Moone asked, then looked at Butler to see her reaction. She huffed, then turned away.

'Yes, me and you, the way the Chief Superintendent wanted it.'

'Well, I've got the fire investigation officer coming to see me at the station later,' Moone began.

'Probably just an electrical fire,' Carthew

said, then started walking across the street. 'I'll meet you back at the station.'

Moone watched her cross the street like nothing was wrong and she had no cares in the world. Butler appeared at his side, staring across the road too.

'She's a complete, manipulative psycho, that one,' Butler said, then turned to face him. 'Go on then, you'd better go and interview Pritchard with her.'

'Could be him. He's linked to Stannard and Sarah MacPherson.'

'You'd better run along and find out then.' Butler turned and walked away, then stopped and looked at him. 'You know she'll be the end of you, don't you?'

CHAPTER 16

Dan Pritchard was sitting at the desk in the interview room, a plastic cup of water at his side. He looked round nervously at the door as Moone walked in, followed by DS Carthew. His eyes followed them as they sat down, questions piling up.

'Am I in trouble?' Pritchard asked.

'Not at the moment,' Moone said, getting comfortable, half watching DS Carthew out the corner of his eye, wondering what news the fire investigator would have for him. He kept seeing his caravan engulfed in flames, then Carthew walking calmly up to him, a look of almost glee in her eyes. He couldn't remember if that's how she had actually looked at the time, or if his imagination had invented it for dramatic effect. 'We just want to ask you a few questions.'

'About what you asked me earlier?' Pritchard was staring at Carthew. 'Is this about the video?'

'This is about Philip Stannard,' Carthew

said.

Pritchard looked confused as he sat back, staring at them in turn. 'Stannard? About the money he stole from us?'

'In a way,' Carthew said, leaning forward. 'When was the last time you saw him?'

'I don't know,' Pritchard said and shrugged.

'The man ripped you off,' Moone said. 'He took a lot of your money. I think I'd remember the last time I saw a man who took all I had and left me doing a job I felt was beneath me.'

Pritchard sat up. 'I didn't say it was beneath me.'

'It's in your voice though, your manner. You thought you'd be running your own business, not working for someone else.'

Carthew leaned in. 'That must hurt.'

Pritchard looked at her, the calculations going on behind his eyes. 'Hang on a minute. Why are you asking about him? He did a runner, didn't he?'

Moone sat back. 'We don't think so. In fact, we think he might be dead.'

Pritchard stared at Moone, disbelief on his face. 'You think someone killed him? That's it, isn't it? You think that I did him in?'

'Sarah MacPherson,' Carthew said. 'We think she took that video of you and that girl...'

'Yeah, so what?' Pritchard looked away and shook his head. 'That's in the past. I'd forgotten about it...'

'Liar.' Carthew gave an empty laugh. 'You don't forget something like that. Did you know it was her that put it online?'

Daniel Pritchard glared at her for a moment, his jaw grinding before he leaned towards her. 'Do I need to call someone? I mean, are you going to arrest me or something?'

'No,' Moone said. 'Not right now. But I wouldn't go far. We'll probably need to talk to you again after we go through your phone records and your online history. We'll be checking to see if you did know that Sarah MacPherson put that film online...'

'I didn't, I...'

Moone held up a hand. 'Save it. You can go now. I'll get someone to see you out.'

Carthew shut the door to the interview room after Pritchard was escorted out, then faced Moone with a subtle smile.

'We make a good team,' she said. 'We should be teamed up, not you and that dragon.'

Moone avoided her eyes, thinking everything through, trying to filter out the images of his burning caravan from the investigation. 'Better the dragon you know.'

'You calling me a dragon?' Carthew pointed at herself, her eyebrows raised.

'No, you know what I mean.'

'You know me. You know me very well. You could know me a lot more.'

He saw the smile, the glint in her eye. 'Do you think Pritchard was telling the truth?'

She stared at him for a moment before she said, 'Yes, I think he was. I don't think he's the one forcing these people to kill themselves. As for Stannard...'

'No, I think our suicide guy is the same person who murdered Stannard. Maybe Stannard knew about them all somehow. I don't know.'

'What about your Madam Revello theory?'

Moone laughed, nodding, appreciating how foolish he'd sounded over the last few days. 'Yep, I think I've been jumping to conclusions lately.'

Then there was a knock on the door and Butler stuck her head round.

'Moone, the fire investigator's here to talk to you,' Butler said, her accusatory eyes jumping to Carthew. But the object of her accusations didn't bat an eyelid, just straightened herself and passed by Butler and vanished from the room.

'Get him in here, will you?' Moone said, staying at the desk, his stomach churning over, expecting the investigator to reveal that an accelerant had been used to burn down his home. Butler nodded, then left.

The fire investigator was a stocky chap, with dark grey hair and a craggy face. He knocked on the door, then stepped in. He was wearing an ill-fitting suit.

'James Scott, I'm the fire investigator,' he said and put a bulky evidence bag on the desk.

Inside it, Moone saw his toaster, which was half melted and charred.

Moone pointed to the toaster. 'Did that cause the fire?'

Scott sat down and put a hand on the bag. 'It's surprising how dangerous toasters can be. Especially if they're not cleaned out regularly...'

'Hang on, I didn't buy it that long ago. And I do clean it out.'

'To me it looks like it was clogged up with lots of breadcrumbs. But it wasn't just that...'

Moone leaned in. 'Go on.'

'Looks like there's a fault in it. I've seen this before with toasters. They heat up, but they don't turn off, so they get hotter and hotter, and because of all the breadcrumbs...'

'A fire starts. Tell me, is there any way you could tamper with this toaster to make it look like there was a fault with it?'

The fire investigator sat back, scrutinising Moone. 'Anything's possible. You'd have to know what you were doing. I mean, if you wanted to start a fire with a toaster, then if you could make it faulty and stuff it full of crumbs...'

Moone sat back, nodding, picturing Carthew's face that night. 'So, it's possible.'

'Anything's possible. You think someone did this on purpose? I mean, I was ready to put it down as an accidental fire. Your insurance...'

Moone held up a hand. 'No, I was thinking about another case I'm working. Don't you worry yourself…'

As he stood up, Scott looked relieved. 'Thank fuck for that. Thought you were going to have me doing all kinds of paperwork.'

Moone smiled, then watched the investigator leave with his blackened and melted toaster. He stood up, suddenly remembering where he got the toaster from. The Realm store. He thought of the pompous, careless Mr Darwin and huffed as he walked out and found Butler waiting for him.

She had her eyebrows firmly raised, her arms folded across her chest. 'So?'

Moone blew the air from his cheeks. 'Says the toaster did it. Could've been faulty. Full of breadcrumbs.'

Butler let out a laugh. 'And there you were, thinking Carthew had torched your caravan. You had me worried.'

'If someone had the know-how to make it look like an accident…'

Butler rolled her eyes. 'Oh, come on, Pete. He said it was an accident, didn't he?'

'It was stuffed full of breadcrumbs yet I hadn't had it that long, and I always make sure I clean it out. You should've seen her face on the night…'

'What about this? She turns up that night, sees your caravan's on fire and leaps at the chance to fuck with your head? Does that sound more plausible?'

He stared at her, realising what a paranoid freak he was sounding these days. Maybe she was right, he decided. She had got to him and wormed her way into his brain. 'I've let her get to me, haven't I?'

'Yes, you have. I'm not saying she's an angel, because she's far from it. We've seen that, and we need to keep an eye on her. But setting fire to your caravan?'

Moone nodded. 'OK. Maybe it was just an accidental fire caused by my toaster.'

'Where did you buy it?'

He gave a laugh full of irony. 'The Realm.'

'From that cheeky bastard's shop? Probably fell off the back of a lorry. Come on, let's go...'

'Where're we going?' Moone asked as Butler turned and started striding down the corridor.

'To The Realm to confront that dodgy dealer.'

'We've got an autopsy to go to!'

'No, we haven't. Parry's moved it to this afternoon. Come on, let's not waste any time.'

Butler drove them to The Realm, and he could see from her profile that she was looking forward to confronting her arch-enemy. She parked up in the car park, and they sat there, the wind whistling and the rain hitting the roof of the car.

'Come on,' Butler commanded, then climbed out and rushed towards the shop and in through the automatic doors.

By the time Moone caught up with her, he could see she wasn't heading up the escalators towards his office, but was instead storming towards the back of the store.

Then Moone spotted him, Colin Darwin showing around a couple of suited men, pointing out things around the store. Moone rushed on, catching Butler up as she reached the middle of the camping section, where Darwin and the suited men had stopped.

'Oi, Darwin!' Butler growled as she flashed her ID.

Darwin looked lost for a moment before his eyes fell on her, then her ID. 'Do you mind?' he snapped. 'I'm in the middle of something! I do apologise, gentlemen...'

'We need a word,' Butler said. 'Now!'

Darwin had a thunderstorm in his eyes as he stared at her, then back at the suits he had been showing around. 'I'm sorry, this won't take long. It's about a security issue. Follow me, officers.'

Colin Darwin, fists clenched at his side, took them to the back of the bottom floor where there was a large pair of delivery doors. He turned and faced them, his eyes burning.

'This better be bloody good!' he snapped.

Butler squared up to him. *'My colleague's caravan burnt down! That was his home!'*

Darwin's eyes jumped to Moone, a smirk appearing. 'You live in a caravan?'

'A mobile home,' Moone said, his anger starting to flicker. 'But not any more.'

'He bought one of your toasters,' Butler said. 'It was faulty and caught on fire.'

Darwin moved away from Butler and stood in front of Moone. 'Is this right?'

Moone nodded. 'That's what the fire investigator said.'

Darwin stared at him for a moment. 'You're sure you bought it from me?'

'Yes, quite sure.'

'Got a receipt?'

'No, I haven't...'

Darwin shrugged, then barged past him. 'Then I can't just take your word for it, can I?'

'I used my card,' Moone said.

Darwin stopped and faced him. 'I don't make them. I just buy this stuff. Cheap. Anyway, I'm guessing your insurance will cover it.'

'I hope so.'

Darwin smiled. 'Then what're you worrying about? Sounds like your toaster did you a favour. Living in a caravan? Jesus...'

'You... wanker,' Butler said, squaring up to him again.

'Didn't you get the message last time?' Darwin asked Butler. 'You know, when I had to have a word in your boss' ear. Can't wait to hear what he says this time.' Darwin laughed, then turned and headed back towards his group of suits again.

'Did that go as well as you expected?' Moone asked Butler, as he turned to see her skin was a reddish hue.

'Marvellous.'

'Now he's going to get on the dog and bone to his chum.'

Butler huffed. 'Can if he likes. See if I care. The Chief Super can kiss my arse too.'

'You don't mean that.' Moone started following Butler as she stormed towards the entrance of the shop. 'All we need is another telling off.'

As they got out to the car park, Butler swung round to face him, her hands on her hips. 'What the hell're we doing, Moone?'

'What do you mean?'

'With this case. We've got nothing to go on. I'm starting to think we're wasting our time...'

'Stannard's dead, murdered...'

'Yes, he is. That's the only case we should be working. We need to be looking into who murdered Stannard. We've got plenty of suspects, plenty of people who might have wanted to knock him off.'

'True. But there's something going on here...'

'Shut up. Let's just go and see Parry. Maybe his autopsy might tell us something and maybe then we can stop chasing our damn tails.'

Moone drove them to Derriford and found the car park was quite packed out. He found a space and they headed toward the main building, where they would take the lift down to the morgue.

'We're spending far too much time here,' Butler said as they reached the entrance.

Moone was about to reply in agreement, but his phone started ringing. It was Rachel calling. Butler shrugged and went on in, leaving him with his regret at not calling her sooner.

'Hey,' he said, standing out of the way of the patients and staff coming out.

'It's Rachel,' she said. 'In case you'd forgotten me.'

'How could I forget?'

'I never heard from you.'

'Sorry. Really sorry. There is an explanation.'

'Ok, I'm listening.' She sounded a little pissed off.

'I got home last night to find my caravan on fire...'

'Oh my God, what happened?'

'Electrical fault probably. Insurance should pay out, hopefully.'

'Are you OK? You got somewhere to stay?'

'I'm staying at a hotel...'

'A hotel? That'll be costing you more money. Why don't you come here tonight? I'll cook you dinner.'

'That's very tempting.'

'Then come over.'

The thought of going back to the hotel and spending the evening alone consumed him suddenly. 'OK. I'll be round as soon as I can get away from work.'

'Good. I'll see you later.'

'OK.' The call ended, and Moone was left feeling a little hopeful. He headed into the building, wondering where his roller coaster life was heading these days. He wondered what Alice would make of him having a much younger girlfriend. His stomach sank at the thought, and he felt like a dirty old man as the lift doors opened and he stepped inside. Nurses and patients climbed in around him as he headed down to the morgue.

He was alone by the time he left the lift and walked along the quiet corridor towards the autopsy room.

Butler was standing, arms folded, in the bright white room, chatting to Dr Parry when Moone stepped in. There was a body on the table, from which a ripe and pungent aroma was rising to greet Moone and twist his stomach.

'That's our victim?' Moone asked, nodding to the table.

'Philip Stannard,' Butler said. 'Matched prints to the ones we've got on our database. He didn't get away with his loot after all.'

'I don't think many Plymothians will shed tears over him,' Parry said.

'Did the blow to his head kill him?' Moone

asked, stepping closer to the table.

'I'd say there were several blows administered to the back of his cranium. Judging by the front of his skull, some of the blows were administered while Stannard was lying on his front. Blows came from your ordinary claw hammer. Blunt end. He was too decomposed to get any DNA evidence from his body, but maybe his clothes might speak to you. He was otherwise quite healthy and had lived a quiet life, but blows to his head caused bleeding and swelling. So, yes, to your original question, the blows killed him.'

'Thanks, Doctor,' Moone said. 'Let us know if anything more comes up.'

'Of course.'

Moone started towards the exit with Butler in tow.

'So, probably not going to get much from the body,' Butler said. 'Typical.'

'Maybe from the clothes,' Moone said. 'Might get some trace evidence.'

'Who's our prime suspect? Seems to me it's half of Plymouth.'

Moone's phone started ringing as he was about to press the lift call button. It was Harding again.

'Boss,' Harding said.

'Yep. What is it?'

'I got hold of Stannard's mobile call log. There's a number that called him a few times around the last time he was seen. Fits in with the estimated time of death.'

'Whose number is it?'

'Don't know. It's a pay-as-you-go...'

'Great,' Moone said, rolling his eyes so Butler could see his disappointment.

'Thing is, boss, that phone had been off. But it lit up again a few hours ago.'

'Where is it?'

'It's off again now, but was near the Hoe.'

'Near the Hoe? Where Pritchard Runs that hotel?'

'Close.'

'Bloody hell. Right, let's get Pritchard back in.'

CHAPTER 17

He slipped under the door of the lock-up, then pulled it down and closed it, cutting off the wind and rain that had started again. He pulled out the latex gloves from his pocket and stepped towards the table he had placed at the back of the space. He'd done his best to keep the place tidy, but there was a little more dust gathering on the shelves. He took out his antibacterial wipes from the filing cabinet in the corner and wiped away the dust. He stuffed the wipe in the black bin bag in the middle of the room, then went over to the shelves where he found his files.

He dragged his fingers across them, reading the titles, the names. Most of them gone now, filed away by the police and local authorities. He smiled at the thought of it, burning at the satisfaction he felt at having changed the world a little and having remained invisible. He'd almost been seen by the uniform that night, but he had managed to get away without her being able to identify him. It was almost a shame the dog had to die too, he decided, but he shrugged it off and then took out the last file.

He opened it up, his eyes scanning over the words he'd printed off, and the collection of photographs he'd snapped from afar. His next *client*. He preferred *client* to victim. Victim suggested, in his mind, that he would be murdering them, and that was distasteful to him.

The man in the photographs was stocky, with short fair hair. He did not have the appearance of a clever man, not in the least. His cranium looked underdeveloped in fact. More brawn than brains. He smiled in the knowledge that his latest client would stand out from the others. When he started it all, two years prior, during a stint of his life that was ordinary, mundane even, he had no idea how excited it would make him to have control over other people, to hold their fates in his hands.

He put down the file, then found the box in one of the other locked drawers. He took out the envelope that bulged a little. He opened it and took out the cash. It was barely over two hundred pounds, the savings of an ordinary young woman. He saw her lying in the bath, her skin so grey. The blood swirling in the water.

The need to do it again pulsed in his brain, and made his chest tighten. He was becoming addicted to the thrill, but he didn't care. Now he understood how a junkie must feel, although he was not on their level, not at all.

He put away the cash when he heard the car coming down the street. He took off his gloves, his heart starting to beat harder, a light panic rising in him, as he tidied everything away. Then he lifted the garage door and peeked out. He let out a breath to see a familiar car parked outside and an even more familiar face.

Daniel Pritchard was taken along to the custody suite, where he was booked in. He was now under arrest. Harding and Carthew had done the honours. Now he was sitting in the interview room, waiting for his legal counsel. Now that he was under arrest, and in their care, a search team could now be sent out to his home, an apartment in one of the new developments overlooking Sutton Harbour.

Pritchard's solicitor joined him, who was a quite young, spectacle-wearing, female. Moone sat down next to Butler, the mobile phone log in front of him.

'You realise you're under caution,' Moone said, putting a pleasant look on his face.

'Yes, I do,' Pritchard said, looking drained. 'I just don't know what you think I'm meant to have done.'

Moone sat back. 'Philip Stannard. The man who ripped you off...'

'I know who he is,' Pritchard said.

'He's dead. He'd been bludgeoned to death.'

Their suspect stared for a few moments at Moone, taking it all in, or seeming to. 'What do you mean?'

'Someone murdered him,' Butler said, dragging Pritchard's eyes to her.

'I'm here because you think I did it?' Pritchard stared at her, his head shaking a little. 'This is a joke...'

'Daniel,' the solicitor said, touching his arm. 'You don't have to answer any more questions. Detectives, do you have any evidence against my client?'

'We do,' Moone said. 'As you know, because your client is under arrest, we can search the property that he was in prior to the arrest...'

'Yes, I'm aware,' the solicitor said, with a sarcastic smile. 'But you can only search for evidence pertaining to the crime for which the suspect has been arrested for. And you have to have grounds for the arrest.'

Moone nodded and sat back. 'Yep, that's right. We have grounds. I was coming to that. A call from a pay-as-you-go phone was made to Philip Stannard not long before he was last seen alive. That same disposable phone was used again several hours ago, allowing us to track it. We tracked it to the hotel that you manage...'

'No, no way,' Pritchard said. 'I don't have a disposable phone.'

'Don't say any more,' the solicitor said. 'Are you going to charge my client? Because I don't see how. You have a phone that could belong to anyone, in a hotel where lots of other people come and go.'

'We're waiting on a magistrate to issue a warrant,' Moone said, watching Pritchard, seeing the colour drain from his face, 'to search the hotel. We won't be charging him yet. But he's not going anywhere.'

Outside in the corridor, Butler said, 'She's a bit on the sharp side, isn't she?'

Moone nodded, letting out a breath. 'She knows her stuff. Did you see the way she kept touching him? Think there might be something going on there. Do you think he did it?'

'Could be. But I don't like the timeline. He and whoever else invested in this health gym or whatever it was, and it was barely a month before Stannard supposedly stole all their money and ran off. But he hasn't run off. He was stuck under the floorboards.'

'But his financial dealings tell us he was hoarding their money. He had fake passports...'

'Yeah, I know. But when did Daniel Pritchard discover he'd been ripped off? And why would Stannard go and meet someone he'd ripped off? Doesn't make sense.'

Moone nodded, hearing his own doubts echo back to him. 'What about this phone?'

Butler shrugged. 'I don't know. Maybe someone else staying at the hotel used it.'

'Well, we won't know until we find it. If we find it.' Moone headed towards the incident room, hoping some kind of result would be called in soon. Any result would do, either way he wanted some kind of direction; his mind and instincts were all messed up and he didn't feel like he knew which way was up. He had been sure the suicides had somehow tied in with the whole Stannard affair, but now the old man was lying in the morgue. What was it all about?

Then his phone rang again, and he sighed, wondering what it might be this time.

'DCI Moone,' he said as he stepped into the incident room.

'The Chief Superintendent would like to see you and DI Mandy Butler ASAP,' Laptew's PA said, filling Moone's stomach full of lead. 'Right, OK. We're on our way.'

'Who was that?' Butler asked.

'Shit. The Chief Super wants to see us.'

'Bollocks to him,' Butler said. 'It's that little fucking shit, Darwin. He's grassed us, the bastard.'

'Well, we're in for it now. I'll be back to DI. Come on, let's go and face the music. Hope you've got your dancing shoes on.'

'Is there a party going on?' Butler asked when they reached the corridor where the Chief Super had his office. Moone looked towards the end office and saw Stack standing there, a plastic cup of something warm in his hand. DS Carthew was sitting on a chair, chatting to him.

'You two got invited as well, then?' Stack asked, took a sip of her drink and grimaced. 'Disgusting. The drink, not you two. Well...'

'What's this about?' Butler asked.

'Don't know.' Stack shrugged. 'Probably a bollocking, but I can't think of any cock ups I've made. You?'

Carthew looked up at him. 'Me? No, can't think of anything.'

Butler stared at her, then looked at Moone. 'What do you think?'

Moone was about to answer when the outer door opened and the Chief Super poked his head out. 'You're all here. Good. Come through.'

After giving Moone a raised eyebrow, Butler turned and followed the others through the outer office, then into Laptew's room.

'What's this all about?' Butler said under her breath.

'I've no idea,' Moone replied and shut the door behind him.

Laptew sat at his desk, while everyone else remained standing, all staring at him, waiting.

The Chief Super looked over them all. 'My apologies for all the dramatics, rushing you down here. I don't know if any of you have been following the news. Well, there's a virus spreading across the globe. Goes by the delightful name of coronavirus.'

'Yeah, I've read about it,' Stack said. 'What's that got to do with us?'

The Chief Super sat back. 'I've had word from up high. We've had our first few cases here, in the United Kingdom. Italy's already up against it...'

'It's just another kind of flu,' Stack said and huffed out a laugh.

'No, it's bloody not!' Laptew shouted. His face was red as he stared up at Stack. 'No, it's not. It's much worse than flu. And there's no vaccine. People are dying all across China and now Italy. We won't be far behind.'

'What does this mean for us?' Carthew asked.

The Chief Super stood up and looked at her. 'It means that we'll soon be in charge of keeping order. There's been lockdowns in other countries, there will be the same here.'

'Jesus,' Butler said. 'This can't be right. What, people under house arrest?'

'To a degree,' Laptew said, a glumness to his voice. 'They're going to try social distancing first. Everyone two metres apart.' The Chief Super sat down. 'So, a few cases, are going to be put on the back burner...'

'You're joking,' Butler said and exchanged a shocked look with Moone.

'No, I'm not, acting DI Butler,' the Chief Super said. 'I wish I was. This whole suicide affair, you haven't come up with much so far, have you? Moone?'

Moone broke out of his dream and shock, then looked at the Chief Super. 'We believe there's a link between the whole Stannard case...'

Laptew let out a sigh. 'But I've been informed it's only a theory. A pretty thin one too. Anything to substantiate it?'

'No, sir. Not at the moment, but...'

The Chief Super held up a hand. 'I've heard enough. You haven't even got definitive proof that these suicides are connected. I'm afraid that will all have to be put on hold for now. As for Daniel Pritchard, it sounds like you've got a good case against him.'

'If we find the phone.'

Stack cleared his throat and looked at Moone. 'The warrant's arrived. You can search his flat.'

Moone nodded. 'OK.'

The Chief Super stood up again. 'Right then, get on with it, and bring me some good news. I've emailed you lots of posters and information on the coronavirus. Start printing it up and reading through it. We've got a tough slog ahead of us all. I know we will come through this together.'

Moone looked at the others, saw the incomprehension on their collective faces as they began to leave the office. He started to follow but the Chief Super called him and Butler back.

'Moone, Butler,' he said, sitting back down at

his desk. 'Get this case brought to a conclusion as quickly as possible. And I mean bloody quickly! Get the evidence and charge your suspect. I'll make an appointment with the CPS as soon as I can. Right, that's it, go on.'

'OK, sir,' Moone said.

'Oh, and Moone, I'd visit your family while you can, before we all get locked down.'

'Can you believe all this?' Butler asked as she drove them back into the car park at Charles Cross station.

'It's hard to take in,' Moone sat back in his seat, staring toward the dirty grey walls of the station. 'Especially our investigation being put on hold.'

'Surely this is all precautionary.'

'Doesn't sound like it. I've been reading up on it. They're saying we're a couple of weeks behind Italy and they're dropping like flies over there.'

'Bloody hell. Anyway, our suicide case, I don't think that'll be picked up again...'

Moone stared at her as he took off his seatbelt. 'Why not?'

'We've got nothing to go on.'

Moone sighed and nodded. 'I know, I know. But there's something going on here. Someone's definitely forcing these people to take their own lives... I'm sure of it.'

Butler pushed open her door. 'You may be

right, but if we've got nothing to go on, then we've no way of finding out who's behind this. They're a ghost. We have to let it go and get the dirt on Pritchard.'

Moone got out of the car, letting out a huff as he did.

Butler shook her head. 'I know that noise. You don't think Pritchard murdered Stannard, do you?'

'I honestly don't know,' he said, then his phone was ringing. It was Sergeant Pinder's number. He stopped just inside the entrance to the station. 'Kevin. What's new?'

'I'm with the search team at the hotel,' he said, voices in the background. 'We've found a disposable phone tucked away behind a vent in a room supposedly used as an office by Daniel Pritchard.'

Moone dragged a hand down his face, letting out another tired breath. 'OK. Bag it and bring it to the station.'

Moone ended the call, then turned and faced Butler. 'That was Sergeant Pinder. They've found a disposable phone at the hotel in a room Pritchard used as an office, squirrelled away.'

Butler shrugged. 'There you go then, the Stannard murder is pretty much solved. Come on, let's have another word with him.'

Pritchard and his solicitor were already seated in the interview room by the time Moone and

Butler walked in and took their seats. Moone kept his eyes on Pritchard, noting how his nervousness was growing, and wondering if guilt was getting the better of him. He was starting to wonder if they did have the right man after all.

It was Butler who took care of the formalities of the interview, and read out who was present, the date and the time.

'I have to remind you that you're still under caution. Do you understand?' Moone said.

Pritchard nodded.

'You have to speak up, for the recording,' Butler said.

'I understand.'

'Are you going to charge my client?' the solicitor asked, looking down at her notebook.

'We'd just like a little chat first,' Butler said. 'To get things straight.'

'You don't have to say anything,' the solicitor said and touched Pritchard's arm.

'It's true what she said,' Butler leaned forward. 'But you'd be an idiot to listen to her advice. This is your chance to explain how we found what we found in your office, in the hotel you work in.'

Pritchard's head sprung up, his eyes widening.

'That's right,' Moone said. 'We found the phone. Hidden away in your office. You might as well tell us about it.'

The solicitor sat up straight. 'As I stated last time, it's a hotel, people come and go...'

'His office,' Moone said, then looked at Pritchard. 'Your office. Hidden behind a vent. We found your prints on it. Can you explain that?'

Pritchard lowered his head, shook it slightly.

'I think I need some time with my client,' the solicitor said and got to her feet. 'Daniel...'

Pritchard shook his head. 'No, I don't need any more time. I need to, I need to get things straight. Just sit down, Caroline. Please, sit down.'

The solicitor sat down, staring at him, her face a little paler.

Pritchard looked up at Moone as his hand tapped at the desk. 'The phone, the one you found, it's mine. I bought it. There's no point denying that. I kept hold of it. I turned it on the other day. The moment I did it, I knew I'd been stupid...'

'Why did you have it?' Moone asked. 'You did message Stannard?'

Pritchard swallowed, then nodded. 'Yes, I did...'

'Daniel, I warn you...' his solicitor began, but the young man turned to her, his hand patting hers as he said, 'It's OK, Caroline, it's OK. I've got to explain.'

'Go on then, this should be good.' Butler folded her arms and sat back.

Pritchard cleared his throat. 'I'm not proud of myself. I want that on the record...'

'It's all being recorded,' Moone said, tapping the recording machine.

'Well, I knew Stannard a little, from before this all started. A friend of a friend did work experience with him. I met him a couple of times at charity events. He said he liked me, looked at me like the son he never had. His wife divorced him years back, he said, and never had kids. I was fine with that, and I thought I might learn something from him. What I wasn't expecting was, well, for him to tell me about what he'd been doing all these years... '

'He told you he was ripping off his clients?' Butler asked.

Pritchard hunched over, putting his hands together. 'Yeah, he did. He said, if I helped him bring in more clients, and tell them about this deal he had going, then I could get in on the action.'

'You helped him?' Butler said, a disgusted laugh leaving her mouth. 'You actually helped him rip people off?'

Pritchard stared at her. 'He ripped me off too!'

'Oh, well, that makes it all right then,' she huffed. 'Poor you.'

Moone leaned towards him. 'I don't understand. If you knew it was all a scam, then how come you gave him your money?'

Pritchard hung his head. 'I know, sounds pretty stupid of me, doesn't it? You have to understand that Stannard was the kind of guy who could get you to believe anything. I never would have gone in for conning people, but somehow he convinced me. Then he's saying he can take our money and make more. I guess greed and, well...'

'Stupidity,' Butler said. 'You got what you deserved. So, then you found out Stannard had ripped you off, you rang him from your disposable phone, got him to meet you at that house and killed him...'

'No!' Pritchard's eyes blazed with fear. 'That's not what happened...'

'But you did phone him?' Moone asked. 'Why?'

'Because I wanted to get my money back. But he wouldn't meet with me, said everything was ok, but he was busy. He kept making excuses...'

'So you tracked him down,' Moone said.

'Or more likely,' Butler said. 'You're lying. You used the disposable phone to get him to meet you at that house. Once inside, you tried to get him to give you your money back. He wouldn't, and you fought...'

'This is all conjecture,' the solicitor said. 'All you have as evidence is a disposable phone that could have been put there...'

Moone stared at Pritchard. 'Daniel, the truth

is very important right now...'

'I know,' Pritchard said, his voice shaking.

'Did you use that disposable to call Stannard?'

Pritchard swallowed then nodded. 'Yes, but Stannard gave me that phone. When all this kicked off, I hid it. That's the truth, I swear.'

'I don't believe you,' Butler said.

'Can we take a break there?' the solicitor asked. 'I think I need a word with my client.'

Moone rubbed his face as he headed away from the interview room and towards the incident room. He could hear Butler behind him, could feel her words building. He spun round and faced her. 'What?'

'What?' She held up her hands. 'Nothing.'

'You think he did it?'

'It doesn't matter what I think.'

'DCI Moone,' a familiar voice said, and Moone turned to see Sergeant Pinder coming towards him.

'Pinder,' Moone said. 'Got any good news?'

Pinder slowed up, looking between them. 'Well, I've got two pieces of info to impart to you. But by the looks on your faces, maybe I should start with a joke.'

Moone raised a smile, but said, 'Just give us the bad news.'

Pinder nodded. 'We went door to door round North Prospect. Got some interesting comments, but we've got a neighbour who puts a young mixed-race lad with a much older gentleman, going in the direction of the house where Stannard was found...'

'Brilliant,' Moone said.

'The punchline? The Chief Super sent a message. Charge him.'

BOOK TWO

CHAPTER 18

Moone sighed as he stared at his hands, noticing the redness between his fingers, the dry and cracked skin there. He had never washed his hands so much in his entire life. Everything had changed in the last few weeks. His usual disgust at seeing his fellow men taking a piss then leave the toilet without washing their hands, had turned to anger.

Coronavirus, he said to himself, staring up at the poster over the sink in the station's small kitchen. The poster reminded him to wash his hands for at least twenty seconds and then to keep a social distance from his colleagues of two metres. It was almost impossible in the cramped station to keep that distance from his colleagues. So much had changed in the last few weeks, and one day he had woken in a surreal world where people were no longer allowed to stand next to each other and some people fought over loo paper. A couple of weeks ago, he had found himself stood at his ex-wife's driveway, talking to his kids, telling them what was happening and how he had to stay away for a while. Alice had promised to keep an eye on everyone, and so he left with a horrible feeling in his stomach.

'You going to bloody well hurry up?' Butler groaned from behind him, stood outside the door.

'I'm going as fast as I can.' He smiled sarcastically.

'Faffing as usual.'

'What the hell's going on?' Moone asked, picking up his mug of coffee. 'When did it become normal to queue up outside supermarkets and fight over wipes and toilet roll?'

Butler let out a breath. 'Never. It's never normal. I went out and bought loads of toilet roll when this all started…'

'Oh, so you're the problem? Fantastic.'

Butler laughed. 'Got to be prepared.'

Moone walked past and stood in the corridor as she went in the kitchen. 'It's our whole case going out the window that's pissed me off. Now here we are, going round telling people off for socialising and fining them. Feels like we're in East Germany.'

'Social distancing. Keeps the riff raff away. I'm all for it.' Butler put the kettle on and started making herself a coffee. 'Anyway, we had no case. Apart from the one against Daniel Pritchard. Now he's banged up in a detention centre, awaiting his trial.'

'I know, I went to his magistrates court when he was denied bail. Flight risk, my arse.'

'Well, there's been no more suspect suicides. If there was a nutter going round forcing people to commit suicide, he must be practising social distancing now.'

Moone started down the corridor, stopping and sidestepping to let one of the uniforms get past. Moone made an apologetic face, but the uniform just shrugged and went on their way. He went into the incident room, where the desks had been moved further apart, two metres to be exact. DSU Stack has taken great pleasure in getting his tape measure out and wielding it at everyone.

Moone sat at his lonely desk, staring round at everyone. There were a few civvies missing as they were considered vulnerable. Harding was also absent, looking after his son who had various ailments. Moone felt bad suddenly, realising he knew little about his team.

'Your ex-wife must be loving it,' Butler said, coming in and sitting miles away.

'Because she's a teacher?' Moone huffed out a laugh. 'She's home-schooling the youngest boy. Not going great by all accounts. This is doing my head in, waiting here, sitting here rotting, waiting for someone to dob in their neighbour for having a mate round or I don't know what. Where's all the crime gone?'

'The criminals are self-isolating, obviously. Anyway, we did solve those series of burglaries…'

'Oh, yes, I forgot. The masterminds that were robbing their neighbours. That took all of a week.' Moone sat back. 'He's out there somewhere.'

'Who is?' Butler started on her paperwork, tapping away at her keyboard.

'You know who. He's planning his next one. This has made it all the more difficult for him, but he'll be back.'

'If he ever existed in the first place.'

Moone ignored her words as his phone started to ring. It was the Chief Super's number. He sighed, then picked up the receiver. 'Yes sir, what can I do for you?'

'Morning, Peter,' he said. 'How's it going there?'

'Quiet. Not much to report. Everyone's keeping their distance. Even the criminals.'

'Good to hear. Listen, I've had a call from Colin Darwin. He's got some information for you…'

Moone sat upright. 'In relation to what? Don't tell me he's going to grass up some civilians for not keeping a social distance.'

'Please don't joke, Moone. It's in relation to your suicide case.'

'I thought that was all done and dusted, sir?'

'So did I. Just go and see what he's got to say. Probably won't come to much, but go and have a word.'

'We will, sir, don't worry.' The call ended and Moone looked towards Butler. 'Come on, we've got an outing.'

Butler folded her arms, narrowing her eyes at him. 'Do I need to bring a tape measure?'

'No, we're off to see your favourite businessman.' Moone smiled as he stood up.

'You don't mean Darwin?'

'That's exactly who I mean. Let's go.'

Butler stood up and started going through the contents of her desk.

'What're you looking for?' Moone asked, heading for the door.

'My latex gloves and mask.'

'You know those masks don't stop anything, don't you? There's no filter.'

'I don't care. They make me feel better. What we going to do about the car situation?'

Moone let out a breath. 'We either take two cars, which is bad for the environment, or I can sit in the back, across from you.'

'A back-seat driver. How lovely.' Butler headed out in front of him, keeping her distance.

'Look at that,' Butler said as she parked and pulled on the handbrake.

Moone leaned over to look through the windscreen to see what she was looking at. Across the enormous car park, that was quite empty, was a long line of people queuing right up to the doors of The Realm store. The queue went right round the edge of the car park, with a little gap between each person.

Butler climbed out, with Moone following as she stormed over to the head of the queue. 'Hey, you lot,' she shouted at the people in the queue. 'Get further apart. Go on, two metres. No, luv, that's not two metres.'

Moone ignored it all and got his ID from his jacket, feeling the now warm sun burning his neck, ready to flash it at the member of staff guarding the door.

'*Get to the back of the fucking queue!*' someone shouted from the line of people.

Moone showed his ID. 'Police. Get back.'

'Don't mean you get to jump the bloody queue!' someone else shouted at him.

Moone ignored the calls and showed his ID to the tall, thickset and balding doorman. 'DCI Peter Moone. I need to see your boss, Colin Darwin.'

'Hang on,' the doorman said and walked off inside the shop and came back with a mask and gloves. 'Put these on.'

'What?' Moone looked down at the gloves and mask. 'Why? If it's OK, I'll just keep my distance.'

'No one sees him without this gear going on them. It's his human right.'

Moone huffed, then snatched the mask and gloves away and put them on. 'Right, where is he?'

'Stock room,' the doorman said, stepping aside.

'Where is he?' Butler repeated.

'Stock room,' Moone said. 'Put on your gloves and mask and come on.'

Butler did as she was told, then followed Moone into the store which had only a few customers inside, spread out, side stepping each other. They all wore gloves and masks as they hurriedly perused the shelves.

The doorman overtook them and directed Moone towards the large double doors near the back. The doorman opened up the doors, then let them through as a warm breeze followed them. As Moone stepped in, followed by Butler, he saw the suited figure of Colin Darwin, sitting behind a desk that had been pushed to the back of the dusty and crammed room.

Darwin got up, put on a mask and gloves and approached them, keeping a good two metres from them.

'My temporary office,' he said, rolling his eyes. 'My proper one's being given a deep clean. Can't be too careful.'

'What did you want?' Butler asked, almost spitting out the words.

'Have you two been tested?' he asked, narrowing his eyes at them.

'No,' Moone said. 'But we'll stay over here, so don't worry. What's this info you've got for us?'

Darwin rested himself on his makeshift desk. 'Yeah, that. I've been giving it some thought, going over what you said. Might be something, might be nothing, but I remembered Jessop talking about this IT whizz he'd found. Think he was after someone to show him how to delete stuff, if you know what I mean...'

'We do,' Butler said, sounding fed up already. 'Get on with it.'

Darwin shot her a look, then turned back to Moone. 'See, thing is, he convinced me to meet with this fella, saying he was God's gift to computers and could rejuvenate my store's system.'

'What did you have to hide?' Butler asked, causing Darwin's eyes to blaze.

'Right!' he growled, his face red. 'I've had enough of your crap!'

Moone held up his hands, turning to glare at Butler. 'I'm sorry, Mr Darwin. Please, we'd like to know what you know. You have my apologies. Why don't you wait outside, DI Butler.'

Butler glared back at him, then turned and stormed off towards the exit, pulling off her gloves as she went.

'She's got a chip on her shoulder, that one,' Darwin said. 'Was always the same at school. Couldn't take a joke.'

'This IT wizard?' Moone asked.

Darwin nodded. 'He came here. Wanted him to take a look at our computer system, but...'

'But?'

'I didn't like the look of him. There was something, well, off about him. I've got a nose for that sort.'

'Really. It's taken you a month to tell us about him.'

'There's been a lot to deal with, hasn't there? What with all this coronavirus business.'

'True. What was he called, this IT whiz?'

Darwin turned back to his makeshift office and picked a small business card from his desk. 'Here. I happened to find this when I was moving my stuff down here. That's what brought it all back really.'

Moone took the card. He read it out loud, 'Ian Speare IT consultant. Where do I know that name from?'

Darwin shrugged. 'Search me, but you might want to ask him a few questions.'

Moone nodded and put the card away, thinking about his partner who had suffered as a child at the hands of the man in front of him. 'How come this place is still open? You don't sell essential items.'

Darwin smirked, then pointed a finger back towards the door. 'You'd think, wouldn't you. But if you walk out that door, then head right, you'll come to a small supermarket *inside* this store. That's why we're still open. We're needed. So, go and do your job, talk to this Ian Speare fella. Go on, run along.'

Moone stared at him for a moment, let his eyes tell him what he thought of him, then turned and headed out of the shop.

Butler was outside, near the car, arms folded across her chest, her eyes scanning the line of customers.

'There's no such thing as karma, is there?' she asked as Moone reached her.

'What do you mean?'

'Well, just look at him, Darwin. He was an evil bastard at school, and now look at him. A billionaire...'

'But is he happy?'

Butler flashed him a look, then unlocked the car and climbed in.

'Ian Speare,' Moone said, once he'd joined her. 'Where do I know that name?'

Butler tapped the steering wheel. 'Ian Speare? I don't know. But, yeah, I know it too. Speare, Speare. Hang on.' Butler got her notebook out and flipped through several pages then stopped. 'Got it. Ian Speare. Madam Revello's son...'

'Revello?' Moone gave a laugh, then nodded, the realisation flooding him. 'That's it. Of course.'

'What?'

'Ian Speare is the IT consultant that Jessop had doing his dirty work for him. What if Speare got hold of sensitive info from Jessop's computer? Maybe he was blackmailing him. That could even be how Madam Revello knows stuff about her clients, because her son looks it all up…'

'Hang on, you can't say for sure…' Butler started the engine.

'No, but it's a bit funny that Speare, Revello's son, knows Jessop or worked for him. I wonder how many of our victims he did work for?'

'Let's find out.'

They parked up outside Madam Revello's house, then climbed out, not saying much, but Moone knew that they were both trying to figure it out, wondering if Speare was the man forcing people to commit suicide. Then Moone chided himself as they reached the front door, knowing that from day one Ian Speare seemed odd to him. Maybe it was the Norman Bates, living with his mother thing, he decided, but there was something not right about him.

Butler huffed and pressed the doorbell.

'What was that?' Moone asked her.

Butler looked at him, a little shame in her eyes, he thought. 'I feel pretty daft. I mean, I will if she's been having me on all this time.'

Moone didn't say anything, didn't dare, because he didn't want to be sceptical right now. The door opening saved him, and they found themselves faced with the man they had come to see, dressed in an old man's cream trousers and light blue shirt, his thick and large glasses in place.

Moone showed his ID. 'Remember us, Mr Speare?'

Speare nodded. 'Did the photos help?'

'I'm sorry?' Moone asked.

'The photos you looked at last time.' Speare blinked at them, quite blank.

'Very helpful. But we need some more information. We'd like you to come down to the station to talk to us. A sort of informal chat.'

The milk bottle glasses blinked at them again. 'Mother. I can't leave her on her own.'

'Can't you get someone to look after her?' Butler asked.

'There isn't anyone,' Speare said. 'Just me.'

'We can get someone here,' Moone said, putting on a sympathetic face. 'Someone to keep an eye on her. I'll call now.'

Moone took out his phone as Speare said, 'Am I under arrest?'

'No, you're not. Like I said, we would like you to come to the station to answer a few questions...'

'What have I done?'

'I'll get someone here to look after your mother, then we can head to the station to discuss it.'

When Moone walked into the interview room, Ian Speare looked up, his hands wrapped round the mug of tea they had made for him. The large bulbous eyes behind his big glasses blinked at him. Moone sat down, then Butler came in and joined him. They sat back, away from the desk, doing their best to keep a social distance from Speare.

'You have a sideline,' Moone said.

'Do I?' Speare asked in a quiet, blank voice.

'Apparently. IT? That ring any bells?'

'It's a hobby,' Speare said, then shrugged. 'I like computers.'

'You ever go to see a man called Colin Darwin?' Moone asked.

'Colin Darwin? As in the owner of The Realm shops?'

'The very same. Did you meet with him?'

'Yes, I did. He wanted his computer system checked over...'

'What about Martin Jessop?' Butler asked.

'Who?' The big, magnified eyes turned to Butler.

Moone took out a photo of Jessop that was used in the Plymouth Herald and showed Speare.

'He looks familiar,' Speare said. 'But he could have been to visit Mother. So many people come to see...'

'We believe you worked on his computers,' Butler said.

'I don't think so...'

Moone leaned forward. 'You did go and see Colin Darwin, though? To see about his computers?'

'Yes, but he changed his mind...'

Moone nodded. 'But that's the thing, because Darwin says that Jessop sang your praises, said you were a computer whiz.'

Speare took off his glasses, gave them a wipe, revealing two tiny, shrivelled-up eyes. He put his glasses back on and stared at Moone. 'Must have me mistaken for someone else. Look, can I go? My mother needs...'

'You're free to go whenever you want,' Butler said. 'But I feel like you're not telling us the truth about Jessop.'

'Am I in trouble?' Speare asked. 'Do you think I did something wrong?'

Moone opened the file he had brought along with him, and took out the photographs of the people who had committed suicide. He put them in front of Speare. 'Do you recognise any of these people, Ian?'

Speare looked down at the photographs. He stared at them for a while, then looked up. 'They might've been to mother. For a reading. I don't know.'

'They did come for a reading,' Moone said. 'Did they make appointments? I mean, they don't just show up, do they? They phone up or book a reading online. That's right, isn't it?'

'Mum likes to prepare herself...'

'You prep her, don't you?' Moone asked. 'You dig around in these people's online history, so your mum, Madam Revello has lots of amazing insights into them. I mean, it must be so easy for you to do because these days everyone puts everything online, posting photos of their daily life, even what they had for dinner, the whole lot. The stuff you must find...'

'I don't, I don't...' There was panic beyond the huge eyes, fidgeting, and right then Moone knew he was right, had hit the nail on the head.

'What did you do for Jessop?' Butler asked. 'What did you erase? Sex stuff?'

Ian opened his mouth a couple of times, looking like a fish out of water. 'I think... I think I need a lawyer.'

'We haven't arrested you,' Moone said. 'We just need you to talk to us...'

Then there was a knock at the door. Harding poked his head round it, his eyes immediately finding Moone's, a look in them of sympathy for the two detectives.

'What is it, Harding?' Butler asked, raising her eyebrows.

'There's a solicitor here wanting to see Mr Speare,' Harding said, then was shunted out of the way by a full-figured, blonde woman in her mid-forties, dressed in an expensive looking trouser suit.

'Helen Sherrard-Cooke,' the woman said, sounding a little sharp, her voice quite well spoken. 'I'm here to represent Mr Speare...'

'How did you know he was here?' Butler asked.

'His mother called me,' the solicitor said,

still stood, folding her arms across her chest. 'She's very worried about her son. As am I. Are you about to arrest my client?'

'Well, this is more a fact finding…' Moone started to say.

'So, he's free to go?' The solicitor raised her eyebrows.

Moone stood up. 'We've still got questions…'

'Then you need to arrest him or let him go. I don't believe my client has anything more to add, do you, Ian?'

Speare looked up at her, then at Moone, still blank-faced. 'No, I don't. I can't help you. I don't want to say any more…'

'Then, I've got no choice,' Moone said, staring at Speare, but then the door opened and DSU Stack's red, stolid face appeared around it.

'A word,' Stack said, a grunt to his voice.

Moone found him outside, leant against the wall, his hands in his pockets.

'What's wrong?' Moone asked, not liking the look in his eyes.

'You've got to let him go,' Stack said.

'But we know he worked on Jessop's computer…'

'That's all you know. Doesn't mean he had anything to do with… whatever the fuck you've been looking into.'

'But the Chief Super told us to look into this, to talk to Darwin…'

'Yes, I know. But you've got nothing to

arrest him on, have you?'

'We need time, we need to talk...'

'Let him go. Get back to your Covid duties. That's an order.'

CHAPTER 19

'They're having a laugh, aren't they?' Moone huffed, staring out of the car window, watching the fields and the houses rushing past as they headed into deepest Cornwall.

'What now?' Butler said, taking them down the eerily quiet stretch of the A38.

'One minute the Chief Super's telling us to go and talk to Darwin, then we're being told to go back to our Covid duties. Are they just trying to wind us up?'

'Of course they are. It's what they do.' Butler signalled, then turned right, towards a caravan park entrance. Already they could hear the distant beat of music coming from somewhere deep inside the park. 'Idiots. Having a party at a time like this...'

Moone's phone rang, and he saw that Rachel was trying to get hold of him. 'Hi, you OK?'

'I'm fine. I was just wondering if you're going to be home for tea?'

He smiled, thinking how far and fast he had

travelled in the last month since the whole virus scare had taken hold. One minute he was living out of a hotel room, the next he was moving in with Rachel. During the lockdown only, they agreed, on a kind of probationary period to see if they could live with each other without one of them killing the other. Things were moving pretty fast, he knew that, but something inside had told him to push on, to ride the wave and see where he ended up.

'I'll try my best,' he said, looking towards Butler and seeing her look that said it all. 'You know, work and everything...'

'I know. Hope you're staying safe.'

'We are, but I can't say the same for the criminals.'

She let out a little laugh. 'Looks like I'm now furloughed. The boss doesn't want to risk getting it.'

'No, I bet he doesn't. Will you get paid?'

'I'll be fine.'

Butler parked the car, then sat back, staring at him with her eyebrows raised. Somewhere the beat of music was still thumping. 'I've got to go. Sorry.'

'It's fine. Maybe we can get a takeaway later, when you get in...'

'Maybe. If there are any open.'

She gave a hollow laugh. 'True. OK, talk later. Stay safe.'

'You too.' He ended the call as Butler got out,

then followed her along the grass verge that ran along the main road of the caravan park. They passed under the huge archway sign of the park.

'I can't believe you've moved in with her,' Butler said, moving ahead, her fists clenched at her sides.

'I know you can't, but I did. It's not for ever.'

Butler swung round and faced him, her hands on her hips, eyebrows raised. 'You're joking, aren't you? So, when this is over, you're going to just up and leave?'

Moone shrugged. He hadn't thought that far ahead, to be fair, and had been playing it by ear. 'We said we'd see how things are when it's all over.'

'Yeah, and this could go on for months. What were you thinking? Oh, I know, you weren't thinking, were you? Little Pete Moone was doing all the thinking.' She tutted and started walking again as they were overtaken by an incident response car heading in the direction of the reception office.

Moone couldn't be bothered to argue about it again with Butler. It was quickly turning into Groundhog Day back at the station and he was tired all over. He steamed ahead when he saw the main office building, which was surrounded by a cluster of trees, separated a little from the rows of neat mobile homes that lined the park in every direction. The beat of music was now very loud and the chatter and screams of partygoers was competing with it.

A tanned middle-aged man in a shirt and tie came towards them, his expression full of tiredness and stress.

'They're over there,' he said, jabbing a finger across the park. 'It's been going on for hours. They just don't care!'

'We'll sort them out,' Butler said, holding up her palm as she stormed on to where the loud dance music was coming from. They took the next turning, where another row of mobile homes lined a short lane. Moone saw the crowd of people spilling out from behind a caravan, some of them dancing like they were ablaze. Others were sitting or standing, a drink in their hands. None of them were adhering to the social distancing policy. As he watched on, the uniforms appeared from nowhere, storming the group, breaking up the rave. The music still blared as Moone stood there, watching some of the revellers make a run for it into the surrounding woods.

'I'm not giving bloody chase,' Butler said, stood behind him.

'Me neither,' Moone said, looking over the other partygoers, some of which he realised were only in their teens. He could hardly blame them, he decided, realising that it must be tough on them having the little freedom they probably felt they had being torn away. He looked across the lane towards another group of young girls where

Sergeant Pinder was taking down names.

Moone sucked in a breath, his heart beating faster as a pair of young eyes met his. 'Jesus... Pinder, a word.'

Pinder looked round at him, his pen poised over his notebook. 'Boss?'

Moone took him to the side, his eyes still fixed on the ones that stared at him, full of worry. Alice. What the hell was she doing here? 'Pinder. This is a bit delicate.'

'OK. What's wrong?'

'One of those girls. She's my daughter. Alice.'

Pinder glanced towards the gaggle of girls. 'Oh right. Yeah, I can the resemblance now. So, what do we do?'

Moone looked down, feeling the heat rise to his cheeks. 'I'm not sure. She needs a good talking to...'

Pinder nodded, looking around the area. 'I'm sure you'll take good care of that. Want to tell them to get lost?'

Moone smiled his thanks, then headed over to the girls, but only staring into Alice's eyes. 'All of you, you'd better piss off. Alice, come with me.'

As the girls dispersed, Moone gestured to Alice, then turned and headed back towards the car. Butler fell in step, and they all walked back in silence.

'You going to tell Mum?' Alice asked a few feet from the car.

Moone turned and faced her, arms folded.

'Where is your mum?'

Alice let out a heavy sigh, looking off towards the road. 'She's at home, working, making sure the kids get their home-schooling stuff or whatever…'

'Where the bloody hell does she think you are?' Moone opened the back door for Alice.

'Said I was popping to the shops.' Alice climbed in, and Moone and Butler followed. 'You're not going to tell Mum, are you?'

Moone turned in his seat and faced her. 'As long as you promise not to do this again.'

Alice looked up, a slight smile on her lips. 'Scout's honour.'

'That's my line!'

Butler started the engine, then turned the car round and took them back on to the A38, heading home.

'Nice to meet you, Alice, by the way,' Butler said. 'Don't worry, Pete, I'll do the introductions.'

'Sorry,' Moone said. 'Alice, Butler. Butler, Alice.'

'Mandy,' Butler said with a huff, then she smiled at Alice. 'Tell me, Alice, has your dad always been a faffer?'

'Absolutely.' Alice laughed.

'Alright you two,' Moone said, shaking his head.

Butler laughed. 'What do you think about his new girlfriend?'

'What?' Alice sat up, her eyebrows shooting

up.

'Butler!' Moone said, then buried his head in his hands. 'Thanks a lot.'

'Whoops.'

'You've got a girlfriend?' Alice said. 'Who?'

'She's pretty young,' Butler said, then tutted.

'She's not that young. Late twenties. Practically thirty.' Moone turned and faced Alice. 'Sorry, I should have told you about her.'

'And he's living with her,' Butler said.

'Alright, what's your name?' Moone stared at Butler. 'Bertie Smalls?'

'Who the bloody hell is Bertie Smalls?'

'Take no notice,' Alice said, sitting back. 'He's a London criminal who grassed up some other London criminals. So, you're living with her? Locked down with her?'

'Rachel,' Moone said. 'That's her name. Yes, locked down, living with her, after my caravan burnt down.'

'Your caravan... what?' Alice sprang forward again. 'You didn't say!'

'Nothing to worry about. Just an electrical mishap. I'm fine.'

Butler drove them on down the A38, then dropped Alice outside her house. Moone climbed out, opening the back door for Alice. He smiled at her, seeing a lot of worry in her eyes, the way she stared regretfully at her home.

'You OK?' he asked.

She nodded, then a glumness overtook her

face. 'When's this going to be over, Dad?'

'I don't know, sweetheart. Wish I did.' Moone stepped closer, put out his arms. She came over and hugged him as she said, 'Is she nice?'

'Not as nice as you.'

Alice let go of him, smiled a little then headed towards the front door, and he watched her for a while, thinking, wondering when it all would come to an end. He pulled himself out of his dream, then climbed back inside the car and sat there, staring out the windscreen.

'Sorry for grassing you up,' Butler said, starting the engine.

'No you're not. But she had to find out sometime.'

'I really don't know what you were thinking, Moone.'

'I wasn't thinking. I was trying to go with my heart for a change.'

'I think you're mixing your heart up with your...'

'Let's just go back to the station, shall we?'

He sat in his car for a moment, feeling how quiet the street had become. There was still the occasional person around, and people queuing up at the shops like sheep, all wearing masks, some wearing latex gloves. Fear had gripped them, tearing at their minds. So many people ready to die, he thought and could almost taste the delicious irony of it all. But he had other business to attend to. He looked across at the cream-coloured house that resided at the top of the grey steps.

He coughed for a moment, the sudden burst of irritation rising through his chest. He took out the inhaler he'd managed to get hold of and sucked on it. It opened up his airways, allowed him a few minutes without a fit of coughing.

He slipped on some gloves, then a green surgical mask that covered most of his face. He put on a baseball cap, then climbed out. He didn't move quickly, just took his time and headed to the front door. People didn't take notice of people that walked calmly, but they might sit up and pay attention to a man in a hurry.

He rang the bell, then waited, half looking round the street, but all was still quiet.

Ian Speare opened the door, his face blank at first, no recollection in the enlarged lenses of his glasses. Then he obliged by pulling down his mask, revealing his face, and making Speare start a little.

'What're you doing here?' Speare sputtered, his eyes jumping past him, staring into the street.

'I need a word with you.'

'You shouldn't be here.' Speare started closing the door, but the man pushed his gloved hand against it.

'You talked to the police.'

'I didn't say anything.'

'Convince me. Let me in and make me a drink.'

'You're not supposed to let...'

The man laughed and shook his head, then showed his gloved hands. 'I'm wearing gloves. I won't touch anything and I'll keep two metres away. Happy?'

'No, not really.' Speare didn't look at all happy, but backed away, leaving the door open.

He stepped inside the dark house, staring round at the place, taking it all in as a thought occurred to him. 'Where's your mother? Madam Revello?'

'Sleeping in the conservatory,' Speare said, then pointed to the front room. 'Go on in. But keep your voice down.'

He went in, his eyes searching the place, the furniture, the thick photo albums on the shelves. The curtains were pulled but not all the way, and a stream of sunlight toyed with the dust in the air. He pulled them shut and faced Speare. 'We don't want to be seen, do we?'

'You mean *you* don't,' Speare said, stood by the door, his face drawn, the worry in his eyes. 'They're dead, all of them.'

'Who do you mean?'

'I mean they died, all those people I helped with their PCs, the ones I gave you info on. Why're they dead?'

He shrugged. 'I don't know. Suicide, wasn't it?'

'What did you do?' Speare started moving towards him, then stopped, catching himself. 'You told them what you knew, didn't you?'

He laughed. 'You think I made them kill themselves? How would I possibly do that?'

'Because you knew what they'd done...'

'They made the choice. What's it to you? Because the police talked to you, now you're worried?'

Speare looked away, then down at the floor. 'I didn't say anything...'

'Good. Because I know all about you, remember?'

Speare stared at him, his fists balling, tears appearing in his eyes. 'You can't keep doing this, and I won't...'

'You'll do as I say.' He stepped closer, making Speare shrink back a little. 'I need more information.'

'No, I can't do it again...'

'You can. You will. You haven't got any choice, have you?'

Speare looked down, shaking his head. 'But the police...'

'Know nothing. They're brainless, I told you before...'

'How come they came to me?'

He smiled, tried to be reassuring. 'Blind luck. Don't worry. One more piece of information and I'll leave you in peace.'

Speare let out a sigh as he said, 'Who this

time?'

He reached into his coat, then took out the information he had put together, sealed in an envelope, including a photograph of the man. He reached out and put it on the edge of the sofa, then stood back. A cough tried to rise to his mouth, but he swallowed it down, as Speare reached out for the envelope with his gloved hands, his eyes raised with suspicion.

The spectacled son ripped open the envelope, read the information, his large eyes, growing even wider, and his face reddening. 'A policeman? He's one of them? I can't, you're mad...'

They both turned their heads when a croaky voice called through the house.

'My mother needs me,' Speare said.

'You wouldn't want her to find out about you, would you?'

Speare had turned, heading towards the door, but stopped, and stared back at him. 'You wouldn't. Please...'

'I won't, if you help me. This one last time.'

Speare held his stare for a moment, then looked back out into the hallway, towards his mother. 'One last time. That's it. Then we're done.'

'Then we're done.' He smiled.

Stack was waiting for them, arms folded, when they entered the incident room. He was resting against DS Carthew's desk, smiling at her, chatting. But his deepest, grumpy scowl found Moone as he entered, followed by Butler.

'Broke up the party, did we?' Stack said, straightening up.

'Yeah,' Butler said, with a sarcastic smile. 'Call us the party poopers.'

'It's not funny,' Stack said, standing close to her, his hands behind his back. 'None of this is funny. People are dying, Butler. Old people, vulnerable people. Have you got elderly parents, Butler?'

'My dad, sir.'

'You wouldn't want him to get sick with this, would you?'

She sighed, went over to her desk. 'Heaven forbid.'

Stack watched her, his face thunderous, then turned his eyes on Moone. 'She's an interesting one, your partner, isn't she, Moone?'

Moone had sat down, busying himself and trying to be invisible. 'Yes sir. She's certainly interesting. Never boring.'

Stack nodded. 'She knows all sorts, Butler does. Rubbed shoulders with every kind of scum. Rubs off after a while, doesn't it?'

Butler stopped what she was doing and faced Stack, arms folded, her face flushed. 'What does that mean… sir?'

'There was a call for you,' Stack said, staring at her. 'Has some information for you, apparently. Left an address. It's on your desk.'

Butler looked around her desk, then pulled a post-it note from her monitor. Moone watched her brow corrugate as she stared at whatever was written there.

'We all know who lives there, don't we?' Stack said, giving a gruff laugh, before he headed to the door. 'Better run along and see what they want.'

Butler beckoned Moone. 'Let's go.'

'Where're we going?'

'Hartley,' Butler said, grabbing her phone.

'Hartley? Who's that?'

'It's a place,' Carthew said.

He looked at her as he was following Butler out. 'Thanks.'

Carthew stared at him. 'Thinking of buying another caravan, or are you nicely shacked up with that teenager you're seeing?'

Moone didn't say anything, just rushed to keep up with Butler.

He stepped out into the hallway, hearing Speare talking to his mother in the conservatory. He crept down, listening to their banal conversation, peering into the darkness. He looked round the door, the put upon son propping up the old fraud, giving her some water. Before Speare came out again, he crept back to the living room.

'She needed a drink,' Speare said, his voice

still filled with suspicion.

'You're a good son.' The man smiled. 'Would be a shame if you spoilt it all now.'

'OK, I'll give you what you need...'

'Good decision. The right decision. But right now, I need to use your toilet.'

'You're not supposed to use...'

'I'll clean it after and I am wearing gloves.'

'Throw them in the bin. There's another pack by the basin.'

'Why don't you get the info, put it on a stick, so I can get out of your hair?' The man smiled, then passed Speare, giving him a wide berth. He headed up the stairs a little way, then stopped, listening out for signs of what Speare was doing. He heard him opening up his laptop, then the chimes rang out, the signal that the machine was booting up. So the man crept back down, careful not to make a sound and then headed towards the conservatory. He stood in the doorway, hearing the harsh sound of the old woman breathing, a snore beginning to build. He stepped in, checking behind him, making sure Speare wasn't in the room. He was a trusting fool, he thought, and found the old woman in her lounge chair, a blanket pulled over her. He looked around the dark corners and saw cushions on the corner sofa, near the curtained off windows. He grabbed one, then gripped it in his gloved hands, feeling his heart begin to thud a little in his chest. His excitement grew, twisting and unfolding, making his hands tremble as he lowered the pillow over her face. He pushed it down, stiffening the muscles in his arms, feeling her slowly awaken, her hands reaching out, clawing. He pushed down, harder, grunting.

Her hands tore a little at his short sleeves as she blindly struggled for air.

Then the hands fell away. He stayed there, holding the cushion over her face for a minute, breathing hard.

He spun round, but the hallway was empty. He threw the cushion on the sofa, then crept back to the living room, where he found Speare sitting at the desk in the corner, typing away, a memory stick inserted into his laptop.

'Have you got it for me?' he asked.

Speare turned round in his chair. 'Yes. What if the police come and talk to me...'

'They won't...'

Speare handed over the memory stick. 'How do you know? They...'

'Because you'll be dead.' The man straightened up, stared at him. Then he pointed a thumb in the direction of his mother's room. 'Your mum's sleeping now. For ever.'

Speare jumped to his feet, his bulbous milk bottle eyes swelling even more with horror. 'What have you done?!'

The man blocked his way, shoved him backwards, knocking him back to his desk.

'You... you, bastard,' Speare spat, shaking all

over, his fists clenching.

'You've not got much left to live for now, have you?'

'Let me help her!' the son made another lurch for the door but the man stood in his way.

'Too late. She's better off now. Shame she didn't see it coming.' He laughed.

The fist swung awkwardly for him, and slow, the swing of a man who had never struck out before in his life. Had only ever been hit. He stepped back, ducking out of the way of the next few swipes, laughing at the ridiculous display.

'Calm down,' he said. 'Breathe. Sit down. Think.'

Speare was breathing hard, tears in his eyes, magnified by his glasses, bent over, looking up at him with hate in his eyes. 'You're evil.'

'Sit down.'

Speare did as he was told, collapsing in the chair, then put his face in his hands. He walked round him, listening to his sobs, realising he didn't have time for chitchat and the usual psychological games he liked to play. He looked up at the shelf of books, then at a metal bookend, formed into some kind of bird. He grasped it, weighing it in his hand, then looked round at Speare.

He raised it, staring at his balding scalp, the thud of excitement rising up again, a burning overtaking him as he brought it down on the son's head.

CHAPTER 20

Moone had noted the pinched look on Butler's face, the way her skin retained the scarlet hue longer than it normally did. That was the thing with Butler, he thought to himself as she drove them into Mannamead, you could piss her off or wind her up, but it was water off a grumpy duck's back after a little while. It was all pretence with her, a big show and a few well-placed huffs. So this was different, the menacing look in her eyes, the hint of trepidation.

Who the bloody hell were they off to meet? Moone kept glancing at her, trying to fathom it out, not wanting to broach the subject too soon.

'Stop it, you wally,' she said, glaring at him, then taking a left turn into a residential street.

'What?'

'I can feel your eyes burning into me, Moone, so stop it.' She put her foot down, then slowed, signalling, taking another turning. 'Hartley. This is Hartley.'

Moone nodded, staring round at the nice

houses, the relatively clean streets, which were empty. One jogger was all they spotted, a chubby, red-faced jogger who looked like he might be heading for a heart attack. That's what the lockdown had done, forced the usual couch potatoes outside, getting them out of the front door more than they had ever been before. Some things about the lockdown he didn't want to change, he found himself thinking.

Butler slowed down outside a large, whitewashed house with a long stretch of gravel driveway. The house had huge windows, an arched set of fancy double doors. Two massive columns guarded the doors.

As they parked up on the drive, the front door opened and a stocky man in a white short-sleeved shirt came out. He had a shaved head, thick, tattooed arms. He stood for a moment, watching them before he came closer, his look of deep concentration fixed on Butler.

What the hell was going on? Moone's gut told him gangster, drug dealer, hit man, or all of the above.

'Palmer,' Butler said, through the corner of her mouth. 'Shaun Palmer. Don't suppose you've heard of the Palmers.'

'No, I haven't.'

'They're a big name round here. You don't piss off the Palmers, don't try any funny business in one of their pubs or clubs.'

Moone nodded. 'I get it. You've had run-ins

with them before...'

'You could say that.' Butler pushed open her door. 'Let me do the talking, London boy.'

Moone shrugged, then followed Butler out of the car and up the drive.

Palmer walked closer, his arms folded across his chest. Another man, almost interchangeable with Shaun Palmer, stepped out of the house behind him, watching.

'How many of them are there?' Moone whispered.

'Six brothers.' Butler sidled up to Shaun Palmer. 'What do you want, Mr Palmer?'

Shaun's grey-blue eyes turned to Moone. 'Who's this?'

'DCI Peter Moone,' Butler said. 'He's with me. Where I go, he goes.'

'Hope he can keep his mouth shut,' Shaun said, staring into Moone's eyes for a few seconds, then he turned and headed back towards the house. 'Come in for a coffee.'

Moone stared at Butler when she didn't move. 'Are we going in?'

'Maybe you should stay out here.'

'No way. We're in this together.'

Butler nodded, then went up to the front door, which was being guarded by another of the brothers. She went in, so Moone followed into a cream tiled hallway that stretched on far into the house. The sun glowed along a line of windows at the far end, while on his right a wide ornate staircase curled up into the house.

'This way,' the man said, turning on the spot to face them and pointing a thumb behind him. 'The kitchen.'

Moone noticed the man wasn't as young as he first thought when he stopped in the huge clinical kitchen, resting his back against a gigantic Aga oven, his arms folded. There were creases round his eyes, grey hair around his ears.

'I'd say welcome to my home,' the man said, a toothy smile on his face. 'But you know you're not.'

'We do,' Butler said, mirroring his stance. 'Why don't you get on with it, so we can get out of here?'

Palmer turned to Moone, looking him over. 'So, they've saddled you with this streak of piss, have they, Mandy?'

'DCI streak of piss, if you don't mind,' Moone said, staring back at the man.

'He's got a sense of humour though. Palmer,' the man said. 'Shaun Palmer. I'd shake your hand, but you know...'

'Covid,' Moone said.

'That too,' Palmer said, as another, younger man came in, his meaty body squeezed into a white t-shirt, tattoos all over his arms.

'Can't believe you're entertaining these fuckers,' the young man said, staring at Butler as if he wanted to spit at her.

'Calm the fuck down, Lee,' Palmer said, then

pointed to his own top lip. 'See this here scar, mate?'

Moone saw a thin scar running from his top lip to just below his nose. 'I see it.'

'A fucking Doris did that. You see, back in the day, you didn't just wander into someone else's territory. You did, you got fucked over. We were Stonehouse beys. One day this little bitch comes into Stonehouse from Devonport. Bold as brass. Walks right up to me and clumps me right in the mouth...'

'You'd stolen my brother's bike,' Butler said and huffed. 'What did you want, Shaun? I'm about ready to fuck off.'

Shaun huffed out a laugh. 'You know my older brother, Neil, right?'

'Course, what about him?'

'You heard what happened to his boy? My nephew?' Shaun shook his head, turned and looked away. 'Fuck. Shit. Poor little bastard. Barely seventeen and they says he killed himself. Jumped in front of a fucking train...'

'I heard. I'm sorry.' Butler looked down at her shoes.

'He didn't kill himself. He had no reason to. Nothing. You lot were too happy to write it off, but it was all bollocks.'

'Why're you telling us this?' Butler asked.

'I heard you were looking into some suicides...'

'How did you hear that?'

'I hear a lot of things.'

Lee let out a harsh breath then faced his brother. 'This is a waste of fucking time... these dickheads don't know anything.'

Shaun put his head close to his brother's, staring him in the eye. 'Shut the fuck up, Lee. Let me handle this. Go on, fuck off.'

Lee stared back, then switched his pissed-off eyes to Moone and Butler before he ambled out of the room.

The word 'cunts' was heard being muttered, which made Shaun laugh.

'You'll have to excuse my brother,' Shaun said. 'Can't stand you lot. But who can?'

'Let's go, Moone,' Butler said and turned to head back out of the kitchen, but Shaun moved fast and cut her off.

'Hang on, I was talking.' Shaun held up his hands. 'My nephew, Daryl, didn't kill himself...'

'There were witnesses that saw him jump in front of the train.' Butler folded her arms.

'True. But he didn't do it voluntarily. I know he didn't.'

'How do you know?'

'Cause he had everything going for him.'

'Sometimes that makes it worse.'

Shaun looked down, shaking his head. 'You always were a...'

'Can I ask a question?' Moone said, walking up to Palmer.

'Maybe you've got more sense, go ahead,'

Palmer said.

Moone leaned against the work surface. 'You had any dealings with Stannard, the solicitor who ripped everyone off?'

'No, why the fuck would I?' Palmer said. 'What's that got to do with my nephew's death?'

'There's the possibility of a connection, but we're not sure.'

'I thought you lot got someone for Stannard's murder, didn't you?'

'We did. What about a psychic? Would your nephew visit a psychic?'

Shaun looked Moone up and down as though he was about to punch him. 'What the fuck? What sort of shite is this, Mand? Psychics? Fucking Stannard?'

Butler sighed. 'We think most of the suicides we're looking into visited a certain Madam Revello.'

'What the fuck? That psychic old dear? What, you think she... what the hell do you think?'

'We can't discuss that,' Moone said. 'I know these sound like strange questions, but if you could find out if your nephew visited Revello, or had his computer fixed lately by anyone professional, say from anyone who came to his house...'

'Sounds like you two are chasing your fucking tails.' Shaun shook his head. 'Right, OK, I'll find out. He had a girlfriend somewhere. I'll get her tracked down and ask her.'

'We'd appreciate that,' Moone said.

'Would you?' Palmer looked at Butler, stared at her. 'Would you appreciate that, Mand?'

'Don't call me that,' she said, her voice barely a whisper. 'I'm DI Mandy Butler to you.'

'Acting DI, I hear.' Palmer gave a big shit-chewing grin.

Butler looked at Moone, her face red, but a subtle smile appearing. 'You know why I punched him? You want to know? My little brother's bike. They stole a little boy's bike. Got it back, didn't I?'

Butler started on her way, nudging Palmer to the side. He didn't say anything for a moment, just watched them leave. As they headed back towards the front door, Palmer shouted, 'You don't tell anyone yous was here, you get me?! I've got a fucking reputation!'

Moone decided keeping schtum was the best course of action as they climbed in the car. Butler slammed the car door, then sat there, still red-faced, staring daggers at the house.

'You're not going to come out with something?' she asked.

'I didn't know you had a younger brother,' he said.

She turned to him and grimaced, as though he had created a bad smell. 'That's what you got from that? My heritage? Yes, I have a younger brother. Step-brother, actually. Hardly see him, cause he turned into a little shit. Quite a thank you for getting his bike back. Won't be doing that again.' Butler started the engine.

'He probably won't need to have his bike rescued from gangsters, to be fair.' Moone smiled, but she ignored him and turned the car around.

'Funny though, isn't it?' Butler said after a few minutes.

'What is?'

'The older brother not talking to us about this. Desmond. He's tried to get away from the family business, and start up his own little sideline, but they usually manage to drag him back when they're in trouble.'

Moone looked out onto the streets, thinking. 'Maybe he doesn't want to get involved or doesn't think there's anything to look into.'

'Exactly. What makes him so happy with it all? What does he know?'

'Are we going to pay him a visit?'

'Not right now, I don't think. Let's wait and see what the girlfriend says.'

Moone started to say something, but his phone started ringing in his pocket. He took it out to answer it. 'DCI Moone?'

'Hey, boss,' Harding said, sounding excited. 'Just had a report of a fire at Madam Revello's house. Thought you'd want to know.'

'Jesus,' Moone said, then ended the call. 'Revello's place. Now!'

They had to pull up and park at the end of Madam Revello's street, as two fire engines were blocking the way. The fire was just about out by the time they climbed out and watched the firefighters dampening down the house and inspecting the scene. The street was lined with neighbours, all watching, mesmerised by what was happening. A couple of the firefighters started rolling up the hoses, shouting commands at each other, running back and forth. The windows and front door were blackened, charred, and smoke still drifted out.

Moone noticed the ambulance parked close by that was getting ready to leave, one of the paramedics climbing aboard. He hurried over, trying to see into the back of the ambulance.

'Have you got a survivor?' Moone asked the male paramedic, showing his ID.

'Yeah, male, smoke inhalation and burns,' the paramedic said. 'Taking him in now.'

Moone nodded, looking inside and saw what looked like Ian Speare strapped to a gurney, an oxygen mask over his mouth. The doors shut, the ambulance went racing off, the siren blaring.

'Who was that?' Butler asked behind him.

'Ian Speare. Where's Madam Revello?'

'I'm afraid she's no longer with us,' a familiar voice said behind him.

Moone turned to see DS Carthew stood there, arms folded. 'What happened?'

'What does it look like?' Carthew asked. 'A fire happened.'

'Don't be bloody funny,' Butler growled. 'Was it arson?'

'Looks like it, they said. Accelerant used all round the living room.' Carthew looked up the street, towards the other houses that curved round the bend. 'You know what I think?'

'No, we're not psychic,' Butler said, catching Moone's eye and tutting. 'Why don't you inform us?'

Carthew stared at her for a few seconds, the burn of anger in her eyes, then looked at Moone. 'I think Ian Speare was our man. For whatever reason, he was learning what he could about these people, blackmailing them for the money and then getting them to kill themselves so they couldn't report him. We were close to catching him, so he starts a fire, so him and his mother go out together.'

Moone looked at her, then at the house, thinking it all over, realising it made sense. 'No one saw anyone else?'

'Not so far,' Carthew said. 'We'll keep knocking though. I think I'm right. What do you think... boss?'

Moone nodded. 'It's possible. Seems to fit. Let's look at the footage of our first victim again, see if we can match the man in the back with Speare. If we're lucky, we can. OK, let's get on it and see if we can find the evidence that links

Speare to all this. Well, done, Carthew.'

Carthew smiled, only slightly, before heading off towards the uniforms going door to door.

Moone turned to see Butler staring at him, eyebrows raised. 'What?'

'Well done, Carthew?'

'Credit where it's due.'

'She has some theory that he's behind all of this. A theory that was pretty bloody obvious.'

Moone turned away, started heading towards the car. 'I wanted to be encouraging. You feel bad after blaming her for my caravan burning down.'

'She wanted you to think that. She's still a psycho. You're so changeable.'

They climbed in the car. Moone smiled, trying to lighten the mood. 'You're jealous.'

Butler started the engine. 'You wish.'

'We can't even visit him in hospital.'

'Why not?'

'Coronavirus.'

Butler sat back. 'Shit.'

Then a phone was ringing, and Butler stared at him expectantly.

'Not my phone.'

Butler huffed, then pulled out hers and answered it. 'DI Mandy Butler. Who's this? How did you get my number, Shaun? Oh, you have your ways, do you? What the bloody hell do you want? Where is she? Right, we'll take care of this.'

When she hung up, Moone said, 'They've located the girlfriend already?'

'Pretty efficient, aren't they? We should recruit them.'

The address Shaun Palmer gave Butler for the girl was a block of flats on Albert Road, not far from the Torpoint Ferry, close to where Moone and Butler had nearly been murdered one afternoon. It replayed in his mind without him realising, his heart starting to pound in his chest. He saw Butler against the wall, her face white, the man and the knife in front of her, cutting off her escape. He pushed it away, looking at Butler as she parked up in a litter strewn side street filled with a few shops and an almost derelict looking pub. He wondered if she ever thought of that day. It had been the day everything changed between them.

Butler pointed the way, across the desolate high street, over to some dirty looking 1930s style flats. Seagulls squawked, hovering in the air, swooping down at some bin bags out the front of the place.

'What do you think you're doing here?' Butler said and Moone's head sprang round to see Shaun Palmer outside the building, leaning against the wall, smoking a cigarette.

'Just making sure you morons do your job,' he said, straightening up and flicking his cigarette into the undergrowth. 'Top floor. Come on.'

'Where do you think you're going?' Butler asked.

'She wants me here when you talk to her,' Shaun said.

'What's your vested interest in all this?'

'What's that supposed to mean? For fuck's sake...'

'I can't see your older brother here. He doesn't seem bothered. Why're you digging around?'

Shaun stepped closer, rage filling his eyes.

'Two metres back,' Butler barked.

Shaun stared at her. 'He was family. No one else seems to give a shit, he's got no one to talk for him, so I'm doing it. Think what you like. You coming up or what?'

Butler took out some gloves, passed a pair to Moone, then nodded at Shaun. 'Lead the way.'

Shaun eyed them both, then turned and headed into the dark coolness of the interior of the building, then up the metal stairway, taking them to the upper floor. It was barren on the top floor and all the other floors, grey, boot-marked floors and graffiti-daubed walls and front doors. Shaun knocked on the middle door, then stood back.

A young woman with dark skin, and black shiny hair tied back answered. She wore a long beige cardie over her slender frame, her arms wrapped round herself.

The girl looked at them, only nodding to Shaun briefly.

'Hi,' Moone said, showing his ID. 'DCI Peter Moone. We'd like a word with you about Daryl.'

She nodded, her dark eyes jumping to Shaun, staring at him. 'I heard. You'd better come in.'

The girl went into a short hallway, the smell of spicy cooking mixing with the gritty and deep scent of marijuana finding Moone's nostrils. She took them through to an untidy, cramped lounge, with a small kitchen to one side. The young woman sat on the sofa, picking up a cigarette from an ashtray and lighting it again.

Shaun stood by the windows, arms folded, watching the girl intently, while Moone kept his distance, his back to the kitchen door. 'We didn't get introduced.'

'Marie,' the girl said, taking a drag, then blowing the smoke upwards. 'It's nice to have some company. Gets lonely here, with all this lockdown business.'

'Hopefully, won't last too much longer.' Moone smiled.

'You're kidding, right?' Shaun said, the anger rising in his voice. 'You think those bastards in their ivory towers will let us roam free again? No fucking way. They'll use this to keep us locked up. They'll want to be able to track us and all that shit. This is just an excuse.'

'You're not helping,' Butler growled.

'Marie.' Moone smiled again. 'I know these are difficult questions to ask, but we need to ask them. OK?'

She took another puff. 'OK.'

Moone nodded. 'Do you know why Daryl took his own life?'

Marie's eyes jumped to Shaun again, then away, staring into space. She shook her head. 'No, I don't. I wish I did. Every morning I wake up and it's there, right in my face. I keep asking myself, if...'

'There was nothing you could've done,' Shaun said. 'Cause he didn't kill himself.'

'Please,' Moone said.

Shaun's eyes jumped to Moone. 'What you going to do, big man? Arrest me for the truth? Go fucking ahead.'

Moone turned to Marie. 'Did Daryl ever visit a psychic?'

Marie looked up, staring at Moone, about to take another puff. 'Yeah, I mean I dragged him along...'

'Do you know the name?'

'Um... this old lady, we saw. Got a funny name...'

'Madam something?' Butler asked.

Marie nodded. 'Yeah, um... madam, like it was an Italian name... or something.'

'Madam Revello?' Moone asked.

'That's it,' Marie said. 'What's she got to do with this?'

'They don't fucking know, Marie.' Shaun took out a cigarette and stuck it between his lips.

'Did he have a laptop?' Moone asked.

'Yeah, his dad bought it for him, but I don't know where it is...'

'Did he ever take it to a shop to get repaired or have someone come round to fix it?'

Marie shrugged. 'I don't know. It was top of the line. Think his dad sorted all that.'

'Listen, Marie. I've got to ask, but did you know if Daryl had any secrets that, well, he really wouldn't want anyone to find out? Anything anyone could use against him?'

Moone saw it, Marie's eyes jumping to Shaun again, then the nervous twitch of her hands, a quick hungry puff of her cigarette. She was hiding something. But the problem would be getting her away from Shaun Palmer.

'No, there's nothing,' she said, before taking another nervous puff.

Moone took out his card, then put it on her coffee table. 'That's my number. Call me if you think of anything, or you want to talk.'

Marie stared at his card, then nodded.

Then Shaun has lurched towards it, snapped it up in his fingers, staring at Moone with a subtle smile, a look of victory in his eyes. 'Nice, yeah, we'll get in touch if there's anything more. Won't we, Marie?'

She nodded.

'Fine,' Moone said, nodding to Butler. 'We'll

make a move.'

They headed out, followed by Shaun, then by Marie, who trailed a little way behind down the stairs and out to the front door.

'That was a waste of fucking time,' Shaun said, lighting his cigarette, as they stood outside the building.

'What's it matter to you?' Butler snapped.

Moone ignored their sniping and looked back at the young woman, who was lighting another cigarette with her last one. She caught his eye and stared at him. Her mouth seemed to open, as if she was trying to communicate something. Moone looked round at Shaun and Butler, listening to them sparring. Then he made a dash for it, a few quick steps towards the young woman.

'Where the fuck're you going?' Shaun shouted, but Moone reached her, getting much closer than social distancing allowed.

'You OK?' he asked.

She hesitated, then lowered her voice. 'He… Daryl, well, he was… gay.'

CHAPTER 21

'I thought he was going to knock your block off,' Butler said and pulled on the handbrake after she parked at Derriford Hospital. The car park, across from the main entrance, near the recently built restaurant complex, was mostly empty. People weren't coming to the hospital, fearful of catching coronavirus, temporarily easing the burden on the NHS.

'He didn't seem pleased,' Moone said, as he climbed out. 'Did he?'

Butler climbed out, then followed Moone as he started towards the main entrance, crossing the empty road, and passing only the occasional member of the public.

'So, she said Daryl was gay?' Butler said, overtaking him as they reached the M&S shop to the right of the main entrance.

'Yep. I suppose that's a pretty big secret to want to conceal…'

'Yeah, if your uncles are psychopathic gangsters.'

They walked through the main corridor, past the restaurant, then headed towards the emergency department.

'You sure we're going to get a look at Speare?' Moone asked, as they walked the unusually quiet corridors towards the Emergency Department.

'I told you, I phoned and the doctor I talked to said Speare's in the green emergency department. That's the non-covid emergency department.'

'Good,' Moone said and headed along the corridor to where the waiting area was, which was usually crammed with waiting patients, either in seats, cubicles or on gurneys. There were few people there, and most of the staff were sitting round doing paperwork or chatting.

He went up to the desk at the centre of it all, right by a row of curtained-off cubicles and showed his ID to a couple of doctors.

'We're here to see Ian Speare,' Moone said. 'I'm DCI Peter Moone.'

Another doctor looked up from a computer screen, then came over. She was a dark-haired, pretty young woman who came over, giving a tired and brief smile.

'Doctor Emily Taylor-Cant,' she said. 'Mr Speare is in a room down the corridor.'

'How is he?' Butler asked.

'Unconscious,' the doctor said. She pointed the way, then walked round them and headed to the rooms back along the corridor. 'He's suffered severe burns and lung damage. His throat was badly swollen, cutting off his air supply. He's intubated right now.'

The doctor opened the door to the room, where Speare was lying on a bed, monitors and wires beside him. He seemed to be breathing, the machine beeping. A nurse was there, taking his vitals, then left after a brief conversation with the doctor.

'What's his chances?' Moone asked.

The doctor faced Moone, hands on her hips. 'He's committed some crime, hasn't he?'

'Possibly. We're not sure, but we'd like to speak to him as soon as possible.'

The doctor made a face, then turned to look towards her patient. 'I'm afraid Mr Speare won't be saying anything for a good while. Even if he was conscious, he has damage to his larynx. We'll let you know if the situation changes.'

Moone nodded. 'How's the covid situation?'

The doctor let out a breath. 'Quiet to be honest. The dirty ITU beds... I'm sorry, that sounds terrible. You see the covid part of the emergency department is referred to as dirty, the non-covid part as clean. I think they're rethinking the labels.'

Moone let out an empty laugh. 'I'm not surprised. So, you haven't got many cases, yet?'

'No, not many, but we've got 300 ITU beds ready for it, for when we supposedly hit the peak.

It's going to get bad, they say.'

'Let's hope it doesn't get that bad.'

The doctor nodded, a little sadly, he thought, and headed off out of the room.

'You know what I keep wondering?' Butler asked, staring at the patient across the room.

'What?' Moone asked.

'What was Palmer trying to hide? Why was he trying to keep us from getting close to Marie?'

Moone shrugged. 'I don't know, but something's not right there. We need to talk to Daryl's father. But first let's go to the morgue and see what Dr Parry's found out.'

Dr Parry was still wearing his green gown and gloves that he peeled off and discarded in a yellow waste bin. There was the pale, bluish, wrinkled DB of Madam Revello lying on the morgue table. Most of her was covered up, but Moone could see the post-mortem scar running up her sternum. A young-looking technician took away her tray of blood and other fluids, ready to be poured down a drain.

'I'm surprised you risked coming to the hospital,' Parry said, his usual wide smile stretching his stubble-covered face. 'Everyone seems to be staying away.'

'We haven't got much choice,' Butler said, putting on her mask.

'I've been tested,' Parry said. 'I haven't got it, if that makes you feel better.'

'What did you find out?' Moone asked, pointing to Madam Revello.

'Well, death during a fire may be due to the effects of breathing in toxic fumes given off by the fire, carbon monoxide, but also cyanide. It could be heat also, and possibly something to do with the initiation of a vagally-mediated "reflex" cardiac arrest following the stimulation of nerve endings in the larynx.' Parry smiled. 'Did you get that?'

'Sort of,' Moone said.

'I hear your survivor is suffering from smoke inhalation and burns.'

'That's right,' Butler said. 'And cutting out the gobbledygook, what about Revello? She die from the fire, smoke, or what?'

Parry indicated to Revello's open mouth. 'I found fibres in her mouth. Polyester, wool type fibres...'

'There was a shaggy, woolly pillow near the body,' Moone said.

Parry nodded. 'I found no indication in her mouth, or lungs, no soot or chemicals, to suggest she breathed in smoke during the fire.'

'So she wasn't breathing when the fire happened?' Moone said and stepped closer. 'That means Speare could've smothered her before he set fire to the house. Doesn't suggest a third person was there.'

'What about his hands?' Parry said. 'We need to check him for fibres, and the clothes he was wearing. If he did press the pillow forcefully on her, then there might be trace evidence...'

'But he could have that innocently,' Butler said. 'Looks like he tried knocking himself off. Couldn't take her finding out what a bad boy he'd been. I think we can lay it to rest with him.'

Parry shrugged. 'Well, you're the detectives.'

Moone looked over the body of the old lady, the woman who once promised to be able to see into people's futures. An ironic thought occurred to him, but he pushed it away for being distasteful.

'She certainly didn't see this coming, did she?' Parry said, his smile stretching wide.

Moone kept his face straight, even though a large part of him wanted to laugh.

'Trust you,' Butler said and tutted, then looked at Moone. 'Come on, let's leave this depraved man with his friends.'

Moone walked out, taking note that it was quiet around him, that the hospital was almost silent apart from an air ambulance helicopter coming down a few hundred yards away, blowing down-draft towards them. It was getting past late afternoon, he noted as he looked at his phone.

'What now?' Butler asked. 'Do we go and talk to Daryl's father?'

'Maybe we should call it a day,' he said, smiling at her through his tiredness.

'You dumping me?' Butler laughed.

'Just for the evening. We'll go and see the father in the morning. Looks like we might've wrapped up the whole suicide thing anyway.'

Butler nodded, then huffed out a laugh. 'I suppose you want to get back to that young girlfriend of yours.'

'To be honest, I wish I was going back to the caravan and then to bed.' He forced a smile, feeling a sadness creep over him that he couldn't quite get a grasp of. Something was unsettling him, and he wasn't sure it was the case or his own life.

'Go on then, I've got paperwork to do before I go home,' she said.

'I thought you'd be rushing to get home.'

'Yeah, right. Him indoors... well, he's a pain, and don't get me started on his daughter.'

'OK, see you in the morning.'

Moone stared at the shiny silver key that Rachel had cut for him about a week ago. He put it in the lock, wrestled to unlock the door, but nothing happened. He let out a breath, leaning on the door, then pressed the buzzer for her flat.

Rachel opened the door, then stood there, a dish cloth in one hand, her eyebrows raised. 'You still ringing the bell? What's wrong with your key?'

He held it up. 'Tried it, but it wouldn't work.'

'Bloody key cutters. I'll get another one cut.' She took it off him, then smiled and kissed him.

'Thanks,' he said. 'I needed that.'

'Bad day?' she asked, turning and heading back up the short flight of stairs to her flat. She went in through the inner door and into the living area, past the bedroom. It was not a massive place, but nice, clean, nicely decorated by Rachel. The kitchen was narrow but modern, clean as always. Rachel put the kettle on and turned to face him as he started to pull his tie off. He started looking round, trying to get his bearings again, wondering how he had got to this place in his life. An image of his family flickered into his mind, making his stomach sink once more.

'What happened then?' she asked. 'People not keeping socially distant?'

He laughed. 'No, not that. The suicide thing.'

'Really? Thought you were off that? Tea?'

'Please. Well, we are really. Looks like we've got someone for it.'

Rachel's head sprung up as she put teabags into mugs. 'Really? Who?'

'Can't really discuss that.' He smiled awkwardly. 'But looks promising, although...'

'Although what?' She stopped what she was doing and came close, putting her arms around his neck, moving her face close to his.

He could smell her sweet perfume, her moisturiser, and the fruity shampoo she used, making his tiredness retreat a little as his desire woke up, stretched and yawned.

'I get this feeling,' he said, then shrugged. 'But it's just self-doubt, I guess.'

'What feeling?' She kissed his lips a little.

'The feeling that something's not quite right, or I'm missing a piece of the puzzle. Am I sounding like a cliché detective yet?'

'A little bit.' She kissed him again, pressing her warm body to his. Then she looked into his eyes. 'But I like it.'

As she went back to making tea, Moone said, 'I've never really asked, but wasn't there anyone else on the scene before me?'

'Like who?'

'A boyfriend. Young, muscular, good looking.' He smiled. 'The exact opposite of me.'

She shook her head. 'You're putting yourself down. But yes, there was someone. But as it went on, I realised they weren't really into me.'

'How's that possible?'

She let out a short laugh. 'Well, he just wasn't into sex, I guess. He got more joy out of his... well, his hobbies. So, we decided to be friends.'

Moone raised his shoulders. 'His loss is my gain.'

'Don't forget it.' Then she looked at him strangely.

'What?'

'Sometimes I think maybe your job might be my competition.'

'Never. I'll quit tomorrow.'

She laughed again. 'You'd better. What about dinner? Chinese or pizza? Everywhere else seems to be shut.'

'Chinese then.'

She passed him his tea. 'I'll order, then we'll have time to fool around a bit.'

'Oh, will we?'

She came over and kissed him again, longer, her tongue slipping into his mouth. He felt like a young man again, having flashes of being in a darkened park or behind the school, against a wall, kissing hungrily before they were caught out.

She stopped kissing him, then looked down. 'Well, looks like someone's woken up.'

They both straightened up when the buzzer echoed through the flat.

'That's bloody quick,' Moone said and laughed.

'I haven't even ordered yet.'

'Strange.' Moone turned to the hallway, facing the door. 'Are you expecting anyone?'

'No, I'll go and see.'

Moone followed her down the stairs and watched her open the door, and heard Rachel say, 'Hello.'

'Hi,' was the only thing the person managed to say before Moone recognised the voice.

'Alice?' he called, moving round Rachel and standing on the front step.

Alice was stood in jeans and a cardie, adorned in surgical gloves and a mask. 'Hi, Dad.'

'What're you doing here?' he asked, a sudden panic rising through him. 'Is everything OK? The kids?'

'It's all OK.' Alice's eyes jumped to Rachel behind him. 'You OK, Dad?'

'I'm fine. Alice, you shouldn't be here. There's restrictions...'

She nodded, then looked down. 'I know, I'm sorry, but it's not like I'm hugging you.'

He nodded, noting a hint of sadness in her voice. 'No, I know. Is everything OK?'

'Why don't you go out there?' Rachel said. 'You can stand and chat a couple of metres apart. I'll go order the takeaway.'

Moone stepped out, while Alice backed up the front path.

'I think you can take that off,' Moone said, pointing to her mask. 'Then I'll be able to see your lovely face.'

She was blushing a little as she lowered it. 'You're so uncool.'

'I try. Anyway, what's going on?' He absently started looking for a cigarette, forgetting for a moment he had quit. 'I can see something's not right.'

She shrugged. 'I just wanted to see you. Been a while...'

'I know. But you can't just show up...'

'Wouldn't she like it?' Alice pulled a child's

upset face.

Moone huffed. 'She's nice, Alice. Me living here isn't a permanent thing.'

'Does she know that? Because you look pretty cosy. Takeaway? Sounds like you've got your feet under the table.'

'I've got a life too.' Moone smiled, suddenly wanting to put his arms round her. 'When this is over, I'll give you a big hug.'

'Don't be soft and pathetic.'

'Maybe when this is over, you can come round and have dinner...'

'Tea, they say round here. Thanks, but I don't think so.'

'Why not?'

'Because she doesn't like me.'

Moone gave an exhausted laugh. 'What makes you say that?'

'The dirty look she gave me.' Alice stared at him, eyebrows raised.

'She didn't...'

'She was behind you, Dad. You didn't see. Anyway, I'm going. I've seen you, I've met her. Now I'm gone.'

Alice turned round and started off down the street.

'Alice!' he called, but she kept on going until she disappeared around the corner.

He watched the flames dancing, the smoke rising from the incinerator bin. He knew he was being hypnotised by the flames. He broke out of his dream, then picked up the bin bag that contained the clothes he had worn when he torched Speare's house. He threw the clothes in the bin, then stuffed them down using a four by two he had found in the shed. The flames started gorging on the clothes, more smoke drifting across to the neighbour's garden.

He coughed, the smoke blowing back at him a little, seeping down his throat. Then he doubled over, coughing harder, feeling like a lung might fly from his mouth. He shivered a little, feeling cold suddenly as the sun slowly went down. Hot and cold, cold then hot. It was the way he had been feeling off and on for a few days. He had tried to ignore it, but now it had gripped him, the fever having seized hold of him. He had all the symptoms, but there was no way he was going to phone the NHS line or visit the hospital. He was young enough to get over it.

He turned and looked at the other bag of stuff he had taken from Speare's house. Evidence. He crouched down over the sports bag, then unzipped it and looked at the laptop he made off with before he set the place alight. He had sat in the car, watching, long enough to see the flames spitting from the windows before he drove off, satisfied that he had disposed of the weakest link in the chain. But he had the information, and enough to carry on where he had left off. He had planned to wait it out, to ride the coronavirus storm and then get back to his calling. But the desire had become too great for him to deny.

He turned his head, hearing the distant ring of his mobile. He got to his feet, then picked up the sports bag and took it inside, through the open French doors.

The phone was ringing and vibrating across the kitchen work surface.

'Hello,' he said. 'Yes, everything's OK. Of course it's OK. I've been thinking. I don't think I can wait much longer...'

He paused, listening, then his heart began to hammer. 'What do you mean? How can he still be alive? How do you know? Oh shit. Well, if he's in Intensive Care, then he won't be talking to anyone. Don't panic. There'll be a way we can fix it, I just need to think. In the meantime I'm going to go ahead with my plan. Yes, yes, it'll be fine. The police officer will be next. I've got plenty of dirt on him.'

CHAPTER 22

It had been bothering Moone all morning, marring his breakfast time and his first coffee of the day. It had put him in a grump, as his mother used to say. Now they were driving towards Plympton, Butler at the wheel, both in silence. His stomach was knotted and when he took his first sip of the takeaway coffee Butler had brought him, it tasted bitter.

'All right, I'll bite,' Butler said as they reached the next set of lights, signs for Saltram House on their right. 'What's got you in a mood?'

'Nothing, it's OK.' He took another bitter sip. 'Has this got sugar in?'

'Sachets on the dashboard. Come on, let's talk it through and dispel some of the bad energy. Isn't that the sort of crap they say these days?'

'Alice turned up last night.'

'Alice? Where? At your new bit of stuff's place?'

'Rachel.'

'Yeah, I know. Rachel. Didn't go down well

then?' Butler took them right, over a small bridge, then left into an industrial estate that was lined with furniture stores and bathroom showrooms.

'I thought it was all right, but then Alice said something...'

Butler pulled up outside a large brick and glass warehouse building. 'What did she say?'

'That Rachel gave her a dirty look. It's ridiculous. Why would Rachel give her a dirty look?'

Butler made a face, then climbed out and headed towards the building that had a big sign that read: Palmer Food Deliveries.

'What was that face?' Moone asked as they reached a pair of large metal doors that were open, several people in light blue uniforms and wearing bike helmets coming out.

'Well, you trust your daughter, don't you?' Butler asked, heading into the interior of the place.

There was a reception desk, with a few uniformed people behind it, all wearing gloves and masks, while beyond them there seemed to be sectioned off counters where cooking was going on, the spicy scent of food, and the sizzle of frying.

'Mostly. But she's probably a bit put out.'

'Can I help?' a masked young man asked.

'Where's your boss?' Butler asked, showing her ID.

'You want one of the managers?' the young man said, looking around him, searching the kitchens.

'No, Desmond Palmer, the owner,' she said. 'Get him, *now.*'

'Where's the boss?' the flustered man said to the masked and gloved young woman next to him.

The woman shrugged and said, 'In his office?'

'Where's that?' Butler demanded.

'Follow the path right down the bottom,' the girl said.

Moone and Butler headed down a concrete pathway that took them alongside the sectioned-off small kitchens where various takeaway meals were being prepared then picked up by delivery drivers.

'You've got to go with who you trust more,' Butler said, looking over her shoulder at him before she knocked hard on the office door at the end of the warehouse.

'Jesus,' Moone groaned and rubbed his stubble. 'Why would Rachel have a problem with Alice?'

Butler let out a tired breath. 'If you don't know that, then I can't help you.'

The door opened and a stocky man in a pinstriped shirt faced them, looking pissed off. He was an older, more grey-haired copy of the other Palmer brothers, Moone thought as he took out his ID.

'What the fuck do you lot want?' Desmond Palmer groaned. 'I'm busy right now, trying to keep my business afloat during this whole fucking mess.'

'We want a chat,' Butler said. 'If that's quite all right with you?'

'Not right bloody now it's not.' Palmer sighed. 'But I don't suppose you lot won't give up easy.'

Palmer retreated into a bare room with dusty concrete floors, a battered metal desk at the back with a PC and monitor sat on it. There was paperwork covering the desk and a large mobile phone. The stocky businessman rested on the desk, and folded his arms over his meaty chest. Moone noted he had tattoos poking up out of his shirt collar.

'Go on, then,' Palmer said. 'What have I done now? You know I'm all above board, right?'

'We heard,' Butler said. 'We're sorry, but we're here to ask about your son, Daryl.'

'I know my son's name.' Palmer straightened up, a dark cloud moving over his face. 'He can't be in trouble, cause he's in Weston Mill. I go every week.'

'It's about his death,' Moone said.

'What about it?'

'We're looking into a series of suicides.'

Palmer narrowed his eyes, staring at Moone as he came closer. 'What? What do you mean looking into? A suicide's a suicide, isn't it?' Then Palmer looked down, seemed to notice how close he was and retreated to his desk.

'Usually it is,' Moone said. 'But we have reason to believe that some people who recently committed suicide might have been coerced into it...'

'Daryl did what he did.' Palmer looked down, hung his head. 'I'll never understand why, but he did. There was footage, caught on CCTV. They used it at the inquest.'

'We know,' Butler said. 'But we were wondering if you have reason to believe someone might've coerced him. Or used some information to force him to do it.'

Palmer stared at her. 'Information about me, you mean? No, no way. What info? Who put you up to this? You didn't just happen by here.'

'We can't divulge that...' Moone began.

'Bet it was one of my fuckwit brothers, wasn't it? Probably Shaun, the fucking moron.'

'Did you deal with Daryl's laptop?' Butler asked.

'His what?' Palmer asked.

'His laptop,' Moone said. 'We hear he had quite an expensive one, bought by you.'

'Yeah, I did get him one. But the thing disappeared. I wanted to look at it, see if there was any clue to... well, you know. But his girlfriend didn't have it. If you find it, I'd like to have it back.'

Moone exchanged glances with Butler before he said, 'Who did any servicing on it, repairs?'

'Never had any,' Palmer said. 'Didn't need any. Brand spanking new. So, what the fuck is this? You think my son killed himself because some bastard made him do it? That's bollocks. My son killed himself because...' Palmer welled up, then looked away. 'It's none of your fucking business, to be honest. But I know I should've been there for him. I should've...'

'You should've supported him over certain things?' Moone asked.

Palmer looked at him, staring at him, seeming to mull it all over before he nodded his head. 'It's cause of where I'm from, our way of life, I guess. You get a reputation as some kind of hard man. So your kid thinks they have to be a certain kind of man... but it wasn't like that. I loved my boy...' Palmer coughed, clearing his throat, and sniffed. Then he sharpened his gaze, fixing it on Moone again. 'You think there's something to all this? Someone made him do it?'

'It's just a line of enquiry we're following.'

Palmer shook his head. 'Na, it's bollocks. Has to be.' Then he stared at Moone again. 'But you will tell me if you find out anything, won't you?'

'If there's something to report,' Butler said. 'If we've got more questions, we will.'

'I'll be interested to find out,' Palmer said. 'Very interested.'

'Bet you would.' Butler huffed, then signalled for Moone to follow her. 'I think we're done here.'

Moone followed Butler to the car, thinking it all over, running the conversation back through his brain, and landing on the laptop again.

'What do you make of this laptop business?' Moone asked.

Butler unlocked the car, then leaned on the roof. 'Don't know. It's possible that Desmond Palmer's lying, and he just doesn't want us to see the laptop...'

'Have they gone through the evidence from Speare's house?' Moone asked and climbed in.

'Ongoing. Carthew is in charge of that job.'

'Let's go talk to her then. See if Speare had a nice new laptop.'

Butler sighed. 'Carthew again. You're obsessed.'

Then Moone's phone was ringing with a number he didn't recognise. 'DCI Peter Moone.'

'Hi,' a familiar voice said. 'It's Ashley, Simon Whittle's widow...'

'I remember. Sorry, I've been meaning to get in touch... Have you got any more information?'

She sighed, making Moone feel awkward.

'There's something I've got for you,' she said. 'Could be nothing, but I received a strange email the other day.'

'Really? From who?'

'I don't know. Seems to be from some kind

of service, with no name. But it's a bit weird, the message I mean.'

'You think It's related to our investigation?'

'I think so. I mean, if you read it too, you might think so.'

'I'll come now. I take it you're home?'

'Well, with this lockdown, I've got nowhere else to go.' She gave a sad little laugh.

'Yep, should've guessed that. I'll be over as soon as I can.'

When Moone ended the call, he looked at Butler and raised his eyebrows.

'Whittle's widow?' Butler asked. 'You're in demand today. Must be your aftershave.'

He gave a sarcastic laugh. 'She says she's got a weird email. Let's go and take a look.'

'Why don't I drop you off, then I'll go and talk to Carthew?'

'You talk to Carthew? You had a lobotomy?'

Butler shrugged. 'Well, I suspect what she'd really like is to see you. Seeing my mug will just piss her off, won't it?'

He shook his head. 'OK, have it your way. Let's go.'

Butler dropped him off at the old village that seemed to be a lot quieter than last time. The only person he saw was on a cycle and they tore past wearing a mask and gloves. It felt eerie as he walked towards Mrs Whittle's house, slipping on surgical gloves himself and preparing for social distancing.

Her door opened before he got to it, Mrs Whittle's face appearing with a subtle smile. She looked even more tired and slimmer than she had before, he decided.

'I'll try and keep at a distance,' she said, back up along the hall.

He nodded and went into the deadly quiet house, hearing a clock ticking loudly somewhere. They went through to the kitchen, where Mrs Whittle stood by a laptop that had been set up on the kitchen table.

'I won't take up too much of your time,' he said, with a polite smile.

'Don't worry. To be honest I could do with the company. I'm here all by myself. Locked down all on my lonesome.' She looked down, somehow swinging on Moone's heartstrings.

'You haven't seen anyone?'

'Not really, a couple of people from the village but that was a short conversation shouted across the street. Oh, Simon's brother popped by a couple days ago to check up on me, which was nice. But that's it.'

Moone nodded, then decided he best not let himself get dragged into a potential witness's sad life. He looked at the laptop and gestured to it. 'So, you got an email?'

'Oh, yeah, see, I nearly forgot that. Going mad.' Whittle turned on the screen, revealing an email that appeared across it. Moone stepped closer, smiling apologetically as Ashley stepped backwards. He leaned in, reading. It had been sent from some kind of phone-email service a couple of days ago, from what he could tell. He read the message aloud:

'Dear Mrs Whittle, you don't know me, but I want you to know I'm so sorry. It's a terrible thing that was done to you. I wish I had time to say more, but I need you to tell them that a police officer is next. He's planning...'

Moone looked up at Ashley. 'He didn't get the chance to finish what he was sending. Which means he was probably interrupted and sent it as it was.'

'Was done to you,' Mrs Whittle said, tears filling her eyes. 'They mean what happened to Simon, don't they?'

'Certainly seems that way. But let's not jump to any concussions...'

'What else could it be? There's nothing else that's been done to me. Simon was murdered, that's what they were trying to tell me.'

'If it's OK, I'm going to send this on to a colleague of mine that might make sense of it?'

Mrs Whittle nodded, staring off into space. He stared at her for a moment, thinking that normally he might even stretch to a supportive hug. Now, even that was not allowed. He sent the email, then straightened up, thinking about leaving, although he was feeling sorry for her.

'I'm afraid I've got to go,' he said, putting on a slight smile.

She nodded. 'Sorry, I didn't even offer you a tea or...'

'Best not to. Cross contamination and all that.'

'Yes, I suppose. It's crazy, isn't it? We go to bed in the same old world, then we wake up to this? When is it going to be over?'

'Not too much longer, I hope.'

'Are you any nearer to solving this?'

He sighed. 'Maybe. I hope. Did Simon have his computer fixed by anyone at any time?'

'He used his laptop, but he wouldn't have let anyone else near it.'

Moone made a strange noise of confusion.

'That's not what you wanted to hear?' she said, her forehead bunching up.

'No, it's fine. You ever heard of or met a man called Ian Speare?'

She shook her head. 'No, I don't think so. I don't know if Simon had. I can go through his work diaries, if you think it might help? Is that who you think is behind all this?'

Moone shrugged, while his mind raced to find the right words or a way he could answer without filling her with false hope. He ran dry. 'Honestly, I don't know. I'm just trying to find a connection to all this. There's something here, but so far it's eluded me. Anyway, I'd better get going...'

'OK, I'll let you know if I find anything.'

'Thanks,' he said, then turned and headed to the door. He opened it and saw a sad and lonely looking Ashley Whittle behind him, looking towards the ground. Before he could stop himself, he found his mouth opening. 'I will find out who's behind this.'

She stared up at him, a little shocked, then with a smile. 'You promise?'

'Scout's honour.'

When Moone called for a nearby response car to pick him up, he hadn't expected to see Sergeant Pinder pulling up outside the house. Pinder nodded as he wound down the window and said, 'Fraid you'll have to sit in the back. Devon and Cornwall taxi service at your beck and call.'

Moone laughed a little, then climbed in, making sure to sit diagonally behind him. 'Didn't expect to see you.'

Pinder pulled away and took them towards the Tamar Bridge. 'Not much else for us to do at the moment. Toothless dogs right now, that's what we are. How's Mrs Whittle?'

'Coping, just about. She's in that house all alone.'

'Shame. I feel bad for her. Wish I could've done more.'

'You did all you could. Wish I had some hope for her.'

Pinder tried to see him in the rear-view

mirror. 'Are you making any kind of progress?'

Moone shrugged. 'Don't know. Our number one suspect's in Intensive Care, and it doesn't look much like he's going to pull through. Could do with some answers from him. Mrs Whittle received an email that apologised to her for what had been done to her...'

Pinder's eyes widened in the mirror. 'Do you think our killer sent it?'

'As a way of saying he was sorry? No, I think whoever sent it has information, and was probably involved somehow. Thing is, whoever sent the message, and I suspect I know who did, said that a police officer is going to be targeted next.'

'Fuck me. That's got to be you, hasn't it? Sorry, but...'

'Yep, I get it. The man in charge would make him a nice catch, wouldn't it?'

'Who do you think sent the email?'

Moone leaned forward a bit. 'Keep all this under your hat, but I think it was Ian Speare. I think he sent it just before our assailant set fire to his house. Speare knew too much, that's for sure.'

There was a low rumble as the car travelled over the Tamar Bridge. Moone leaned towards the window and stared up at the massive construction, feeling quite small suddenly. He sat up straight, wondering if he was too small, in the grand scheme of things, especially when it came to his job. He was a salmon battling its way back up stream. He sighed and watched Plymouth getting closer. Then he saw his caravan burning, then the face of Rachel, the young woman he had grasped hold of to keep him buoyant. He searched himself for his feelings, as he had done on several nights lying next to her in the dark. He came up empty every time.

CHAPTER 23

The first thing Moone did in the morning, after he'd made himself an Americano and put it in his mug flask, was pop to the hospital to see Ian Speare. He wasn't allowed in to see him properly, as he was now in isolation. His lungs were in bad shape and that made him particularly vulnerable to Covid 19. Moone saw him briefly through the window, staring at him, recalling his conversations with the man, trying to make up his mind whether he could be the person that enjoyed forcing people to take their own lives. As much as he tried, he couldn't make it fit. Yes, he was probably the person who collected the blackmail material, but not the one who did the coercing.

Most of the team were in the incident room when he got back, but all spread out. The civvies had been put in a conference room, manning phones there so they could all be more spread out. It was surprising how quickly they had all adapted to the new routines and what he called the coronavirus shuffle, which was the dance they all did in the corridors or other tight spaces to get out of each other's way.

Moone sipped his home-made Americano and grimaced as he looked over the whiteboard and all the photos. Ian Speare's photos were there now.

'What's the latest on Speare's laptop?' Moone turned and focused on DS Carthew.

'I told DI Butler,' she said, looking up briefly.

'Now tell me.'

She stared up at him, her eyes burning into him. 'His laptop wasn't there. There was a drawer in his desk that had a laptop power cable in it, but no laptop...'

'Check the cable, see what make...'

'I already did. Was a Mac. An expensive one.'

'Interesting.' Moone smiled.

'Not really,' Carthew said, a slight smirk on her face. 'Turns out Madam Revello wasn't short of a few quid. She could've paid for it. The laptop's not old, so I've started going through her finances...'

He nodded, aware the whole room was listening. 'Good. Well done. We need to find out the exact make of the one Daryl Palmer had.'

Butler came in with a paper cup of coffee, her face set in a grimace. 'Jesus. I just paid fifty pence for this shit. That's the bloody problem with this bloody lockdown, you can't get a decent cup of coffee...'

She stopped talking, then looked round the room at everyone. 'What? You can't.'

Moone shook his head. 'Where have you been?'

'To see if Barry can deal with your mysterious email.'

'Can he?'

'Can you believe it? He's self-isolating out in the middle of bleeding Cornwall! Health issues or something. We need to call him, if indeed they have phones there.'

'Hey,' Molly said, quietly. 'I'm Cornish!'

'It was only a joke,' Butler said, huffing.

Moone ignored it all as he opened up a laptop and called the number he had for Barry. It took quite a few rings before a pale, tired-looking Barry came on the screen.

'Yeah,' Barry said, very raspy, and rubbing his eyes.

'DCI Moone. You OK, Barry? You don't look too hot.'

'Ongoing issues,' he said. 'You got a job for me?'

'I forwarded an email to you. It was sent to a witness from some mobile phone email service.'

'I know the kind. I'll have a look now. Sorry, been dead to the world.'

Barry started typing as his pale face took up the screen. He kept stopping to blink and drink some Lucozade before he would carry on typing.

'I see it,' he said. 'An email sent from a

mobile, via a messaging service. I've seen this before. It'll take a while, but I'll be able to tell you who sent it hopefully.'

'Hopefully?' Moone said, leaning towards the screen, eyebrows raised.

'I'll let you know,' Barry said blankly before the call ended.

'I'm sure Barry will come good,' Butler said.

Moone let out a sigh, nodding. 'What's the chances Speare has Daryl's laptop?'

'I wouldn't like to bet on it. You think Speare sent the email to Mrs Whittle? Why would he do that? More psychological games?'

'My theory is that Speare is the information man. He gleaned info for his mum, so she knew what to say… '

'Sceptic.'

He smirked. 'Somehow, he ends up feeding info to our suicide obsessed killer, or whatever you want to label him. What if Speare sent that message as a warning but didn't get to finish? What if the killer came back into the room? What if he murdered Madam Revello too before setting fire to the house?'

'You've got a lot of questions and no answers.'

'Thanks for your input.' Moone looked up when he saw Sergeant Pinder. He went over, followed by Butler, all of them trying to keep two metres apart and failing.

'What is it?' Moone asked, resting against

the wall.

'Got a witness,' Pinder said with a nod. 'If you two are planning on getting married? No, not funny?'

'Get on with it, Kev,' Butler said with a deep huff.

He rolled his eyes at Moone. 'Got an elderly gentleman who reckons he saw a white male walking down Speare's road not long before the fire...'

'Description?' Moone asked.

'He's frail, white-haired, probably about sixty-five.' Pinder smiled.

'You get worse,' Butler moaned.

'Ok. I'll be serious. White male, but he was wearing a surgical mask and a baseball cap, he thinks.'

Moone buried his face in his hands. 'Of course he was! Cause everybody's wearing a fucking mask!'

'What're we supposed to do with that?' Butler said to Pinder.

Pinder shrugged. 'You're the detectives. Check CCTV in Mutley. Maybe this bastard's car gets picked up, if he drove.'

'Why don't you get on that?' Moone said, pointing at him.

'I asked for that, didn't I?' Pinder nodded, then sloped back out of the incident room.

'I think I've got something,' DS Carthew said, as she stared at her monitor.

Moone moved closer to her desk. 'What is it?'

She looked up. 'I've been going through Madam Revello's and her son's finances. Seems she lost lots of money a couple of years ago...'

'You're not going to say what I think you are?'

'Stannard,' Carthew said. 'She lost her savings. She wasn't quite as flush as I first thought.'

'Bloody hell,' Butler said. 'Looks like everyone's got a bloody motive for knocking off Stannard. Doesn't matter though, cause we've got his killer locked up.'

'Have we?' Moone turned to her. 'I'm starting to have my doubts. 'What if Daniel Pritchard's innocent?'

'Then maybe he'll get off when it comes to his trial.' Butler shook her head. 'But we had him, bang to rights. We've got no reason to believe Speare murdered Stannard.'

Moone looked towards the photos on the board, staring into the eyes of Speare, his driving licence photo. 'We need to talk to him.'

'Good luck with that.' Butler sat at her desk.

Moone rubbed his hands over his hair. 'We need to go over his house again...'

'To find what?'

'To find a link to Stannard or the other victims...'

Butler put her face in her hands, then

looked up at him. 'We're just chasing our tails here.'

'Then what do we do?'

'I don't know. He's got the laptop! If Speare was feeding him the info. If. It's a bloody big if. If he was, then he's got the evidence, and probably the rest of his intended suicides, or murders...'

Moone hung his head, knowing she was right and he had little. As usual he was out of his depth, sinking under the water, and everyone in the room knew it. His eyes jumped to Carthew and he noticed a look on her face, an expression of what he thought was satisfaction. He looked away, scrambling around in his head. 'What about the other thing?'

'What thing?' Butler sat up.

'In the email sent to Mrs Whittle, it said a police officer was next.'

'If that email even meant that, or was even sent by Speare.'

'It was, I know it.' He didn't know it, but he was praying that Barry came back with something concrete.

'What are you suggesting, that we lay a trap? How do we do that?'

'You ever seen the film Manhunter?'

'What?'

'I have,' Carthew said, getting up. 'You're suggesting we put something on the news to piss him off, make one of us the target.'

Moone pointed to Carthew. 'Exactly.'

Butler let out a laugh. 'It's not going to work. For one thing, this bastard's picked out his victims because they've got a terrible secret that they never want anyone to ever know about. Have you got a terrible secret? Have you?'

Moone looked round the room, seeing everyone waiting. He let out a breath. 'No. But if we antagonise him...'

'He'll come after you.' Butler shook her head. 'No, we need to know who he's targeting in the police. But none of them are going to volunteer their terrible secret, are they?'

'It's me.'

They all stopped talking, then slowly turned towards the voice. Harding was looking down, by his monitor.

Moone stepped closer. 'Harding? What do you mean?'

'I should've said something,' Harding said, looking up. 'I'm sorry...'

'Right, come with us,' Butler said, crooking a finger at him.

DC Harding slumped into the chair in the interview room, his face red, his eyes furtively looking Moone and Butler over as they sat down. The DC coughed out a laugh as he said, 'I feel like I'm a suspect.'

'Shut up,' Butler said, folding her arms. 'Just tell us what the bloody hell's going on?'

Harding took a deep breath. 'About a year

ago, I had my PC looked at. Took it to this shop in Peverell somewhere. Don't think it's there now. Speare worked there, I'm sure of it. I recognised him as the bloke who fixed my PC…'

Butler leaned in. 'So, there was something on your PC, I take it?'

Harding looked down, nodding. 'Yeah…'

'Jesus, what was it?'

Harding looked up. 'I'm not going to bloody say, am I? Let's just say that it's nothing I want people knowing about.' He looked between them. 'It's not like that, if that's what you mean! I'm not a perv!'

Butler narrowed her eyes. 'So you say. I don't know who you are any more, Harding. If that's even your name!'

Harding stuck up his middle finger.

'Stop it,' Moone said.

Butler glared at Moone. 'It's only banter. I've known this arsehole for years, I know he's not a perv.'

'Cheers.' Harding lowered his head, shaking it a bit. Then he looked up at Moone. 'What do I do?'

Moone sat back. 'This is what we do. Like I said before, we get hold of Carly Tamms, get her here and fill her in on some of this. We get Harding to talk to her, say how the guy we're after is a sicko, perv, whatever will wind him up… No, actually, I've got it. A thief. He took money off those people. He's just a lowlife common thief. Scum of the earth.'

Harding widened his eyes. 'Do we want to wind him up or get him to stab me?'

Moone held up his hands. 'Hopefully he'll contact you somehow. Try and get money from you. Then we go from there. What do you reckon?'

Butler stared at him. 'What do I reckon? You want me to be honest or tactful?'

'Honest.'

'I think you're mental. We don't even know if it's Harding he's targeting!'

'What the bloody hell do you suggest!' Moone heard the barked words pop from his own mouth, his heart hammering a little, feeling hot all over.

Butler glared at him. 'All right, calm down, London Boy. Fine, we'll give it a shot, but my gut tells me we're barking up the wrong tree. Go on, call Tamms.'

Butler came up with the idea of meeting Tamms somewhere away from the station, just in case the killer was watching them. So they arranged the meet in Devonport park in the afternoon, not far from the cafe and the monuments. They saw the occasional dog-walker or puffy faced jogger going past. Butler and Moone stood with their backs to the trees, watching the rest of the park, while Harding, looking rather uncomfortable, walked up the pathway, deeper into the park.

'What do you think it is?' Butler asked, staring towards Harding.

'His secret?' Moone asked, craving a cigarette. It would be the perfect time to smoke one, he decided, resting in the shade of the tree. Besides, he'd just read something about smokers being less likely to get Covid.

'Yeah, of course his secret.' Butler folded her arms. 'I can't think what it can be. It's got to be porn, hasn't it?'

'I don't know, and I don't want to know. All that matters is that we have a chance of catching this bastard before he coerces anyone else into taking their own life.'

'Do you think anyone could get you to do yourself in?' Butler turned to face him.

'I don't know. I've been to some pretty bad places. Depends what state you're in, if you're close to it anyway, or...'

'Some fucker's got the dirt on you.'

Moone nodded. 'If you already feel that bad about the thing, whatever it is, then, who knows?'

Moone straightened up as he spotted Carly Tamms coming from the direction of the cafe, striding forcefully towards Harding. Harding looked up, then seemed to tidy himself as she approached. Tamms walked round him, then started turning, heading for Moone and Butler. Moone sighed, then kicked himself away from the tree as she stopped about six feet from them.

'We're not really meant to be meeting anyone at the moment,' she said, narrowing her eyes at them both.

'Still keeping a social distance,' Butler said.

'What's this all about?' Tamms asked.

'We need a favour.' Moone smiled.

'OK? What sort of favour?'

'You know.'

'Yes, you want me to put something in the paper for you. Is this to do with the suicides?' Tamms folded her arms.

'Yep. The officer you ignored. Behind you. We need you to interview him. He knows what to say.'

Tamms kept staring at Moone. 'You're of more interest to me. My readers too, I think...'

'I'm very boring.'

Tamms stepped closer. 'You're a hero. A hero far from home. I'd like to interview you.'

'No way.'

'After you do this,' Butler said. 'Do this and you'll get your interview.'

Tamms nodded, then turned on the spot, and started heading for Harding.

'That was embarrassing,' Harding said as he stormed across the incident room to his desk and slumped into his chair.

'You did great,' Moone said, watching him from across the room. Then he came closer, lowering his voice. 'At least you didn't have to say too much.'

Harding nodded. 'Yeah, I know. Do you think it'll work?'

'It'll get some kind of reaction, I guess.'

Then Moone turned when he heard the ringing coming from the laptop on his desk. Barry was video calling him, so he sat down and answered it.

'Give me some good news, Barry,' Moone said as Barry's tired face filled the screen.

'I hope it's good news. The laptop used to send the email was the same make as the one you said disappeared. I traced the email too, and it was sent from the address you sent me.'

Moone let out a sigh of relief as he sat back. 'Thanks, Barry. That's great. Now get some rest.'

Barry nodded, then the call ended, leaving Moone to stare at himself. He looked away, unable to stare into his own tired eyes any longer.

'Good news?' Butler asked as she came into the incident room.

'The email was sent from Speare's address...'

'That's just more reason to believe he's our assailant. If he is, we won't get anything from this interview in the paper.'

'We'll see.'

He sipped his water, staring across the car park, towards the calm sea. There was hardly anyone around, and the restaurant behind him was shut. There was a car that had pulled up a couple of minutes ago, a lone person at the wheel. A woman, in her late forties. It had to be her.

He wanted to move his car closer, but he didn't want to grab her attention just yet. He took out his burner phone, the one he'd used to get her to the beach in the first place.

He wrote a text: 'You came. Well done.'

He sent it, then watched her, and smiled when he saw her fish her phone out.

She stared at the message, then her head darted up, looking all round for him. He put on his covid mask, then his gloves and finally his baseball cap, and climbed out of the car. When he shut the car door, she looked up and watched him approach, frozen.

A dog-walker went past, glancing at him, but he didn't panic, for he was just another masked, frightened fool. When he looked back towards her car, he saw that she had turned in her seat, trying to get a look at him. He stood by her window, staring at her, watching her stare back at him, tears in her eyes. He signalled for the window to come down. Obviously flustered, she blindly searched for the button. The glass came down, so he said, 'I'll get in the back. Don't want to contaminate each other, do we?'

She didn't say anything, just watched him climb in, then turned forward and stared at him in the rear-view mirror.

He smiled, even though she probably didn't see it under the mask. 'You should probably wear a mask,' he said. 'You can't be too careful.'

'What do you want?' she asked. 'What's this all about? Do you want me to call my husband?'

'Does he know about it all?' he asked, raising his eyebrows. 'Does he know all the dirty little details?'

She bent her head down, shaking, trembling as the tears came again. He felt the surge of pleasure pour over him again, making him burn all over.

'Why're you doing this?!' she demanded to know as she took out a tissue and wiped her eyes. 'What do you want? I suppose you want money? Is that it?'

'Do you have money?'

'I can get money. Maybe a few thousand...'

'What do you have on you?'

She looked up at him in the mirror, the mascara darkening her eyes as she blinked, full of confusion. 'I don't carry a lot of money...'

'I mean, what do you have on you, in your purse. Cash.'

She kept staring at his reflection. 'You're joking. Is this some kind of sick joke to you? Do you want me to call him, my husband?'

'You won't. We both know you won't. How much do you have on you? Have a look.'

She glared at him, then found her handbag and took out a dark red purse. She had a quick search through, then stopped, staring out towards the calm sea. 'Barely forty pounds...'

'I'll take it.' He held out his gloved hand.

'Then you'll ask for more. It's never enough, is it?'

'On the contrary. It's more than enough. I would have taken five pounds. It's not about the money, you see.'

She turned round in her seat, staring at him, obviously trying to work him out as she held out the money. 'You're telling me you don't want any more than that? Do you think I'm stupid?'

'No, I don't. Although you were pretty stupid to make those little movies for your boyfriend. Very graphic...'

Her face burned as her eyes dug into him. 'What are you going to do with them? Please, please don't...'

'I won't, if you do me one more favour.'

'A favour?' She looked as if she had tasted something truly disgusting. 'Oh God, what do you mean?'

'Nothing like that. I want you to kill yourself.'

'What? You sick little...'

'You either kill yourself, or your husband and the whole of the internet community see your movies. Your choice.'

'You're evil, aren't you?'

He shrugged. 'If there's such a thing... Anyway, I'll be in touch to find out what you've chosen.'

He climbed out and walked away, smiling to

himself, feeling the pulse of pleasure in every one of his cells.

Seconds later, as he reached his car, he heard the engine behind him. He looked round to see her car reversing and then coming forward.

He turned back to his car again, still full of the ecstatic feeling he'd grown to desire more and more.

Then the engine sound was louder, blaring and revving. He spun round, seeing the car racing towards him, her eyes, so full of hate, so wide and white, coming for him. Pure hate.

He froze as the car came closer and closer, roaring like a wild beast.

Then he dove, throwing himself out of the way, and rolling over the front of his car.

Her car rushed past, clipping another parked car, taking off its wing mirror, heading for the cliffs. Then the car was swerving, heading for the wall that carried on from the side of the cafe.

The smash of the car echoed round the car park. The engine was still moaning as he shook himself out of his shock, then climbed slowly to his feet. He looked around, expecting to see people rushing towards him. His heart hammered as he stepped closer to the driver's side. She was slumped over the wheel, her dark hair covering her face. He opened the door, crouching down, moving her hair.

She made a sound, a pain-filled moan.

'You're hurt,' he said. 'Don't move.'

'He… help… help… me,' she said, her words a deep, scared whisper. Blood caked her head, her nose.

He looked around, then put his gloved hand over her mouth and nose, grasping her tight, even when she weakly fought to get him off. He covered her mouth, grasping tighter as he felt her lungs empty.

He stayed there for a while, staring at her still face, staring at her crushed chest, checking for movement. A dog barked behind him, disturbing the moment, their wonderful moment together, like lovers lying together after the act.

He let go and ran to his car.

CHAPTER 24

Moone rode the dirt track towards the beach, feeling every bump and hole in the makeshift road. There was a sign for a National Trust car park on his left. Uniforms were stood on guard, and beyond them was an ambulance and a fire engine. The fire crew were stood back he noticed when he parked up at the end of the track. The car was crumpled against the wall. He noticed the closed cafe and his stomach tried to devour itself. He stepped closer to the scene, showing his ID, then getting under the cordon.

There was a middle-aged female inspector observing, her greying blonde hair being toyed with by the breeze. Inspector Tremain, he said to himself, then smiled politely as she turned round to face him.

'DCI Peter Moone, I presume?' she said, then showed her gloved hands.

He nodded, making sure to keep his distance, while noticing some uniforms further down another track that led down to the beach, talking to a few dog-walkers. 'You presume right. What happened?'

The Inspector stepped closer to the car, her eyes on the paramedics collecting equipment. 'We're not quite sure. Apart from this poor woman drove at speed and, well, you can see for yourself.'

'No cameras?' He looked around.

'There's one on the front of the cafe, but it's been turned off. Even so, it wouldn't have picked this up.'

'I wonder what she was playing at?' Moone stepped closer, bending down to look at the woman. Her head was back, her curly dark hair half hanging over her face. He was automatically thinking suicide, but that seemed to be his default mode these days, so he switched his mind, tried to clear it out. 'ID?'

'Yes, that's the thing. She's one of us. Or at least was. Former Detective Constable Pauline Stack.'

Moone lost all warmth, the breeze having seemed to turn icy. He straightened up, staring at the Inspector. 'Pauline Stack?'

'You know her?' The inspector showed little sympathy.

'No, but...' Moone turned when he heard a car pull up and saw Butler at the wheel. He hurried over, greeting her as she climbed out.

'Love this place,' Butler said, stretching and yawning. 'Beautiful view.'

'Pauline Stack.'

Butler lowered her arms, staring at him. 'What? Why're you talking about Stack's missus?'

Then she must have read his face. Her eyes jumped to the car, her body beginning to move towards his in a hurry.

He cut her off. 'There's nothing to be done.'

She stopped, still staring at the car. 'I didn't know her very well. Met her at a couple of dos. Jesus, poor fucking Stack. Anyone told him yet?'

Moone shook his head, then looked off towards the car.

'I suppose it's down to me.' Butler took in a deep breath. 'I'd better call him. Get him here.'

Moone nodded. 'Sorry.'

Butler sighed, then walked away, taking out her mobile. He took out his phone and made a call, reporting the incident and asking for the SOCOs to be brought to the scene. He wondered why she had been there, then headed to the Inspector who was now sitting in the back of a response car, filling out some paperwork.

'Did you find her phone?' Moone asked. 'That might tell us something.'

The Inspector looked up. 'No, no mobile. Which is unusual, but then not everyone has one.'

Moone nodded, partly agreeing, but feeling something cold travelling down his spine. 'Did anyone see anything?'

'Dog-walker heard the engine roaring as he was coming up the path. Said he thought he saw a man running, but wasn't sure.'

'A man running? Running away?'

She pointed her pen in the direction of the beach. 'I don't know. One of my constables has taken his statement. If you head down there you might catch your witness.'

Moone was off, half jogging across the sandy car park, then down a pathway through the undergrowth that seemed to snake down to the beach. Just a few hundred yards down he could make out a uniform talking to a tanned, bald man, a small fluffy dog by his side.

Moone headed down, nearly tripping over stones and roots, until he reached the uniform and the man, quite out of breath.

Moone took out his ID and showed it as he caught his breath and said, 'You saw what happened?'

The man stared at his warrant card, then up at Moone. 'Sort of. Heard it really. Heard a crash. When I got up there the car was just there, against the wall. I called you lot.'

Moone nodded. 'You saw a man running away?'

'He seemed in a hurry...'

'What did he look like?'

The man raised his shoulders, let out a harsh breath. 'Didn't see him properly. He had a baseball cap on. Blue, I think it was. One of those masks. Oh and I think he had gloves on. Surgical ones.'

'Did you see if he had a car?'

'No, sorry. He just vanished.'

Moone stepped back, the tingle racing up his spine. He looked at the uniform. 'Did you get all that?'

'Already have, sir.'

Moone turned and headed back up to the beach, breathing harder as he struggled back up, grabbing hold of the bushes as he climbed. Then he reached the car park, then looked round at the scene, trying to play out what had happened in his mind.

'Where did you run off to?' Butler said, looking pale and deflated.

'Witness saw a man fleeing the scene. Baseball cap, mask, gloves.'

Butler glared at him, folding her arms across her chest. 'Everybody's wearing...'

'No, they're not.' Moone pointed a finger at the car, aware his voice was louder, filling with annoyance. 'She wasn't! The dog-walkers aren't. Look at them!'

Butler huffed, then looked across the beach. 'OK, so what? You think that our suicide boy came here...'

'She's a former police officer. She's Stack's wife. They'd make a pretty big target for us, wouldn't they?'

Butler seemed to lose her disbelief, her

eyes softening as she looked around again. 'The bastard. The fucking... we've got to keep the lid on this for the moment. Stack's on his way...'

'How did he sound?'

'How the bloody hell do you think?'

Somehow it had grown darker by the time he heard the engine grumbling, getting louder as the car came up the track towards the car park. Moone felt cold all over as his shadow stretched out over the sandy tarmac.

'Here we go,' Butler said behind him, then he watched her stride over to the car that Harding was driving. Stack was in the passenger seat, his face straight, unreadable. But then he was out, pushing the door open before Harding had a chance to park. He jogged then ran to the car, but stopped short, staring. Even from where Moone was, he saw his eyes grow red, his fists clenching. Butler rushed to him, her arms grasping him as he began to sob.

Moone looked away, staring over the water, seeing the sun sinking down, the orange and red of it colouring the clouds.

He needed something to help take his mind off things, but didn't want to go home, his temporary home with Rachel. As much as he felt a kind of desire at the thought of seeing her, he knew it was an empty one, free of any true feelings. Butler was right, he had made a big mistake.

No, he wouldn't go to Rachel's place just yet. He thought of Simon Whittle's widow, all alone. He nodded to himself and brought up her number, just to check up on her, see if there was anything he could bring her.

He stood there, watching Butler and Stack, and the scene being secured, Mrs Stack being removed carefully from the car after the SOCOs had done their thing.

There was no answer, just the constant ringing. Maybe she had gone out somewhere, he decided, but then recalled that she had been reluctant to even leave the house.

Moone found himself heading for his car, deciding to check in on her before heading home for the evening, his eyes glancing over to Butler who was still comforting Stack. There was still a lot he didn't understand about their relationship, whatever it might be. He didn't want to know, it wasn't his business, he told himself and climbed in his car and started the engine.

It was much darker by the time Moone drove along the narrowed country lane, past the closed pub, the old church. He found Mrs Whittle's cottage, parked and climbed out.

He headed towards the cottage and rang the bell, then tried to look into the darkened windows for a sign of her, but there seemed to be none. Where could she have gone?

'She's not there,' a voice said, from across the street.

He turned round to see a middle-aged woman who had stepped out of her house across the street, a Labrador at her side.

'Where is she?' he asked.

'Hospital, I think. An ambulance was there yesterday. I wonder if she's got it.'

Moone smiled, nodded, his mind racing, wondering what had happened to her as he hurried back to his car. He started the engine, getting ready to head for Derriford Hospital.

'I'm sorry, but if she's in the Covid ward,' the receptionist said to Moone, not sounding like she had a lot of sympathy. 'You won't be able to visit. There's a lot of restrictions at the moment.'

The receptionist was masked up, with surgical gloves on. Moone nodded, smiled politely. He was in the A and E department, at the main desk, trying to avoid any contact with the few other people waiting.

'Can I find out if she's OK?' he asked, looking round, noticing the rest of the hospital was strangely quiet.

'I'm sorry, I couldn't tell you. I can try and get in touch with someone. It depends if they're in the suspected Covid ward or the confirmed.'

'OK. Her name is Whittle. Ashley Whittle.'

'I'll see what I can do.' She gave a brief smile.

Moone turned away, watching two

uniforms with masks and gloves on, trying to help an elderly couple. He rubbed his face, wondering about Simon Whittle's widow, hoping she was OK, trying to figure out how she had got infected, if indeed she had got infected. It was a waiting game. There was little he could do. He took out his card, then pushed it across the desk towards the receptionist who was now on the phone.

'Call me?' he asked.

She nodded, sort of smiled, then turned her back on him. He felt rather empty as he headed out into warm air, looking round the hospital streets and hardly seeing anyone. Even the ambulances were parked up, empty. He shook his head, thinking about heading home.

Then his mobile rang. He looked at the number calling and didn't recognise it.

'DCI Peter Moone,' he said.

'Hi, you might not remember me,' a young woman's voice said, the sound of a cigarette being sucked coming over the line. 'I'm Marie, Daryl's friend... I don't know if you remember...'

'Course I remember. How are you?'

'I'm, I'm OK. I just, well, I wondered if we could meet up.'

'Is everything OK, Marie?' Moone made his way across to the car park.

'Yeah, everything's fine. Just got some info for you, I think.'

'Why don't you come in, talk about it?'

'No.'

'No?'

'Sorry. I'd rather not. If it's all the same. Could you meet me at Desmond's work?'

'Desmond Palmer's? Why there?'

'Cause I'm going to go and talk to him. I'm on my way there now.'

'OK, I'll be there soon.'

The call was ended, and Moone was left in the mostly empty car park, wondering what Marie might know that she hadn't already told them. But as he unlocked his car, he recalled that they had always talked to her in the presence of Desmond's younger brother, Shaun. Maybe, he thought this was her way of getting him to tell the truth.

Moone pulled up in the small industrial estate to find it almost dead. He parked opposite the building where Desmond had his food delivery business, but the shutters were down. He rubbed his beard, staring at the sign taped to the shutters, which he couldn't read from where he was. He climbed out, hearing voices far down the strip of buildings, and headed to the sign.

"Temporarily closed due to Covid. We'll be open again soon. Sorry for the inconvenience."

Moone stood back, wondering where Marie was and if she had found the same sign and left.

Then he heard heavy footsteps crushing the dirt, seeming to come down the lane that ran parallel with Desmond's building. Moone stepped towards the sound, then looked up the lane.

'Shit,' he said to himself, the penny dropping right on top of his thick skull.

Shaun Palmer, followed by a meaty, dark-haired gentleman came towards him. Shaun had a smile on his face as he came towards Moone, getting about two feet away. Then the yob looked down, laughed, and said, 'Oh no, I seem to be breaking the social distancing laws. What a wanker I am.'

'What do you want, Shaun?' Moone looked around him, trying to casually look for an escape route. But all he saw was a thick-set brother, who was standing close to Moone's car, arms folded. Shit.

'What do I want?' Shaun looked around him. 'I want to know what happened to my nephew. You fucking well know that. Don't act stupid. But you are a pig, which probably means you are thick.'

'Nice one. What's your plan? Beat it out of me, Shaun? That's not very smart, is it? Assaulting a police officer.'

He lost his smile as he stepped closer, his fists balled at his sides. 'No, it wouldn't be very smart. But you've got an ex-wife, kids...'

'Don't even mention my kids...'

Shaun held up his hands. 'I won't have to, not if you do as you're told and start telling me who made Daryl kill himself. Plus, if you do, I can give you a little bonus to your pay packet. How about that? I mean, we're all struggling in these tough economic times, aren't we?'

'Bribery? Blackmail?' Moone laughed, looking around again, wondering how the hell this was going to end. 'No thanks, Shaun. I'll take my chances, and I'll put a guard on my ex-wife's place.'

'You do that. But they won't let you have a copper on her door for ever, will they? That costs money. When they've got bored of guarding her, then that's when one of my lads will make a visit...'

Moone felt the anger twisting the muscles in his neck and shoulders, making his heart begin to pound. He was a few seconds from taking a swing at the smug-looking wanker. No, that would be stupid, he thought.

Then he heard an engine. He looked round and a black BMW was turning into the industrial estate, its lights beaming.

The car parked, then the doors opened. When the two figures climbed out and stood there watching, Moone sighed with relief. Desmond Palmer had been driving, while Butler was his passenger. Questions popped into Moone's mind, but they disintegrated as Desmond Palmer started storming towards Shaun.

'What the fuck do you think you're up to,

Shaun?' Desmond shouted.

Shaun stood his ground, poking out his chest as he folded his arms across it. 'None of your fucking business, is it?'

Desmond took a sudden step, slapping his hand against his brother's chest, knocking him backwards. 'It is my fucking business! Look where you are, you little shite!'

Shaun stayed on his feet, his face reddening, his fists clenching. 'I'm trying to fucking find out what fucking happened to Daryl! But you don't fucking care!'

'Course I fucking care!'

Moone watched on, saw both men tensing up, as if one of them might strike out at any moment. Butler walked up to him, standing shoulder to shoulder with him.

'Putting on a good show, aren't they?' Butler said.

'Yep. So, how did you know I would be here?'

'I didn't. Just blind luck.'

'Then what were you two...'

'Leave it.' Butler folded her arms across her chest.

'Why don't you fucking do something?!' Shaun growled, his face red. 'You just walk away, pissing about with your fucking takeaways... look at me, I'm respectable now. Fucking pussy...'

Desmond snapped forward, letting out an angry grunt. Shaun backed away, his face suddenly full of fear.

'Yeah,' Desmond said. 'Look at you. Fucking pissing yourself. You're not a fucking hard man, Shaun. You get your boys to do your dirty work, don't you...'

'Fuck off.'

Desmond laughed, but it was full of sadness. Then he looked around, biting the inside of his mouth, nodding to himself. 'All right, Shaun. You want to know the truth? Why I didn't do anything? Because I know who's to blame for Daryl's death...'

Shaun stared at him, then stepped closer. 'Who?'

'Me.' Desmond jabbed a thumb at himself. 'Daryl was scared to talk to me. Scared to talk to me, his hard man father, scared to tell me who he really was. But I fucking knew!'

'What the fuck're you talking about?'

Desmond stepped closer to him. 'Daryl was gay. You hearing me? He was gay.'

'Fuck off.' Shaun turned away, started walking towards his car. 'You're fucking mental. You've lost it.'

'He was, Shaun,' Desmond shouted.

'Fuck you!' Shaun said, then climbed into his car, followed by his two henchmen. The car roared, coming down the lane, taking a swerve towards Desmond, who didn't move. The car missed him, but the elder brother stormed after it, staring at it.

'What the hell do we do now?' Moone asked

Butler, but she just raised her shoulders, then walked over to Desmond.

'Des, forget about it,' she said and put a hand on his shoulder.

He shrugged her hand off, and turned to her, and Moone, his face rigid, cold-looking.

'I don't know if what happened to my...' Desmond stopped talking, swallowed, looked down for a moment. Then his eyes rose. 'I've got information for you.'

'You've got info for us?' Butler let out a laugh. 'You? Desmond Palmer, the big...'

He held up a hand. 'Fuck that. I'm done with those fuckers.'

'What's the info?' Moone asked.

Desmond took a breath. 'I know who murdered Stannard. It's not the bastard you've got locked up for it.'

CHAPTER 25

Butler was about to step into the interview room where Desmond Palmer was waiting, but Moone stopped her with a tug of her arm.

'What?' she said, frowning, staring at him as if he'd grabbed hold of something more personal.

'I've got to ask,' Moone said, backing up against the wall. 'What were you two doing?'

'Saving your bacon.' Butler folded her arms.

'Yep, but what were you doing there in the first place?'

'We have history.' Butler looked down the corridor.

'I'm starting to think you've got history with everyone.'

She huffed. 'Say that again and you'll be history. Look, I went to have a word with him, OK, to dig around...'

'You called him Des.' Moone raised his eyebrows.

'Like I said, we've got history. Now, can we

get on?' Butler shook her head, then went into the interview room.

Desmond Palmer was sat back, watching them, a plastic cup of water at his side next to a face mask.

'Here she comes,' Palmer said. 'And here's DI Mandy Butler too.'

Moone stared at him, trying not to show any emotion as Palmer and Butler laughed.

'Sorry,' Butler said to Moone, then sat down, facing Palmer. 'Mr Palmer, you know you can have a solicitor, don't you?'

'Mr Palmer?' He laughed. 'Yeah, I know. Don't need one. Don't need to hide behind anyone any more.'

Butler turned to Moone. 'Shall I do the formalities?'

'Go ahead,' Moone said, then stared at Palmer as Butler turned on the recorder, then read out all the details.

'Your name is Mr Desmond Palmer?' Moone asked.

'Yes, it is.' Palmer leaned back, folded his arms. 'What do you want to know?'

'Let's start with Philip Stannard's murder,' Moone said.

Palmer picked up his cup of water and took a sip. 'All right. What do you want to know?'

'For the record, you told us that you knew who murdered Philip Stannard,' Moone said, staring at the ex-drug dealer, trying to read his tanned granite face. 'Is that true?'

Palmer looked at Butler, then back at Moone. 'Yeah, that's right. I was there the night it happened.'

Butler let out a breath. 'Is any of this true... Mr Palmer?'

'I'm afraid so, acting DI Butler,' he said, and there was a strange sadness to his voice. 'Some might think I should've come forward sooner, but I couldn't, could I?'

'Why not?' Butler asked. 'Because of your big man reputation? The no grassing policy that you criminals have?'

Palmer smirked. 'Something like that. But I was up to my neck in it. Listen, this fella you've got locked up for Stannard's murder. Daniel Pritchard. He didn't do it.'

Moone sat forward. 'Tell us how you know.'

Palmer tapped the desk. 'Because I know who did. Look, I met Pritchard around that time, just before actually. Stannard introduced us...'

'Hang on,' Butler said. 'You were involved with Stannard? You were in on his little con trick?'

Palmer huffed. 'Gone down in your estimation, have I? Well, I was short of cash, my pubs and everything was causing me a cash flow situation. I couldn't be seen to have walked away from the family business to fail at my own business, could I?'

Moone rubbed his eyes. 'So, you were

involved with Stannard? So, what, you and Pritchard realised you were being fiddled by him too, and you planned on getting your money back?'

'That's basically it,' Palmer said. 'Pritchard was meant to call Stannard on his burner, get him to the house, you know, one of the ones he was going to get redeveloped...'

'Where we found his body?' Butler said, a hint of anger in her voice.

Palmer nodded. 'Thing is, me and Dan were parked up the street, watching the house. Then we see Stannard turn up and go inside. We were just about to follow, when this weird-looking bloke turns up. Glasses like milk bottles...'

'Ian Speare?' Moone said, hardly able to believe what he was hearing.

'That's right.' Palmer nodded. 'His mum's one of them psychic frauds. Every gullible fucker in Plymouth goes to see her...'

'They did,' Butler said. 'She's dead. Her son's in intensive care. Someone set fire to their house.'

Palmer narrowed his eyes at her. 'There an accusation in that? Wasn't me.'

Butler laughed. 'Funny that. But looking at your younger, wilder days, you did set a couple of fires...'

'Oh come off it.' Palmer laughed emptily. 'That's not me. Yeah, I did those things when I was a little shit, but not now. Listen, Speare goes into that house. We wait, then I see him like...

stumble out, face white as a sheet. I knew the look on his face, I knew he'd done something to Stannard. I push past him, into the house. There he is, head caved in. I'm thinking I could be tied to this. So, I hide the body, knowing that given enough time there won't be much evidence for you lot. I tell Speare to have it away, to forget it ever happened. That's the end of the story.'

'Until we found his body,' Butler said. 'And Daniel Pritchard ends up banged up for his murder.'

Palmer nodded. 'Shame about that. Poor kid. Never told on me. He's a good lad.'

Butler huffed, then sat back. 'You know we'll do you for aiding and abetting, don't you?'

'Obstructing justice.' Moone nodded.

'I'm terrified,' Palmer said. 'Don't you realise I don't give a shit any more? That's why I'm here. Telling you thick twats this. Daniel didn't murder Stannard, Speare did. So, there you go, charge me, do your worst.'

Palmer sat back, arms folded, turning to face the wall.

'We'll have to get all this on paper, with dates,' Butler said.

'Fine.' Palmer didn't look round.

Moone stood up, signalled for Butler to follow him out into the corridor.

'What do you think?' Moone asked. 'Is he telling the truth?'

'Doesn't have much to lose, does he?' Butler

asked.

'Unless he did it and he's putting the blame on Speare. The other charges get him a lighter sentence.'

'I don't think so.'

'Neither do I.' Moone looked towards the room. 'We'll have to formerly charge him. Then we go over his house, his computers, just to make sure. We search for Daryl's laptop.'

'OK.' Butler let out a heavy breath. 'I can charge him.'

'Mrs Whittle's got Coronavirus,' Moone said. 'Or suspected.'

'Oh dear,' Butler said. 'You been to see her?'

'Yes, but couldn't get near. I've been wondering how she got it. Far as I know she's been on her own for weeks.'

'You went to see her?' Butler gave a laugh. 'Maybe you're typhoid Pete!'

'I hope bloody not. I saw her alive the other day. I'd better check up on her.'

'Calm down, London boy. I'm sure you're not. Have a test if you're worried.'

Moone nodded, giving it serious thought.

'By the way, Parry's been in touch. He's performed the autopsy on Mrs Stack.'

'How is DSU Stack?'

'Not good, as you'd expect. He's off on sick leave. Poor bastard. Anyway, why don't you go and see Parry and I'll charge Desmond Palmer.'

Moone nodded, then looked at his phone,

noticing it was getting late. 'OK, do that, then get home. I'll see you in the morning.'

Moone put on some overalls, gloves and a mask, then stood behind the glass screen that separated him from the post mortem room. Dr Parry and a technician were pushing a DB from the room on a metal gurney. The doctor returned and gave a wide smile to Moone. How anyone could be that happy in their job, he just couldn't understand, but smiled a little and nodded.

'You're here for Mrs Stack,' Parry said, losing his smile as he put on some gloves.

'Yep. Terrible.'

'It is. Never good when it's one of your own.' Parry stepped towards the metal table where the DB, covered in a green sheet, was lying. He pulled down the sheet, revealing Mrs Stack. She had the usual fresh post mortem scar running down her sternum. There were other lacerations and deep purple bruising across her otherwise pale chest.

Moone took in a harsh breath. 'Cause of death?'

'Her thorax had received some serious damage. Her ribcage was crushed in, causing her right lung to collapse. She would have had trouble breathing.'

'So, she suffocated?'

'It's hard to tell. There's not a great deal of head trauma, so she would've been conscious, but for how long, I don't know. There is a little petechial haemorrhaging in the eyes, but that could come with her fight to breathe.'

'But it could be something else?' Moone asked.

'It's going to be hard to tell, to be honest,' Parry said, with a shrug. 'Sorry, I know that's not what you need to hear. You're thinking your suspect finished her off?'

Moone sighed. 'I don't know. But a masked, gloved man was seen fleeing the scene. If it's the same masked man that was spotted approaching Speare's house...'

'But you haven't got much evidence?'

Moone shook his head, feeling a little depressed again, knowing he wouldn't have many answers for Stack. He was a policeman, not just a grieving husband, and he would demand answers, some kind of justice.

'Thanks anyway,' Moone said. 'Please send your report and let us know of anything useful.'

'Always.' Parry put on his wide grin, but Moone turned and walked back out of the post mortem room and out into the corridor. He removed all the protective equipment he was wearing, his mind whirring, trying to make sense of everything and coming up empty. He was a fraud, a pretender to the detective throne.

Then his phone was ringing. He breathed out, saw it was Butler and answered. 'Butler, how's it going your end?'

'Fine. He's not giving me much trouble...'

'Not much to go on with Mrs Stack, I'm afraid, nothing concrete... We need to go over Stack's computers...'

'He's not going to like that. Anyway, listen. Got an update on Ian Speare. He's not well, at death's door.'

'Oh, Jesus. Complications?'

'Sort of. He's tested positive for Covid.'

Moone waited at the end of what they called the green Covid ward, the part of the Emergency Department that was for non-Covid patients. Speare had been delivered to the red Covid ward, which was a better name than the dirty ED, he decided. Speare was fighting for his life. Unfortunately, the lung damage he had sustained from the house fire had made him susceptible to pneumonia and other complications.

Shit. Moone bent over, feeling tense all over, worried that he would never get to interview Speare and find out exactly what his role was in the whole suicide business.

His head jumped up, turning towards the sound of footsteps down the end of the corridor. A figure had stepped along it, decked out in overalls and mask, the whole PPE shebang. Then the figure went into another room, and Moone sunk back down in his seat. One of the doctors working on Speare had been asked to come and talk to him, but of course they were busy. The rest of the hospital was quiet, hardly any patients around. It was a ghost town.

'Are you the police officer?'

Moone spun his head round, then got to his feet. A mousey-haired, young and tired-looking doctor stared at him. He was wearing scrubs and a mask.

'DCI Peter Moone,' he said, showing his ID.

'You came to see Ian Speare?' the doctor asked.

'That's right. How's he doing?'

'I'm afraid we lost him a few minutes ago. His lungs were badly damaged from smoke inhalation...'

Moone sunk back to the chair, only half listening to the details that the doctor went into. He was dead, unable to give his version of events.

'Did you know the deceased?'

Moone looked up. 'Only met him a couple of times. He was a witness.'

'I see. It would be helpful to know who he's come in contact with so we can trace the virus.'

'What about me? I was recently in contact with him.'

'Were you a social distance from him?' The doctor checked his watch.

'Well, it's difficult not to get close.'

The doctor nodded. 'OK. I'll get someone to swab you. Might be a bit uncomfortable at the back of your throat.'

The doctor hadn't been wrong. Moone could

still feel the swab as it had been dragged across the back of his throat, making him gag as he headed through the quiet hospital, towards the cafe and the exit. He was near the door when his eyes jumped to the only other person coming towards him, a man in a grey suit, a surgical mask over his mouth and nose. The man's eyes jumped to Moone with a flutter of recognition in them.

'DCI Moone?' the man said, a little muffled through the mask.

'Do I know you?' Moone asked.

'Michael Whittle. You were investigating my brother's suicide...'

Moone nodded, telling himself off for not recognising him, even though of course he was partly hidden by a face mask. 'Yes, of course. Sorry. I suppose you're here to visit your sister-in-law, Ashley?'

'Yes, that's right.'

'They won't let you in. I've tried. Any covid patients, suspected or otherwise are in quarantine. I hope she's OK.'

Michael smiled. 'She's a fighter. I should get some flowers...'

'They don't allow them these days. Health and safety gone mad. Maybe you can get a message to her.'

'That's a good idea.'

Moone smiled, feeling the conversation had run dry, and wanting to head off. 'I wonder how she got it.'

Michael shook his head. 'Not from me. I'm perfectly healthy. No coughs or fever.'

'Well, you can be asymptomatic, pass it on without having any symptoms.'

'I see. Well, I'd better get myself checked, then.' Michael smiled. 'I'd best get on. By the way, I hear you're living with Rachel? How's that going?'

Suddenly Moone felt uncomfortable, as if he was talking to a parent or brother of the woman who he was undoubtedly going to give the elbow to sooner or later. 'Fine. Good.'

Whittle nodded, his face taking on a serious look. 'Be kind to her, won't you. She puts on a front, but she's quite delicate. She had some trouble years ago, and well, I think it's stayed with her.'

'Trouble?'

'She's never talked about it much, but, well, she puts on a happy go lucky front. Sorry, probably shouldn't have said anything.'

'No, it's fine. I'll try and be kind.' Moone smiled, then gestured to the exit. 'I'd better get moving.'

Whittle nodded, smiled and headed off.

As he drove, Moone started to wonder more about how Speare had caught Coronavirus, and how they had interviewed him in a small room not that long ago. But he had no symptoms and it had been a few days since he had interviewed Speare. It was unlikely he was infected. He drove back towards the station, mulling it over.

Their killer came to mind. He would have had to get close to Speare when he had tried to kill him. Moone smiled, getting a buzz along his neck as he put his foot down, racing along the mostly empty streets.

By the time he had arrived in the incident room, he had developed a plan of action.

'How is he?' Butler asked, standing by the whiteboard and writing notes.

'He's dead.' Moone ran his hands down his face. 'He had Coronavirus. I've just been swabbed. Hopefully that'll come back negative. We need to know where Speare caught it.'

Butler nodded. 'You're thinking this suicide bastard infected him?'

'Maybe. We need to find Madam Revello's appointments book.'

'I've got that,' DS Carthew said from across the room.

'Good. We need to find everyone she saw and see if they've had the virus or symptoms.'

Carthew looked around her desk. 'If they don't, then maybe Speare's killer infected him.'

'Track and trace the virus, find our suicide nut job.'

'Boss.'

Moone looked round at Harding, who was pointing towards the doors of the incident room.

When Moone looked, he saw a figure hunched over in the corridor beyond. It took him a couple of seconds before Moone realised it was Stack. He had a jumper and jeans on, his head lowered to the floor.

'I'll talk to him,' Butler said, turning towards the doors.

'No, I will.' Moone pushed through the doors, making Stack raise his eyes to him. His boss made a sound in his throat which was unidentifiable, so Moone just stood there for a moment.

'You're married, aren't you?' Stack said, in a hollow, broken voice.

Moone thought he could smell alcohol, maybe whisky. 'That's right. I can't imagine...'

'At least you can understand. You get what I'm feeling.'

Moone nodded.

Stack looked at his hands as he balled them into fists. 'Are you any closer?'

'I think so. I think the bastard killed Ian Speare, Madam Revello's son. Speare just died of Coronavirus...'

'I see. I see what you're thinking. Anyone could've infected him.'

'But the virus is not as wide spread down here. I think we can trace it.'

Stack let out a huff. 'What about Palmer? You've charged him, yeah?'

'Not with all this. It's not him.'

Stack's eyes rose to him, burning into him as he stood to his full height. 'You'd better be sure. You'd better get this fucker, Moone.'

'I will. I promise.'

'I don't care how he comes. You understand?'

Moone tried to hold his burning gaze, but he felt like he was looking into a raging volcano or into a black hole. He looked down, nodding. 'I understand. We'll bring him in.'

Stack nodded, then looked at his hands again. 'See that you do. There's going to be a service in a couple of weeks. Not many people allowed. You know, what with all this shit. I'd like you and Butler to come.'

'We'll be there.'

Stack didn't say anything more, just turned and headed back along the corridor, leaving Moone with the voice of self-doubt in his head. He was once again putting all his chips on one number. He rubbed his tired eyes and turned, then almost jumped back a little.

Carthew was stood there, arms folded, face blank. He smiled awkwardly, wondering where the fresh-faced young PC had gone, and whether that version had ever existed at all.

'Can I help?' Moone asked.

'Where are we going to interview these people?' Carthew asked.

'We'll call them, get them to come in, maybe do it in the car park. Spread out, social distancing and all that. We'll get the hospital down here to swab them.'

'Good idea, boss.'

He nodded, not knowing what else to say. Then a bubble of questions rose into his throat. 'You OK?'

She narrowed her eyes at him. 'What do you mean?'

'I don't know. Getting on OK. I know things have been a bit... well, shaky between us. You know we were once...'

'Close?' She leaned against the wall, her arms folded.

'Yes...'

'I used you. I wanted to get ahead.'

Moone found himself staring at her, unsure whether she was joking or not, and soon realising she wasn't. 'Well, you got ahead. You got what you wanted.'

'Don't feel bad, boss. Do you want to know what I think?'

'OK?'

She stepped towards him, lowering her voice. 'I think you're scared...'

'Scared?'

'Of me. Or maybe it's all women? Have you always been scared of us?'

Moone put on a smile, because he didn't know what else to do, and he didn't want her knowing that she was getting to him. 'Well, when you're the boss, I'll be doubly scared.'

She smiled. 'Yep, you should be. It won't be long. Not long at all.'

CHAPTER 26

Moone was reluctant to go home. But it was late as Butler reminded him and practically frogmarched him to his car. She didn't seem that keen on going home either, and for a little while he wondered about her home life these days. But tiredness overtook him, so he started driving. It was ten minutes before he realised he was driving towards Whitsands and not headed towards the flat he was sharing with Rachel. It was wishful thinking, he felt, although he couldn't help but feel drawn to her sexually. Then he thought of Michael Whittle's comment about her past, and how vulnerable she was underneath. He felt a tinge of regret as he changed direction, heading back towards the city and Rachel's. When would be a good time to have 'the conversation'? Never.

Rachel was cooking in the small kitchen when he got through the door. She came over, kissed him briefly, then went back to the stove.

'You're actually cooking us dinner?' he

asked, taking off his tie.

'Don't look so surprised,' she said, narrowing her eyes. 'I can cook, and we can't live on takeaways for the rest of our lives.'

Her words rang in his ears. The rest of their lives. He shoved it away, as he watched her draining some pasta. 'I bumped into your boss today.'

'Mike?' she asked, looking up at him. 'Really? How is he?'

'You haven't talked to him lately?'

She shrugged. 'Not really. Haven't had much need, now I'm furloughed. I've popped into the office to do stuff for him but he's never there.'

'He mentioned…' Moone stopped himself, realising that he was probably stepping on rocky ground.

'What? What did he mention?' Rachel stopped what she was doing, her hand on a spoon that was deep in a pan of bolognaise.

'It was nothing.'

'No, there's something. Go on.'

'Well, he gave me one of those men-to-men things, the sort of thing an older brother does.'

'Oh, I see. He told you to look after me. That it?' She shook her head and started stirring the sauce again. 'I think he's a bit overprotective of me. Did he tell you I was delicate?'

'He might've done.' Moone smiled, trying to take the sting out of it all.

Rachel nodded to herself, her jaw seeming

to tighten as she turned off the gas. Then she stood back, folding her arms over her chest, staring intently at him. In all his years as a copper, he'd learnt that body language like hers was never good.

'He's partly right,' Rachel said. 'I suppose I used to be delicate. But I'm OK now. I just don't stand for any shit. Some men don't like that. Before you say anything, I'll tell you what happened to me. When I was in my mid-teens, I was in a pub. I grew up in a little village in Cornwall. There was this pub where the landlord would serve us, 'cause he didn't care. One of the lads in there had upset this local. Turns out he was a few sandwiches short of a picnic. He brought a knife into the pub...'

'Jesus...'

'Yeah. But he wasn't there. So he just started stabbing people. Two of my friends got stabbed. Jane...' Rachel stopped talking, then swallowed, her eyes filling with tears.

'You don't have to...'

She held up a hand. 'She didn't make it. My other friend, Sam. Samantha, she was badly injured. She pulled through, but she was never the same.'

'How did...'

'How come I survived? Unhurt? I hid under a table, just watching it all. Watching it happen to my friends.'

As she started to cry, Moone swept his arms

round her as she sobbed. He said comforting things, but all the time he was remembering how he had planned to give her 'the talk'. He pushed it all aside, and held her tighter, and kissed her mouth when she looked up at him.

In the morning Moone was kind of glowing inside, but he didn't really understand it. Somehow Rachel's grief had turned to a sad kind of passion. They had gone to bed for a few hours before they decided to eat.

He was seeing her differently somehow. She was no longer just a beautiful young woman that seemed to like him for whatever reason. She had other dimensions, and so dark and complicated, he found himself sinking deeper into whatever was going on between them.

'You going to get out?'

Moone flickered to life, turning to see Butler staring in at him, her eyebrows raised. He climbed out, then leaned in to pick up his Americano and Butler's cappuccino.

'Thanks,' she said, taking her drink. 'What were you dreaming about? Don't tell me, Rachel?'

He huffed out a laugh. 'Right. I need to have the talk with her, but just found out she's a lot more vulnerable than I thought.'

'Well, you can't bloody leave her now, can you? You're on lockdown with her. Just wait until this is over. You get yourself in some bloody messes.'

'I know. Right, let's get these gullible clients in.' Moone went to head for the entrance, but Butler grabbed hold of his elbow. 'What?'

Butler sighed. 'Chief Super's here.'

'Oh shit. What's he want?' Moone clamped his hand on his face.

'Not sure. But can't be good if he's come all the way from Crownhill, risking getting the lurg from us lowlifes.'

Moone sipped his coffee, and gave an empty laugh as he went into the building and up to the incident room. As soon as he got inside, his eyes fell on Chief Superintendent Andrew Laptew, decked out in a mask and gloves, who was standing a couple of metres away from DS Carthew, chatting about something. He didn't want to know what, but his stomach churned at the mere sight of them.

'Moone, Butler,' Laptew said, his gloved hands squeaking as he rubbed them together. 'Good. Good. Just wanted to congratulate the team...'

'What for?' Butler asked, her voice full of exasperation.

'The suicide investigation,' Laptew said, narrowing his eyes at Butler. Then he smiled at everybody around the room as he said, 'Great work. Even in these difficult times, you've all proved yourself invaluable...'

'Sir,' Moone said, raising his hand.

'Don't do it,' Butler whispered behind him,

but it was too late, as Laptew had turned his attention to Moone.

'Yes, DCI Moone?' Laptew said.

'Well, the thing is, we aren't quite sure that Ian Speare was the person forcing his victims to take their own lives...'

Laptew stared at him, his brow furrowing. 'I'm sorry, but I was under the impression that you linked one of the victims' computers to Speare?'

'Well, yes,' Moone said, exchanging looks with Butler. 'We believe he sent a message to Mrs Whittle, Simon Whittle's widow, using the laptop of Daryl Palmer. But that still doesn't mean he forced them to take their own lives. We think he was the person obtaining the information. For one thing, when Mrs Stack was...'

Laptew held up his hand. 'Hang on a minute. What's this got to do with DSU Stack's wife?'

'We believe Stack's wife might be one of the suicide victims... '

'Have you lost your mind, Moone?'

'No, he hasn't,' Butler said, an annoyed grunt in her voice. 'I've talked to Stack about it, and he's in agreement...'

'Stack is suffering with grief,' Laptew said, shaking his head. 'He's hardly thinking...'

'Sir,' Harding said, raising his hand and sitting up.

'Yes?' Laptew said, gruffly, turning to him.

Harding looked awkward as he said, 'I meant DCI Moone. Sorry, sir.'

'What is it, Harding?' Moone asked, his gut knotting even tighter.

'I've been searching through the CCTV footage around the beach and beyond the time Mrs Stack, well you know...'

'Yes. What've you got?' Moone stepped closer to his desk.

'Well, obviously there isn't that much traffic on the roads right now, so I quite easily picked up Mrs Stack's car. Then I managed to pick out a few other cars heading in the direction of the beach...'

'And?' Butler asked.

Harding looked around at everybody before continuing. 'Well, there's quite a few cars, and we'll have to talk to them, but there is a particular car that heads in that direction with one person at the wheel. It's a man...'

'Let's have a look,' Moone said, heading round to Harding's desk.

'Two metres remember!' Laptew said, giving Moone a stern look.

'Yes sir.' Moone kept back from Harding's desk, watching as the DC brought up the grainy still taken from the CCTV footage. It was a man at the wheel, a cap pulled down over his face. The lower part of his face seemed to be obscured by a mask.

'That's him,' Moone said. 'That's our suicide

man. Can't really make him out though. Wearing a hat and mask...'

Laptew huffed. 'So, we've got a man in a hat and mask? Not very conclusive, is it? Could be just someone off to walk their dog.'

'No dog from what I can see,' Moone said. 'A man with a cap and mask was seen running from the scene of Mrs Stack's accident. And outside Ian Speare's house before the fire...'

'But you don't know who this man is?' Laptew said and shook his head. 'And nothing really solid to prove anyone else was involved in all this apart from Ian Speare. Mrs Stack's accident could've been just that...'

'Sir,' Harding said.

Laptew and Moone looked at him, making him spin his eyes between them before he said, 'I managed to get a shot of the registration number...'

'Really?' Moone felt his heart pump to life. 'Who is he?'

Harding made a face that caused Moone's heart to sink again. 'What is it?'

Harding said, 'The car belonged to Stannard. Sorry, boss.'

Moone gripped his face, letting out a sigh.

'But that proves it,' Butler said. 'Whoever's driving that car, they're our killer. We need to find that car. We need to pull CCTV from all over the city. We can track it down!'

Moone looked up at her, surprised by the

enthusiasm in her voice. 'You're right.'

Laptew looked round at them all, nodding. 'Maybe I spoke too soon. Maybe you're onto something. Ok, I'll make sure you've got the resources. Find that car and bring the culprit in. Stack was an ex-police officer, one of our own. So, get out there and get this done. Well done everybody. Good work.'

The Chief Super gave a wave, then signalled for Moone to follow him out into the corridor.

'I'll be back in a minute,' Moone said, hesitantly, then stepped out into the corridor, where Laptew was standing with his hands behind his back.

'You've certainly done some very good work, Moone,' Laptew said, nodding, a half smile on his face. 'Find whoever did this and you'll soon be going places.'

'I sort of like where I am,' Moone said, but Laptew seemed to miss his joke and nodded, his eyes seeming to jump back towards the incident room.

'I hear DS Carthew has been a real asset to the team,' Laptew said, returning his eyes to Moone.

'She's certainly...'

'I'm thinking of pushing her on and up. Giving her the chance of passing the inspectors' exam...'

'Really?' Moone turned and saw Carthew at her desk, working away, a bad feeling rising in his stomach.

'You don't approve?'

Moone looked at him. 'Just seems a bit...'

'Fast? That's fast tracking for you. It's the way it works. Between you and me, having someone like Carthew rise up the ranks... well, it looks good.'

'I see.'

'Anyway, I think it'll be good all round. Carry on with the good work, Moone.' The Chief Super smiled briefly, then turned on the spot and headed off down the corridor.

Moone turned back to the incident room, watching Carthew, thinking it all through, replaying the moment where she saved himself and Butler, then almost beat a man to death. Then his caravan on fire. Carthew coming out of the shadows, her face lit orange by the dancing flames.

No, she didn't do it. Just a malfunctioning toaster.

He pushed through the door, back into the incident room, clapping his hands like his old boss used to. 'Come on then, people, we need to trace this car. It can't be that hard, because there's really not many cars on the road.'

'You'd be surprised,' Butler said, looking up from her desk, her phone cradled in her neck. 'I've seen plenty of traffic out and about lately. Loads of idiots trying to come into Plymouth or head into Cornwall... Morons think they're immune.'

'Boss,' Molly piped up from her desk.

'Molly?' Moone smiled. 'Forgot you were there.'

She blushed, looking awkwardly round the room. 'Some of Madam Revello's clients have turned up.'

'Right. Good. Not sure when the medical team are getting here. Anyone know?' Moone looked around the room, but everybody just shrugged. 'Great. I'll give them a bell then. Then I'll meet you all in the car park. Gloves and masks, please.'

'Oh great,' Butler huffed.

'I just wanted to find out how Ashley Whittle's doing?' Moone said, as he headed down the stairs towards the car park. 'It's DCI Moone from Charles Cross.'

He listened to a distracted receptionist tell him how busy they were.

'Yeah, I appreciate it must be mayhem there. It's just I need to know, for my investigation...'

He was told to hang on, so he did and stepped out into the warm day, with only a few clouds hanging over the car park. It was a like a summer's day. Trust it to be this nice when most people, and their kids, were trapped indoors, he thought.

There were three rows of people, most young, the eldest perhaps in their thirties. Butler and the rest of the team were asking questions at a distance, masks over their faces. Some of the witnesses were wearing masks and gloves too. He looked out for a man of average build wearing a baseball cap, gloves and a mask. No such luck.

'Hello, yes, I'm here,' Moone said, walking towards the line of witnesses. The gates were being opened and an ambulance directed into the compound. 'So she's in the actual Covid ward? So it's confirmed? Ok, I understand. Thanks.'

Moone put away his phone and watched the ambulance's doors open. A couple of female nurses climbed out the back, all decked out in overalls, masks, gloves and a plastic shield over their faces. They had medical kits with them, that they started to open, getting ready to swab the witnesses.

'How is she?' Butler asked, muffled by her mask, as she stepped away from the line of witnesses.

'Sounds like she's got Coronavirus. She's doing ok, but they couldn't tell me much.'

Butler nodded, then seemed to scrutinise him. 'I hope you're not getting too involved.'

'What do you mean?'

'Well, she's a widow, all on her own...'

'No! No, way. It's not like that. It's just that, well, she doesn't sound like she's got anyone...'

Butler let out a sigh. 'OK, just remember you've got a girlfriend. Although, the widow's closer to your age.'

'Ha ha,' Moone said. 'Thing is, I keep wondering how she got it.'

'Same as everybody else. Someone sneezes, coughs, whatever...'

'Yes, I get that. But she's been out there on her own.'

'No visitors?'

'Her brother-in-law, but apparently he didn't even go inside. And far as I know he's not got any symptoms.'

Butler shook her head. 'You know it's not your job to go round investigating how people catch coronavirus...'

'It is when it comes to all this.' Moone gestured to the people lined up. 'If we can find the person who gave her covid...'

'It's a bit thin. Anyone could've given it to her.'

'The killer would've got close. Speare started displaying symptoms a few days after the fire. It fits.'

'What about your test?'

'I'm clear. You need to get swabbed too.'

'Yes, boss.'

Moone looked round when he saw one of the nurses approaching.

'No temperatures,' the nurse's muffled voice said through all her protective gear. 'No symptoms, but of course that doesn't mean anything. We'll let you know the results as soon as we can.'

'We appreciate that.' Moone nodded and smiled, then watched the medical team taking their equipment back to the ambulance.

'So now we wait?' Butler folded her arms. 'How long?'

'Not long.'

'Waste of time. He's still out there, sticking his fingers up at us.'

'We'll find Stannard's car...'

'Will we? He could have it stashed anywhere.'

'Come on, let's go back inside and see how everybody's getting on.' Moone headed inside with Butler's words still playing around in his head, her doubts echoing his, putting his hopes on a car that might never show up again. He was trying not to show it, but he felt the defeat creeping in all around him. He shook it all away as he went back into the incident room.

'Boss,' Harding said, poking his head over his monitor. 'I found something.'

'What?' Moone's heart coughed and spluttered into life again.

'Stannard's car. The Peugeot?'

Moone hurried closer to his desk. 'Really? You've found it?'

'Not exactly found it. I started looking through ANPR back around the time this all started. I found Stannard's car going towards Charlene Bale's boyfriend's place late the night before she died. Then it doesn't appear past the train station until the early hours of the morning.'

'So, that means our suicide nut job was using Stannard's car right back then as well.'

'Yes, boss. I think we're close to catching the bastard.'

CHAPTER 27

Moone sat at his desk, Butler hovering close by as he brought up the only images they managed to capture of the driver of Stannard's Peugeot. It was dark, the images were grainy as always. Moone bent forward, enlarged the image.

'It's no good,' Butler said with her usual huff. 'It's too pixelated. You can't make him out.'

'Male,' Moone sighed. 'Average build. Looks white. Just like the man seen in the back of her car.'

'That's because it is the same man. We just don't know who he is.'

Moone put his hands over his face and let out a harsh breath, smelling his own coffee breath. 'Bloody hell. One step closer, two steps back. Who is this bastard? Why's he doing this?'

'Because for some reason he's obsessed with suicide...'

Moone stood up, staring round the room at his team. 'Right. Everyone. Let's think about this. Why's he doing this?'

Harding shrugged. 'Because he can. He's a psycho who likes to see people do themselves in.'

'But why?' Moone turned and looked at the board. 'There's got to be a reason. There's a motive. Like the last one, Stack's wife.'

Moone tapped the board where Stack's wife's photo was now taped to it. 'The motivation? To wind us up. Make it personal.'

'We can't let him get to us,' Butler said, sitting at her desk and sipping her coffee.

Moone folded his arms. 'There's a reason for all this. A deep-seated reason. Something messed him up. Maybe a member of his family killed themselves...'

'Maybe,' Butler said. 'Maybe he just likes to get his kicks from having the power over people...'

Moone nodded, pointed to Butler. 'Exactly. The power over life and death, and making someone choose death over humiliation. It gets him off. Then he takes their money, even a couple of hundred pounds. The final humiliation.'

'So,' Butler said, sitting back. 'We're dealing with a sick and twisted bastard. Where does that get us? He could be targeting anyone next.'

'What if he's got no more targets?' Moone asked, thinking of Speare who was undoubtedly on the way to the morgue.

'What do you mean?' Butler asked.

'He means,' DS Carthew said, coming over. 'Speare is dead. He was the information man.

Like he was for his mother. They took bookings, took details of the people coming to see them. That gave Speare time to research them.'

Butler huffed, but Moone said, 'Faith's right. Speare did the research, used the info on their victims' laptops. Maybe Speare even saw it as a money-making scheme, I don't know. But our suicide obsessed killer, he just wants the power. So, who are we after?'

'Speare was a killer himself,' Butler said. 'We know that.'

'Yes.' Moone sat up. 'But that was done in the heat of the moment...'

'You don't know that,' Butler said.

Moone ignored her. 'Speare wasn't a cold-blooded killer. But let's think about the whole thing. Palmer sees him go into the house, then helps him dispose of the body. What if our killer witnessed it all too? Maybe that's what he had on Speare, held it over him.'

'But who? Could be anyone that happened to pass by.'

Moone was about to speak when Harding said, 'Boss?'

Moone stood up, stretched a little. 'Good news I hope, Harding?'

'Stannard's old car again,' Harding said. 'I've picked it up heading towards Sarah MacPherson's the day she died.'

'Jesus, the bastard,' Butler said, standing up.

'Also got it...' Harding stared at his screen.

'Yeah, got it out and about the day of the fire at Revello's place.'

Moone nodded, his mind suddenly clearing a little. 'Let's think about this for a moment. Like, how did our killer get hold of Stannard's car? What? He thought, Stannard's run off, I'll nick his car?'

'He knew he was dead,' Carthew said.

Moone pointed at her. 'Exactly. He was either involved in Stannard's death or witnessed it. But he had to have known he was dead long before us.'

'So what now, then?' Butler said. 'We keep chasing this car?'

'Yes, we keep an eye open for it. We have every incident response vehicle, every officer we have on the street keeping an eye out for it. We also need to talk again to all the people living around North Prospect Road that might've seen something that night.'

'Right,' Butler nodded, and picked up her phone. 'I'll get your favourite, Sergeant Pinder to start the uniforms on door-to-door.'

'Good.' Moone heard his phone ringing, then took it out. 'Let's keep going on the CCTV footage too, we're bound to get a better look at the bastard. He hasn't always worn a mask, so let's concentrate before the virus hit.'

Butler widened her eyes, a slight smile on her face. 'You're even starting to sound like a real detective.'

He laughed, half noticing an unrecognised number on his phone. 'I'm starting to feel like it too.'

Moone slipped out of the incident room and stood in the corridor as he answered his phone. 'DCI Peter Moone.'

'Hello, Mr Moone, I'm David, calling from Peacock Insurance...'

'I was waiting to hear from you lot.'

'Yes, I'm afraid I've got bad news concerning your insurance claim...'

'What do you mean, bad news?' Moone backed himself up against the wall, his gut twisting.

'I'm afraid Peacock Insurance are rejecting your claim. I'm very sorry...'

'Hang on, Dave. Why? There was an accidental fire. My caravan burnt down. My home...'

'I'm very sorry for your loss, but the claim was rejected, as there was some evidence of tampering with the electrical item that started the fire...'

'Wait a minute. You're suggesting I tampered with the toaster to start a fire? I'm a bloody policeman. I'm a detective!'

'I'm very sorry. I can understand you're upset. The report will be sent to you...'

'So that's it? I don't get anything? I'm homeless?'

'I'm very sorry. If there's anything else I can

help with…'

Moone hung up and stood there, seething, picturing his home burning right in front of him. There was evidence that the toaster had been tampered with. What evidence? He recalled what the fire investigator had told him about the crumbs, how if the toaster didn't switch itself off and there was a build up at the bottom…

Jesus. They were basically accusing him of starting the fire himself. He pushed through the door and went into the incident room, still seething from the phone call, swearing under his breath.

'What's wrong with you?' Butler asked. 'Someone pissed you off, or are you having a nervous breakdown?'

'Maybe both.' Moone sat down. 'My insurance company aren't paying out.'

'What a surprise. Why? What sneaky reason did they give?'

'Apparently there was evidence of tampering with the toaster. Do you Adam and Eve it?'

'Tampering? What? What do they mean?'

Moone shrugged. 'I don't know. When I talked to the fire investigator, he said there might be a way you could stop the toaster from turning itself off and jam it full of crumbs to cause a fire. But he said you'd have to know what you were doing.'

Moone watched Butler's head turn, her eyes

taking in someone across the room. Moone followed her eyes, saw she was staring at Carthew. Moone shook his head.

'Were there loads of crumbs?' Butler asked.

'I'm not sure.' Moone hung his head. 'I'll just have to, you know, buy another caravan I suppose.'

'You're living in a flat, remember? With your very young girlfriend.'

Moone pulled a face, showed her his discomfort. 'I know. Don't remind me. But I can't stay there for ever. I'm sure she understands that.'

'You don't get women, do you? No wonder you're divorced.'

'Funny. I need to get hold of that fire investigator.'

'Yeah, you do.' Butler stared intently at him. 'Because it sounds like someone did tamper with your toaster. They started that fire on purpose.'

Moone turned round to look at Carthew, who was looking at him, but looked away.

'You think...?' Moone lowered his voice. 'Carthew did do it?'

'Who else?'

Moone shook his head. 'No, it can't be. Let's just forget all this and get on.'

Nature had done the job for him. He smiled as he contemplated the fateful feel of the whole situation, as if the seas and mountains were parting for him, making his life more fruitful. When he started out, he never thought that what he was doing would have some kind of divine intervention, but he had to admit that it seemed very much like it had. He didn't believe in God. If he did, he wouldn't be doing what he was doing. He would live in fear of sending souls into the blackness. That's what awaited them, no more no less. No afterlife. He was sure of that.

He lived for the look in their eyes, when they were faced with their choice. Be exposed or end their misery for ever. But that was the beauty; they had no choice at all.

He turned and faced his car. No, not his car at all. Stannard's dark grey box of a car, like all the others on the road. It sat in his dusty garage, staring back at him. It had given him pleasure, as well anonymity to drive around in the dead solicitor's car, but now the police knew of the old man's death. It was too risky to keep driving around in it.

He had a flash, the image of the woman, the ex-policewoman driving towards him, the fire in her eyes. She had tried to kill him but had lost control of the car. Fate had intervened and saved him and taken her. He glowed at the thought, prickled with excitement. He felt untouchable. His only regret was, that he had spent so many years in a boring job, serving the same stupid faces over and over. Now he was doing what he loved, enjoying his work.

He started coughing again, feeling the pressure on his lungs, the constant ache. Shit.

He bent over, coughing, taking out his handkerchief and holding it to his mouth. He had it, he was sure of that. But he didn't have the time to get himself checked or admitted to hospital. The cough was with him all the time, making sleep broken. He'd sometimes wake up shivering, then boiling hot. There was no way he was going to hospital. He would ride it out, weather the storm.

He had work to do. For one thing, he had to get rid of the car, but that wouldn't be possible until dark. He knew somewhere where he could dump it, but he couldn't risk them getting any evidence or DNA. He would take a can of petrol and set it on fire. After all, he now loved fire, admired its all-consuming beauty. He'd always found himself staring at the dancing flames at bonfires or lit hearths. He had been standing outside Speare's home as the flames rose in the windows, his only regret that he hadn't been able to see the place burnt to the ground.

Speare was dead, he had learnt that much through his contact. It was a relief and now there was no link between him and the spectacled idiot and his fraud of a mother. They had brought him a large pool of potential victims, which had been whittled down with the help of Speare to a more manageable number. A few with dark secrets that could be exploited.

He turned and went over to the shelf again, where he kept his files, all the information about his victims. There was nothing much left. He felt disappointment when he once again realised that his pool of victims had all been but extinguished. But he knew it would be the case, that he could only get away with it for so long before someone raised the alarm. But it had come far too soon.

He took out his latest file, which he had hastily put together himself. Another policeman. A detective.

He took out the information he had typed up and printed out. It wasn't much to go on, but it would be enough. It was surprising how much information could be gleaned online. There was a photo of him too, found on an online news site, taken when he was still at the Met. He looked much younger, clearer of the eyes, not so tired.

DCI Peter Moone.

He smiled to himself, staring down at the photo, then nodding, almost agreeing with the notion that had risen in him. He would take him somewhere, and talk to him about his life, his failings, then coerce him to do the only sensible option available to him.

But that wouldn't be enough. Surely, he'd need more of an inducement. He smiled as he thought of something, knowing from his research that DCI Moone had family. Estranged, but there would be feelings there, especially guilt.

He smiled, tapping the photo of the policeman, already imagining the moment he realised he would have no choice but to kill himself, and the beautiful look in his eyes.

Moone found himself back on Ian Speare's street, following Harding and DS Carthew and a few uniforms as they went door to door, hoping someone might have spotted Stannard's car and might be able to identify the driver. Chances are, Moone thought, their suicide obsessed killer might have visited Speare long before the outbreak of the virus, and would therefore have arrived without a mask. He knew there wasn't a great chance of finding anyone who might remember the car or the driver, but it was the only thing they had. The tests had come back from their horde of potential witnesses, Madam Revello's former clients, and none of them had the virus. The killer was infected, he was sure of that, and was still out there spreading the illness, potentially killing anyone vulnerable he came in contact with. There were now two reasons to stop him.

Moone stopped, raised his coffee flask mug to his lips and took a careful sip. He grimaced. It was an Americano blend of instant coffee he'd hurriedly poured before heading out. It just wasn't the same, not by a long stretch and he prayed for normality to return and the coffee houses to reopen.

His mind turned over as he watched the team hit the doors like a bunch of desperate politicians before an election, falling short of kissing babies as they tried to get answers. His eyes had jumped to Carthew, his brain still trying to convince himself that she had been the one who tampered with his toaster, jammed it full of crumbs and managed to fake a fault in it that would prevent it turning itself off. It seemed pretty simple and clever, something that might be overlooked. And he felt it might have been overlooked if he hadn't raised concerns with the fire investigator, and he'd have his pay out.

Now he was living with a young woman who was certainly beautiful, charming and everything really, but not what he was looking for. She was too young, and undoubtedly would seek marriage and kids one day. He was too old to start again. He felt it deep in his bones. So what to do, how to finish it?

'Hey, boss!'

Moone broke out of his dream and saw Harding striding towards him, his thumb pointed behind him at a house.

'What is it?' Moone asked, meeting him halfway.

'A woman living in the house behind me,' Harding said. 'Says she saw Stannard's car parked here a few times.'

'You showed her the photo of his car?'

Harding nodded, taking out the photo as if it was proof. 'Yeah, I showed her. She seems pretty certain it was parked along here a number of times.'

'Let's talk to her,' Moone said, not getting his hopes up too high that they might be onto something.

Harding went ahead and rang the doorbell of the ordinary, quite narrow terrace house. A woman answered, possibly in her mid-fifties, with dyed long dark hair and a freckly face. She was quite tall, slender. A small, white fluffy dog came with her, yapping angrily up at Moone and Harding.

'This is my colleague, DCI Moone,' Harding said to the woman. 'This is Mrs Carroll.'

The woman looked quite glum, and unimpressed as she looked Moone over.

'Are you back about the car?' she asked.

'Sorry to disturb you, Mrs Carroll,' he said.

'Shut up!' Mrs Carroll snapped at the dog. 'Sorry. She gets excited. I told your colleague that I've seen the car parked here, that's all I know really. Parks right outside my house, like he owns the bloody street.'

'Do you know who the driver is?'

'No, no idea, but I'd like to know. Give him a piece of my mind if you get hold of him, would you?'

Moone nodded and smiled politely. 'Did you get a good look at his face?'

Moone crossed his fingers in his pocket, made a deal with himself to stop smoking, never have another if she could tell him who the driver was.

'No, not really. Probably about forty. Short brown hair. Last couple of times I saw him he had a mask on. Afraid of getting sick, but not frightened of parking outside my house in my space.'

'So, you've seen him without the mask?'

'Yes, but he usually has a cap on. You know, a baseball cap.'

He nodded, then turned to Harding, lowering his voice. 'Let's get Butler down here and a sketch artist. Butler has this thing she does to help witnesses remember things...'

'Doesn't beat them up, does she?' Harding asked, his voice lowered, his eyebrows raised.

Moone ignored him and looked at the witness. 'One of my colleagues will be by with a sketch artist, if you could give us a description.'

The woman sighed. 'OK, I suppose. What's he done anyway?'

'We can't really discuss that, but it's very serious.'

The woman narrowed her eyes at him. 'Yes, I guessed that much.' Then she shut the door, leaving Harding and Moone to walk away.

'So, we might have a sketch of the bastard soon?' Harding said.

Moone stopped and looked at him. 'We

might have. I feel like we're getting closer all the time. Just wish I knew who he might be targeting next, cause this guy isn't just going to stop by himself.'

CHAPTER 28

He used his own car to drive to the house. It was a large house, owned by the former MP, Carl Mathieson. He had read about what happened, and DCI Moone's involvement in the case. He was a hero for the second time in his career. He had a medal to prove it. He sat back in his car, staring towards the house and the drive, the large windows. He guessed there would be a piano somewhere, but no one would play it, just an object they had collected because they could afford it.

He had been there two hours, drinking a cup of tea from his flask. He had to lift his mask to take sips of his drink, but there was hardly anyone around, and after all, he had his cap pulled down over his head. The more he learned about DCI Moone and his past, the more he realised that fate had thrown him the perfect next victim.

The door to the house opened. He shuffled down in his seat when the young woman stepped down from the front door, a shopping bag in her hand, one of the bags for life type. He nodded to himself, watching the young woman, her short, lithe body, her light hair. Yes, she was the image of her policeman father. She turned and headed towards the shops that were situated a few hundred yards away. He started the engine and followed her, edging along, trying not to bring attention to himself. But she didn't stop at the shops at all. She kept going, heading past the shops and far along the high street until she came to a small, enclosed park. He parked up and watched her enter the park, stuffing the carrier bags in a nearby bin.

He decided to climb out, curious to see what the young girl was up to, and followed her into the park that was dappled with shade from the large chestnut trees that surrounded the puddle shape of grass at the centre. The young woman was called Alice, as he found out as a young lad stood up from a bench and waved her over. He was quite tall, skinny, with a mop of dark brown hair. With him was another young girl, who remained sitting.

He smiled when he saw Alice approach the young man, her face flushing as he took her hand. Then they kissed, passionately, but briefly. A policeman's daughter breaking the social distancing laws, he thought and smiled as he leaned against a tree.

He wondered how often she made these

secret assignations, and started to plan to be there for the next one. He would need to be prepared and bring some restraints. Yes, he would certainly need to be prepared for her, he told himself, then turned away, feeling the sun flicker through the trees, warming his skin.

Moone sighed when he sat back, the completed artist sketch in his hand. There were two images, one with mask and cap, the other with just the cap. The face had little detail, a thin mouth, a square, slender head and face. It could be any man.

'Not very helpful, is it?' Butler said behind him.

He turned in his chair, faced her and saw her standing, arms folded. He shook his head. 'No, pretty useless. But the eyes. They're familiar, sort of.'

'You should get the dog walker to have a look.'

Moone nodded. 'Yep. I'll get onto that. Thanks for doing that.'

She shrugged. 'Didn't do much. I want to catch Mrs Stack's killer as much as anyone. We owe him that much. He can be a tosspot, but he's one of us.'

'I wonder where he is right now, what he's thinking...'

'Who he's planning on knocking off next?'

'He's making it up as he goes along, which

makes him reckless. He's going to make a mistake.'

'Is that what we're counting on? Him making a mistake? Biting off more than he can chew?' Butler sat at her desk.

'Sort of. And waiting for the car to turn up. We've got two fast response teams ready to go.'

'With Kev at the wheel? Good. That'll keep him out of trouble and making bad jokes.'

Moone let out a breath, then looked out of the window. The streets were quiet, only a few cars and a bus passing by, heading round the roundabout. 'How hard can it be to spot a stolen car at a time like this?'

'Very difficult if he's onto us and he's dumped it.'

'We should've kept Stannard's death quiet. I made a mistake.'

'We didn't know he had Stannard's car. What about Pritchard?'

Moone looked at her. 'With Palmer's testimony, he should be out soon. And we look like crap again.'

'Come on. You and I both know we were pressured into that...'

'But we take the brunt. It's our necks on the line, not Laptew's.' Moone let out a harsh breath and faced his desk again. Then he looked at Butler. 'Have we got a photo of Stannard's car on the local news?'

'No, not yet. Don't want to frighten him into

disappearing.'

Moone nodded, but his gut twisted. 'But he might be done. What if he's planning on doing what we thought Stannard had done? What if he's got Stannard's money?'

Butler shrugged. 'It's risky. It's your choice.'

'I just have this gut feeling if we don't put it out there...'

'Like I said, your choice. Just give the word.'

Moone lowered his head, putting the two choices in his head. Then he did ip, dip, dog shit in his mind.

You. Are. Not. It.

'Do it! Get it out there!'

It was an itch he couldn't scratch. He had headed towards home, to safety, but halfway there he found himself seeing the daughter of the policeman. Alice. A pretty name. A pretty girl.

What if the police were onto him? They could grab him any second. He had carried on home, got the equipment together, the cable ties, the sleeping pills mixed into some coffee. He poured it in a flask, grabbed his masks and gloves and loaded it all in Stannard's car. It was risky, going out in it again, but he couldn't risk being seen with a kidnapped girl in his own car.

He had been standing there for a while, staring at the car, trying to make up his mind.

Fuck it, he decided and climbed in, started the engine. He had put on a mask, his cap, and gloves, and headed out of the garage.

She was still there, laughing and cuddling with her boyfriend. They had a secret between them. He bet her father didn't know. He was trembling at the prospect of grabbing the girl, having her under his power, and therefore her policeman father. The ultimate power.

He took out his phone, got the local news up. He checked the Evening Herald's webpage to see what info the police had let out. He was flicking through, then he saw an update. A photo, grainy from a traffic camera. His heart started to thump, panic flooding his body.

The car. Stannard's car, the car he was sat in. His head spun round, looking at where he was, out in the open in a car the police were looking for. He needed to get out of it and run.

Even though his heart was hammering, he managed to calm himself. He started the engine. He would drive it away, dump it somewhere, set fire to it. He put it in gear with a trembling hand. Then he looked over to the girl, across the park, who seemed to be saying a slow, lingering goodbye to the young lad.

He looked down at his hands. It was never about getting away, not really. It was about having the power over someone, making them choose life or death.

The policeman would be the ultimate prize. He had time before they caught up with him.

If he had her, he'd have time to bargain

with.

He grabbed the restraints, and the knife, then quickly got out, pulling his cap over his face, looking down, keeping his head low, even though he was pretty sure there was no CCTV nearby. His mask was in place, his gloves.

She had turned towards him, smiling to herself, happy in her useless little life. The daughter of a policeman, a stupid policeman, a lapdog to the government. He headed towards her, smiling beneath the mask so it showed in his eyes.

He controlled his breathing, calmed himself as he said, 'Alice Moone?'

Of course, she looked surprised, then a little guilty.

'Who're you?' she asked, finding her voice.

'Your father sent me,' he said. 'DCI Moone...'

'I know who my father is... who are you?'

'I work with him...'

'Your name?' She raised her eyebrows, folded her arms across her chest.

Her father's daughter. Time was wasting, his heart beating faster, feeling as if the eyes of the law were already staring at him across a desk.

'DS John Taylor,' he said, plucking a name from the air, trying to sound confident.

'Where's your ID?' More eyebrow raising from her.

He stepped towards her.

'Stay back,' she said. 'Two metre rule,

remember?'

'That didn't seem to bother you or your boyfriend.' He regretted the words as soon as they left his mouth.

'What? You going to tell my dad on me?' She huffed, started moving round him, heading for the exit. 'I don't think you know him, so get lost before I call the police.'

He turned and watched her, his annoyance growing, his heart beginning to beat much faster. He snatched at any idea he could. 'Call him, if you don't believe me.'

She stopped and looked at him. Then she took out her phone. 'Maybe I will.'

He stared at her, edging a little towards her, grasping the ties in his pocket. Then she turned her head for a moment, looked away from him. He lurched out, swiping his hand down, knocking her phone right out of her grip. As it clattered to the path, he wrapped his arm around her from behind, trying to grab her arms behind her back. She was tougher than she looked, and her hand came from nowhere, her nails scratching down his cheek. In amongst the blur of his anger and fear, he saw the thick tree a metre away. He forced her towards it, pulling her off her feet with the last bit of strength he had left. He grasped the back of her head and thumped it against the bark. He did it twice, hearing her groan then slump.

He was breathing hard as he let her fall, a

moan coming from her. She was only dazed, so he needed to act fast. He was bent over, breathing hard as he turned his head towards the entrance of the park. His car was far away, or seemed it. Too far for him to drag her by himself. He got the cable ties out and attached them to her pale arms behind her back. Then he heard a dog bark and swung round towards the other side of the park where a brown dog bounded around. He nearly ran, but kept his cool and looked down at her. He grabbed her feet and dragged her towards a large bush and hid her behind it.

He watched the middle-aged woman who threw a ball around for her dog as he got his phone out. He would need help, and called the only person he could.

Moone leaned back in his chair, then put his face in his hands, enclosing himself in darkness. Then he took them away and looked round the room, seeing everyone sat apart, wondering how they had entered this strange alternate world. One minute everything was OK, or thereabouts, the next they had entered a zombie apocalypse movie. Now they were waiting, trying to spot a car that the temporary owner probably would have got rid of by now. He sighed again.

'You OK?' Butler said, narrowing her eyes at him as she typed away.

'Yep, just tetchy.'

'Yeah, you sound it. Cheer up. Might never

happen...'

He sat up. 'Exactly.'

Then a phone was ringing on the desk and Moone jumped up to reach for it. Butler snapped it up and poked her tongue out. 'DI Mandy Butler. Yeah, really? Right. Are the team on their way? Good.'

She hung up and raised her eyebrows at him.

'What?' He stood up. 'Who was it?'

'Kev. Says they're off to find the car. Was spotted about twenty minutes ago near Ebrington Street.'

Moone followed her as she headed towards the doors. 'Ebrington Street? Ebrington street... hang on, that's not far from here!'

'Well done, London boy, we'll make a local of you yet.'

There weren't many cars parked opposite the walled park where the car had been sitting. The incident response cars of Sergeant Pinder's team were lining the park side of the road, ready to rush off if needed. Some of the uniforms were searching the area.

'Where was it parked?' Moone called to Sergeant Pinder who was standing across the road, and had just stopped talking into his radio.

'Right where you're parked,' he said and walked across the road.

Moone looked around, feeling the quietness

of the place, hearing the tweets and songs of the birds in the trees above that would usually be drowned out by the traffic. There were some good things about the lockdown, he decided.

'Shit,' he's gone. 'We missed him.'

'I'll check ANPR,' Pinder said and started talking on his radio again.

'Wonder what he was up to,' Butler said behind him.

'No idea. He could be up to anything...' Moone heard his phone ringing and took it out, then sighed when he saw it was his ex-wife. That was all he needed. He was about to hang up when he saw he also had a text from her.

'Have you heard from Alice?' the text read. 'Call me. Please.'

He was about to call, his heart fluttering to life, when he saw he had a missed call from Alice. No message. He rang her back, walking up the road a little way, praying she would answer. It went to voicemail.

'You alright?' Butler asked, with Sergeant Pinder in tow.

He looked round. 'I don't know. My ex-wife text me about Alice. I've got a missed call too.'

'From your ex-wife?'

'No, Alice. But no answer. She should be at bloody home! Where the hell is she?' Moone walked past, then turned into the archway of the park as he put his phone to his ear and tried Alice again. He could hear ringing. He lowered his mobile and listened out, hearing the ringing coming from somewhere close by. He turned off his phone, started walking round, but the ringing had stopped. He shook his head, certain he was going mad. He tried Alice's number again.

There was ringing again. He recognised the tune of the ringtone too, a song that Alice liked.

'You get hold of...' Butler started saying, but Moone held up his hand and shushed her.

The ringing was coming from a bush near the stone wall. He crouched and spotted it, the screen glowing, 'Dad' written in white letters across it. He nearly put his hand out and grabbed it, but stopped himself. He took out a glove from the pack he now carried, then carefully picked up the phone. He groaned as he got up and held it up for Butler and Pinder to see.

'Who's that?' Butler asked.

'Alice's phone.' Moone scratched his head, looking round, trying to make sense of it. What the fuck was her phone doing here? His stomach was flooded with black moths, all charging towards his mind.

'What the bloody hell's her phoning doing here?' Butler asked, looking at him like he'd dropped his trousers.

'I don't know. But a bit of a coincidence that we've just had a spotting of Stannard's car not half an hour ago, isn't it?'

'No, you don't think...'

'You want me to get her photo out there?'

Pinder asked.

Moone stared at him, then at her phone. 'She wouldn't go anywhere without her phone. Yes, get her photo out there. I'll message you one.'

Moone sent the photo, then got hold of her mum, filling her in on what had happened. All hell broke loose like he knew it would. Of course, it was all his fault. He didn't tell her about the car, just that he had found her phone. He got off the phone after promising on his life that he would find their daughter, and asking his ex-wife to send the numbers of her best friends.

'Any luck?' Butler asked after he walked back towards her and Pinder.

'Got the numbers for her friends,' he said, then carefully held her phone out towards Pinder. 'Get this tested will you? Might get prints off it, but I'm not holding out any hopes.'

Pinder nodded, then took the phone with a gloved hand and turned to walk back towards the entrance.

'Want me to contact her friends?' Butler asked.

'You can call some, I'll do the rest.' Moone walked past her, heading back towards their car. He crossed the road, still thinking, imagining the worst, that their suicide obsessed killer had hold of her. If it was true, what was he hoping to do? Get her to...

He shook away the thought, refusing to entertain the horrific notion. His stomach nosedived again as he climbed in the car, staring down at his phone. He called a few of the friends but most of them hadn't seen Alice since the lockdown had begun.

Then he called a girl called Jessica.

'Is that Jessica?' Moone asked, then listened as the girl said it was with a suspicious tone in her voice.

'Who's this?' Jessica asked.

'DCI Peter Moone. Alice's dad.'

'OK...'

'Just wondering if you've talked to her or seen her lately.'

There was a pause, then she said, 'We're on lockdown...'

'Yep, that's right...'

'Don't really go out...'

Moone sighed. 'You're not supposed to, but have you seen her or heard from her at all?'

Another, longer pause.

'Listen,' Moone said. 'You're not in trouble. Alice is missing. I just found her phone in a park off of Ebrington street...'

'Oh, right...'

There was a shakiness to her voice. 'Jessica? What do you know, Jessica?'

'Nothing...'

'Yes, you do. Let me tell you, if you don't tell me something I need to know and something happens...' He left his words hanging in the air, hardly noticing Butler open the passenger door and climb in.

'All right. Alice met this lad today... Mason. He's all right though, he wouldn't...'

'In the park, on Ebrington street?'

'Yeah. She wouldn't just...'

'I know. What time were they there?'

'We all met, about...'

'You were there?'

'Yeah.'

'Did you see anyone hanging round? Anyone suspicious?'

'No, nothing like that.'

'Have you got this boy's number?'

'Yeah, just a sec...'

When Moone had read out the number for Butler, he ended the call, and started the engine. 'Can you call him? Make sure Alice isn't with him?'

Butler nodded, then made the call as Moone started driving. He didn't know where he was going, wasn't really aware of the roads around him. His mind was ablaze, panicked thoughts flashing horrible images.

'She's not with him,' Butler said and stared at him. 'She'll be all right.'

He ignored her. Then he heard his phone ringing, and quickly pulled over. It was Harding and not Alice. His heart sank. 'Tell me something. Anything.'

'Sorry, boss,' Harding said, sounding confused. 'We had a call for you. It was a muffled voice, asked for you, then hung up.'

CHAPTER 29

He pulled the garage door shut, closing off the late afternoon sun. Then he turned round in the darkness of the interior and looked towards her. She was lying on the ground, on her side, her hands tied behind her back. He had put a gag round her mouth. He couldn't risk the neighbours knowing she was there. He was concerned about the cut on her head, which looked ugly. He cleaned it, and also checked her pulse. She would be OK, he decided and stood up as he heard her moan and mumble through the gag. Her eyes were fluttering a little, and soon all hell would break loose. Not just from her.

He walked over to the desk in the corner and picked up his passport, held it in his hand. Then he looked at his own photograph, the image of an ordinary man going about his ordinary life, his boring job. No more. After this, no one would think he was boring or ordinary. He'd had the power of life and death over other people, like some kind of god.

He looked at her again, watching her start to move. She had been surprisingly heavy and it had taken two of them to get her to the car. A police officer's daughter. He had raised the stakes. He looked at his passport again, realising there was nowhere to go, nowhere to run to. Coronavirus had seen to that, closing off foreign travel. He was feeling a little better now, the illness seeming to have left him. He occasionally coughed, but that was all and now it was at least bearable.

She moaned louder through the gag, and turned a little, her eyes flashing open, taking in her environment, and found him standing close by, a smile ready on his face.

She tried to pull herself back, her eyes widening, anger and fear creeping over her pale face. Words, all muffled and incomprehensible to him, started puffing away through the gag. Her body shook, her eyes becoming wet.

He held a finger to his lips, tried to shush her, but still the tirade came.

'I don't wish you any harm,' he said, trying to sound soothing. 'My argument isn't with you. It's your father. He's the one who challenged me, and brought this on himself.'

More muffled berating from her, so he shook his head and started to busy himself by collecting together his files and papers, which he planned on burning later.

When she seemed to have stopped and sank

back, obviously exhausted, he approached her again. 'Are you hungry? Thirsty?'

She stared at him, the anger still flickering in her eyes.

'It's no good starving yourself. I don't think your father would approve.'

Some muffled words from her.

'I suppose you're wondering what I have planned for your dad, aren't you?' He smiled, nodding to himself.

'Yes. I bet you're very curious to know. Well, I'm going to meet with him, somewhere out in the middle of nowhere. I've already got an appropriate place in mind. Then I'll convince him to kill himself.'

She was crying now, but he just smiled and collected his files together in a bin bag.

'Have they traced the call?' Moone said, as he raced to Harding's desk. Harding looked over his monitor, flustered, red-faced.

'Er... still working on it,' he said. 'Sorry, boss.'

Moone nodded, taking a breath, the panic rising and falling in his heart. Did he have her? Was their crazy suicide nut job with her right that second? The puke rose to his throat.

'What's happened?' Carthew said as she walked across the room.

Moone looked at her, not really seeing her,

or anyone but the imagined horror firing across his mind. 'My daughter. She's missing.'

'Bloody hell. Have you got a photo? We'll get it out there...'

Moone smiled, or tried to, but his face muscles would hardly move. 'It's taken care of. Uniforms are out and about.'

'She's probably just...'

'I think he's got her,' Moone said and sat down at his desk, trying to grasp a clear thought, a plan.

'Who?' Carthew came over, her face looking almost genuinely sympathetic.

'Our suicide nut job.'

'We don't know that for sure,' Butler said as she came through the door carrying two coffees. She pushed one opposite Moone. 'Why would he take her?'

'This is about him versus us,' Moone said, looking at his coffee, hardly able to contemplate drinking or eating anything while Alice was out there. He put his face in his hands. 'I made us a target. I pushed his buttons...'

'You only did what any of us...'

The phone was ringing. Harding scooted over to it, ready to grab the receiver, as they all turned to look. Moone jumped up.

'Let me,' he said and watched Harding retreat. Moone stared at the phone, starting to tremble a little as his heart began to pound. He walked round the desk, past Harding, no longer caring about social distancing. Bollocks to it all.

He picked up the phone. 'Charles Cross incident response line...'

'DCI Moone,' the muffled male voice said. 'I want to talk to DCI Moone.'

He looked at Harding, then nodded and watched him as he grabbed for another line.

'Speaking,' Moone said, trying to control his voice.

'Quite a game we're playing,' the man said, a smile in his voice.

'That's how you think of it? As a game?'

'What other way is there?'

'Where's my daughter?'

There was muffled laughter. 'She's with me. Safe and sound.'

'Where does she come into your game? Because you'd better not lay a finger on her.'

'Why would I?'

'Because you like forcing people to take their own lives...'

'Force? That's an interesting way of looking at it. I just confront them with the truth...'

'Your game is nearly over. We're coming for you. Best thing you can do is hand over my daughter...'

'It's been nice talking to you... see you very soon.'

The line went dead, leaving Moone to look round the room, seeing the sympathetic eyes staring at him. 'Well, do we know where he made the call from?'

Harding stood up. 'We traced the first call. It came from a phone box not far from North Prospect.'

'Right, let's go then,' Moone said, heading for the door.

'He's not going to still be there,' Butler said, standing up.

'What else do you suggest we do?' Moone turned to her, surprised to hear the annoyance in his own voice. 'Sorry, I just... you know...'

'It's all right, I get it. We'll go.' Butler looked towards Harding. 'Let us know when you trace the last call. Maybe we'll get some kind of position. And get Pinder to have his response team ready to roll.'

'Will do.' Harding sat down again, reaching for the phone.

'Come on, then,' Butler said to Moone. 'Let's go.'

The phone box was up the street a little way, one of the few working public phones in the area. They were halfway between the Weston Mill cemetery and the new build houses along North Prospect way. Hardly anyone was about, only the occasional bus or dog walker. No kids.

Moone sipped the coffee Butler had made for them, poured into a flask. He grimaced, but it wasn't the bad tasting coffee, more the images flashing in his mind, one after another, an assortment of horrific scenarios. He shut them down, tried to think of something else.

'She's going to be OK,' Butler said, sitting behind the wheel.

She didn't know that, he didn't know that, but he had to hope. He managed a nod. 'He chose a phone box close to where we found Stannard.'

'You think he's trying to tell us something?'

'Rubbing our noses in it. Look how stupid we've been, how slow we've been.'

'He thinks he's got the power.'

Moone sat up. 'That's it. Exactly. This is what this is all about. *The power*. He gets off on the power he has over people. Knowing their darkest secrets, able to get them to kill themselves rather than…'

'Well, he's fucked up this time. He's picked the wrong victim. He fucks with one of us, he fucks with us all.'

Moone smiled at her, nodding, but his mind was still in panic mode, the terrible images still racing around his brain. What could he do though? He had no idea where their suspect was or who they might be. Not a clue, and all the time he had Alice. He could've broken down and cried. After all the shit he'd been through, all the killers he'd tracked and none of them had brought it home to his family. He rubbed his eyes, trying to think, to get some kind of idea of what the killer might do next. But he knew, of course he did. He meant for Moone to be his next victim; don't kill yourself and Alice dies. He clenched his eyes shut. That's what fathers are meant to do, die for their daughters, protect them no matter what.

'I know what you're thinking,' Butler said, splitting his thoughts in two.

'What?'

'You're a martyr.' She narrowed her eyes, scowling at him. 'The whole world on your shoulders... you're not a martyr, you're not going to die.'

He laughed, but he heard the emptiness of it. Then his phone was beeping at him. He took it out, expecting another message from his ex, but it wasn't her, but a number he didn't recognise. He opened the message.

'You have to come alone if you want to see sweet Alice again. Keep this to yourself,' the message said. Moone looked up, his mind spinning.

'Who was that?' Butler asked.

He hesitated. 'Rachel. Checking up on me.'

'See, she's got you right where she wants you.'

Moone laughed, his stomach sinking. Then he brought up Harding's number. 'Harding must have traced the other bloody call by now.'

Moone got through to him after a few rings.

'Yes, boss?' Harding said.

'Have you traced the second call?'

'Phone box in Plympton. Just came through. Want us to send a car?'

'Yes, but unmarked, plain clothes. Tell them to keep a low profile.'

'Where was the other call made?' Butler asked after he hung up.

'Plympton.' Moone hung his head, staring at his phone, thinking about the last message. Alice. What was he doing to Alice? Jesus. The anger rippled through him, burned his insides.

'You want to check it out?' Butler started the engine.

'He won't be there. Harding's sent some unmarked cars to keep an eye out. But he won't be there. This is the run-around.'

'Then what do we do?'

'Who is it? Who the fuck's doing this?'

'I don't know. But we're going to get her back. Don't do anything...'

'What?'

'Reckless.'

'When have I ever done anything reckless?'

Butler huffed, started driving them back towards the station. But Moone's mind was in reverse, travelling back to one of his last cases in London, where if he had been a bit more reckless, or even brave, he might have saved a few more lives. It made him sick to look at the thing he hadn't truly earned. He wouldn't hold back this time and would do whatever it took to get Alice back.

Moone let Butler go on ahead, and stared at her as

she went up the stairs and disappeared along the corridor. He found a quiet corner and sent a reply to the number that had text him.

'What do you want?' he asked, knowing full well what was expected.

No answer came. The message didn't deliver, which meant the number was out of action. He wasn't stupid and probably had burner phones.

Another text came through. Different number: 'Are you ready to do the sensible thing?'

'What do you want?'

'It's simple. You die and Alice lives.'

'You're sick.'

'Some might say. But some of us have to take charge, have the power. You just follow like a good little boy. Bet you've been a good little boy your whole life, Peter Moone. Good little Peter Moone.'

'Prove to me Alice is alive.'

Then nothing for a while. His heart started to race, his stomach churning, convinced that he'd pushed him too far and he was going to do something...

A photo came through. A close-up of Alice, wearing a gag, her eyes staring up at someone, full of anger, a newspaper held in her hands. Today's date.

Moone backed up to the wall, tears filling his eyes. Don't lose it now, he thought. What the fuck did he have to do to get her free? Kill himself?

'Good little Peter Moone couldn't save his colleagues, could he?'

'Fuck you.'

'Couldn't save DS Kirsten Payne. I bet bad Peter Moone would have. Good guys finish last.'

The anger rippled and burned through his heart as Moone typed: 'That was you, wasn't it? A good boy all your life, overlooked. The girls didn't fancy you, did they?'

Then nothing for a few minutes. Moone stormed up and down the corridor, waiting, swearing at himself for over playing his hand, now he was pissed off, probably angry. What would he do to Alice?

Nothing. It wasn't her he wanted.

A message came through: 'We need to meet. Come alone.'

Moone typed: 'Where?'

'I'll let you know, but it'll be soon. Needless to say, if you bring anyone, you'll never see pretty Alice again.'

'I'll be alone. Don't harm her.'

But there was no reply, and all he could do now was wait. He trudged up the stairs, back towards the incident room, his head spinning, trying to figure a way out of the mess. But nothing came back, no clever way out. He was stuck.

Alice. He stopped outside the incident room, letting out a moan as he clasped his hands to his face, feeling tears building. He controlled himself, went into the incident room, put on a mask.

'How we doing?' he asked the four corners of the room.

Everyone looked at him with the same kind of sympathetic look that made his stomach turn over. He looked down.

'Her photo's everywhere, boss,' Harding said. 'Uniforms are all over it. We'll find her soon, don't worry.'

Moone raised a smile, then turned round and let out a breath as he saw a masked Chief Super staring at him through the doors. Laptew pushed open the door, holding a hand out to the room. 'Carry on, everyone, I just wanted a word with DCI Moone. Moone…'

He went out the doors, following Laptew down the corridor a little way, noting he had his usual blue surgical gloves on, wondering with a heavy heart what he was going to say now.

Laptew faced him, but it was hard to tell what his expression meant over the mask. 'Moone… I just wanted to lend my support. I heard what happened. I can't imagine…'

'I just need to get her back, her mother…'

'Anything. Ask for it and you've got it. We will find the bastard. You can count on that.'

Moone nodded, thinking back to the text he'd received.

Laptew stepped closer. 'Have you heard any

more? I mean, does he want a ransom or what?'

'No, it's not about a ransom. It's a power play.'

'These sick bastards.' Laptew shook his head. 'Where do they keep coming from?'

'I wish I knew. I'd close the fucking factory down.'

'That's the spirit, Moone.'

Moone heard his phone ringing, took it out with an apologetic look at his boss and looked at the number. Ashley Whittle. She was still with them, alive and well. He was glad. 'Sorry, sir. Got to take this.'

'I understand,' the Chief Super said and turned and headed away.

'Hey,' Moone said, backing himself against the wall.

'I'm alive,' a whisper of a voice said on the other end, but he hardly recognised her voice. 'Barely. How are you?'

'Well, things have been better. I'll tell you all about it when this is over. By the way, how did you get the dreaded bug? I thought you were self-isolating.'

'Me too. Only person to visit me was Michael...'

'Right. That's right. But he stayed outside...'

'No, he came in. Naughty really. And he gave me a hug.'

Moone was staring at the opposite wall, picturing Michael Whittle hugging Ashley, close enough to infect her. The brother of Simon. Dead Simon. Was he close enough to infect Ian Speare?

CHAPTER 30

Michael Whittle undid the padlock, slid the bolt across and opened the bedroom door. Alice was awake, her large eyes staring at him, the same look of hatred and fear in them. She moved awkwardly up the bed as much as she could, trying to get herself away from him. There was a small lamp that lit the room from the bedside table. He'd put blackout blinds over the windows. He carried the cup of tea across to the bedside table and put it down. Then he smiled as he took out a plastic straw and placed it in the cup.

'Sorry,' he said, and looked at the straw. 'It's plastic. Not very environmentally friendly, I know.'

There came mumbling from her gag.

'Drink your tea. You have to stay hydrated. I don't want you to die. Believe me. I just want, rather *need* your father to die. He'll be the icing on the cake, as they say. The cherry on the top. Then I can retire.'

He leaned towards her, his gloved hands

reaching for her gag. She recoiled further. 'Now, you have to let me undo your gag, so you can drink.'

With her eyes tight shut, her body quivering with obvious repulsion, he quickly undid her gag.

'Don't bother screaming, the neighbours are deaf,' he said, then handed her the mug. 'Drink up. I brought the straw in case you have sensitive teeth.'

She looked at the tea, the straw being held out to her. Then she opened her mouth and began to drink.

'That's a good girl, Alice,' he said, her angry eyes finding his. 'Such a pretty name.'

'He won't do it,' she said, her voice harsh.

'Won't do what? Kill himself? To save his precious little girl? I think you'd be surprised.'

'He'll find me...'

'No, I don't think so. He hasn't got a clue who I am. I've been here, right here under his nose the whole time and he's never once looked my way. It's insulting really. I was quite surprised when he came to see me, asking about my poor dear departed brother. But he didn't understand, didn't see what was right under his nose.'

'What was under his nose?' Alice sat up, trying to hide her fear under curiosity, but he could see it clearly.

He smiled. 'My brother. He was always the golden boy, my mother and father's favourite.

They didn't care for me, at least my father didn't. He smoked heavily, ended up breathing through a tube. It didn't take much to smother him, and of course they didn't waste much time looking into it. It was several years later that I found myself searching for something, feeling lost. Something was missing. I was bored. I wasn't like the other young men my age, I didn't long for fornication. Then I knew what it was. I used to take walks on Dartmoor, just me, and the sky, the ground. As I walked, I saw this young man standing on the viaduct. He seemed unsteady, staring down at the ground. I soon realised he was high, high as a kite. He was depressed, hence the drugs. There seems to be an inexplicable amount of young men these days who become lost in our society. He was one of them. I talked to him, and listened and he poured his heart out, told me his troubles, which seemed pretty trivial to me. But they were obviously mountains to him that he could never hope to climb. I realised he expected me to offer some kind or support or solution... so, do you know what I did?'

Alice stared at him, then shook her head.

He smiled at her, pausing for effect. 'I slowly convinced him that the world was as dreadful and hopeless as he suspected. I convinced him that he should jump.'

Alice kept staring, that look in her eyes, as if she expected a punchline.

'I'm not joking, Alice. I did it. Maybe it was

the drugs that helped, but slowly I wore him down. In the early hours of the morning he stepped off. I looked over and there he was. I don't know how long I stood there looking down, thinking over what had just happened, replaying it over and over, expecting some kind of remorse. But nothing. Nothing but pure unadulterated pleasure. I had to do it again, but with someone who wasn't addled by drugs. Then one day I saw a man enter a house, an abandoned house. In North Prospect. The man had killed someone in that house. I entered his life and soon realised he had certain talents, talents that could help me find the most vulnerable people. Like my brother, who I managed to convince was worthless and his wife hated him because he couldn't give her a child.'

Whittle found himself laughing, the same way he had the night he had watched his brother jump from the top of the car park. 'I'm sorry, it just amuses me.'

Alice started to cry, tears slowly running down her face.

'Don't get upset, Alice. As I said, I'm not going to hurt you. It's your father. Let me tell you about your dad. Did you know he's been having intercourse with my PA, Rachel?'

Alice looked away, her skin losing the little colour it had left.

'Sorry, I should leave out the gory details. But at least you know what sort of man he is...'

'He's not a sick bastard like you.' She was looking at him, her eyes burning again.

He smiled, nodded. 'I understand. You've just had disappointing news...'

'I already knew.'

'You saw them together. I know. I just didn't know you were aware of their relationship.'

She looked away. 'Fuck you. Can't wait to see my dad lock you up. You freak.'

He laughed. 'I hate to disappoint you, but that's not going to happen. Anyway, you need to get ready, as we'll be leaving soon. Drink your tea.'

He picked up the mug and passed it to her. 'You need to be hydrated when I hand you over.'

She stared at him, then at the mug of tea. She took a few sips, then sat back, looking away from him. Then she was blinking, shaking her head.

'I feel funny,' she said.

'That'll be the tablets,' he said and smiled. 'Can't have you making a fuss. You'll be fine.'

She spun her head to him, the anger rising, then falling as her head lolled. She sank back, her eyes closing. They opened again, and she mumbled something.

He stood there for a moment, staring at her, watching her breathing change, smiling a little. All was right for now and he had the upper hand.

Moone pushed through the doors to the

incident room, the beat of his heart filling his ears. He looked around the room, focused on Butler.

'I know who we're after,' he said, turning his eyes to the whiteboard, looking over their victims.

Butler shot her head up. 'What?'

'I know who it is. Who's been doing this.'

DS Carthew stood up and he saw her coming over out of the corner of his eye.

'Who?' Carthew said.

Moone took a marker and wrote Michael Whittle in large letters. Then he stood back, thinking. 'We need his address. We need cars there now.'

Butler stood up, reading the board. 'Michael Whittle? Simon's brother?'

Moone nodded. 'It makes sense now. He's a solicitor. Maybe he rubbed shoulders with Stannard... maybe he knew what he was up to...'

'How did you find this out?' Butler asked.

Moone looked at her. 'I just talked to Ashley Whittle. The only person who visited her was Michael. He hugged her. He told me he didn't even go in her house. He lied!'

Butler shrugged. 'Maybe he lied so he wouldn't get in trouble for breaking the social distancing rules.'

Moone stared at her, noticing the disbelief in her eyes. 'He gave her covid. Someone gave Speare covid. So far everyone Speare came in contact with has tested negative. It has to be Whittle.'

'Does it? Have you got anything else?'

'We need to search his home. Alice...'

'We need a warrant. Nobody's going to give us a warrant on those grounds.'

'He's got Alice!' Moone stared at her, the hurt and desperation rising, beating over his chest.

'I buy it,' Carthew said.

'You would.' Butler glared at her, then looked back at Moone. 'We need something concrete.'

Moone lowered his head, ready to cry, trying to think.

'Check his phone records,' Carthew said. 'See if we can place him anywhere near the victims' homes.'

Moone spun his head round to Carthew, almost contemplating hugging her. 'Yes. That's great. Can you get on it?'

Carthew smiled and hurried back to her desk.

Moone faced Harding, who was standing watching it all play out. 'Harding, can you go and find the Chief Super. Get him in here?'

Harding broke out of his dream, then nodded, and hurried out of the incident room, leaving Moone to face Butler.

She had her eyebrows raised, staring at him.

'What?' he asked.

'You're putting everything on this...'

'I know. He's got her. I know it in my gut. There was something about him. Something...'

'Let's get a selection of photos,' Butler said. 'Put him in amongst twenty maybe, show them to our eyewitnesses...'

'OK, but we haven't got much time.'

'Yeah, we have. He'll come to you. He's got Alice. It's all about you now. He wants you. He'll keep Alice safe until he's got you.'

Moone nodded, praying she was right. She had to be right.

'Don't worry, I'm a woman. We're always right.'

He managed a smile, but let it go, looking at his own hands. He needed to call his ex-wife and tell her what was happening, but his gut churned when he thought of hearing her scared and angry voice.

Butler patted him on his shoulder.

'Fuck social distancing,' she said. 'I'll get those photos together and get them to our witnesses.'

Moone nodded, then sat down, ready for the wait, praying to anyone who might listen to save his daughter and keep her safe. He took out his phone and stared at it, hoping it might ring.

'You know what you need to do?' Butler said, appearing in the doorway.

'What?'

'Get hold of your girlfriend. She works for him. She might be able to shine some light on this.'

'What do you mean? How would she know anything?'

Butler shrugged. 'I don't know. Isn't she his PA? She might know his whereabouts on certain days. She might have an idea where he is right now.'

Moone stared down at his phone, thinking, considering she might be right. He picked up his phone, then went past Butler, hardly acknowledging her as he brought up Rachel's number.

'Hey, you,' she said, sounding bright and cheery.

'Hey. Sorry, but I need to ask you something.'

'OK. You sound strange…'

'Alice is missing…'

'Oh God. Is there anything I can do?'

'Do you know where your boss is?'

'Michael? Why do you want to know where he is?'

'I can't go into it, but I need an address.'

'Right, OK. I'll text it to you. Has this to do with Alice? I mean, I can't…'

'I can't talk about it. Have you noticed anything strange about your boss's behaviour lately?'

There was a long pause. 'No. Ok, you're scaring me. Has he done something?'

'I'm sorry, Rachel. Just text me the address

and I'll see you later...'

'OK, I'll text it now...'

He hung up, then felt bad he had been so abrupt. But it was the way his personal life had suddenly been tainted by his work life. He didn't like the smell of it.

'Did she know anything?' Butler asked from behind him.

Moone turned round. 'No. But she's going to text his address.'

'Can you trust her?'

Moone felt tired all over, too tired to take her questions. 'That's enough. We'll get his address and go and see him, ask him a few questions.'

'Fine. But I think you need to keep an eye on her. She could be warning...'

'Butler.' He got to his feet, the stress digging into his shoulders, his back and neck. A dark cloud of a headache had arrived over his head. Then his phone beeped and he looked to see that Rachel had sent through his address.

He let Butler read the message. 'Where's this?'

'Out near Dartmoor, Yealmpton. Nice and quiet, the perfect place to hold a kidnap victim.'

Moone lowered the phone, nodded, feeling sick to his stomach. Then he looked over at Carthew. 'Butler's got photos here. Show them to our eyewitnesses, would you?'

Carthew nodded. 'Anything to help find your daughter.'

'Thanks. Let us know if any of them ID him. Come on, let's go and pay him a visit.'

Whittle was driving, heading down the lonely road, the barren land all around him, just the misty outline of tors in the distance, the white cloud like the outline of sheep. Ponies were there too, in small clusters, munching grass. A car came the opposite way, tearing past, just a blur. He kept on going, careful not to speed as he headed towards Princetown. He had flashes of that morning, which seemed years ago, not weeks, taking the girl out into the snow to die. It was a beautiful moment, seeing her raising the knife with tears in her eyes. How many cuts did it take? He'd lost count.

He was brought out of his daydream by his phone ringing. He was now in his own car, so much more comfortable than Stannard's old banger. He'd stolen so many people's money, but hadn't really given himself the chance to spend it. He pressed the button on the steering wheel that allowed him to talk, hands free to whoever was calling.

'Michael Whittle,' he said, cheerfully.

'It's me, Rachel.'

'Hello, Rachel. I haven't got a lot of time to talk.'

'Where are you?'

She sounded worried. 'Is everything OK? You sound upset.'

'Moone called me. Peter...'

'Ah, your boyfriend. How is he?'

There was a long pause.

'Rachel?'

She cleared her throat. 'He's on to you.'

He flicked his eyes down to the phone, trying to catch his breath. 'I'm sorry?'

'He knows it's you. He knows you have his daughter.'

'How? Forget it, it's not important. Well, he's not as useless as I first suspected. Never mind. It's all to play for now, isn't it?'

'This isn't a game.'

He heard sniffling. 'Don't cry, Rachel. We knew it would come to this. I told you...'

'We have to get away, like we planned...'

He didn't say anything for a moment, just looked at the seemingly endless road ahead. He listened to her starting to cry, the building torrent, barely being held back. 'I'm not going anywhere.'

'What? You have to...'

'No, I don't. I'm playing this to the end. I'm going to finish the game...'

More crying. 'You can't leave me. I can't go through...'

He sighed, listening to her sobbing, almost able to picture her red puffy eyes, the tears glistening on her cheeks. It was time to end it all. 'Rachel, calm down. Listen to me.'

She sniffed, waiting.

'I'm leaving. I'll be gone, to prison more than likely. You'll be on your own.'

'I can't, I can't...'

'Yes, like before. Before we found each other...'

'I... I love you.'

'I've told you before, I'm not like other men. I don't have those... longings. It's time to go. You should think about that.'

'Think about what?'

'Remember how all your friends left you? What about the night you came home and found your friend, Lisa? How beautiful did she look? So still, so free. Remember how you told me that? How you longed for that peace?'

'I remember.'

'You've always longed for that kind of peace, Rachel. You can have it at last.'

'I don't know. I want it, but...'

'If it wasn't for you, all the others, like my brother, wouldn't have found that peace. We saved them. You saved them. You can save yourself.'

'I don't know if I can.'

'*You can*, Rachel. I'm going to hang up now...'

'*No! Please. Stay with me...*'

'You'll do it? You promise?'

More sniffling and tears. 'Yes, yes... I will. I promise.'

'Good girl. I'll stay, I'll be here.' He reclined a little, listening to her tears, the sound of her taking her phone across her flat. Then the running of her bath as more tears came. It would be a long, drawn-out process, but he didn't mind. He had a little time.

Butler pulled up at the end of a winding, narrow lane. The wind was up, tugging at the trees that had barely begun to produce leaves. In front of them was a farmhouse, a couple of metal barns either side. A couple of windows were broken, and Moone could hear something squeaking in the wind.

'Doesn't look like anyone lives here,' Butler said.

Moone pushed open his door and climbed out, looking around at the overgrown bushes and grass, listening to the wind whistling and the crows squawking down from the trees, sounding a little like they were saying his name.

Butler climbed out. 'He's not here. She lied.'

Moone looked at her. 'Why would she lie? He must have...'

'She lied. You know why. Let's go and talk to the bitch.'

Moone looked back at the place, then made a call and got Sergeant Pinder to come down and search the house and the grounds. He climbed back in the car and nodded. 'Let's go and see Rachel.'

CHAPTER 31

They climbed out of the car, parked out the front of Rachel's flat, Moone's new home. His stomach sank as he headed to the front door, reaching for his door key. He stopped himself, then pressed the buzzer a couple of times.

'Forgot your key?' Butler asked.

'Doesn't feel right, letting myself in. Not in these circumstances.'

Butler nodded, then pressed the buzzer. 'Nothing.'

Moone took out his phone and rang Rachel. No answer. He let it keep ringing until her answer phone message came on. He hung up, then took out his key, his stomach churning even more, wondering if Rachel might even be with Whittle.

He stepped into the quietness of the flat, listening out, then went to the narrow stairs to the living area. He caught sight of something out the corner of his eye as he heard Butler coming up the stairs behind him. He looked towards the bathroom and saw her. Then he was jogging, racing towards her slumped body, her skin so white, as he fixed on her dark hair that covered half her face. The water was red.

His eyes looked beneath the dark water at the outline of her arms. He reached in, grasping her forearm and pulling it out, feeling the still warm water. There was a deep cut running lengthways along her wrist. She had done it properly. This wasn't a cry for help.

'Rachel,' he said, grasping her chin, lifting her head to him. Her eyes were closed and her skin was chilled. 'Rachel!'

'She's gone,' Butler said, standing in the doorway, her phone in her hand.

'Call it in. Call an ambulance. Now!'

His voice echoed round the bathroom, hollow, dead.

Butler lifted her phone to her ear and turned away, while Moone struggled to pull her from the bath, the water sloshing. He dragged her over the side, then flopped back to the lino, her in his arms. He looked over her wet hair, staring down at her wrists. Both cut.

He laid her down, then started CPR, pressing down on her chest, shouting her name. He looked up briefly to see Butler watching, staring down at him.

'You're all over this place,' she said.

'What?'

'Your stuff. Your clothes. If they know

you've been living here, it won't look good.'

'Fuck it. I don't care.'

She crouched down, suddenly close to him, her eyes digging into his. 'Yeah, you do care. I'll start getting your stuff out. Fingerprints, DNA won't matter. You're here now. Doing this.'

Moone looked away as he kept pressing her chest. 'Rachel! Can you hear me?'

Butler reached out, put her fingers to her neck, looking at him. 'She's gone, Moone. I'm sorry, but it's too late.'

'No, it's not...'

'She's cold. Stone cold. You have to think about you. Your family. The job. I'm sorry.'

Moone stopped pressing her chest, then sat back, breathing hard, trying to think clearly.

Then he saw it, her phone on the floor, by the bath. He nodded to it, so Butler took out a pair of gloves and pulled them on before picking it up.

'Whittle,' she said, letting out a harsh breath. 'Michael Whittle. That's who she called last. About two hours ago.'

Moone looked around, then awkwardly clambered to his feet. 'Go and wait for the ambulance.'

Butler stared at him, a question in her eyes, then she got to her feet, shrugged, and walked out.

He sat down on the side of the bath, looking around, ready to cry, trying to avoid looking at her.

A flash of Alice smashed into his mind. His family. He got up, feeling like his legs were about to turn to dust, and made his way out of the bathroom. Butler was trudging up the stairs, staring at him, looking concerned.

'You're as white as a sheet,' she said.

'Get rid of it. All of it. Get it out.' He moved past her as she nodded, the vomit threatening to rise up and pour out of him. He went down the stairs and into the overcast day, grey clouds gathering.

'I came as soon as I heard,' a voice said and he looked up to see DS Carthew standing a couple of metres away, near her car.

He nodded, then saw an incident response car crawling along towards them. Pinder was at the wheel.

'Want a lift back?'

He looked at her, shook his head. 'I'll go with Pinder.'

'Well, hope you're OK. Who's the victim?'

He stared at her, feeling his pulse rise, a bubble of anger and desperation soaring with it. 'Is this what you do now?'

'Sorry?'

'Pretend to be concerned? Playing your little games. Did you do it?'

She was blank-faced, maybe a spark of something in her eyes. 'Do what?'

'Burn my caravan down?'

'Mobile home, you mean?' She smiled.

'Did you?'

'Have you got any proof?' Her smile faded.

'No, but I'll get some or I'll stop you somehow. You won't be my boss while I've got any breath left in my body...'

'Then we'll have to see about that.'

He looked at her for a few seconds, her eyes burning into his.

His phone beeped, but he ignored it as he climbed in beside Pinder. 'The station.'

'What were you talking to psycho Mary about?' Pinder started the engine.

'I think she might've burnt down my mobile home. But I haven't got any proof. She's much cleverer than me.'

'Don't sell yourself short. We'll get her.'

Moone looked at him, saw his smile of reassurance that almost convinced him that everything would be ok in the end.

'I'll settle for my daughter right now.' Moone looked at his message. His heart rushed back into action as he saw he'd had another message from an unknown number.

Message: 'Bickleigh viaduct. Now. Come alone or you know what happens to sweet Alice.'

Moone was staring down at the message, trying to fathom what to do. Did he go alone or what? Did he risk telling anyone about it? His thoughts spiralled, imagining Whittle having Alice somewhere locked up, at a location they knew nothing about. They might never find her, and if they arrested Whittle it would be the only bargaining chip he had.

'Everything OK?'

Moone jerked his head up and stared at Pinder, having almost forgot he was there. 'Yep. Fine. But could you drop me off near Bickleigh Viaduct?'

'On Dartmoor? OK. Why's that?'

'Just got to check something out.'

'Ok. Let's go.'

Sergeant Pinder pulled up along the road, then pointed to the narrow path leading away to their left.

'It's up there,' Pinder said. 'You can't miss it. Do you want me to come?'

Moone looked towards the path, his stomach churning, his heart beginning to pulse. 'No. You head back to the station.'

Moone climbed out, feeling the wind attack him, prodding him backwards. He looked at Pinder, who was staring at him, the engine still running. A large part of him wanted to ask him to stay, but he decided he couldn't risk it.

He nodded to the sergeant, then started walking up the path, trying to see the viaduct. He heard the incident car pull away and head off, making his stomach take a massive nosedive. Then he saw it as the path grew steeper, the familiar low walls on either side. The massive drop. The wind had picked up, pushing him to one side as he looked up at the viaduct and saw a shape in the distance. Whoever it was saw him and reacted, put their hand in their pocket.

He got closer, slowly, now able to see the baseball cap wearing man, whose eyes stared at him over a blue face mask.

Michael Whittle.

'Where is she?' Moone asked, walking round him, his eyes jumping to a shape on the ground. His eyes widened when he saw Alice lying behind Whittle, close to the edge, where there was a gap in the brickwork and railings blocked the way.

Whittle lowered his hand as he stepped in Moone's view, showing him the long and sharp kitchen knife in his gloved hand.

'I can stab her,' Whittle said, crouching beside Alice. 'Or even cut her throat before you can get to me...'

'It's over, Whittle,' Moone said, his voice trembling. 'Where are you going to go?'

Moone looked around, his stomach turning over as he looked down at the drop and the sight of Plymouth so far away. 'Everyone's looking for you.'

'So? I've waited for this moment my whole life.' He smiled, reaching the knife out towards Alice's neck. 'You came alone, didn't you? You stupid fool.'

'Come on, this isn't about her. It's me. You want me...'

'Yes. You're quite right. Probably for the first time in your useless life. I want you to turn around and climb onto the wall.'

Moone looked behind him, his heart pounding in his ears, wishing he'd made Pinder stay. He was an idiot, a bloody stupid fool.

'Is this where you made that boy jump from?' Moone asked, hoping to buy some time.

'I'm not talking to you about all that. You can talk to your daughter about it. I talked to her. She was a good listener.'

'Rachel?' Moone asked, staring at him. 'Do you know what she did? Yes, of course you do. She called you.'

Whittle laughed. 'It didn't take much to persuade her. She's been... fucked in the head for a long time. She sucked you in to our little game, didn't she? She brought all this to me, showed me the way. Now, stop stalling and climb up on the wall. Be a good little policeman. Save your daughter.'

Moone looked round at the wall, then at Alice, and the knife being held out to her, trying to calculate if he had time to move.

Then Whittle was coughing, bent over. His eyes soon jumped up to Moone, the knife raised and pointed at Alice.

'Don't move!' Whittle shouted.

'Still with you then?' Moone said and laughed even though he felt like throwing up. 'Bet you thought it had gone.'

'I'll be fine.'

'They'll treat you in prison, I suppose. Maybe they won't and you'll die a slow and painful death.'

Whittle laughed emptily then started coughing, even harder, the knife hand wavering.

Without thinking Moone started running for him, watching the knife, reaching out his hands to grab for it. Whittle's eyes jumped up to him, glaringly white, his knife hand and his whole body turning towards Alice. Moone lurched towards him, grasping his back, sweeping his arm round his neck. He tried to pull him back from Alice, but Whittle tore forward, thrusting his knife hand towards her, a desperate growl coming from under his mask.

Moone saw the metal bars of the small fence and used all his weight to force Whittle towards it. As his knife hand was over the highest metal rail, Moone grasped his wrist and slammed it down onto it. Whittle let out a shout, and tried to bend his arm back towards Moone, to try and stab him. But Moone gritted his teeth, letting out a growl himself as he slammed his knife hand down again on the barrier. He managed to knock Whittle's hand down twice before the knife slipped from his grasp and dropped over the edge.

Moone let go of him and staggered back.

Whittle looked over the edge for a moment, then spun his furious eyes back on Moone. Then he was looking at Alice as he grasped her, trying to drag her to the edge.

'Leave her!' Moone lurched at him, grasping his hands and pulling them away from Alice.

Moone's head spun to one side, his jaw stinging. Whittle had punched him, and was staring at him, his fist still drawn.

Moone raised his fist, throwing it at the masked solicitor and landed a punch right on his nose.

Blood poured out as Whittle grasped his face, half whimpering, backing up to the barriers.

'You're finished,' Moone said. 'Michael Whittle, I'm arresting you on suspicion of murder...'

But Whittle didn't seem to hear him as he stood up, looking at his hands and the blood smeared on them. He looked around, his eyes jumping to Alice then to the sky. He was turning, grasping for the barrier, his right leg getting a foothold.

'Wait!' Moone shouted, putting out his hands to pull him back.

Whittle went, falling down without a sound.

Moone leant over, feeling the cold of the barrier on his palms as he looked down to see Whittle lying at the bottom, sprawled awkwardly. There was blood trickling from his head. It was over, he told himself, and Alice was safe. He was looking down at her, lying beside him, when he heard movement behind him.

Hands landed on his back, jerking him forward, toppling over the barrier. He was half over, gripping at the metal railing, staring down at the ground and Whittle's body. He gathered his thoughts. Someone had pushed him.

Then he felt someone grasp his legs, lifting them, forcing him over the edge.

'No!' he shouted, still grasping on to the rail, now dangling over the edge, his legs kicking out at nothing. He looked up, seeing a shape above him, someone looking over the edge at him. For a moment it looked like it was a woman.

'*Stop!*' he shouted. '*Help me!*'

The figure was gone, leaving him grasping onto the railing, scared of looking down. Already he could feel his hands losing grip, so he clasped tighter, but the metal was cold, slippery. He wouldn't be able to hold on for long.

'*Help!*' he shouted, his pulse thudding in his ears. Everyone was on lockdown, so hardly anyone would be out and about, especially not taking their dogs for a walk along a viaduct in the middle of nowhere.

Don't look down, he told himself, feeling the icy sweat dripping from his armpits.

He was going to die. Sooner or later, his hands wouldn't be able to hold on, and he would drop. No, stop it. Don't think like that.

He looked up, the railings and the bridge

just a blur. '*Help! Please! Anyone! Help!*'

No one was coming. Then he remembered Alice was lying close by.

'Alice!' he screamed. '*Wake up! Please! Alice!*'

Nothing. She must have been drugged, he decided, starting to worry why she wasn't awake yet. Then his right hand started to slip, losing grip on the railing. He gritted his teeth, trying to keep hold. He couldn't. His hand was about to let go and he couldn't do anything.

'*Please!*'

Then he saw something. A shape breaking the sunlight. Someone was looking over the edge at him.

'I can't hold on,' he said.

'Jesus!' Pinder's voice said. Then he could see the sergeant moving, clambering over the railing, then slowly crouching down to reach out his hand.

Pinder's face was red, his teeth gritted as he put out his hand towards Moone.

'Grab hold of me!' Pinder said.

'I can't move!'

'Yeah, you can. It's either that or die.'

'Is Alice OK?'

'She's breathing. Come on, give me your hand.'

Moone let go of the railing and grasped hold of Pinder. He found himself being dragged up over the railings and back onto the ground. He laid there for a while, staring at the blue sky that was dotted with wispy clouds and the occasional bird. It was so peaceful. He almost didn't want to move, but then he found himself turning towards Alice who was being examined by Pinder.

He turned over, and got to his feet.

'Shall I call for an ambulance?' Pinder asked.

'Let's get her to your car. We can take her.'

As they lifted Alice between them, Pinder asked, 'How did you end up down there?'

Moone hesitated. 'I was pushed.'

'By who?'

'I don't know. But I have my suspicions.'

CHAPTER 32

He wasn't really supposed to be there. Not supposed to be by her bedside, but he'd be damned to hell if anyone was going to try and make him leave. He was almost begging for the fight, waiting anxiously for one of the nurses or doctors to remove him. But no one came as he watched the pale, and frail looking figure of Alice under the starched bedsheets. She was in a separate room, away from the proper wards. Moone had a mask on, gloves, everything they had demanded. But he wasn't leaving.

He wanted to put out his hand and grasp hers, but he didn't want to give them any reason to throw him out. She would need to be tested for covid after spending time with Whittle. Same for himself.

It was another couple of hours before Alice's eyes fluttered and she looked around her.

'Alice?' he said, making her tired looking eyes turn towards him.

'Dad...' her voice was weak. 'Sorry.'

He shook his head. 'Why're you sorry?'

'I told Mum I was going to the shops.'

'Well, let's talk about that another time. I'm sorry he came after you because of me...'

'He did it, not you.' Alice tried to sit up, but ended up resting on her elbows. 'You did your job.'

He smiled. 'I wish your mum saw it that way. I got a right earful on the phone...'

'I'll straighten her out.' Alice smiled. 'I feel so wiped out.'

'You'll be fine.'

'Promise?'

'Scout's honour.'

'Oi, Moone,' Butler called from the doorway. 'Your wife is down the corridor.'

'Ex,' Moone said and got to his feet. 'I'd better scarper. Talk soon.'

'OK, Dad.'

He reached the door, looked back at her. 'Love you.'

'You too. Go on, before you get in trouble.'

Butler started the engine, then took them out of Derriford Hospital and towards the city. She kept eyeing him, and Moone could feel it all the way as he stared at the dribbles of traffic and masked pedestrians they passed.

'What do you want to say?' he asked, looking at her, feeling barren inside.

'Well, I talked to Pinder,' she said. 'Seeing as

you've not been very forthcoming. How the hell did you end up hanging over the bridge…'

'It's a viaduct.'

'Whatever. What happened?'

'Someone pushed me over. I was staring down at…'

'Hang on, so Whittle's gone over, you're looking down and someone pushed you over?'

'Yep.'

'Who the fuck did that? Did you see them?'

'I think I've got a pretty good idea.'

Butler glared at him. 'Who?'

'They burnt down my mobile home, but that obviously didn't satisfy them…'

'Jesus, bloody hell. That cow… What're you going to do?'

Moone shrugged. 'What can I do? No eyewitnesses. No cameras. My word against hers. Can you imagine it when they ask if I saw who pushed me? No, I didn't. Not really.'

'Wait till I…'

Moone put a hand on her arm. 'You can't. I've made Pinder swear to it, now I'm asking you. We don't spill the beans on this.'

'Fuck that. She gets off scot-free?'

'No. We are going to find a way to get rid of her. Me, you, and Pinder. Together.'

Butler drove them into the police car park and pulled up in a space close to the entrance. 'You'd better come up with a plan of action then.'

Moone pushed open the door, then headed

into the station and up the stairs to the incident room with Butler following.

He went into the incident room and nearly jumped out of his skin when Harding and the rest of the team cheered him. There was a banner too, which was pink and read: *Congratulations, it's a girl!*

'Sorry about the banner,' Harding said, producing a bottle of cheap looking champagne. 'You know, lockdown and all. Not much choice.'

'It's fine,' Moone said, looking round the room and seeing a gloved and masked Chief Super coming towards him.

'Well done, Peter,' he said, nodding. 'There's a lot of loose ends to deal with and well, you shouldn't have gone there on your own. But that's a telling off for another time. Enjoy your day.'

Moone took a mug of champagne from Harding and sipped at it, then grimaced.

'Not great, is it?' Harding said and walked away.

Moone looked up to see Carthew staring at him, a mug in her hand. She had a strange kind of smile on her lips. 'No, not great.'

She looked him over, then into his eyes as she walked up to him. 'You know, I've heard people say you resemble a dog, a whippet or something. I can't see it myself.'

'Really?'

'No. I think you're more like a cat. A cat with

nine lives, you keep on surviving. But you'll run out of lives eventually.'

Moone stared at her, choosing his words. 'You're never going to be my boss...'

'Who's going to stop me?'

'Me.'

'Unless I get in your way first.'

He smiled, but his stomach knotted. 'We'll see in the end.'

Then she raised her mug. 'Here's to that. May the best person win.'

Moone huffed, then walked away and stood shoulder to shoulder with Butler. 'We have to stop her. I think I know how.'

'Good. Now shut up and finish your bubbly. Even though it tastes like shit.'

Moone sipped the drink, staring across the room, watching Carthew, who was now laughing and chatting with Laptew. But every now and again, her eyes would find his and he could see the intent and danger in them. He didn't show it, but he was fearful of what she might do next. There had to be an end to her, whatever way he could think of. He had a terrible feeling come over him, like something bad was rising, a sense of doom was somewhere on the horizon, and it was coming for him.

GET TWO FREE AND EXCLUSIVE CRIME THRILLERS

I think building a relationship with the readers of my books is something very important, and makes the writing process even more fulfilling. Sign up to my mailing list and you'll receive two exclusive crime thrillers for FREE! Get SOMETHING DEAD- an Edmonton Police Station novella, and BITER- a standalone serial killer thriller.

Just visit markyarwood.co.uk

or you can find me here:

https://www.bookbub.com/authors/mark-yarwood

facebook.com/MarkYarwoodcrimewriter/